KILLER ON THE ROAD

ALSO BY
STEPHEN GRAHAM JONES

THE INDIAN LAKE TRILOGY

My Heart Is a Chainsaw
Don't Fear the Reaper
The Angel of Indian Lake

NOVELS

The Fast Red Road
All the Beautiful Sinners
The Bird Is Gone: A Manifesto
Seven Spanish Angels
Demon Theory
The Long Trial of Nolan Dugatti
Ledfeather
It Came from del Rio
Zombie Bake-Off
Growing Up Dead in Texas
The Last Final Girl
The Least of My Scars
Flashboy
The Gospel of Z
Not for Nothing
The Floating Boy and the Girl Who Couldn't Fly (with Paul Tremblay)
Mongrels
The Only Good Indians

The Babysitter Lives
I Was a Teenage Slasher
The Buffalo Hunter Hunter

NOVELLAS

Sterling City
Mapping the Interior
Night of the Mannequins

SHORT STORIES AND COLLECTIONS

Bleed into Me: A Book of Stories
The Ones That Got Away
Zombie Sharks with Metal Teeth
Three Miles Past
States of Grace
After the People Lights Have Gone Off
The Faster Redder Road: The Best UnAmerican Stories of Stephen Graham Jones

COMIC BOOKS

My Hero
Memorial Ride
Earthdivers
True Believers

KILLER ON THE ROAD

STEPHEN GRAHAM JONES

LONDON **NEW YORK** TORONTO
AMSTERDAM/ANTWERP NEW DELHI SYDNEY/MELBOURNE

AN IMPRINT OF SIMON & SCHUSTER, LLC

1230 AVENUE OF THE AMERICAS, NEW YORK, NEW YORK 10020

For more than 100 years, Simon & Schuster has championed authors and the stories they create. By respecting the copyright of an author's intellectual property, you enable Simon & Schuster and the author to continue publishing exceptional books for years to come. We thank you for supporting the author's copyright by purchasing an authorized edition of this book.

No amount of this book may be reproduced or stored in any format, nor may it be uploaded to any website, database, language-learning model, or other repository, retrieval, or artificial intelligence system without express permission. All rights reserved. Inquiries may be directed to Simon & Schuster, 1230 Avenue of the Americas, New York, NY 10020 or permissions@simonandschuster.com.

This book is a work of fiction. Any references to historical events, real people, or real places are used fictitiously. Other names, characters, places, and events are products of the author's imagination, and any resemblance to actual events or places or persons, living or dead, is entirely coincidental.

The Babysitter Lives copyright © 2022 by Stephen Graham Jones
This title was previously published in 2022 in audio format by Simon & Schuster Audio
Killer on the Road copyright © 2025 by Stephen Graham Jones

All rights reserved, including the right to reproduce this book or portions thereof in any form whatsoever. For information, address Saga Press Subsidiary Rights Department, 1230 Avenue of the Americas, New York, NY 10020.

First Saga Press trade paperback edition July 2025

SAGA PRESS and colophon are trademarks of Simon & Schuster, LLC

Simon & Schuster strongly believes in freedom of expression and stands against censorship in all its forms. For more information, visit BooksBelong.com.

For information about special discounts for bulk purchases, please contact Simon & Schuster Special Sales at 1-866-506-1949 or business@simonandschuster.com.

The Simon & Schuster Speakers Bureau can bring authors to your live event. For more information or to book an event, contact the Simon & Schuster Speakers Bureau at 1-866-248-3049 or visit our website at www.simonspeakers.com.

Interior design by Lewelin Polanco

Manufactured in the United States of America

1 3 5 7 9 10 8 6 4 2

Library of Congress Cataloging-in-Publication Data is available.

ISBN 978-1-9821-6767-7
ISBN 978-1-9821-6768-4 (ebook)

for my brother Spot, who I can talk trucks with for days

His brain is squirming like a toad

—THE DOORS

CHAPTER
0

"Thanks for the ride," the hitcher says, climbing in from the sheeting rain.

"What's the old joke?" the driver says, clocking his mirror to ease back up to speed. "I ask you—no, you ask *me* if I'm a serial killer, and I say no, I'm not worried about that. The chances of two serial killers randomly being in the same car are through the roof, right?"

"Something like that," the hitcher says, taking the towel the driver's dug up from behind the seat, nodding thanks over it.

The driver clicks his headlights from bright to normal then back again, trying to see through the rain.

"More like I should ask if you know how to handle a submarine," the driver says, easing them ahead.

"Biblical out there," the hitcher says, strapping his seatbelt across.

"Belly of the whale," the driver says back.

"You don't listen to talk radio, do you?" the hitcher asks, squinting through the blurry windshield at the road ahead of them.

"Maybe I do?"

"Good," the hitcher says. "Me too. Can't get enough."

"Or maybe I don't."

"Me either. Hate it. Talking heads, floating voices. Puts me on my meds."

"You're medicated?"

"Not right now, don't worry."

The driver considers this for a handful of seconds.

"Just to be transparent here," he finally says, and pushes his hand down alongside his seat, comes up with a chunky snub-nose.

"I get it," the hitcher says. "Road can be a dangerous place."

"I don't usually do this," the driver says. "Pick someone up, I mean."

"And I usually don't manage to catch a ride when it's raining," the hitcher says.

"Firsts for both of us, then."

"Just two killers heading west."

The driver chuckles, likes that. Switches hands on the wheel and looks over to the hitcher. "Confession time," he says. "My radio's actually on the fritz—why I stopped for you. So you can help me stay between the lines. Know any scary stories to keep us awake?"

"Work for my supper, got it," the hitcher says, scooching down in the seat for a comfortable position then straightening back up.

"I'm driving either way, man," the driver says. "Just"—easing over for a whirr of the rumble strip on the shoulder—"am I over here or not, right?"

"I could drive, you want," the hitcher says. "License is good and clean in Wyoming."

"Thanks, of course, but . . . you know."

"I get it, yeah," the hitcher says. "So, a story . . ."

The hitcher narrows his eyes to dredge the right one up.

"You heard the one about the guy picks up a girl who turns out to be a ghost?" he asks.

"You telling me I'm talking to a ghost?" the driver says, very ready to thrill a smile up.

"There's the one about the vampire thumbing rides at night to get his dinner."

The driver lifts his revolver again, makes like he's peering into the back of the cylinder, says, "And here I am without my silver bullets."

"Think that's werewolves," the hitcher says, folding the towel that wasn't folded before. "You know about the lot lizard who kept working after she was dead, and ended up getting pregnant with something?"

"Sounds like a cautionary tale," the driver says, raising his hand to shield his eyes from a bright car on the other side of the divided highway.

"Here's one," the hitcher says. "You hear it everywhere, last year or two."

"Everywhere like . . . hobo camps?"

"If this was 1932," the hitcher says with a tolerant smile. "Rest stops, truckstops. Lock-up. Tunnels when it's raining like this, or under bridges."

"This isn't the lot lizard one?" the driver asks, his disappointment nearly theatrical.

"Better," the hitcher says. "It's one of us—dudes looking for rides. Deal is, this Bucketmouth guy climbs in like I just did and after a while he asks you if you'd rather be dead or missing a finger."

"He just asks it out of nowhere?" the driver says. "Out of the blue, like?"

"Kind of a conversation killer, yeah."

"Is Bucketmouth his name?"

The hitcher shrugs sure.

"Finger, obviously," the driver says. "You've got ten fingers but just one life. Easy call, especially if it's hypothetical."

"Thing is," the hitcher says, "it's not. He'll give you a knife or something to cut it off if you can, then he makes you sit there while he takes it and"—miming a tiny cob of corn—"he eats the meat off it while you watch."

"A *cannibalism* story," the driver says, his lips peeled back from his teeth in appreciation.

"Except this one's true," the hitcher says, and opens both his hands, presses them into the dashboard for viewing, all his fingers there through his fingerless gloves, except... the pinky on the left.

The driver jerks the car over, away from this, the tires thudding over the reflectors embedded in the shoulder, then he flutters his right hand over his beating heart.

"I'm awake now," he says, making himself breathe big in and out, the seatbelt tight across his chest from all his moving around.

The hitcher chuckles, his hands still pressed onto the dash.

"You've done this before, haven't you?" the driver says at last.

The hitcher unfolds his pinky finger, waggles it.

"What if you really met this guy, though?" the driver asks, undoing his seatbelt to reset it, guiding the strap back down to the buckle, having to dig and adjust to find it. "No, no—what if it's *you*, and this is how you prep me for what's about to happen?"

"Already had my finger for the day," the hitcher says, looking at all his own, still spread out perfect on the blue vinyl of the dash.

"Not me," the driver says, and presses the snub-nose barrel of his revolver against the hitcher's pinky where it connects to the hand, and pulls the trigger.

The sound in the cab of the car is massive.

The driver drops the revolver to press this finger to the dash, catch it before it can fall into the floorboard. The hitcher reels away, pushing hard with his feet, his butt climbing the seatback, but then he realizes: the *gun* in his lap.

He fumbles it up, trying to hold it and stop his new stump from gouting blood up into the headliner.

"You, you, you," he says, and pulls the trigger at the driver again and again.

There was only the one bullet.

The driver lifts the still contracting finger up like thanking the hitcher for it, then inserts it neatly into his mouth, rotating it a little on insertion like getting it just how he likes it.

"Where you headed, mister?" he says as if starting them over, dialing them back to when the hitcher got in. His words a bit muffled by the finger in his mouth, but it's only the pinky.

The hitcher doesn't respond, is still climbing his seat.

"What?" the driver answers in his own voice, leaning forward over the steering wheel, the raw end of the finger still protruding from his lips. "You mean this *isn't* the highway to hell?"

He laughs and laughs about this, then sucks the finger all the way in.

The hitcher fumbles at his door handle but the lock sucks down.

He elbows the window but is wearing so many layers that they pad his blows.

"*What the fuck are you?*" he screams to the driver.

"Bucketmouth, evidently," the driver says around the thick finger. "I know I don't get to, like, select my own name, that's not how the big machine works, but what does Bucketmouth even *mean*?"

He leans forward to inspect his mouth in the rearview mirror, work it open and shut a couple times to confirm that it's just a normal mouth. Then he sees something that needs attention at the base of his jaw on the right side. He angles his head over so his fingertips can pinch up a skin tag.

He tugs gently on it, then harder, longer.

His whole face peels off, leaves just muscle and fat and tendons and dripping blood, and something cloudy and viscous coating it all, like the saliva of someone who's been sucking on a Vaseline lollipop.

He inspects himself in the mirror again from all sides, nods that he likes this, yeah. This is good.

He tosses the face he just peeled to the hitcher, who flinches away hard enough that the back of his head shatters the window out at last. The interior of the car swirls into a madhouse, burger trash and receipts and emptied-out Fritos bags whipping around everywhere, then sucking out into the night.

"What are you, man?" the hitcher says, weaker.

"More like *who*, sir," the driver says, unlocking the doors with his master control and then reaching across the hitcher to pop the door open, push him out, leave him rolling in their lane, the headlights of the semi behind them coming on fast and unavoidable, the horn blaring at what probably looks like a trash bag of something. At least until it goes under the wheels.

Alone in the front seat, the driver looks in the rearview again, winces when the headlights behind him turn sharply away. Then he angles the mirror onto himself, says, "Bucketmouth?"

He shakes his head in wonder then turns his functional radio on, hums with the Roger Miller coming through, and clicks the headlights off, slips ahead, into the darkness.

CHAPTER
1

There might have been a better way to do it, Harper knows.

Also, she could have packed.

And, just spitballing, but what if she'd thrown less of her mom's precious collector's plates across the living room? What if she hadn't lifted the couch up by one end and, in trying to send it flying after the plates, jammed it against the ceiling?

No way was she taking back what-all she'd said, though.

On Harper's list of things she hates now and always will, forever amen, around number six or seven would be people simpering back after a big blowup, saying how they didn't really mean to say that.

What they mean with that, actually? It's not that they hadn't meant to say that, it's that they got pissed enough that they said what they really meant, and now kind of wish they could reel that back in, do you mind? Can we all just forget, pretend that never happened, keep moving forward?

No, Harper tells them in her head. No do-overs, no takebacks.

As of two months ago—graduation—she's eighteen, so doesn't have to play nice anymore. Granted, there's her little sister Meg to keep in mind, who in a perfect world wouldn't have been watching this big blowup from the hallway, but . . . had Harper had anybody watching out for *her* when she was in seventh grade? No. It was just and only her, twenty-four/seven, and she made it through . . . not completely unscathed by Mom, but she wasn't a smoking husk, either. Not yet, anyway.

But she could have packed.

When her mom disappeared back down the hall, came storming back up with Harper's laundry to throw at her on the porch, yeah, it wouldn't have been terrible to have held onto some of those dirty clothes. But it had felt so good too, hadn't it? Flinging it all over the front of the house, screaming how this was a clean break, that she didn't want any reminders of this place, that she didn't need any of them, that this podunk Wyoming shitkicker town wasn't going to hold her back anymore? That she had better opportunities anywhere than this. That her friends were her real family anyway.

That last part . . . Meg hadn't still been listening from the living room, had she? Because she didn't mean it *that* way. Her and Meg would forever be sisters. Just, Harper could not stay in that house even one second longer. Sorry, Meggie. But if Harper made it this long, so can she, right? Anyway, it's not like Harper can take a little sister along. Really, it's just her for this big exit. Those friends she calls family *would* be there for her, but two of them have already zipped their sleeping bags together and taken off for Yellowstone to work for the summer, one of them's blasting off for college in Salt Lake next month, doesn't need this kind of distraction, and the other one, her many-times ex Dillon, they aren't exactly talking, and probably won't be until the ten-year reunion, which Harper does *not* plan on attending. So there.

In ten years she's going to have a room above a bar in Seattle or Los Angeles, her right arm's going to be full-sleeve, her left arm waiting for her thirtieth birthday, and she's going to wear mostly leather vests, keep her hair always pulled back unless she's shooting pool and doesn't want the night's mark seeing her eyes.

Her mom isn't going to have any idea where her daughter is, either. Guaranteed.

Meg? Maybe she can know, sure. No reason to hide from her. But, too, Meg'll be in college by then, or just getting done, Harper can't math it out perfect. Maybe Meg'll even have found the perfect guy or girl by then. They'll backpack through Australia, send Harper postcards with spiders and snakes and kangaroos on the front, not the elk and bears and cowboys of idiotic Wyoming.

Harper kicks a rock ahead of her, tracks its vaulting gallop down the asphalt into their shared future. Hers and the rock's.

Her one consolation for the moment is thinking about her mom trying to work the couch down from the support pillar it is now. It's up there tight. When that puffy arm had caught against the ceiling, Harper had backed off, given it her shoulder, all her hundred and forty pounds plus whatever her rage came to, but the couch hadn't had even one ounce of budge in it. She'd backed off then, stood in the soft rain of the popcorn acoustic and sparkly glitter scraped off the ceiling.

In fifth grade, her and her dad had blown that ceiling up there together, the air compressor over by the back door in the kitchen so they wouldn't all asphyxiate, and her mom had said no glitter in the living room, but Harper's dad had let her sneak a handful into the mix anyway, and it had been beautiful, like twinkles of secret gold.

This of course being five years before Mom ran Dad off.

That of course, Harper figures, being pretty much the official beginning of the end. The last good summer.

Write it in your memoir someday, she tells herself, and passes the rock she kicked. She doesn't kick it again.

It's hot now but this is Wyoming in July. Come dark there'll be a chill. Which is why she's not going to be outside. Also, if things go right, she's not even going to be in Wyoming anymore. Maybe if she runs hard enough, if she never looks back, she can forget she's even from this place at all.

And she's *not* fucking crying, okay?

"Happy last summer before real life," she says to the idea of her mom. "Thanks for all the laughs, it was a riot."

A big rig grinds past her—the on-ramp to the interstate is right there—and she hunches her shoulders against the dust and sound it's dragging then sneaks a peek at the back of the trailer. Just to see.

Her dad, whatever trailer he was dragging that week, he would always draw a rough circle in the grime on the back of it, lower right, then lick a different finger, dab some hashmarks in for the idea of numbers. A short slash and a long slash, then—careful not to cut a piece of pie from this circle—and . . . it was a clock. It was supposed to be his way of telling all the tourists on his roads that he was on a schedule, that he had places to be, that he had a family to be getting back to, that he didn't have time for RVs drifting from this lane to that, for sports cars passing on the right side, for minivans flipping lanes to get to the next tourist attraction twenty seconds sooner.

That's Harper's first tattoo, so far: the round, slightly oblong face of a clock on her right scapula. She'd told the guy to just put the hands pointing at whatever time, it didn't matter. It wasn't about the time. It was about who she was. It said she had places to be, thanks. Places very much not here.

Another thing that's going to be out here on the road with her tonight, she knows, is stars. Wyoming stars, which she has to admit she might come to miss someday. Lying under them she's going to be eleven years old again in the living room, the ceiling above glittering and sparkling.

Too late, just for the gesture of it, just to show she's committing to this enterprise, she hikes her thumb up for the trucker's mirrors but he's already hauling his big wheel over to the left, reaching for a lower gear, to ride the on-ramp into America proper.

When the truck doesn't slow, Harper lowers her face, thrusts both hands into the kangaroo pocket of her pow-wow sweatshirt—Meg's, oops—and stifflegs it under the eastbound then westbound bridge to make that big left onto 80 as well.

In her head she does her blinker, and, coast clear, swings her right leg around, pivoting on her left foot, taking that important first step away, into something better, something real. Something not here.

CHAPTER 2

Because the staties will stop to have words with you for hitching on the actual interstate, the ramps are where all the rides are, Harper knows. Well, the ramps are what work when your mom might be cruising slow through all the pump islands of town.

That's the way it always works with her mom: I hate you I hate you I hate, followed by I'm sorry I love you come back you're the most important thing in the world I could never lose you please.

So: the ramp, which is just a ramp by name, not by actually angling up or down more than three or four feet.

Because West Laramie's a blink-and-miss-it joke, Harper's the only one sailing her thumb out at five thirty in the blazing afternoon. Which is good. In her current state she doesn't need any Bobby McGee tagging along.

The first big rig that rumbles past has too much speed to waste it on a runaway who's probably a minor, and the second and third rigs—a Mack cabover, a Freightshaker like her dad's—both already have riders perched up in the passenger seat. Yeah, one of those riders is a dog, one's a woman her dad would have called a seatcover, and all the trucks had sleepers she could have napped in just fine for three hundred miles, but screw it.

Is it the big stenciled feather on her back that's warning the drivers off? Are Indians automatically trouble? If so, then it's good she stole Meg's sweatshirt, isn't it? Otherwise the drivers would have to wait to ditch her until they saw her hair, her skin, her face.

I could be Mexican, though, Harper says to those drivers, her eyes slit hard at them. Except this is Wyoming, yeah. And except for this big feather on my back. More like a bullseye.

Thanks, Mom.

If these drivers knew her dad had been a gearjammer *and* white like they maybe are, would they be lining up to give her a ride? Probably to the first exit, yeah. Where they could turn around, trash their schedule to deliver this little girl back to where she belongs.

Screw that noise.

An hour later Harper is sitting by the last reflector pole down the ramp, her back to Laramie, her face west, west, always west. Now she's thinking it would have been nice to pack some clothes and *also* her headphones, wherever they are.

Big gestures don't always involve forethought, though. And anyway, it's not like this is the furthest away she's ever made it, right? Her junior year she made it all the way down to Colorado before a waitress called her in for approaching trucks in the back row. According to the cops, that waitress maybe saved her life.

Her comeback when the cops told her that: What life?

The younger one told her yeah, she'd been seventeen once too.

When tires finally crunch onto the shoulder behind her, Harper hauls herself up, no smile, ready to give whatever bluff or attitude she needs to make this work out. Maybe even a smile. Extreme circumstances call for extreme measures, all that.

It's an old long Thunderbird, faded red with a vinyl roof peeling away in a thousand tiny curls of white.

Her eyes flash to the car's rearview first of all. It's how she's trained: will there be an eagle feather there, or some baby moccasins, a little beaded headdress? All of those would be acceptable, as would a twirling iridescent CD, meant to scatter radar guns. What'll send her scampering for cover will be a dreamcatcher. What's there in this Thunderbird is a cross that's really purple yarn wrapped around and around two popsicle sticks, with a secret and surely meaningful strand of yellow or gold in there.

Don't run, don't run, you need this, Harper tells herself, even though her genes have been programmed to know the church is the boogeyman for Indians—it's the hand that grabs you by the scruff while the other hand's already drawing back in a fist.

The passenger door opens, takes forever to *stop* opening because this car is long enough to be a train, practically, and both the passenger and the driver get out that side. For safety.

Harper, her face pleasant, hair threaded behind her ears, tries to see into the backseat. No one. Good. This can work.

The woman approaches first. She's got this long skirt and sandy-colored beehive do under a scarf—she should be wearing cat-eye glasses, Harper thinks. Next is the acne-scarred white man putting his sports jacket on, trying to guide his combover back into place and get his glasses resettled on his face.

The woman leads with a bottle of water fresh from a cooler, with a glow-bracelet threaded through the label for increased visibility at night.

Shit.

Do-gooders. Holy rollers.

Harper takes the bottle, twists the cap off and takes a polite sip.

"Do you know where it is that you're going, dear?" the woman says. This is probably their script: the woman carries the conversation load when the hitchhiker is female, so as not to spook her. Or maybe it's to establish sisterhood or be a mother figure.

The question is a loaded one, of course.

"To hell?" Harper says, to just get it over with.

The man looks back up the on-ramp, his cheeks crinkling around his eyes, his chest thrust out from the way he's stretching his shoulders back, his hands wrapped into thumb-swallowing fists from the strain.

"Next hundred and fifty miles are—they're like the Bermuda

Triangle for travelers, do you know that?" he says, finally bringing his pasty face around to Harper.

"Thought it was the Snow Chi Minh Trail," Harper says right back. It's what her dad used to call 80 in the winter.

"He's talking about all the people who go missing, dear," the woman says. "You've seen the posters in the windows at the gas station, haven't you? Not just . . . *walking* people either. Drivers too."

"Just because people don't call to check in doesn't mean they're missing," Harper says. "Just means they don't want to get found."

"No, I mean—" the woman starts, then starts again: "One of the young women from our congreg—from our flock, she's kind of a data expert, see, it's her job, and she's identified this stretch of interstate as statistically more—"

"Thanks for the water," Harper says, being sure they can tell she's already looking on down the road. "Don't worry, I recycle." She tips the bottle off her forehead, saluting them bye, but they're on a mission, are blind to any and all social cues.

"Just last month," the man says with apologetic finality, guiding his hair into place again, passing a slick photograph to Harper.

She doesn't take it but she can't help but clock it.

It's the head and shoulders of a dead man in the dry grass of what's probably the ditch—no, this is deeper into the BLM wasteland, isn't it? Harper can tell from the snow fence this man's been leaned up behind, that's tilting him forward. His eyes are gone, probably taken by birds, and his mouth has been hollowed out as well, and his skin's been baked to leather. In the winter he'd be a corpsicle, but in summer like this he's just a mummy.

Harper sucks air in through her teeth, almost a hiss. It's not so much from the shock of seeing this with no preparation, it's from—it's stupid. Right after her dad didn't come back from his last run, this was where she'd spent all her time: studying what photos she could find of unidentified men found in proximity to the interstate. At first she'd been able to eliminate some of them by hair length, but after a couple of years her dad could have grown his hair down to his shoulders. So now all she had was facial hair versus no facial hair. Her dad had none when he left, and had always been against it, said it creeped him out when he could see it out the bottom of his eye. This dead guy maybe had the same hang-up. Clean-shaven.

"You okay, dear?" the woman asks.

"Scared straight, ma'am," Harper says. "Thanks, thank you. Wouldn't have a sandwich for a lonely traveler now, would you?"

Ten minutes later, the Thunderbird people gone, Harper bites into the first of the three sandwiches she was able to talk them out of. It's pimento cheese, which is paste with chunks in it that are a slightly different temperature, or texture. After two normal chews and four longer, slower ones Harper gags it out, thinking of that dead guy's dry, empty, open mouth, damn those holy rollers to hell.

"That won't be me," she says, making it so by saying it out loud.

And it isn't her dad either, she adds, in secret.

CHAPTER
3

Two and a half sandwiches in her kangaroo pocket now, Harper finally just decides to stand, hoof it. She's got the glow-bracelet on her wrist, right? Doesn't that make her practically bulletproof?

Half a dozen steps later, another set of tires crunches in behind her.

Harper cringes, doesn't need any more salvation, fuck you very much. But, at the same time, she knows she probably should load up on water, if there's water to be had. And maybe a handful of tissues too, since she's now committed to walking away from all indoor bathrooms.

She turns, her most pitiful face on like a mask, and it's—it can't be. Cropped-short orange hair in the passenger seat, a perfect white smile over the steering wheel. *Kissy and Jam?* Who are supposed to be in Yellowstone for the whole summer, chasing wolves and tagging bears?

Harper holds her arms out so they can see how flabbergasted she is, how out of the blue this is, and then she holds them there a bit longer, shoulder high, her face trying to maintain the same shocked expression. But she's processing now: if they were in town for the day, for the weekend, for whatever, then . . . they were in stealth mode? not looking her up? avoiding her?

What kind of bullshit is that supposed to be?

Jam slithers up from the passenger side of the blocky-old four-door used-to-be-white Forest Services looking truck—*Park* truck, Harper's just now registering—crosses his arms over the roof and flops his head over to the side like to see Harper better, or slower, make this moment last.

"We leave for two months and you're already sacrificing yourself to the interstate gods?" he says.

"*Harper!*" Kissy yells from behind the wheel, tapping the horn three times in celebration, the third time long and loud.

Harper has to smile.

Her hands thrust back into her sweatshirt pocket, she sashays up to Jam's side—short for 'James' since junior high—and leans in to hug him, reaches past him to hold hands with Kissy, which has been her name since forever, for obvious reasons.

"Figured you'd be pregnant already," Harper says to her.

"Not for lack of trying," Jam says around the back of his hand and not even close to a whisper, and Kissy hits him in the hip with the side of her fist.

"There's bears up there!" Kissy says, about Yellowstone.

"Bears and pic-a-nic baskets, yeah," Harper says, looking down the ramp to a clump of three choppers riding in formation. "Y'all are going back?" she says into the cab real casual, trying not to load it with anything.

"We swung by your house," Jam says, quieter, shrugging it true. "Your mom was, um, redecorating?"

"She'll be moving on to my room next," Harper says, rolling her top lip in between her teeth. "Now that she can do what she wants with it, I mean."

"I'm sorry," Kissy says, batting her eyes like she's a deer in a Disney movie. The bad thing about Kissy, which is maybe the good thing too, is that she's put together just like the cartoon Pocahontas in the movie Harper took Meg to last week: impossible cheekbones, bustline that won't quit, shampoo commercial hair. Never mind that she's not enrolled at Wind River, or anywhere. On all her applications she checks the ethnicity box she has to draw in,

"Cherokee Princess." It kind of fits, sick as it is. It makes her everybody's grandmother, just, when that grandmother was hot.

"You look good," Harper says to her. "Pre-pregnancy suits you."

"This is all I've got cooking in me," Kissy says back, extending her middle finger slow like a bun rising in an oven.

"I've missed this," Harper says. "Been kind of a long summer."

"Tell them where you went looking for her next," a voice calls over the backseat, even though the backseat's . . . empty?

Harper lowers her eyebrows to Kissy about this but is already stepping back to look through the rear window.

Dillon, kicked back across the bench seat, his down-at-the-heel boots chocked up on the passenger side armrest.

"We thought y'all might be . . . back together," Jam says, as apology.

"And he's going back to the Park with you now?" Harper says.

"I was worried about you," Dillon says. "I know how you can be. I mean, if anybody does."

"You fixed my mom's couch, didn't you?" Harper says to him, disgusted.

"I did," Jam says, raising his hand to take this heat. "We didn't have loverboy with us yet then."

"That's one name for hi—" Harper says, looking up the ramp and catching almost immediately on the side-profile of her mom's pale Buick, cruising out from under the bridge like she gave the car some pedal a quarter mile back, is just riding that out in silent mode.

Harper rolls to the truck, flattens herself against it, and, easy as anything, Dillon slips the door open, pulls her in, his hand to the jut of her right hip, his other hand guiding her head below the level of the window.

"She's stopping, she's stopping . . ." Kissy announces, tight to the rearview, her foot revving the engine even though they're not in gear.

"Shit shit shit," Jam says, bouncing in his seat, drumming one hand on the outside of the door.

"Go already!" Harper says from the floorboard of the backseat.

"She'll know," Dillon says, and then kicks the door open decisively, takes one step out into the grass, and lets loose with a harsh arc of pee, leaning his whole body back from it.

Halfway through, his staged emergency over, he looks up like just seeing the Buick up there. He turns to it, waves big, probably some other part of him waving as well, and Harper's mom puts her foot to the gas now. When Dillon leans back in, breathing hard with excitement, Kissy passes a baby wipe back to him.

"You can just pee any time like that?" Jam says, impressed. "Never knew that about you."

"Full of piss and vinegar, my mom always said," Dillon says, leaning back to zip up. "That's half-true, anyway."

"You could have faked it," Harper says. "She can't see detail that fine all the way from up there."

"That *fine*?" Dillon says after a beat.

He balls the wipe up, tosses it into the grass.

"Listen, thanks," Harper says to Kissy and Jam, her voice ramping up to goodbye—no way does she need to be taking any road trips with her ex, thank you—"but y'all probably need to be getting back to—"

"Ho," Jam says, his hand cupping the side mirror, holding it steady against the engine's vibrations. "You weren't the only rabbit hiding in this ditch, were you?"

All of them look back, and, goddamnit: it's Meg, standing from the drainage part of the ditch she'd evidently ducked down into at the last moment, probably after sneaking out the backseat of their mom's Buick at the gas station—oh, of course: she saw the Park truck, knew it from Kissy and Jam stopping by, and . . . shit. Here she is, right where she should never be.

She raises a hand hi, her smile sheepish, seed heads floating all around her.

"Caught," Kissy says, and before Harper can say anything the truck is reversing *up* the down-ramp, one tire on the shoulder, one on the blacktop, Dillon standing on the running board, his arm wrapped around the window post as easy as anything. Which Harper kind of hates, since it's kind of precisely what she used to love about him—how he doesn't have to think about complicated dangerous scary stuff, just does it like it's the most natural thing ever. In another era he would have stepped up onto a moving train just the same, never had to look down at tracks or the big steel wheels or anything.

Kissy stops right alongside Meg.

"What the hell?" Harper says to her.

Meg shrugs, her lips covering her new braces.

"Mom thinks you're sleeping in the backseat, still?" Harper goes on, trying to make her eyes hot and mad, not about to cry from seeing Meg.

"You broke my plate too," Meg says with a shrug, and Harper has to concentrate to keep all these plates spinning in her head. But then it slows enough for her to see it: the one Meg got off that infomercial because the dog on it looked like Sheba, her dog that had got parvo two summers ago. Harper had camped in the backyard with her and Sheba for four nights until . . . until.

"Shit," Harper says, and reaches through the window to pull Meg's head to her shoulder. "Shit shit shit, girl. I'm sorry."

"I tried to put it together, but Mom—Mom—" Meg says, which is the last thing Harper hears before the world becomes sound and stinging gravel: a shiny Kenworth's taken the left onto the ramp fast to keep its momentum, really dive down onto 80, but that means it's riding the bright white line of the shoulder. The one their truck is straddling.

The Kenworth's air horn opens, splitting the afternoon in two, filling all their heads with instant panic, with certain death, and then Kissy straightens her arms against the steering wheel and stomps the pedal in.

For a moment, a lifetime, the truck stands there on its one spinning tire, Jam screaming, his left hand pushing up into the headliner like that can possibly save him, that Kenworth's grill filling all their mirrors, its horn filling all their heads, but then the Park truck's one spinning tire catches and they bolt forward, and it doesn't matter that Harper is trying to clutch onto Meg, to keep her safe. It doesn't matter because Dillon's stepped back onto the running board, is cupping her body with his, holding her and Meg both safe. Just another thing he does so natural, without having to even think about it.

Goddamn him.

By the spit-out of the ramp they're doing forty, the tired engine chugging, smoke billowing behind them, and a half-mile later they're up to a shuddering unsteady sixty, the truck's absolute limit, and then Kissy is crying and driving and trying not to hyperventilate.

"Any . . . *time*," Dillon says through the open window, still riding the running board, and Kissy eases them off the next ramp, the one that's all motels and truckstops.

The Kenworth slams past, at speed now, its air horn blasting the whole way.

"I-I think I prefer bears," Jam says, trying to smile, his eyes shiny.

Kissy glides them into the scrub nobody cares about and leans into the steering wheel, her hair draping down through the shifter and blinker and whatever.

"Thank you," Harper says to Dillon, over Meg's head, and Dillon shrugs like it was nothing, is already stepping down, looking ahead, tracking that Kenworth.

CHAPTER
4

It turns out that the Park truck Kissy and Jam are driving is why they're in town. Just for the day. Yellowstone is getting a new fleet, selling off the old, and Kissy's dad always needs another. Donny, their legendarily gruff supervisor, had given them eighteen hours to Laramie and back for show and tell—breakfast cleanup to last call—to see if her dad wanted the truck.

Turns out, he didn't. The arrowhead emblem on the door is cool and distinctive, especially half-faded like this one's, but Park trucks have spent their lives grinding down two-tracks in first gear, are better left to that than trying to come to town, put on a suit and tie.

"So . . . you were here all day today?" Harper says.

"That's what you get from that?" Dillon says, impressed.

"Family *lunches*," Jam says, emphasizing the plural. "As in, over at my mom's, then my dad's, then Kissy's parents?"

"Good to eat something that doesn't taste like smoke," Kissy adds, guilty. "But two lunches probably would have been enough."

"What was the fight about this time?" Dillon says to Harper.

"Usual," Harper says, eyeing the interstate, all-too-aware Meg is right there listening. "It's good that it's almost dark."

"True that," Kissy says, patting the truck like the sad thing it is. "Old Whitey here kind of has . . . *overheating* issues."

"Interested?" Jam asks, playing. "Our other buyer turned out to be actually smart."

"I mean," Harper says, about it getting dark. "Just—we're already on trucker radar, right? That little stunt on the ramp? All the drivers headed east on 80 know to be on lookout for a truck with a big stupid arrowhead on the door."

"As in, they want to be sure we make it to our destination?" Jam says, innocent and hopeful as ever.

"As in we're number one on the shit list," Dillon says.

His dad's a driver as well. It was the first thing that brought Harper to him.

"Meaning?" Meg asks, reminding Harper that her little sister was too young to ride the doghouse with her dad on his short runs.

"I think what Harper's saying," Kissy says, drilling an index finger theatrically into each of her temples and closing her eyes to better focus her psychic powers, "is that . . . a revenge-minded semi or two might be razzing us."

"Two inches away at eighty miles per hour," Dillon says, slamming his open hands past each other to show, the palms scraping. "Horn blasting, bombs flying."

"*Bombs?*" Kissy says.

"Bottles of pee," Harper fills in.

"Fun," Jam says. "Who needs amusement parks when there's the Wyoming interstate?"

Harper studies the truckstop across the field.

"Y'all can drop me at Rawlins," she says. "That's where you turn up to the Park, right? What, hundred miles?"

Kissy gives a tolerant smiles, says, "Harp, we're not just going to—"

"And you," Harper says to Meg. "You're calling Mom from that phone."

She points and they all follow that across the field to the payphone koala'd onto the side of the truckstop. The lights glow on over it just then, like Harper staged this.

"But—" Meg tries, only to be stopped by Harper's serious eyes.

"I can't take you with me," Harper says. "I don't even—I don't even know where I'm going. It's not safe."

"For you?" Meg sort of objects.

"For *you*," Harper says. "Why'd you . . . I mean, Mom likes you. You're the good daughter."

"And that's better?" Meg asks, her chin pruning about . . . probably about "expectations," and it being so impossible to live up to them. With their mom, you've either already let her down, or you're soon to.

Harper pulls Meg to her, rests her chin on top of her head and blinks fast.

"Listen," Jam says, "let's *all* go back. We can sleep in my mom's basement. We'll tell Donny the truck overheated. He'll understand."

"He'll understand that we're lying," Kissy mumbles sheepishly.

"But nobody'll be walking on the shoulder of 80 at *night*," Jam says to her, importantly.

"I've *got* this," Harper says, showing off her useless glow-bracelet.

"That a deterrent or a target?" Dillon says.

"And you're not going to be late because of me," Harper adds, argument over, then turns to Dillon: "And—mister smartass, you can stay with her until my mom picks her up?" With Meg.

Dillon just watches Harper's eyes about this.

Finally, "Can we talk?" he asks, tilting his head out past where the group can hear, his bangs falling into his eyes, which is *another* thing Harper despises about him. For reasons.

They walk out, Harper's fingers trailing out of Meg's until the last moment. It almost feels wrong to Harper, not leaning into Dillon. But this isn't old times. This is new times.

"What?" she says to him when she can.

"I'm not letting you do this either," he says. "You're right about it not being safe for Meg. But it's not safe for you, either."

"You don't get to say what I do and don't do," Harper says back.

"I'm saying this as someone who cares about you. It's not—I mean—"

"You're trying to protect me because I'm a girl," Harper tells him. "Thanks. Not insulting at all, Dillweed."

He flashes his eyes up to her about this use of her old name for him.

She glares it true, lets the ghost of a smile curl her lips.

"My brother's shop's in Rawlins," he says. "We all ride there together. Hour and a half. If you still want to get out there, start walking, then I take that old Camaro he has, bring Meg back myself."

Harper looks past him, to Laramie. To the idea of it. Then she comes back to Kissy and Jam, Jam with his hands on an imaginary steering wheel so he can re-enact Kissy's slow-motion facial expressions with that Kenworth bearing down on them. Meg's laughing, her braces flashing, her hand coming up to cover her mouth.

"We can't make them late, deal?" Harper says to Dillon.

"Think I want to single-handedly bring down the national park system?" Dillon says back with a smile.

"And we're not even close to getting back together," Harper adds, just to be sure.

"Wasn't even considering that," Dillon says, falling in behind her. "I hate everything about you, remember?"

Harper hip-checks him, doesn't look over.

CHAPTER
5

They're on the road exactly two and a half miles before the first rig steps up onto the highway stripes, brings its passenger-side front fender close enough to the truck that Kissy reaches out with her hand to push it away, which results in the Park truck drifting onto the right shoulder. To prove this actually just happened she holds her now-grimy palm out to all in the cab.

"Shit," Jam says to Harper. "You weren't joking about them hating us now, were you?"

"That a bird?" Meg says, directing them all to the road ahead of them.

"Crow," Harper says, watching it because Meg's right: it's a big black bird flapping up from the road, into the dusk, but . . .

"What's it carrying?" Dillon says.

"Roadkill," Kissy says, thoroughly grossed out, at which point the crow wheels back over the road, away from a pair of smaller birds divebombing it. The result: whatever it had in its talons, it's falling now. Not like a flattened snake or the rubbery intestines of a deer, either. More like it's caught an updraft swirling up from the heat the asphalt's radiating, but its weight is still pulling at it, so it's just drifting. Down, down . . .

Onto the windshield.

Jam screams loud enough for all of them, is pushing back, over the seat.

It's a face. The skin of a man's white face, which isn't a thing Harper's ever considered before, or considered having to see. It's a mask, she realizes, the backsides of her own cheeks crawling. Just look through the eyeholes, line the mouth up so you can speak through it.

"Shit," Dillon says.

The truck whips from side to side, not quite enough to tip over at sixty, but it is top-heavy with its gone shocks and spongy tires, so, nearly enough.

Harper holds onto the back of the front seat and reaches forward like to touch this face on the glass, says, "Do I know him?"

"What?" Kissy says, and, on automatic, just using her palm not her fingers, like that'll mean she's touching this face less, she does the wipers.

The face slides with the wiper to the side of the windshield and then the wind has it, is flopping it over to the side mirror on the driver's side.

Kissy dives away, isn't interested in driving anymore, just needs distance from this.

Harper surges over the seat to take the wheel but it's a short-term fix. In the moment of stillness she has, she looks over to the face on the rearview—just skin and blood, mostly—and says, "Combover."

It's the guy from the Thunderbird. She can tell from the pastiness, from the acne scars, from the bags under the eyeholes.

And then he's gone, slipped behind them.

Everyone but Harper turns to track the face.

"Kissy, Kiss, brakes . . ." Harper says, way too calmly, about the ten-wheel dumptruck they're about to drive up under.

Kissy moves back over, takes the wheel, veers them away from that certain death and into another: the splatty gravel of the shoulder, then the slick grass of the ditch. After flattening two mile markers, she finally slows them to a ragged stop, their headlights splashing out into the pasture, everyone breathing hard.

"I saw—I saw my life flash before my eyes," Jam says, laughing with nerves. "It was mostly sex scenes."

"I'm *done* driving," Kissy says, turning the key back and stepping out all at once, Harper just managing to reach through the window to grab her shoulder, pull her back from the rig slamming past deep in the shoulder, a hairsbreadth from clipping their cocked-out rear bumper.

Kissy stands with her back to the truck, Harper's hand holding her there, and cries in a breathless way, her whole body shuddering. Jam slithers up from his window, walks across the cowl at the back of the hood, drops down by her, pulls her close.

"Got her?" Harper says.

He nods.

"Harp?" Meg says.

"I don't know," Harper says, and checks the front rearview for headlights before stepping out, whipping around the front of the truck to stand in the ditch, think.

Dillon's there waiting for her.

"You knew that . . . him?" he says.

Harper waggles her uncracked glow-bracelet, says, "He gave me this."

"Guess he stopped to help someone else too," Dillon says. Then, a beat later: "Hey, your friend's back."

Harper looks up.

The crow. *A* crow, anyway. Just perched on a fencepost, an eyeball in its beak, hanging by the pulpy stalk. The stalk is longer than Harper would have guessed. It makes her aware of her brain in a new way, like it's thick with cords waiting to be pulled.

"They're close," she says, casting around the pasture.

"They?" Dillon says, ducking from the bird flapping up, coasting over them nearly at head-level to settle down on the cab of the truck.

"We need a—" Harper says, is cut off by Dillon slinging a rock at the crow.

It doesn't connect, but it's close enough that the crow squawks back, having to spread its wings for balance, its meal of eyeball falling away.

An instant later the rock connects with the hefty grille guard of a Volvo rig barreling past at ninety. The rock comes back like birdshot, takes the rear window of the Park truck out in an explosion of glass.

Harper's already running for the cab, dragging Meg out.

"You all right, you all right?" she's saying, patting Meg's shoulders, checking her face.

Meg, half in shock, touches her own face, looks back to the truck. Her hair sparkles with pebbles of glass.

"*Stupid!*" Harper yells back to Dillon.

He licks his lips, doesn't look away.

"What the hell was that?" Jam says, side-hugging Kissy, walking her around the front of the truck.

One side of his face is sparkling, too. Then, kind of all at once, bleeding, a hundred little pinpricks welling blood.

Kissy looks up, sees it, wants to wipe the blood away but it'll cut her hand.

"Shit," Dillon says, turning around, sick with himself.

"We're going to get you home somehow," Harper's saying to Meg, both of them on their knees now, Harper pinching the glass from Meg's hair.

Meg nods yes, that, please.

"You shouldn't have followed me," Harper tells her.

"Do you think it's my favorite place, there with her?" Meg says back, a tear slipping down her face.

Harper tilts her face back to keep from crying then turns to Dillon, snapping his fingers back to all of them to get their attention.

"What?" Harper says into the quiet he's made.

"Your friend with the face," he says, directing them to taillights out in the pasture. "Who used to *have* a face. Was he driving a mid-seventies Ford? Red?"

"Thunderbird," Harper says, standing to see, a passing rig throwing her shadow out ahead of her then ripping it away.

CHAPTER
6

With Kissy ignoring everything to try to pincer as much shattered glass as she can from Jam's face, Harper stations Meg by the fence, well away from the road, and forges out into the pasture with Dillon, walking in the tire tracks the Thunderbird left. She doesn't want to, but she has to see, too.

"What happened?" Dillon says.

"Nothing good," Harper says back.

The Thunderbird is maybe a hundred yards out, still idling and in gear, only the parking lights on. It's pushing against a tall weathered snow fence that's not giving, just groaning and creaking, like still complaining about being rolled into. Meaning the Thunderbird was hardly moving by the time it nosed out this far.

Harper and Dillon stop a few steps out, look to each other for confirmation that they're doing this.

"Remember," Harper says. "One of them won't have an eye anymore."

"And the other's missing a face, check," Dillon says, taking the driver's side, leaving the passenger for Harper.

"I just *saw* them," Harper says, stepping ahead, careful of making sound, like that might spook the Thunderbird, send it flapping deeper into the scrub.

"Maybe you should let me—" Dillon warns, to the open driver's door now. "Empty," he calls across the roof to Harper. "Gone."

"Got somebody," Harper says back, wrenching the passenger

door open and trying, through the open window, to hold the beehive woman steady. She flops half out so Harper has to catch her.

Harper looks over the woman's shoulder at Dillon, reaching in over the bloody white bench seat to twist the ignition off, moving carefully so as not to leave any fibers or skin that might incriminate him.

The Thunderbird keeps right on idling.

"What the hell?" he says, holding the key up to be sure he's actually got it.

"Old car, worn out key," Harper says, obviously, then: "Little help, please?"

Like that Dillon's to her, already guiding the woman back into her seat.

She's the one with the missing eye. The crow probably sat right on top of the door, right in the open window.

"Impact broke her neck," Dillon says, nodding to the awkward bulge on the side of the woman's neck. The bulge that has to be bone. The skin around it is discolored.

The woman gasps a ragged breath in.

"She's paralyz—she can't move!" Harper says, not sure where to hold her, how to hold her that won't hurt her worse.

"So where's the driver?" Dillon says, standing to cast around in the darkness. "He just leave her here?"

Harper registers Dillon walking around the trunk to reach in the driver's side again, pull the headlights on. They light the snow fence up, and a little brush past it, but don't show any driver stumbling around out there, his face removed.

"He's out there somewhere," Dillon says. "Shit. What do we do?"

He turns to Harper, and she one-hundred percent knows he's doing what he always does: using her like an external conscience. He doesn't want to go crashing around in the dark for the rest of the night, looking for a man with no face, but if she says to, he will.

"I don't—" Harper starts, and then a red bubble slowly expands over the woman's dry lips, goes back down before it can pop. "We need to—we need to get help," she says, reaching in to . . . she doesn't know: put a pillow behind the woman's head? clear her airway somehow? raise her feet above the level of her heart?

Then the one eye the woman has left opens, wheels around in terror, settles on Harper and Dillon.

The woman gasps, choking on her own blood, unable to change the angle of her throat. Harper reaches forward, takes her limp hand.

Dillon steps up onto the bumper, waves both arms to Jam and Kissy.

"Bring the truck!" he calls, just as another rig lays on its air horn. "Shit!" he says, jumping down, slapping his open hand onto the trunk, the car edging forward maybe three inches from his jostling.

The trunk opens too.

Dillon looks down into it, confused.

"Their *bags*," Harper says, nodding. "There's—we need to make a bandage, get something!"

Dillon hauls the one duffel out, closes the trunk just because that's what you do, and that last jostle is just enough to break that one important splinter keeping the snow fence upright, evidently.

Moving slow in the way of massive things, it leans back, the Thunderbird pushing it, pushing it, and then it falls all at once, in an exhalation of splinters.

The Thunderbird surges ahead over it, both doors closing when they encounter broken boards, and like that the big red car is easing deeper into the pasture, *with* the paralyzed holy roller.

Harper starts to run after but Dillon has her wrist.

They watch the car bump and roll, and then both step back when the next panel of snow fence falls over. And the next.

Like dominoes going either way from this one panel tipping over, the snow fence falls, and falls, dust sighing up into the air.

"It wasn't us," Dillon says.

"It was us," Harper says, and turns back to see if headlights are slowing on the interstate.

They aren't.

"We've got to—" she says, and, holding Dillon by the hand, pulls him away from this.

——— ———

They walk back up on Kissy and Meg calling out into the pasture for Jam.

"What?" Harper says. "You were supposed to stay together, I told you to—"

"He took the, you know, the *wipes*," Kissy says. "Three lunches in one day, plus the trauma of—?" She does her fingers around her face to show what she means, why Jam is out there looking for something to squat behind.

Harper looks out into the darkness but not very hard, has no desire to see Jam's head at stomach level.

"How's his face?" she asks.

"I still love him," Kissy says back.

"Were they out there?" Meg says.

Dillon shifts the big duffel to his other shoulder, says, his eyes skating away from Harper's, "Just the car."

Harper blows air out her nose at this. Is he protecting Meg from getting a version of what they just saw, or does he really want to have never been out there, should the law come asking how two hundred yards of snow fence got knocked over? To say nothing of the two corpses sunrise will reveal. The same way he's always been easy with dangerous things, lies have always been second-nature to him too. Just the grease necessary to get through the day in one piece. Which wasn't reason *one* why they're not together, but it was pretty much three through ten, anyway.

Still, Harper lets it slide, doesn't want Meg thinking about the one-eyed beehive lady out there, paralyzed and choking in the passenger seat, her big red car nosing forward for a gully, a creekbed, a sudden canyon.

The headlights are on, though, Harper tells herself. That means the taillights will be a flare for the rest of the night. Once they call this in, the Thunderbird will be easy to find, provided its battery lasts.

"Any time, James!" she calls out into the darkness.

"Pinch it off!" Dillon adds, needlessly. Grossly.

Maybe two minutes later—six rigs, only three of them spattering gravel at the Park truck—the shape of Jam totters up from the bushes. He's buttoning his shirt. Harper doesn't ask.

"My turn!" Kissy says and bounces out past him, taking the baby wipes he's holding up like a baton to pass to her. But he's at the end of his leg of the race, too, is weak, spent, half-gone.

"Does it hurt?" Harper asks when he's close enough.

He looks up to her, his eyes startlingly white in that half-mask of blood.

"I'm sorry, man," Dillon says.

"I just want to get back on the road," Jam says with considerably less humor than he's been having so far.

One quick pee later, Kissy's back.

"Was that all the snow fences falling down?" Meg asks, still looking out into the pasture.

"What's in the bag, big man?" Jam asks Dillon.

Dillon looks to Jam about this—big man?—but just shrugs, sloughs it off his shoulder, into the bed of the truck.

"Bibles and pimento cheese sandwiches," Harper says.

"So we're robbers now too?" Kissy says.

"Too?" Harper says.

"Let's go," Dillon says, checking the road to step around to the driver's door.

"Whoah, whoah," Kissy says. "Donny—like, our boss—he says only Park personnel can drive Park trucks."

"Like he'll know?" Harper asks.

"Not your ass," Jam says, delicately touching a pebble of glass from his top lip.

"Then you," Dillon says to Jam. "Can you see good enough with . . . all that?"

"He forgot his license," Kissy says, face down to deliver this news.

They all look to Jam about this.

His defense: "I—I haven't needed it all summer! It's . . . it's at the bunkhouse, I think. Top drawer. I'll just run up and get it right quick." He laughs about the hopelessness of this and rubs his top lip again, gingerly.

"He can't drive," Harper says. "He can barely see."

"I've got it," Jam says, swallowing loud as if with resolve. "It's just my face that's hamburger, not my eyes."

"But what if we get stopped?" Harper says. "You don't have a license."

"Said the church mouse," Kissy says.

Dillon sputters an accidental laugh about this—it's an old joke, that Harper's always on the straight and narrow—but he holds his hands up to show how not-involved he is with this.

"I think it's choirboy," Jam says. "Church mice are, like, poor, aren't they?"

"It's altar boy," Harper says. "And I'm not one."

"Altar girl?" Meg tries.

"You're not involved in these deliberations," Harper says, flashing her eyes at Meg.

Between headlights and air horn blasts, they load up.

Jam adjusts the rearview, sees himself at last and sags back, lets a deep cough out. The gagging kind.

"You're not going to throw up, are you?" Kissy says from the passenger seat, trying to distance herself from him. "Are you throwing up? Tell me if you're throwing up."

Jam shakes his head no then is throwing up over his knees, into the floorboard.

"Window, window!" Dillon says to Kissy.

"Think you already took care of that," Kissy says with a protective glare, about the back window.

"This is like an afterschool special," Harper says. "Reasons not to run away, one through five."

"How much longer to Rawlins?" Kissy asks, still holding Jam's head so it's pointed more out the window than in.

"Ninety miles," Dillon says, standing up a bit through the broken back window to catch a breath.

"Ninety miles," Harper repeats kind of hopelessly. "So we're . . . like three miles from Laramie? Four? Where's the next turnaround?"

"Emergency or civilian?" Dillon asks.

"What, are you a robot now?" Kissy asks him.

"I don't want to get stopped without a license," Jam explains. "Civilian."

"Highway 12," Dillon says. "Four miles, five."

"That Herrick one?" Jam says, maybe done puking. "That's—Sand Creek, right? There's no phones there, man."

"Hunt Road, then," Dillon says. "We can call in from that gas station. Fifteen minutes. Well, twenty at fifty-five. If it's open, I mean. Sound like a plan?"

"You really are a map," Meg says up to Dillon.

"My dad said if I was going to ride with him, that meant I was the navigator," Dillon says with a shrug. "I took it serious, I guess."

"You have to sit down in the seat," Jam says back to him. "One of us up here doesn't have his license with him, remember?"

"We don't need to get stopped," Kissy seconds.

"Unless we want, you know, *medical help*," Harper mutters. "Or want to report a wreck with fatalities."

Dillon slides back down, clearing the chance of glass out of the way.

"Nice air freshener you got in here," he says to the front seat.

"My own personal blend," Jam says back, lowering the truck into gear, his foot on the brake, eyes in the mirrors.

"Twenty minutes," Harper says to Meg, and pulls her close, holds her there.

CHAPTER 7

Three minutes later, maybe not even that, Kissy is enumerating the night's bullshit so far: Harper's big blowout with her mom, Kissy and Jam finding their best friend in the world in the ditch waiting for a serial killer, all three of them kidnapping a minor—"Do you think your mom's reported her missing?"—all the truckers in Wyoming targeting the Park truck for destruction, a human *face* on the windshield, and then two missing Bible-thumpers, a quarter-mile of snow fence knocked down, and a boyfriend who looks like he cut himself shaving a hundred times in a row.

"I miss anything?" she asks, eyes glittering over the back of the front seat.

"That the truck's overheating," Jam says, studying the gauge. "If that counts."

"Shit," Harper says, slumping further down into her seat.

"Turn the heater on," Dillon instructs. "That pulls the heat from the engine."

Almost instantly the cab is muggy hot, tastes like antifreeze.

"Welcome to hell night," Kissy says, giving up.

"Up here," Dillon says, pointing, and Jam coasts them into the pullout he means. It's nose-to-tail with sleeping truckers, sleeping rigs.

He kills the truck before Dillon can stop him and they all just sit there.

"Should we—" Meg says, trying to figure out the best way to

say it: "Should we have left a little pyramid of rocks on the side of the road back there? For the ambulance to find?"

"I could have hung this on a mile marker," Harper says, holding her glow-bracelet up. "Also, I could have *looked* at the mile marker."

"The one Kiss ran over?" Jam asks, trying to grin and immediately wincing from the effort.

"It's not all on you to save the world, to think of everything all the time," Dillon tells Harper.

"I'm the big sister," Harper says, and pushes her door open before he can come back with anything.

The night air is crisp, and sticky with diesel exhaust. One or two of the rigs are idling. Harper can feel the steady grumble in the asphalt. It's comforting, reminds her of childhood.

"There bathrooms at this one?" Jam asks, kicking his door open as well.

"Again?" Kissy says.

"Ammo dump," Dillon says, looking around at all the sloshing-full plastic bottles.

"Say what?" Jam says, not making the connection.

"Where you store your pee bombs," Harper says, already bored with it. "No, no facilities, Jam. Sorry."

"World's full of facilities, man," Dillon says, opening his arm to the big, dark night.

"You just wanted to look at your face, didn't you?" Meg says, taking a chance—being the kid, talking with the adults. Or, the closest thing to adults.

Jam looks away instead of answering. It's how Harper knows Meg was right.

"Is it drying into a scab?" Harper asks Jam, her right hand lifting not exactly to touch his face, more to almost touch it, like to pad it with a cushion of air.

Jam flinches back all the same, his arm coming up to protect.

"Sorry," Harper says.

He shakes his head no, not to worry about it. But he's not smiling anymore either.

"We should get some water," Kissy steps in to announce in her perky way. "For the radiator."

"Where?" Jam says, holding his hands up. "This isn't a rest stop. It's just a . . . is there some cool trucker word?"

"Hunh," Dillon says, then to Harper, "What *are* these? Nap trap or something?"

"We can call them whatever we want," Harper says like it even matters, leaning over the bed of the truck. "Swingout, how about?"

"Park 'n' nod," Meg says with authority.

"Park 'n' nod," Harper agrees without hesitation.

"Y'all making that up?" Kissy asks.

Meg shrugs and they all turn their heads to the buttery line of running lights coming on, outlining the cabover and trailer of a rig in front of them. Instant Christmas.

"Somebody wants us off their lawn," Dillon says, smiling in appreciation. "Flashing the porch lights at us."

"Shhh," Harper says to all of them.

The lights glow off in what Harper can tell is a surly way.

"It's like we're sneaking into the cave with the bears that want to eat us," Jam says, the ghost of a smile at the corners of his mouth now, his teeth seeming larger for some reason—maybe because they're so white in all that red. Harper wants to smile with him. She wants to smile just because he still *can* smile.

"He's just trying to sleep," Dillon says about the afterimage of the yellow lights still burning in all their eyes.

"Or she," Kissy says.

"Hungry, M?" Harper says to Meg.

Meg shrugs.

Dillon holds his eager hand up.

"I *know* you're hungry," Harper says, and hauls herself up into the bed of the truck, pulls the duffel bag over.

"You sure?" Kissy says, standing on the other side of the bed now. "This like breaking and entering?"

"They're both dead," Dillon says. "Think they can spare us a . . . what was it? Cold grilled cheese sandwich?"

"Pimento," Harper corrects.

"How do you know they're both dead?" Meg asks, not letting that slip past.

Harper rips the zipper down all at once so Dillon won't have to answer.

The duffel isn't Bibles and ziplock baggies.

Clothes? Not even folded?

Dillon steps up with her, the truck shifting with his weight, and Jam comes around to the bumper, his fingers nervous on the top of the tailgate. Harper looks up, finds Meg watching through the missing rear window.

"What is it?" Kissy says.

"Men's clothes, I think," Harper says, and starts pulling them out.

She's right, but that doesn't mean the clothes make sense. There's grimy hitchhiker gear but there's a pinstriped suit, and then a bright yellow sweater vest of all things—

"Easter egg disguise?" Dillon asks about it—and, pulling hard, a thick leather biker jacket, patches all up the left arm.

"These don't—" Harper starts, trying to make this make sense. "The guy who was in the car, he was . . . he didn't dress like this."

"Probably Goodwill stuff to like pass out on the road to people, yeah?" Jam says. "Didn't you say they were good samaritan types? Fairy godmothers of the interstate?"

"Ding ding ding," Dillon says, dropping the sweater vest back in.

Harper pulls it up to her face, smells it.

"Thrift store stuff usually smells like formaldehyde," she says. "It's that spray they use to delouse or whatever."

"What else?" Meg asks.

Harper pushes all the clothes out and to the side, reaches in for . . .

"Baby food?" she says.

Meg reaches above her, clicks the cargo light on over all this.

Baby food jars, yep. Probably twenty of them, each wrapped in rubber bands to . . . to keep them from breaking against each other?

Harper lifts one to inspect, shakes it, the contents runnier than apple sauce or strained carrots are supposed to be, and, and—

She flings it away.

It lands on the motorcycle jacket.

Delicately, Dillon two-fingers another jar up, holds it to the cargo light.

Swimming in the murky suspension is an eyeball.

"Holy shit," Kissy says. "I was just joking about the serial killer thing."

Harper passes Dillon another jar.

Finger.

The next jar is a finger as well, then a stubby thumb, then what looks to be an ear, maybe.

"What the living *hell*, Harp?" Kissy says. "I thought you said these people were proselytizing or whatever?"

"Some gospel," Dillon says, lining the looked-at jars on the rail of the bed.

"He was just . . . normal," Harper says. "Stupid and nothing and normal."

"I'll tell you what happened," Jam says, nodding with this, figuring it out as he goes. "They were pretending to be helping hitchhikers. Really they were . . . doing this. But they tried to do it to someone who didn't like it. Bam, justice."

"Guess that tracks, yeah," Dillon says, impressed.

"Then he's still out there," Harper says, looking behind them.

"Who?" Meg asks.

"Whoever cut that guy's face off," Jam says with more certainty.

Harper nods, keeps nodding.

"We can't keep this," she says about the bag, the clothes, the jars.

"It's proof," Dillon says.

"It's in our possession," Kissy says.

Jam says, "We can give it to the first cop—"

"I'm not riding with it anymore, I mean," Harper says. "I can—Meggie and me can get out here, if y'all want to keep riding with that."

Meg nods, agrees.

"This an Indian thing about . . . about associating with a corpse or something?" Jam asks, and Kissy looks in for the answer too, which is like seconding that stupid question.

"It's a human thing," Harper says. "But yeah, Indians like us, being a subset of humans, we don't like riding around with pieces of murdered people. Bad karma."

"Isn't karma Buddhist?" Kissy says.

"Shh," Harper tells her. "You're on our side here."

"Well then," Dillon says, upping this ante by rolling the wheel of the lighter already in his hand somehow.

"He's right," Kissy says to Harper. "We can't just leave it in the trash."

"We can leave it by the fence," Jam says, pleading. "We can tell the cops it's three posts down from the exit, whatever."

"Fire is burial," Meg says then, just out of nowhere. "That's a Viking thing."

"*What?*" Jam says to her.

"Let her," Harper says.

"It's the only burial they'll get," Meg says, shrinking under the attention.

"And the oracle has spoken!" Dillon announces, way too loud.

Harper shushes him back down to their level.

"I mean, I guess I don't want to get caught with that stuff either," Dillon whispers, "right?" With that he hauls the duffel over, pushes the line of jars back into it.

"These too," Harper says, picking the strewn-around clothes up like a load of laundry, working them into the bag Dillon's holding open.

The trash barrel closest to them is full but Dillon stands in it to pack it down. Harper smushes the duffel down in after.

"Anybody want to say anything?" Dillon says, holding the lighter to the corner of the bag.

"That we're destroying evidence, yeah," Jam says.

"Good riddance," Kissy says with a sneer.

"Do it," Harper says.

Dillon lets the flame catch, then when it's too slow he simply lights the trash under the bag. A flare later the duffel is enshrouded in flames six feet high. Then ten.

The jars pop in muted succession.

"Smells like cinnamon?" Meg says.

It does.

"Must be what that water in the jars was," Harper says.

"Freak," Kissy says, disgusted.

"Freaks *plural*," Jam corrects. "It was a man and a woman, right?"

Harper nods, lost in the dancing flames.

"Truck's cool enough now, I bet," Dillon says, leading the group back to their parking place.

Harper's the last to fall in, and then the first to look back.

"Shit," she says.

They all turn around.

Shit is right.

The trash in the fire is floating out, lighting the dry grass, is already spreading too fast to ever hope to stomp out.

"No no no," Dillon says.

"Go, go!" Kissy says, and pushes Meg into the front seat, Jam climbing in behind the wheel.

"What do we do?" Dillon says to Harper.

The fire is licking at the tires of two of the rigs, is going to be under all of them inside a minute.

"We can't let them burn," Harper says, and takes off running to the closest truck, the ones the flames are already to. She hauls herself up with the grab bar, slams her open hand on the window until the light inside comes on.

"Fire, fire!" she screams, and then is running to the next truck.

She looks back and Dillon is running the other way, waking the truckers parked at the other end.

Harper falls in the gravel, rises, stomps hard on the diamond-plate step of the next truck, comes up slamming her hand on the window again. When the light doesn't come on she closes her eyes and crashes her elbow through the glass, reaches in, pulls hard on the air horn strap in the ceiling. There's enough pressure that it bellows, splits the night with sound. Ahead, taillights are coming on.

From around the seat she's leaned across, a man in a pushed-up sleep mask and ear plugs rouses, tire beater in hand.

"Fire, fire, fire!" Harper yells, and then is gone, stepping back down into a field of flames. She steps ahead and draws back from the heat, is about to try another way when the Park truck skids in beside her, the rear passenger door opening, Dillon in back.

"C'mon, c'mon!" Kissy's yelling, the tired engine of the Park truck bogging down from how far she has her foot in it.

Harper looks back to all the trucks with fire already under them and then she lets Dillon pull her into the bed, wrap her in the biker jacket she must have forgot to burn.

"Oh no," she distinctly hears Dillon say, as Jam's accelerating them up the ramp.

Harper looks to where he's looking: a tanker truck, its lights still off, a beagle jumping at the driver's window, the driver probably conked in back.

"No, we've got to—" Harper says, trying to fight out of the jacket, save that truck, that dog, this pullout, but Dillon bundles her tighter, saves her from herself.

With a touch of distance, the pullout, glowing, is almost beautiful. Until one of the truckers, half-asleep and panicked, tries to grind his rig out of its slot but catches on the rear bumper of another rig, pulling it with. And then they both shake when a rig slams into them from behind. Another's trying to climb the grass up to the asphalt but its front tires are on fire, and now it's rolling over sideways, so slow, back into the flames.

Thirty seconds later the tanker truck explodes.

It's a perfect orange mushroom cloud.

Harper turns away from this, stares ahead, numb.

"It wasn't our fault," Dillon says.

"Then whose was it?" Harper asks back. "There somebody else back there setting fires?"

She thrusts her hands into the pockets of the jacket, feels a cool lump in there, through the fabric—biker jackets are made of pockets—and pulls her hand out fast, shakes it like she might have caught something.

"What?" Dillon says, suddenly there, all around her.

She shakes her head no, no, pulls forward, away from him.

The cargo light is still on, making her shadow crisp.

There through the center hole of the spare tire is the eyeball the crow dropped, staring back up at her.

She reaches up, clicks the cargo light off.

CHAPTER 8

"They're gonna love us even more now, aren't they?" Kissy is saying through the missing rear window. "All the truckers?"

Harper blinks, her hair stinging her face, the tall collar of the leather jacket held tight around her neck.

"Let's—" Dillon says, and guides her through the window into the rear seat, an awkward process since standing up higher than the cab delivers them to the sixty mile per hour wind. He follows, settles in right beside her, Kissy wriggling back into her place in the front seat. It's what micro people like her can do.

Harper holds her hand out to Meg and Meg melts through the window more than really crawls, as *kids* can do.

"Dad," she says.

Harper pulls her close. She can't stop thinking that either: their dad could have died just this way. From stupid kids playing with lighters.

"He wasn't there," Harper says.

"He who?" Jam says to them in the mirror.

"Nothing," Dillon says, though Harper knows he knows, is probably thinking about his own dad right now. Harper wonders if he's on a run right now. Could he have been back there?

No—why pull over for some shut eye so close to home? That'd be a dick move, even if it is just Dillon waiting for him at their trailer.

"My elbow matches your face now," she says ahead to Jam,

hiking her arm up to show, except it's the elbow of a worn-out leather jacket now.

"Hilarious," Jam says, switching from his left hand on the wheel to his right hand at the top of the wheel. It's as close as he can come to turning his back on everyone in the cab.

"She's just joshing," Dillon says, some bite to his tone.

"It's not her face," Jam says back with just as much conversation-killing bite.

"Here," Kissy says, scooching over to him, opening the wipes.

Jam draws away and raises his right shoulder higher, keeping it between her first-aid and his raw skin.

"I just want to get the blood off," Kissy says. "It's not even cut on this side, is it?"

"Music?" Harper says hopefully.

Kissy slides back to her side, thumbs a cassette in on the way. Gordon Lightfoot. "Not mine," she assures them all.

"Yellowstone approved," Jam adds.

Kissy narrows her eyes at him about this.

"Whoah," he says back, and pulls hard onto the shoulder without losing any speed.

They all look back, and *whoah* is an understatement: one of the rigs made it out of that pullout. But now it's trying to outrun its own flames—it's trying to put them out with speed. Its trailer is burning down to nothing, must be wall to wall with cardboard boxes—shoes or VCRs or linens. The rig slams past like the Park truck's standing still, leaves big black flakes swirling in its wake.

"What if he'd been hauling corn, right?" Dillon says.

Harper looks over to him.

"Popcorn," he says, forcing a smile.

"Or chickens," Jam says. "I could go for some fried-right chicken."

"Pigs," Kissy says like a challenge.

"Mmmm," Jam says, stabbing his arm out his window, plucking imaginary strips of bacon from the wind.

A mile later, in the eastbound lanes, it's all blue and red sirens whining in on this explosion.

"Where they coming from?" Dillon says, in wonder.

"Laramie too, I bet," Harper says. "Just, we can't see those."

"We—we can't call that wreck in now, can we?" Kissy says.

"Why not?" Meg asks.

"Because we need to never have been here at all," Jam says, a step ahead.

"He's right," Kissy says.

"But it was an *accident*!" Dillon says. "And we tried to—"

"We left the scene," Harper says. "It's what guilty parties do."

"This doesn't feel like a party," Meg says.

"The jars," Harper says then. "We have to tell them about the jars anyway, don't we?"

Jam cocks his face into the rearview, says to Dillon, "The two people doing that are . . . you said dead, right?"

Dillon nods.

"Then we call in about whoever did that to them," Harper says.

"It was probably self defense," Kissy says.

"Cutting someone's face off is self defense?" Harper says back.

"Maybe that was the birds," Meg says.

Harper shakes her head in disgust, tracks one set of blue and red lights, pushing hard to catch up with the rest. "This is probably how Bonnie and Clyde started out," she says. "Mickey and Mallory."

"That old movie with Arthur in it?" Kissy asks, not following.

"She's talking about Mickey and Mallory," Dillon says. "From last year? That guy from *Cheers*? Jam?"

Jam flashes his eyes into the rearview like caught, then, slowly, and with not much confidence, he nods.

"Your mom hated that movie," Kissy says.

He nods that she did, yes. Obviously.

"She loved it," Kissy says. "She wore that KISS makeup for Halloween, even."

Harper looks from her to Jam, isn't sure what's going on.

"*Shit!*" Jam says then, banging the heel of his right hand on the steering wheel. "I just figured out what those jars were. Y'all've heard of Bucketmouth?"

"Bucket-what?" Harper says.

"Like the fish?" Dillon says. "Isn't that what they call bass?"

"Bass?" Jam says, turning his actual eyes to the backseat for this.

Dillon shrugs, says, "Fishermen call largemouth bass bucketmouths. Smallmouth are . . . yeah, *bronze*backs. You don't know this? Thought you were mister anglerman?"

"There's mostly trout at the Park," Kissy says.

"Catfish are mudcats," Dillon says, listing. "Crappie are speckled perch, and my dad calls steelhead—"

"Why 'Bucketmouth,' though?" Jam's saying, adjusting the rearview to not miss a single thing Dillon's saying.

"Because their mouths are, you know, *large*," Dillon says obviously. "But they're bass, right? A bass eats everything it can long as it's flopping or twitching or chirping, doesn't worry about it till later, just scoops it up, lets digestion do the rest."

"Hunh," Jam says, nodding with this explanation. Liking it, it seems.

"Why does this matter?" Harper asks. "We just burned down a pullout, and now we're talking about fish?"

"Just wondering," Jam says, angling the rearview mirror back to normal. "Nothing."

"You figured out the jars, though?" Dillon prompts, then, for Harper: "That relates to . . . what just happened."

"What we just *did*," Harper corrects.

Kissy is just watching Jam.

"Oh yeah, the Bucketmouth story," he goes on, switching hands on the wheel like this is a Sunday drive they're on. "He's this, like, highway boogeyman, I don't know. You really haven't heard of him? If he eats a piece of you, he can turn into you, something like that. Don't remember exactly. I was thinking that maybe he keeps jars in a bag like that the same way James Bond might keep a suitcase of disguises."

"Quick change," Dillon says, nodding with this explanation. "Let me just nibble on this ear right quick."

"Gross," Meg says.

"To us, yeah," Jam says.

"You're really saying that this, this urban legend or whatever," Harper says, "that those body parts in cinnamon water back there were from that? *For* that?"

"For *him*," Dillon corrects.

"Then we destroyed all his shit," Kissy says.

"Unless he thought ahead, buried some along the way," Jam says.

"Buried *jars* along the way?" Kissy says.

"This fencepost, that utility pole," Jam says with a shrug about how obvious this is. "It'd be smart, wouldn't it?"

"It'd be stupid," Harper says. "It would mean he's running up and down the same stretch of highway over and over, asking to be caught. That's the problem with these bullshit campfire stories. Apply logic and they're not so scary anymore. The only monsters out here tonight are us. Ask that guy whose truck blew up back there, if he's even still alive. Ask him if he's more scared of this Bucketmouth or of stupid kids with matches."

The cab is quiet for a quarter-mile after that.

"Don't take Harp to the carnival," Dillon finally says. "She spends all her time popping little kids' balloons."

Harper elbows him.

"It's more fun to believe!" he says, protecting his ribs now.

"Bullshit monsters digging jars up from the ditch don't make the world better," Harper says. "They just let you put off the world you're actually living in a little longer."

"Not much longer . . ." Jam says then, leaning back to get a showy angle on the temperature gauge. "Where's the next place we can stop?"

"Still Herrick," Dillon says, leaning over the seat to see the needle. "We're not exactly making great time."

"Herrick's not a place," Harper mumbles. "It's just an exit."

"That gas station on 59," Dillon says then. "Hunt Road."

"You are a robot," Meg tells him.

"Don't talk to him," Harper warns.

Dillon robot-dances his arm out beside him as best he can in the limited space, does his jaw up and down like it's on pistons. Meg smiles and Harper has to look away.

In the front seat, Kissy, on her side of the bench seat, is still studying Jam.

"What?" he finally says.

"You didn't use any wipes," Kissy says, holding them up.

They all look to her, Gordon Lightfoot crooning about sundown but seeming to listen too, while he strums his 12-string.

"What do you—?" Jam starts, but Kissy's already there: "Nature called back there, or nervous squirts, too many lunches, whatever, right? I get it, whatever, who cares. But . . . but—"

"She said 'butt,'" Dillon leans over to say to Meg.

Harper shushes him, is watching this closely.

"—but you didn't use any of the wipes, did you?" Kissy finally completes. "I know how thick this was when you went out there. It was the same when you handed it to me. And you're never, shall we say . . . thrifty, are you?"

"Dry run," Jam says. "False alarm. 'There I sat so brokenhearted—'"

"You were gone *forever*," Kissy says, throwing the wipes into the floorboard in a huff.

"Sorry?" Jam says, mostly for Dillon and Harper and Meg, Harper knows. To get them on his side.

"What are you saying, Kiss?" she asks.

"What drawer were you talking about, where your driver's license might be?" Kissy says then, her voice ramping up into a real fight.

"I think that's where it is, geez."

"No, I mean—are there dressers or nightstands at the bunkhouse I don't know about? Because we all use footlockers, Jam. *Trunks*."

"We work at Yellowstone, right? That's why we have this truck?"

"Nobody who works there calls it 'Yellowstone,'" she says. "'Yellowstone' is a dirty word. It's the Park, Jam. The *Park*."

"Listen, I don't know what you're—" Jam says, reaching across the seat to help her down from her indefensible position. She shies away hard, offended.

"Who are you?" she says. "What is your name even short for? Tell me that."

"My name?" Jam says, letting his foot off the gas.

"Just tell us your full name, yeah," Harper says. "Don't look in your wallet either."

"He doesn't have his license," Kissy says, watching him so closely now.

"You're buying into this?" Dillon asks Harper, a little awed. "You think . . . what? He told us that Bucketmouth story because he's actually Bucketmouth? *Jam* is Bucketmouth?"

"*Why won't you let me see your face?*" Kissy screams then.

"Because it's fucking ruined!" Jam says right back. Then, right to Kissy, "Here, you want to see? You really want to see?"

He jerks the wheel over and stomps the brakes, locking the rear tires up. The truck skids and fishtails, rocks and almost rolls, comes to a harsh stop half-in half-out of the ditch, the harsh scent of burned drums and hot rubber washing in through the missing back window. The truck sputters out and the headlights dim a notch, are shining across the two lanes of the westbound, are in the sky by the eastbound, like searching for something up there.

"C'mon," Jam says, opening his door without looking, storming around to the front of the truck—the headlights.

"What the hell is this?" Dillon says.

"Kiss, don't—" Harper says, reaching over the seat for Kissy, but she's already got the door open, is rounding the front of the truck as well, isn't going to let this die.

She comes back for the wipes, holds them up to all in the cab like proof, slams the door after her.

Her and Jam meet in the headlights, are two glowing angels.

Harper opens her door to go up there with them but a station wagon whips by honking, startles her back.

"Just let them," Dillon says, his hand around her wrist. "You know how they are."

"Harper . . ." Meg's saying, her tone rising into panic.

Harper moves over to her, leans ahead to see what's happening at the front of the truck.

"She's—she's gotta be wrong," Harper says.

"About Jam being Bucketmouth?" Dillon says with a smile.

"About Jam not being Jam," Harper says, no smile at all. "When would it have even happened, this big switcheroo?"

"While he was . . . using the facilities," Meg says quietly, and sort of with a gulp.

They both look to her, and then, with different eyes, over the hood again.

"But it probably takes a while," Harper says, mostly to herself.

"What takes a while?" Dillon asks.

"Bucketmouth," Harper says. "After he—he eats a finger, an ear, whatever. It's got to take a while for him to . . ." She does her fingers over her face to show what she means.

"How long was he out there in the bushes?" Dillon says back, not looking away from Kissy and Jam in the headlights.

Kissy has a wipe stretched over her finger now, is pointing that finger up to Jam's face delicately, like a girlfriend, but then the light isn't right. He switches sides with her and they lower down to the driver's side headlight, disappear except the glowing haze of their hair.

"I thought it was the other side of his face," Meg says.

"It was," Harper says, and then jerks back hard when Kissy is pushed up and away, her feet not in contact with the blacktop for maybe a whole second.

It's timed perfectly for the next rig slamming past—probably the last one to pass the pullout before it was blocked off.

It doesn't just hit her, it *bursts* her, and, because Harper's looking right at her, is trying to reel her back in just by not breaking eye contact, she has to see it in high detail: the round passenger-side headlight carving Kissy's face into a clean half-moon, the bumper passing through her like she's a Jell-O sculpture, Kissy's left shoe flinging up alongside the fender for an impossible snapshot of an instant, before the front tire grabs it, pulls her under.

What sticks for Harper is the look on Kissy's face. It's not satisfaction for having been right about Jam not being Jam, and it's not the surprise and shock she would expect. It's the same look Kissy had when they were seventh graders, using her mom's old Polaroid camera to take pictures of each other jumping into the swimming pool at the Y, before the lifeguard cued in, made them stop.

In one of the Polaroids that turned out, Kissy had a look on her face, in her eyes, like she knew the cold dunk that was coming, but she wasn't scared of it, she was ready for it. She couldn't wait.

That's how she looked in that last split instant, her full head of hair lifted all around her.

And now—now it isn't just seventh grade that was gone, it's all the grades since, and all the grades to come. Not college, none of them are thinking more school, but jobs, and marriage if her and Jam made it that far, kids even, grandkids. Checkers at the grocery store giving her the eye when she's not looking, wondering how killer she must have been twenty, thirty years ago.

But she still would have been just as killer, Harper knows.

She's Kissy.

No: she *was* Kissy.

Now she's a scream welling up from Harper's . . . from her soul, her core, whatever's most secret and pure at the very center of her. It's like—it's like Kissy was a *part* of her, a part now being ripped away at eighty-five miles per hour, a part that's now just a breath of red mist hanging in the halogen light, a breath of red mist and a long strand of black hair hanging there.

The part of her mind that's off to the side, that's not building a shriek and pushing it out, it's whispering to her that she's never been this close to death, has she? Sure, on runs with her dad, she's seen a rig blow its driver's side front tire, step over the line, onto a little Datsun or Toyota, but her dad would always reach across, pull her face into his chest.

He's not here now.

Harper can't turn away.

Kissy is . . . she's gone, she's dead, she's nothing. All her years of living, all her experience, all her bad jokes, that way she had of never remembering her jacket, even when it's cold, it's all gone in less than a tenth of a second. And the driver who hit her, he doesn't even have time to honk or brake or anything, maybe isn't even aware he's hit anything. Any*one*.

Harper collapses over the front seat, her right hand reaching, scrabbling uselessly at the dash, her insides cold.

They get colder when Jam stands, wiping his face himself, carefully, dab by dab, looking at the wipe after each slow wipe then applying it again, stretching his neck to tighten his skin, remove each fleck of blood, each smear of red.

Slowly, all the blood and chunks come off, and his face isn't pebbled with glass at all. He's just Jam. But not.

He shrugs one shoulder about Kissy like what you gonna do, like she brought it on herself, then, moving heavy like this is the chore part of these proceedings, he reaches to the small of his back, comes around with a shiny snub-nose revolver that Jam definitely didn't have on him, either before or ever.

"Bucketmouth," Harper says, as sure as anything, and now Dillon, more aware of what that little pistol means for them, is bellowing her name, diving across the front seat to twist the ignition.

The Park truck rumbles to life.

Jam holds both hands up like impressed, like obviously outgunned. He smiles, cocks his head over, watching this small drama play out through the windshield.

"You killed my best friend, asshole," Harper says, and drops the transmission all the way into first just as Dillon, half in the front seat now, slams the accelerator down with his hand.

The Park truck burps forward, catches this Bucketmouth in the midsection, tosses him back into the shoulder like a ragdoll. He rolls through the glowing grass, all the dust in the headlights swirling golden over him.

The Park truck putters out from the effort.

"Shit, shit, shit!" Dillon says, fumbling up for the key again.

In the headlights at first it's just Kissy's bones and Kissy's shiny insides, splattered across thirty or forty yards of asphalt. Until Bucketmouth stands, unkinking his back, shaking his head like breaking cobwebs, like impressed that they actually *hit* him with the truck.

Then he holds his right hand up, opens and closes it in wonder, doesn't have the snub-nose anymore. He looks in his left hand. It's not there either.

He chuckles at how ridiculous this is and Harper turns the headlights off, his bright smile still burning into her eyes.

"He can't find it in the dark," she says.

"Go, go, go," Meg is saying from the backseat, quietly.

"Put it—in park," Dillon says, straining from his awkward position, legs in the backseat, body across the front, arms in the floorboard.

Harper does. Dillon grinds the starter, feathering the pedal. The battery drags, drags, and then, finally, the engine roars to life again.

"*Gas*," Harper says, an order not a request, and Dillon lays into it with his hand again. She waits until the RPMs are screaming to drop the truck into gear.

It surges forward and she clicks the headlights on an instant later, to see Bucketmouth go under the front bumper.

He's not there anymore.

What the tires are crunching through now, it's the bone parts of Kissy.

"Go," Meg pleas, her voice small.

They do.

CHAPTER
9

What Harper can't stop looping in her head is that Kissy didn't have to die. That her best friend could still be here—could still be up in the passenger seat, her hair casually, maddeningly perfect, her purse stuffed with a thousand things she was never going to need but had to have with her all the same.

It's so fucking unfair. It's so stupid.

How could Jam not be Jam? How could there really be monsters who can become other people just by eating a piece of them? What was Jam—no, *Bucketmouth*, what was he even hoping to do? Is that what counts as fun for him, fooling people into believing he's whoever he looks like? Does playing with his food make it taste better?

And, and: what about Jam, lying naked back in the bushes where the Thunderbird went through the fence?

They're both dead, Harper realizes.

It's like she has to keep telling herself that every few seconds. Because it won't stick, it won't stay real.

Kissy, Jam. They're not in the world anymore, and never will be again. Just like that.

"And all because they stopped for me," Harper says, wiping her nose with the sleeve of the leather jacket, tilting her head back to keep her tears in. It doesn't work.

"What?" Dillon says, though he had to have heard.

He's at the steering wheel, Harper in the passenger seat, Meg between them, in some sort of shock. The backseat is a wind tunnel. Gordon Lightfoot's not singing about sundown anymore, but the *Edmund Fitzgerald* going down. It feels right.

"This can't be happening," Harper says. "People can't just change like that. This isn't *The X-Files*."

"Then," Dillon says, picking through all the bad answers, "then that would mean it was really Jam, wouldn't it? It would mean his switch flipped."

"He didn't have that kind of switch," Harper says. "That wasn't him. He would never . . . not Kissy. He would never hurt her. He wouldn't know how."

Dillon nods, knows.

"Then what was he?" Meg asks in monotone. It's how she deals, Harper knows. It's the flat affect she retreats to after a big blowout between Harper and their mom.

Harper doesn't have any answer to what Jam was. "Bucketmouth" doesn't seem like a legitimate answer.

"Two-thirty, two-forty . . ." Dillon reads aloud, not liking the truck's temperature.

"What'll happen?" Harper says.

"It'll seize, maybe crack the block," Dillon says.

Harper expected something like that.

"Good thing her dad didn't buy this truck," she says, forcing a single chuckle that feels more like a sob.

"If he had, we wouldn't be in it now," Dillon says back.

He's practical like that, always sees the straight line between A and B, even if the rest of the alphabet is completely out of sight. Still, B isn't bad. You've got to get to B before all the other letters.

"Do you remember that first December?" she says across to him.

Dillon looks across to be sure, then nods.

It's where they met: December of their eighth grade year—one year ahead of where Meg is now. Dillon was already sitting on top of the apartments his mom was living at when Harper stepped out from the stairway, bundled up against the snow because she wasn't coming down until she saw her dad. But she'd thought it would just be her. She wasn't the only one with a dad slipsliding his way home for Christmas, though. She wasn't the only one who knew these apartments had a bird's eye perfect view of 80.

For four hours they sat up there hardly saying anything, just watching rig after rig lose it on the ice, their trailers coming around in slow motion, churning up snow and dark earth from the ditch. The first one that tumped over, Harper gasped, held her hands over her mouth, and Dillon had put his arm around her, and together, in secret, they promised that they didn't care if their dads made it home that night, that they didn't want them to, that they wanted them to be at a motel in Cheyenne or Salt Lake, warm and safe, watching *Law & Order* on the television. They didn't care about Christmas, they cared about forever.

By the New Year they were promising each other that it was the two of them against the world, that they'd found each other just like they were supposed to, they didn't need anybody else from here on out.

That was how Kissy and Jam had always been, too. Even when they were fighting.

Harper wipes her eyes with the sleeve of the leather jacket, which doesn't wipe shit away.

"I can't believe they're gone," she says, her voice hitching.

"What was he?" Meg says.

"Bucketmouth, I guess," Harper says. "He told us, right? Had either of you heard that story before?"

Dillon and Meg shake their head no.

"I know about that ghost girl who hitchhikes—" Dillon starts.

"Not her," Harper says. "She's just scary, not hungry. Why wouldn't we have heard, you think? We live right on the interstate."

"Maybe he's just getting to Wyoming," Dillon says.

"Or maybe everybody he tells the story to, he . . . you know," Meg says.

"Yeah, that," Dillon says. "He croaks them before they can spread the legend."

"Meaning we're still on his list," Harper says. "He can't let word of what he's doing get out. What he *can* do, whatever he is. But—there won't be any more drivers through there for hours, now. He won't be able to hitch a ride."

"So we're good?" Dillon says.

"We're in an overheating truck we don't own and we just blew up about twelve semis and we left a paralyzed woman to die in her car and I'm wearing some dead guy's jacket and we just saw our two best friends die and there's a killer after us who can change his face and likes to eat people," Harper says. "Yeah, I'd say we're great."

"Us, I mean," Dillon says. "December."

"Long time ago," Harper says. "I was thinking about . . . I guess Kiss and Jam's December would have been band camp, sixth grade, right? That's where they got together the first time?"

"Nerd alert," Dillon says.

"I'm in band," Meg says.

"Idiot alert," Harper says about Dillon. "And no, we're not together. I'm leaving, remember?"

"You're still doing that?" Meg says.

"Does Mom still live in Laramie?" Harper says back.

"I'm going with you, then," Meg says.

"Like hell," Harper tells her.

"That the only reason we're not getting back together, though?" Dillon says. "Because you're leaving?"

"Also because we're probably both dead by sunup," Harper says, wedging her knees up against the dash and holding her hair back with her hands.

"Both dead?" Meg says.

"Not you," Harper says. "You live, always."

"We need a code word," Dillon says. "For if he, you know." He holds his hand up with the ring finger folded down as if bitten off.

"He couldn't remember the bunkhouse," Harper says, nodding with this. "He gets the face, not the memories, has to make it all up on what he sees, or hears, what he can figure out. He knew Yellowstone because of the truck, but he didn't know what it was like to *work* there."

"Band camp," Meg says with finality. "We'll ask where Kissy and Jam fell in love."

"Band camp," Harper says.

"Nerd camp," Dillon says. "Sure. Comes up in natural conversation all the time."

"Temperature?" Harper asks him.

Dillon peers down, shakes his head no, does his lips like steam hissing out, and reaches down to see if he can open the heater up any more.

CHAPTER
10

They have to stop at the exit for 12 whether there's anything there or not.

"Isn't there a creek around here?" Harper asks.

"We'd need a bucket, a hose, and it'd clog the radiator up besides," Dillon says. "You're supposed to use distilled water."

"And this matters to us because we care about this truck so much," Harper says back. "All we need is to get to the first phone."

"There," Meg says.

They're sitting at the bottom of the off-ramp. Under the bridge they can just see signs of life past the eastbound lanes. Not a payphone, but structures anyway.

The truck clatters and almost dies but Dillon feathers it and pats the dash lovingly, eases them under, to the lone light over past the eastbound lanes.

It's a house, some outbuildings.

"Salvation," he says, and coasts them in, past the house to the tanks up on ten-foot racks, all of it painted dull industrial silver, dust and seed heads painted right in with.

"Gas, gas," Dillon identifies, coasting past the tanks, then, braking: "Bingo."

"A hand pump?" Harper says.

"Cleaner than a creek," Dillon says, and puts the truck up in park.

"Turn it off?" Harper says.

"Got to cool it down first," Dillon says, and the way it works is Harper pumps the pump—it's greased, silent—and Dillon directs the thin, once-green hose over the steaming radiator slow at first, touching his palm to the cap over and over, Meg at the gas pedal to keep the truck alive if it tries to sputter out.

Twenty agonizing minutes later—long enough for Harper to cycle back into Kissy and Jam being the forever kind of dead about six times, and come back with a lump in her throat each time—Dillon can finally hold his bare palm to the steel cap.

He backs it off slow, one stage at a time. It hisses at the first stage, doesn't have any steam left by the second.

"If we put too much cold water in while it's still super hot," he explains, "it'll crack. Got to go slow . . ."

"Thanks, shop teacher," Meg says ahead to him, and Harper has to smile in spite of how many times she's cranked the hand pump's lever up and down already.

Dillon eases the water in a spurt at a time, letting the engine suck it up, massaging the top hose to be sure the thermostat's opening, narrating each step as he goes just like, yes, a shop teacher, and then the water's surging up out of the mouth of the radiator and Harper can stop pumping.

"Sounds better already," he says, patting the nose of the truck, easing the hood down and giving it his weight at the very end, trying to close it without slamming it.

"Sounds better for the *moment*," Harper says.

"Guys?" Meg says, and when they look back they see what she means: the shirtless fifty-year-old man approaching with a shotgun.

"Whoah, whoah," Dillon says, stepping forward, hands high, directing the shotgun away from Harper, she's pretty sure.

"Got the gas locked up," the man grumbles. "Think I'm an idjit?"

"Just the water, just the water," Dillon says. "Truck was hot, we hung the hose back up, were going to leave some . . ."

Harper holds up all the cash she has on her: two fives.

Moving slow, she stuffs it into the wire hanger of the pump.

"Just water," the man says, lowering the shotgun. He sniffs the air, can smell the antifreeze now it looks like. "It's well water," he adds.

"Truck's older than me," Dillon says back with a smile.

The man looks up and down the truck.

"It's for sale," Harper says.

"No thank you, ma'am," the man says, then smiles and winks. "I hear it's got kind of a hot temper."

Harper smiles with him, flashes her eyes to Meg, which is the only reason she catches the slight movement behind the truck, coming in from the road.

"Hey—" is all she's able to get out before the blacked-out chopper, engine off, sweeps past at forty miles per hour, the helmeted rider swinging a chain or piece of wire, it's too dark to be sure.

Whatever it is, it takes the man's throat with it, leaves him standing there.

He fires one barrel into the dirt at his feet, and the other barrel into the top of his right foot, blossoming it up into hamburger meat that just keeps coming.

He teeters over, burbling frothy blood down his bare chest.

"Jam," Dillon says, backing off.

"Bucketmouth," Harper hisses.

She runs to the falling man but only gets her arms bloody holding him, can't do anything.

Out in the darkness Bucketmouth pops the clutch, the chopper's throaty exhaust filling the night.

He turns the headlight on, runs the face shield of his helmet up so they can see how perfect his Jam-face is, and stands on his left foot to spin a neat donut, swirl all the dust up into the air, exactly as Jam never knew how to. Then, still throttling high, he unplants his left foot, settles it on a peg, and accelerates right past them, swinging the—it's a chain, yes—swinging it at Dillon, who manages to slide underneath, but just barely.

The chain hooks onto the driver's side open door of the truck instead, Meg squealing back, and the sudden pull yanks Bucketmouth off the back of the bike, sends it careening off. It crashes into the house.

"You asshole!" Harper screams, running from the dead man to Bucketmouth.

On the way she picks up a stray piece of rebar, is already holding it behind her like a broadsword.

But then Bucketmouth looks up at her with Jam's face, says, "Harp? That you? What's happening?"

She stops, the rebar still cocked behind her.

At which point something sparks in the wrecked chopper. It's not an explosion, just a flare of flame that catches the dry grass.

When Harper comes back to Bucketmouth, he's gone again, just the helmet where he was.

The first place she looks is to the truck, but Dillon's already guarding Meg, a board in his hand, his eyes everywhere at once.

"We should leave," he says.

"And maybe we shouldn't, like, *stop* anywhere else?" Meg adds.

"First, this," Harper says, walking to the tumped over chopper. "We're not leaving another fire."

She kicks and stomps it out, then stares down where it was, daring it to come back.

"Let's go, let's go!" Dillon says to her. "He's still here, Harp!"

"How did he get here so fast?" she says back to both of them.

"Like that," Dillon says, tipping his head at the westbound lane, not exactly *jammed* with headlights, but there's a steady enough stream now.

"The eastbound lane's turning around," Harper says in wonder. "Because of us. Because we started that—because we burned his stuff, now they're all lining up to . . . he can refill his little jars."

"With us," Meg says.

———

"We've got to call it in," Harper says once they've merged in front of a little brown Audi, since none of the big rigs are even considering letting *this* truck have anything.

"Anonymously?" Dillon tries.

"I don't care anymore," Harper says. "We'll explain. We'll explain for five days, until they believe us."

"If we all have the same story," Meg adds.

"It's not a story," Harper says. "It's what happened."

"Think he's hitching to catch us?" Dillon says, clocking his mirror.

"Do I think it's a game to him?" Harper says. "Yes. That motorcycle was too easy for him. It didn't make us scared, the way he likes. I think—I think this is so easy for him, he likes to have fun. We're tonight's fun."

"That . . . that gas pump man," Meg says, her breath hitching.

"He was even—" Harper says, figuring it out as she goes. "When we thought he was Jam, he was telling us how he does it, wasn't he? The jars, the, the different faces he can put on. He said it would be smart to have buried them for emergencies. We didn't destroy his stash. We just burned what he was carrying around."

"They've got to be miles apart, though, wouldn't you think?" Dillon says. "How many people can he have bitten a piece off of?"

"Seen all the missing posters in the gas station windows?" Harper says.

"He's one guy," Dillon says.

"You're right," Harper says. "He's a monster, but he's also . . .

human. Like us. We hit him with the truck. It wasn't a hard hit, but it knocked him down. He can be hurt."

"He *did* get back up," Dillon notes, slowing to let an Oldsmobile in, to keep an impatient trucker off its rear bumper.

"We've got to assume he's like us," Harper says. "Mostly."

"Because that's less scary?" Dillon asks.

"If he's not," Meg says, her tone half reverent. "If he's not, then he could be however old, couldn't he?"

"Y'all got some old Arapaho boogeyman stories about him, you mean?" Dillon says.

"Most of our boogeymen stories are about white men," Harper says back, holding her hand up for Meg to slap a sisterly five.

"He is white," Dillon says.

"For now," Meg says. "Temperature?"

"She likes doing just fifty like this," Dillon says, patting the dash with his right hand. With his second pat there's an explosion on the windshield. He brakes hard, the rig behind them having to lock it up as well, but then he raises his hand out the window for the driver to see all's well, eases up to speed again.

"Pee," he says, looking for the wiper knob.

Harper cranks her window up almost fast enough.

Once they can see again, Dillon lifts his finger to a new crack in the windshield. His finger comes away wet. He smells it, crinkles his nose.

"Baby wipe," Meg says, digging them up, passing him one.

"This night," Harper says.

"Maybe we should paint the door," Dillon says.

"Or abandon truck," Harper says.

"Some of us aren't as committed to thumbing it as you are," Dillon says. "I'm a dude. Picking me up off the side of the road is a risk. You're pretty. Both of you are. Picking women up is a chance for a good time."

"Fuck you and fuck that," Harper tells him.

"Just saying it like it is," Dillon says back.

"Don't listen to him," Harper tells Meg.

"Would you pick me or you up first?" Dillon says then. "Being honest, I mean. I'm in my Sunday best, you're wearing that sweatshirt."

Harper considers, considers, then looks away, doesn't want to talk about this anymore.

"*He's* not having any difficulty finding rides," Harper says. "He even got a motorcycle to stop."

"We don't know that," Dillon says. "For all we know, dude stopped to drain the lizard, got jumped by mister bloodyface."

"Jam," Harper says. "He looks like Jam now."

"As of ten minutes ago," Dillon says.

"How long do you think it takes him to change all the way?" Meg asks.

"I don't think you can watch it happen like a special effect," Harper says. "But, look away for a few minutes, an hour?"

"Shit," Dillon says. "He probably stuck around, ate a piece off that guy with the shotgun, think?"

It makes sense.

"Everybody," she says. "He's everybody. He could be anybody."

"Band camp, band camp," Dillon says.

Meg smiles from that.

"Don't," Harper tells her. "He's not funny."

"Just ruggedly handsome," Dillon says, making like studying his look in the rearview, then flinching back and jerking the wheel when another pee bomb explodes on the windshield.

Thirty seconds later, wipers waggling through the oily residue—"What was he *drinking*?" Harper asks—Meg wipes a dot of wetness from her cheek, then another, then pushes fast over the backseat.

The crack in the windshield is worse, now. Leaking urine.

"Will it cave in on us?" Harper asks Dillon, her hand to the escape lever the door handle is.

"Not just from the wind," Dillon says, pushing against the glass with his fingertips to test it for give. "They keep using us like a urinal, though..."

"*Stop, stop!*" Harper screams, hating the shriek in her voice, her arms locking her against the dash not because she told them to but because that's what arms do in situations like this.

Dillon stomps the brakes again, harder, sees what he was missing beyond the windshield: the ass end of a livestock trailer.

"No," he says about what he's seeing in the rearview, and Harper looks around, sees the cabover maybe a foot and a half from their rear bumper, the driver leaned over his wheel, waving his hand in front of his nose about the smell coming from the livestock trailer.

"Pigs," Meg says.

The rig beside them eases tire-deep over into their lane so there can be no doubts about whether this is intentional or not.

"I hate pigs," Dillon says.

The smell is so thick there's particles to it.

Meg, the only one of them thinking, dispenses three baby wipes from the soft bag, passes one each way and presses her own over her nose and mouth, draws deep through it.

Harper does the same. Dillon too, going by the gagging sounds over there.

"You're not throwing up," she instructs him, which is just the puke trigger he needs, evidently.

His vomit is thin, sprays around the edges of the wipe onto the wheel, the dash.

He cranks and cranks on his window, leans out, loses everything else.

The three trucks hotboxing them all lay on their air horns in celebration.

"Ditch, ditch," Harper says, and Dillon nods, steers them over and has to come right back: staties are spaced out on the shoulder to keep traffic moving. To keep cutters from cutting, causing more accidents.

"They knew," Harper says.

"Of course they know," Dillon says, still breathing in an upchucky way. "They can see everything from up there."

"And talk about it on the, on the radio," Harper says, and that's her limit: she's cranking her window down, puking down the side of the door.

When she comes back in, Meg's face is mummied with wipes, her back ramrod straight, like she's pretending to be somewhere else completely.

"Did you, did you cover the decal on your side at least?" Dillon asks.

Harper has to laugh. Her eyes are already crying from throwing up.

"They'll never know us," she manages to get out, and then Dillon's laughing as well and Meg's a mummy, not acknowledging any of this, and that's how they ride the next three miles out, until the exit opens up beside them like the gates of heaven.

"Hunt Road," Dillon proclaims.

"We've got to call," Harper says, hanging her head out the window for fresh air.

"On that phone?" Meg says, a wipe peeled hesitantly from her right eye.

The payphone line snakes back like a rollercoaster ride.

Akal Travel Center.

"The gas station is *open*, ladies," Dillon says, presenting it to them in all its ungloriousness.

He's wrong though, Harper thinks. It's not a gas station, it's a circus: with the interstate piled up for miles, this place is an oasis in the nighttime desert of Wyoming. All the truck parking is nose to tail, and rigs are lining both sides of the road as well, the ground shaking with idling engines, the air sticky with diesel.

Dillon cruises past, looking for parking. It's hopeless.

"I've been here . . ." Harper says, clocking the low red roof that's like a stubby Stuckey's. She turns to Meg all at once: "This is the place with those, you know—bathrooms."

"*That* place?" Meg says, bringing a wipe back up to cover her mouth.

"I'm sure they're better now," Dillon says, pointing to the Women's line with his chin. It's snaking down the aisle, out the door, either merging with or intersecting the payphone line.

"Shit," Harper says.

"Exactly," Dillon says back.

CHAPTER
11

Where they have to park is a good quarter mile up Hunt. To try to avoid getting walled in by truckers with a score to settle, Dillon turns the headlights on and eases them deeper out into the pasture. That way if the rigs want them they'll have to chance their tires finding a soft spot, which will be an instant tow-truck situation, and on a night when all the tow trucks in Wyoming are already tied onto something.

"Wait," Harper says twenty steps from the truck, and goes back for Kissy's oversize purse. "I gave all my money for the water," she explains.

"What about . . . you know," Meg says.

Harper tracks where she's looking: the shotgun guy's blood on her leather sleeves, splashed on the thighs of her jeans.

"Will this night never end?" she asks.

"Sand," Dillon says, and works some up from the grass—dirt, anyway—cups it to Harper's arms, gets off what he can. Because the blood on her legs is still tacky, the dirt just sticks, but at least it just looks like grime. Somewhat.

"You didn't pack any extra clothes for the road?" he asks.

"Let's go," Harper says, hooking Kissy's heavy purse on her other shoulder, threading her hair out from under the strap.

"We should, you know," Dillon says, "split up."

Harper looks to him about this, brows furrowed, eyes waiting.

"They saw us puking our guts up out the window?" he says with a shrug. "They know there's a dude, an Indian girl, and a kid."

"Truckers don't need that decal on the door to ID us anymore, you mean," Harper says.

"He's right," Meg says.

"Well I can't stop being Indian," Harper says, and, to Meg: "And you can't grow up in thirty seconds."

"But we can stop being three," Meg says.

"Can it not just be over with them already?" Harper says. "What, are they elephants, they hold a grudge forever?"

"Elephants do that?" Dillon asks, falling in behind her.

"They remember things," Harper says, not looking over to him.

"We did catch some of them on fire," Meg says.

"They know that was us already?"

"What's CB move at?" Dillon asks. "Speed of gossip?"

"What do y'all want in there?" Harper asks. "Kissy was . . . I guess they just got paid."

She has to blink fast to keep from thinking more about Kissy.

"How much does she—did she have?" Dillon asks.

Harper slows, digs into the purse, past the weatherproof journal—Kissy was always the romantic—past the Park ID badges, past the economy size box of rubbers, past the *extra* baby wipes, into . . . at last: the wallet.

"Pay day," she says, fanning out six twenties, all facing the same way like fresh from the bank.

"How about we each get our own stuff?" Dillon says. "Less suspicious."

"No magazines," she says, passing him a bill.

"I mean . . ." he says, squinting a guilty squint. "Probably not, yeah, but what if they've got the new—"

"Okay, okay, your money," Harper says, and gives a twenty to Meg as well.

"That enough?" she asks her.

"We need gas?" Meg says back.

"Five-eighths," Dillon says. "They must have filled up in Laramie. But, if I had some *more* money, I could buy water for the radiator, should we need it before Rawlins."

Harper gives him another twenty, hates the way she's calculating "forty" in her head, and trying to figure how far that'll get her, food and bed and the rest of her life-wise.

"We're still going to Rawlins?" Meg asks.

"Our best chance," Harper says.

"My brother's shop is still there," Dillon says. "Meg's ride home."

"I'm not going home," Meg says.

"His Camaro," Harper says. "Yeah, that. Good."

"Were you thinking of just sticking your thumb out, starting here?" Dillon asks.

Harper looks to the line of headlights trailing west, shrugs.

"You've got the truck," she says. "Laramie's closer than your brother's shop. I can get off here, you keep asking."

"I'm not going home if you aren't," Meg says again.

"Rawlins," Dillon decides out loud, pulling ahead to singleton it into the travel center, and then he turns around to deliver the last of it: "More time to talk you out of this, bring you home with her."

Harper shakes her head, impressed with his hopefulness.

"Why's he even try?" she asks Meg.

"He's not that bad," Meg says back.

"You're looking at him with junior high eyes," Harper says, watching Dillon push his way through the glass doors. "Wait till you've dated a few of him, you'll see."

"You've only dated one of him, right?"

Harper can't argue with that.

"I'm still not going home," Meg says, walking ahead to be one-of-one as well, not one-of-three.

"Why do *I* even try?" Harper says to herself, and tracks an ambulance screaming down the eastbound lane, lights flashing.

Does it mean they found the shotgun man, the original chopper guy, the Thunderbird woman, the Thunderbird man with his face peeled off, Jam minus one finger and all of his life, or does that burning pullout just need every paramedic in Wyoming tonight?

"I'm sorry, Dad," Harper says, and blinks that away as best she can, turns to the lights of the store, pushes her way in as well.

Akal Travel Center is wall to wall bodies. A morgue shuffling around for salt and sugar, their mouths hanging, eyes shell-shocked, hair every which way.

Standing in the forever line for coffee, breath mints wrapped in her hand for everyone who's been puking, Harper watches two guys Meg's age load their forty-four ounce fountain drink cups up with candy bars before filling them with a revolting mix of root beer and Sprite.

Over the aisles, because he's tall and obvious, Dillon is easy to track. At first he's trying on sunglasses, leaning down to look in the little square of mirror, but then he spots the magazine rack right there and's squeezing in to scope for anything archery related, as if he doesn't already have every single article of every single issue for five years back memorized.

"You're supposed to be eating," she says to him, evidently out loud enough that the trucker in front of her looks back, delivering his scent back to her. "Not you," she says, eyes either burning or moldering, she's not sure.

"You my dietician, darling?" he asks, the fluffy lap dog in his arms waking.

"Forget it," Harper tells him. "I was talking to someone else."

The dog rouses more, dredged up to awareness by . . . its nose? Oh shit, its nose, definitely. It's keyed on the blood Harper's slathered in. The dog leans far enough out of the trucker's arms that it gets its tongue into contact with the sleeve of Harper's jacket, which dials its yapping up to frantic, desperate, want want want.

She turns away but the walking dead are slowing to look. And not just at the dog. At the girl in the bloody jacket.

"What are you wearing?" the trucker asks. "A slaughterhouse?"

"Ketchup," Harper says, loud enough for all. "My burger exploded."

"Burger?" he says, his mouth cracking into a devious smile. "There's not a decent eat-em-up for—"

"Little America," Harper says, holding his eyes steady in hers.

He shrugs like sure, whatever, cups his hand over the dog's muzzle, getting it shushed, and steps ahead with the line but isn't turning around to face forward yet. The rubberneckers waiting for a dog attack—it would have been more like t-ball practice with a stuffed animal—go back to their browsing.

"Sorry about Sheba here," the trucker says, lifting the dog to show who he's talking about. "She is an animal, though. Got instincts."

"That's her name?" Harper says, casting around for if there's any chance Meg might have heard this. A random dog named after the dead dog you still carry a torch for, that's something. Especially when you just lost that dog's collector plate.

"My little queenie, yes'm," the trucker says, roughing up the hair between Sheba's alert ears. "Funny thing about her, too. Turns her nose up at ketchup. Kind of spoiled for a canine, you ask me."

"A dog that doesn't like spilled human food?" Harper says.

"Depends if it's *from* a human or not," the trucker says, letting Sheba reach across for Harper's sleeve again.

"Allergic," Harper says, trying to keep her jacket away from the dog's nose.

"To questions, yeah," the trucker says, then grins without parting his lips. "You, you know, working?"

When he asks it, Harper's narrowed in on the sunglasses rack again, is finally keying on what Dillon was doing—looking for a *disguise*. But then the trucker's words and meaning finally process, and she hears what he evidently thinks she is.

"What makes you think that?" she asks, giving him her full and undivided attention.

"Knew a girl looked like you," he says with a shrug.

"Oh," Harper says. "This skin, this hair?"

"Close enough," the trucker says.

"I'm not her," Harper says evenly, so there can be no misunderstanding.

The trucker does his shoulders like he had to ask and Harper tries her best to stare literal daggers into the craggy back of his neck.

"Don't mind him," the man behind her says, his voice both low and booming somehow. "Been a while since he stumbled into a rainbox, I'd say. We might should pass the hat, take up a donation."

The trucker in front of her comes around like filling his mouth with something smart to say about who does and doesn't need a shower, but then he swallows it back down, lets his eyes keep roving across the store, his lap dog growling for him, because he knows better, apparently.

Harper looks behind her and then up and up again to the driver. She can always tell who drives for a living, who doesn't. It's not about what they're wearing—some truckers are rhinestone cowboys, some go commando in gym shorts and flip-flops—it's how their eyes focus, like they can see all of America from their rocking chair. Like they're seeing it all for the hundredth time.

"Maybe it's the dog," she says.

The tall driver shrugs maybe, sure.

"John Henry," he says by way of greeting, smoothing both his bushy red-grey muttonchops with a single huge hand.

"Ava," Harper lies. It's her mom's name, the first that came to mind. "And, John Henry like the song?"

"You a little young to know something that antique?" John Henry says.

"There an expiration date on Johnny Cash?" Harper says back.

John Henry grins wide, his eyes crinkling up from it. He says, "You're maybe thinking of Big Bad John, little miss. But thank you. Either Jimmy Dean or Johnny Cash'll get you where you're going, I figure."

That's the thing about truckers: they know every song that's ever gone out across the FM or showed up on cassette.

"Which way you headed, you don't mind me asking?" Harper asks.

"To my bunk if I can ferret it out in the dark," John Henry says. "But my schedule, that's going straight to hell—pardon my language."

"This isn't Sunday school, last I checked."

"Lot more beef jerky than I remember, if it is," he says back, nodding over to the rack of plastic bags.

Harper looks, comes back.

"Why's everybody coming back this way, you think?" she asks, just an innocent traveler.

"Spot of trouble up the road a bit."

"Trouble?"

He gives her his full and unfiltered attention, says, "Some semi-pro kids torched a pullout up towards Love Town."

"Anybody di—any fatalities?"

John Henry shrugs, is watching her closer now.

"They catch them?" Harper asks, just a concerned citizen now. "Those pickup truck kids?"

"How'd you know they're in a pickup?" John Henry says, stepping back to better appraise her. Maybe check if she fits a general description.

"You *told* me," Harper says, insulted. "That's what my dad meant when he'd say 'semi-pro,' anyway. What?"

"Your father drives?"

"He had me talking on the CB before kindergarten."

"What was your handle?" John Henry says friendly-like, sidling back in now that Harper's not the one who lit that pullout up. "This would have been . . . ten, fifteen years ago?"

"You coming through here a lot back then?"

"I've been everywhere, man," John Henry says with a grin—another lyric.

"I supposed to say I used to be Teddy Bear?" Harper asks with the same grin.

"Jackson Street 229," John Henry says back, the address from that song, and somehow neither one of them break down in tears, standing there.

"I'm not on the air anymore," Harper says, "haven't been since . . . for years." Then, taking a flier: "Ever hear the term 'bucketmouth' through the static?"

"You're not even twenty, are you?" John Henry asks.

"Not certain where I heard it."

"Think that's one of the old ones," John Henry says, rubbing his scratchy-sounding chin.

"Something with a fish?" Harper tries.

"Somebody who moves their mouth like a fish on shore, I guess," John Henry says, stepping ahead with the line. "Far as I recollect, it's a motormouth on the citizen band, not giving anyone space to even lay their twenty down, deal in to the chatter. Opposite's a . . . it's a sandbagger, yeah. That's what *my* dad called them. Just listens in, never says not word one."

"It's not talk radio," Harper says.

"Copy that," John Henry says, watching her eyes. "Short stuff? That your handle back then?"

"It was a long time ago," Harper says, looking around for Meg. "Galaxy far, far away from where I am now."

"None of my business, of course," John Henry says, "but which way you headed tonight?"

"Was Cheyenne," Harper says. "See my aunt. I guess not anymore."

"Rodeo Town," John Henry says for her. Then: "Coming from Yellowstone?"

"I wish," Harper says, then, with no hesitation, "Salt Lake," and logs that info: Ava is headed to Cheyenne, out of Utah. And she stopped for a sloppy burger at Little America, which she guesses makes her a Little American. "We're in a brown Audi?" she adds. "Seen us out there scurrying around?"

"Like a prairie dog amongst the buffalo . . ." John Henry says, nodding solemnly ahead that it's her turn.

Harper steps forward, fills her cup hot to the brim. The coffee's burned, she can tell from the smell, but still, it's coffee. She's trying to get her lid on without collapsing the side of the cup when a commotion at the register makes her look up.

It's the boys with the candy-filled cups. One of them's spilled his all over the counter, making a mess and blowing their scam. The other's light on the balls of his feet, ready to blast out of this place, keep running all night.

"Idiots," Harper says with a smile—that's her and Dillon, four years ago—and turns away taking that first careful slurp, which is when she sees Jam's red head at the mostly-plundered beef jerky rack. He's following his finger down to the bigger bags at the bottom, but when he leans down for one the two peanut jugs he's already hugging to his chest go tumbling down to the loud metal shelving.

Not Jam. Bucketmouth. *Here.*

He gathers the peanuts with the beef jerky, feels enough eyes on him that he stands wheeling his face this way and that, already chewing a long pink piece of taffy that's hanging limp from his mouth like a severed tongue.

In a single desperate step Harper's standing back in front of the fountain drinks, her breath deeper than she means, her coffee splashed onto the front of her pow-wow sweatshirt, the lapel flap of the leather jacket, the tops of her thighs.

"Ma'am?" John Henry says, because she's pressed right up against him.

"Sorry," she says, and curls around him for the other side of the store, the other side of the world, wherever, please. Just away, away, away. She lifts a camo cap from a hanging string of them, pulls it down low over her eyes, shoves the tag up by her temple.

Calm, calm, she tells herself.

At which point Dillon stands from the magazine rack, waving a magazine for Harper like he's just found buried treasure: the new issue!

"No," Harper says, pleading with him to be anybody but who he is, but he's tall, he's waving that magazine, he's the same Dillon as ever.

Bucketmouth zeroes in on him, bites his taffy off, lets his jerky and peanuts and candy bars slide down his front. He steps over them, looks around, finds Harper in a mirror almost instantly.

He tracks down from the reflection to her, says, "Wait, wait, shouldn't *I* be wearing the camo here?"

He steps over, pulls the same camo cap up from its hanging strip of plastic and seats it on his head, trying to keep both Dillon and Harper in his line of sight. Except they're opposite each other—on either side of him.

A passing clerk with a dolly of water bottle cases says, "Sorry, sir, but you have to pay for that before—"

Bucketmouth steps forward with no hesitation, launches her

into the medicine rack. Lip balm and aspirin explode all over the aisle, and one of the shelf's metal fingers pokes up through the clerk's cheek, has her hanging there, mouth open.

"Just stay there," Bucketmouth says, holding his hand out to keep her there, still trying to track Dillon and Harper both.

Finally he just shakes his head no, admitting he can't do this.

"Didn't mean for it to come to this already," he says, and steps forward, to the books-on-tape display, hauls Meg out into Harper's view, her throat in the crook of his arm, her fingers pulling uselessly at his forearm. Then he turns around so Dillon can see who he's got, too.

"No!" Harper barks, stepping forward, into this.

The crowd parts for her.

Bucketmouth smiles, nods yes to her, yes yes yes, and takes one of Meg's wrists, struggles her skinny arm up and up until her hand is at his chin, her fingers in front of his theatrically snapping teeth.

"Hey," one of the register clerks says, stepping forward, and, without even looking back, Bucketmouth frees up his snub-nose and points it back at him.

The clerk stops, dutifully raises his hands, and when Bucketmouth comes back around to Meg, six of the customers standing close to him are looking at him over the barrels of their pistols.

"Oh yeah," he says, holding his up, finger very clear of the trigger, "this is Wyoming, isn't it?"

Moving slow, he reaches across to the shelf opposite him and Meg, drops his pistol into a large plastic jug of loose jaw breakers.

"Better?" he says.

Slowly, reluctantly, the six other pistols lower, most of them finding holsters.

"I just wanted some chips!" Bucketmouth says then, loud, to everyone, still holding Meg. "Maybe something to drink?"

A bottle of orange juice slow-rolls out to his foot. He laughs a sick laugh.

All Harper can think: Meg, Meg, Meg.

"*I know who he is*," she says then, loud enough for the whole store as well. All eyes settle on her.

She looks from face to face, to be sure she has every trucker's attention, every armed customer's eyes, and then she finally settles on John Henry, his cup of coffee raised to his mouth.

"He's—he's that one in the Yellowstone pickup!" Harper says all at once, the words tumbling from her mouth too fast. "The one who started the fire!"

Bucketmouth looks at her, dumbfounded, then around to all the glowering faces.

He takes a step back, says, "It's her, it's her! I saw her get out of that truck."

"Where's it parked, then?" Harper says, stepping forward again.

Bucketmouth glares at her.

"It's a quarter mile down Hunt," she says. "Back in the pasture. We saw you get out of it, followed you in."

"Just for the hell of it?" he says back. "This what you do?"

"We thought the two of you were up to something," Harper says. "Gonna rob the place, maybe."

"I saw it out there," a voice confirms. Trucker probably. "That one with the arrowhead on the door, right?"

Bucketmouth turns to Harper about this, thins his lips in appreciation, says, his last try: "*Two* of us, you say?"

Harper reaches into Kissy's purse, says, "My sister you've got there, she saw your girlfriend throw these away in the Ladies'."

Going just by touch, she extracts Jam's and Kissy's Park badges. The ones with their faces on them. She steps forward, sets them on the chest-high shelf Bucketmouth parked his pistol on.

"I saw her leave them in the trash when—"

John Henry sets his coffee down and steps forward, peels the two badges up with a kind of brutal formality, the same way a professional wrestler might walk into the ring with the whole coliseum watching his every move. The first badge is Kissy's. He compares it to both Harper and Meg—both of them together aren't half the Cherokee princess Kissy was—and then it's Jam's badge.

He holds it up alongside his angle on Bucketmouth.

"That was *particularly* careless, what you did to my brothers back there," he says, his voice somehow leaning forward, into this.

"You don't, it wasn't, I've got—" Bucketmouth says in Jam's voice, with Jam's mouth, and John Henry just shakes his head no, steps forward.

Bucketmouth swings Meg around like a shield but then a log of Copenhagen arcs up behind him in a fast, short swing. It connects with the back of his head and Meg pulls free of his arm, falls to her hands and knees, is already scrabbling away.

John Henry's big hand lifts Bucketmouth bodily from the floor by the scruff, which is when the clerk finds his voice again: "*Outside!*"

John Henry looks over to him and, hands still up, the clerk says, "Please?"

The mob of truckers scrum around Bucketmouth, deliver him through the door, the cowbell above the door dinging over and over, and Harper finally finds Meg in all the bodies.

"We've got to—" she says, and the two of them hold each other up, walk down the closest aisle, grabbing random chips and peanuts on the way. Passing the register, Harper lays all three of her twenties down, keeps walking.

CHAPTER 12

"Well," Dillon says, shifting in the driver's seat of the Park truck, "Think it's safe to say he's not going to have the same face anymore, yeah?"

They're up on 80 again. Harper's just staring at the taillights of the camper in front of them. Maybe it got turned around at the burning pullout, or maybe they're letting traffic through. Does it even matter?

Where Dillon found her and Meg was walking alongside the westbound interstate.

On the backseat are the two cases of water bottles he stood in line for, because all the gallon jugs were gone. On his face are the surfer sunglasses with neon-yellow arms he's disguising himself with. Never mind the arrowhead on his door, under the crusty puke.

"They're going to hate us even more now," Harper says.

"Once they figure out it was us, you mean?" Dillon says.

"It *was* us," Harper says.

"Jam really was in this truck," Dillon says, trying to get their defense in order. "That part wasn't a lie."

"I'm the one who wanted to burn those jars," Harper says.

"You can't blame yourself for everything, Harpo," Dillon says.

"Don't call me that."

"Were y'all ditching me back there?" he asks back, leaning

forward to rest both his forearms on top of the steering wheel, his posture all about how the answer doesn't matter either way.

"More like saving you," Harper says.

"Without saying goodbye."

"Thanks for the water," Harper says, taking another drink.

Meg isn't drinking hers, is just sitting there.

"Do you think it's over now?" Harper says to Dillon.

He shrugs, checks the mirrors.

"He didn't look like that guy with the shotgun," he says.

"He probably can't do it too many times," Harper says. "At that—in the gas station. Before he saw us. He was getting all the snacks he could. I think he needed to replenish."

"Calories," Dillon says, liking that. "Growing a new face that fast, it probably leaves you hungry like football—like two-a-days."

"More than that."

"You ever do two-a-days?"

Harper takes another drink, holds it in her mouth and closes her eyes.

"Think he has to pick people who are the same height as him?" Dillon's saying. "What about hair? teeth? scars? tattoos? What if he bites a piece off that big fucker who was carrying him outside? Will he be that big, or just have the same face?"

"How far to your brother's shop?" Harper asks, too drained for these mental calisthenics.

"Seventy, seventy five miles," Dillon says.

Harper slumps down in the seat, leans her head against the window for about two seconds, since the Park truck's about as smooth as a rollercoaster grinding up and up. Kissy's dad was smart not to buy it.

"Maybe they killed him," she says, leaving a lot of silence afterward for someone, anyone, to agree. "Maybe Bucketmouth's dead."

"Hey . . ." Dillon says instead, letting off the gas so the rig already passing them can pass them faster.

It's a white-on-red Kenworth cabover done up with the BJ McKay swooshes coming up from the nose, around the sides—what her dad always called Irish eyebrows, which has to be racist, Harper suspects.

Her and Dillon watch it with the kind of awe you save for a blue whale, cruising past your kayak. No, it's more. They watch it like a dragon slithering past through the air, flying low, still crackling from having slipped from its world to this one for a moment.

"What?" Meg says in her scared voice, when Harper and Dillon can't even conjure words.

"You're too young," Harper says, watching that truck's taillights, now.

"That monkey I smell?" Dillon asks, sniffing at his open window.

Harper can't help but smile.

"Kissy saved us back there, didn't she?" she says once the truck's past.

"Jam too," Dillon says.

"What are we going to tell his mom?" Harper asks.

"We need to make it through ourselves first," Dillon says.

"He's dead," Harper says. "Bucketmouth. Gotta be. John Henry killed him."

"We never got to pee," Meg sneaks in like an apology.

"Some of us might have found a tire to water," Dillon confesses, shrugging like sorry it's so much easier for him and his kind.

"Yeah, well, some of us maybe didn't," Harper says. "Where's next?"

"Arlington," Dillon says. "Few miles up. But that little gas station's never open."

"Next?"

"Wagonhound, I think?" Dillon says, switching hands on the wheel to better focus on the map in his head. "Twenty minutes. There's a rest stop there, south side? We used to, um, go there, remember?"

"That place," Harper says.

"That place," Dillon says.

It's where they used to sit and park facing west and dream of being anywhere else. It's the first place they ever left a rubber's square package torn open at the corner, never mind all the truckers grinding past, all the senior citizens walking their dogs, all the sketchy men and women standing in the blasting wind like they can outlast it.

You can't outlast it—this is Wyoming—but you can roll the windows up with someone you love, or think you maybe love. Someone you love for however long this moment lasts. And when you're done, there's anonymous restrooms right there.

"Hold it?" Harper says to Meg.

"I'm not five years old," Meg says back.

"I've got to go too," Harper says, and tears open the barbecue chips she knows she's going to hate.

"Whoah, whoah, *down* . . ." Dillon says, talking quiet for some reason, using his flattened hand to show them what he means, what they need to do.

Harper and Meg scrunch down and Dillon pulls Harper's camo hat off her head, tries to fit it onto his own. Then—Harper can only tell this because she's known him so many years—he settles in behind the wheel in what he thinks is a different way. In what he thinks is the way someone not named Dillon might drive.

"What?" she whispers up to him.

"Shh, shh," he says, smiling the fakest smile, moving his upper body ever so slightly with some beat he's pretending to hear.

Slowly, and partially because Dillon's slowing even more than he did for the *BJ and the Bear* truck, a car passes them. Harper can tell it's a car because a rig would be looking right down at her, and a pickup's roof would be cresting through the window past Dillon.

"It him?" Meg says, ready to panic.

"La la lala la," Dillon sings, not not *not* looking into the left lane.

Finally Harper peeks up, sees the trunk and rear window of a Buick with a single driver, a woman. Same off-white as a certain Buick she knows. Same NATIVE PRIDE bumpersticker. Same nine-foot whip antenna coming up from the right rear fender, arcing forward to the front fender like the feather in a Robin Hood hat.

"Mom?" she says. "What's she doing here?"

"Shh, shh," Dillon says, trying not to use his lips, and then the Buick slows, falls back beside the Park truck.

"Oh shit oh shit oh shit shit shit," Dillon says.

"Duck, duck!" Harper tells him from the floorboard.

"Can't look, can't look," Dillon says through his teeth, at which point an air horn blasts at this Buick slowing down in the passing lane, clogging up traffic, slowing down commerce, blowing everyone's schedules right to hell.

The Buick accelerates—Harper can hear it, knows that rattly exhaust—and in thirty seconds it's passing the camper in front of them, is mostly hidden by the Mack riding its bumper.

"Why is she all the way out here?" Harper says to Dillon. "She never comes out this far!"

"Because of, um . . ." Dillon says, taking the hat off to adjust it out to his size, not looking at Meg but definitely meaning her.

Of course. Harper's not worth the gas it takes to scour the interstate, but, Meg? Their mom'll burn tank after tank, chasing her. She's the last chance to get it right, isn't she?

Harper guides Meg back up onto the seat with her.

"Can he, you know," Dillon says, looking over under his new brim to catch Harper's eye, "do you think he can, like, change into a woman? He sounded like Jam, didn't he? That mean he can sound like anybody?"

Harper stares at the bumpersticker of the camper still in front of them. *RV THERE YET?*

She shakes her head, wondering what this night can possibly still hold, which is when Meg, without looking over, says in her small, little sister voice, "What was the fight about anyway?"

Harper winces inside, lowers her face, studies the floorboard between her sneakers.

Dillon, who's not completely clueless, thumbs Gordon Lightfoot back in, leans against his door, turns the camo hat around so the wind whipping at him won't pull it out the back window.

――― ―――

It had started out as a good day. Good enough.

The night before, Harper and Meg had watched a baseball movie from the grocery store's rental rack. Not because either of them cared even one little bit about baseball, and they weren't watching for Charlie Sheen or that blond guy from *LA Law*. It was Omar Epps. He'd been in a football movie the grocery store had too.

The baseball movie had been funny, but it could have played on mute and that would have been just the same. Her and Meg were entranced by Omar Epps, giggling to rewind it, play his scenes again in slow motion, even though that made tracking lines roll up the screen and, according to Meg, stretched the videotape out for the next viewer.

When their mom had come through the room on the way to the store for spaghetti noodles, she'd scooped the tape case up.

"It rewound?" she said, holding it up.

Harper was lying on the couch with the fingers of her left hand spread out above her, so she could tap each hard fingernail with her right fingertip. At first she'd been humming a tune to it, but now she wasn't sure what exactly she was doing, really. Just nothing.

"It's still in the VCR," she said without breaking her rhythm, whatever her rhythm was, or was going to be.

Her mom shook the case and held it there like waiting for Harper to rise, fill it.

"Can we get another tonight?" Harper asked instead, finally looking over, doing her eyes all big like Kissy's.

"Ninety-nine cent shelf?" her mom said back.

"As always," Harper said back, turning back to the deliciously spread fingers of her left hand.

"Are you on something?" her mom asked.

"Life," Harper said. "Want some, or you already used up what you had?"

"I don't have time for this, Harper," her mom said, tossing the tape case onto Harper's belly. "Unless you want to make dinner?"

"Not hungry."

"You don't work tonight?"

Harper turned her left hand around so the palm faced her now, said, "Are my hands like Dad's, do you think? Where do I get them?"

"The tape, please," her mom said.

"So we *can* get one?" Harper asked back.

"Not something stupid this time, right?"

"Are you watching with us?"

"Not if it's stupid, I'm not."

"Don't worry about it, then," Harper said, studying the ceiling now. The field of glitter.

"I still need to take that one back, though," her mom said.

"We'll just watch it again," Harper said. "Late charges are the same as renting another, so it'll be like we rented something else."

"*Harper*," her mom said.

Harper turned her head to study her mom, and thought what she always thought: *me plus twenty, minus happiness*.

"It's the same ninety-nine cents, Mom," she said. "Why's it some big hairy deal?"

"Because—because watching the same movie when you could be watching something else, that's not . . . it's like throwing money away."

"Throwing a dollar away."

"Dollars count."

"But it's the same dollar, isn't it? Whether we rent something new or watch this one again?"

"Nobody does that."

"Here," Harper said, and straightened her legs to uncrumple a lone dollar from between the two fives in her pocket. She dropped it on the table like cleaning her fingers of it. "Better?"

"No," her mom said. "It's not about the money."

"So every dollar doesn't count? Is this a new kind of parenting, where you contradict what you were just telling me? Am I learning a lesson here?"

"You already know how to be a smartass."

"Obviously."

"Are we really going to do this again, Harper?"

"Do what? We just want to watch the movie again. Meg fell asleep, missed how it ended."

"I heard the two of you in here," her mom said. "There was no sleep happening."

"We like baseball," Harper said. "It's our new favorite sport. We might go pro. Are you going to crush our dreams before they even start?"

"I'll believe that when I see you playing."

"Is it such a big crime to want to watch it again?"

"It's not using your time well."

"Mom, I go to work, I do my job, I pick Meggie up from school when I can to help you out. All work and no play—"

"Relax, sure. You're doing a good job of it right now, looks like."

"Past tense. I *was* doing it just now."

"Watching the same movie two nights in a row, Harper. You can't see how that—it's going nowhere."

"That's what this is about? Really? My future? My decisions? Is it five o'clock already? That's lecture time, right? Shit, where's my notebook, I need to write some of this down, see if it's the same list as last time . . ."

"You don't get *that* from me," her mom said.

"What?"

"That attitude."

"Survival mechanism."

"And watch your language in this house."

"Because it's such a special, special place."

"This is my punishment. Ungrateful daughters."

"Singular, Mom. It's just me saying this."

"Training your sister to."

"She's checked out on my headphones, which I *let* her borrow this time."

"You don't even see how much she idolizes you."

"Smart girl," Harper says.

"With limited role models," her mom says right back.

"And that's *my* fault, that what you're saying? Dad didn't come back because I didn't win the science fair, or dominate in basketball?"

"No, I'm just saying that if you would—"

"Go on, you're getting there."

"Harper."

"No, please, please, I know it's coming, Mom. I'm like Dad. I just want to take enough deliveries to pay the bills, never make any extra."

"Anything that was said between him and me is still between him and me."

"I think the confidentiality on *that* one's expired, Mom, thanks. And when I say that I mean thank you so much for running him off, saving us from his bad influence. I probably never would have graduated if I'd had him here at home. Know what? I bet Meg doesn't even get braces if Dad's still around. I bet the macaroni wouldn't have burned to the pan last night if—"

"Not so loud," her mom said, stepping closer, her lips just opening enough to let her words out now. "Your sister will hear."

"*Meg! Meg, come here!* See, nothing. Or, do you want to take this out onto the lawn like last time? Give the neighbors the Mom and Daughter show again?"

"I don't know what to do with you anymore. I really don't."

"Nothing, Mom, I want you to do nothing with me, how's that? I want you to let me and Meg watch whatever we want to tonight."

"I don't care what you watch."

"Then why are we having this discussion? There's no judgment going on, is there? It's just a stupid baseball movie, Mom. Geez."

"It's not that."

"You hate Charlie Sheen, then? What?"

"Just give me the case thing. We can forget about this. Just eat dinner and go to bed."

"But we want to *watch* it, Mom. Again. Your stupid senseless daughters want to ruin their minds with the same movie, did you forget?"

"I don't have time for this, Harper, I've got to get—"

She brushed past Harper but Harper beat her back to the couch, stepped back holding the case high.

"*Harper*," her mom warned.

Harper stepped back again and it was far enough that the case bumped into the open-faced china hutch filled with commemorative plates. They both looked back, tracked the very top one wobbling on its wooden stand, then tipping, tipping—

Harper lunged forward, caught it with both hands, the case

falling underfoot, but she had enough momentum that she tapped the plate she was saving into another one that hadn't even been in danger.

It held its shape for a moment just like a cartoon, then shattered, fell down the front of the hutch. Her mom turned around, stared at the ceiling for serenity.

"Mom, I didn't—" Harper said, holding the good, *saved* plate out, but her mom came around so fast, so mad, that her lead hand sent the plate flipping away.

They both watched it go end over end, hit the wall behind the TV, shatter.

"Have I forgot to tell you how fortunate I feel that you've stayed here so long after graduation?" her mom said.

"So long?" Harper said, incredulous. "I know, right? Two months? Oceans have risen and fallen, all the stars have shifted into different places—"

"You make it feel like a lot longer," her mom said. "Theatrics like this."

Harper refocused her eyes trying to mentally digest this, then she shook her head, smiled, stepped over to the sacred fucking china hutch of idiot plates.

"Theatrics?" she said. "You mean like *this*?" She took one plate from high, sailed it across the room.

"That the best you've got?" her mom said. "Breaking things I care about? Do you think this is where that starts? Do you think you haven't been blundering into—"

"What, it's almost dinner?" Harper said. "Here, let me set all the plates out, *Mom*."

Before she could stop herself, she was grabbing onto the back of the hutch, planting a foot on the wall, and pulling everything down.

It fell and fell. The crash was tremendous, sent all the dust on the back of the hutch airborne, where it stayed.

They both looked through it upstairs, to the chance of Meg having heard that. She had to have.

"Feel better now?" her mom said, her voice level and pointed. "Think it hurts, that you're really getting to me with this pathetic outburst?"

"I. Just. Want. To. Watch. That. Movie," Harper said. "*Again*."

"Where?" her mom said, looking around. "Living room's kind of upside down now, isn't it?"

"Not yet," Harper said, which was when she stepped up to the arm of the couch, dug her hands underneath, and lifted it as hard as she could, trying with everything she had to flip it as well.

Her mom stepped back, expecting the couch to come her way. When it didn't—couldn't, was too tall to go end over end—she just shook her head, said with mock wonder through the falling ceiling texture, "Look, Harper. The stars you and your dad planted, they're all falling down . . ."

"*I hate you!*" Harper screamed. "I hate you I hate you I hate you! You ran Dad off—"

"He just didn't come back."

"—you try to control every part of my life! I wish you were dead! I wish you'd left instead of him! Then I could, then I could, then I could watch the same stupid movie every night of my stupid life! And get nowhere and become nothing and maybe, maybe, be happy!"

Her mom stepped back, opened her hand, presenting the front door as if it had been there all along. Harper stormed through it, not giving her mom the satisfaction of even slamming it, and was standing on the front lawn opening and closing her hands for control when a load of her own laundry hit her in the back.

"Don't say I didn't give you anything, dear," her mom said from the porch.

"You've given me more than enough," Harper said, and started picking her clothes from the grass. Halfway into it though, she bubbled over, slung them back up at the house. "I don't want anything to remind me of my life here," she said.

"You'll be back," her mom said.

"Bye, Mom," Harper said, already leaving. "Thanks for everything."

Which isn't exactly what she tells Meg.

What she tells Meg, Dillon still taking great pains either to not listen or to pretend not to hear, is that it was about that Omar Epps movie.

"I never even saw the first one," Meg confesses.

"Not worth it," Harper says. "He's not even in it. I don't even know why you make a movie without him in it."

Meg smiles into her chest and finally opens her water bottle, takes a drink.

"That'll help you not have to pee," Harper says.

"Pee on you," Meg says, shouldering Harper.

"Ladies, ladies," Dillon says. "Don't make me pull this car over, now."

Harper looks out the window.

"That black dude really better looking than me?" Dillon's half-whispering to Meg, in some way distant part of the truck. Harper places a barbecue chip in her mouth, closes her eyes to get past the taste, and ends up looking at the back of her hand, the fingers spread.

Her mom, she knows. That's where she gets her hands.

She can tell by the way they destroy everything they touch.

CHAPTER
13

Dillon's right about the little gas station at the Arlington exit: dark windows, no action.

"They could be cleaning up, night like this," he says.

"I never even turned my—this, on," Harper says. She holds her wrist out, the glow-bracelet circling it. "When we were walking," she clarifies.

"I still saw you," Dillon tells her, trying to overpack it with meaning, she can tell.

"It's not about 'look at me,' it's about 'don't not see me,'" Harper says, ignoring his subtext. "Those Bible-thumpers, they were trying so hard to save me. If I'd have just, I don't know, let them? Then y'all never pick me up. Meg walks home. None of this ever happens."

"Why stop with that?" Dillon says, turning Gordon Lightfoot down. "If your mom hadn't royally pissed you off. No, no. If *Major League II* hadn't been on the shelf for you to rent. No, no, if—"

"You know *Major League II*?" Harper asks.

"Just because we're not together right now doesn't mean we don't still watch the same movies," Dillon says. "Right, Megalator?"

"We were never dating," Meg tells him, her lips pressed together so she won't quite smile. She can't hide her dimples, though.

Harper elbows her.

"You're going to make me pee," Meg warns.

"It'll smell better than the throw-up in the floorboard," Harper says.

"And the throw-up on the doors," Dillon adds.

"And the eyeball in back," Harper says, only cueing in a moment later to Dillon and Meg, both turned to her about that. "That lady from the Thunderbird," she explains, and bursts her hand over her own left eyeball to show.

"It shot out?" Meg says, not wanting that to be true, Harper can tell, but thrilling from it all the same.

"Oh yeah, that bird had it in its beak . . ." Dillon fills in, nodding.

Harper holsters that hand-pistol into a different pocket of the leather jacket, comes out with . . . a baby food jar?

"No," she says.

"That's where that one went," Dillon says.

"I've had this all along?" Harper says.

"Motherfucker," Meg says.

"Language," Harper tells her.

"She's right," Dillon says.

"Throw it out?" Meg says.

Harper cranks her window down, turning the cab into an instant tornado. Well, into even more of a tornado. At the last moment, though, her hand out in open space, she doesn't let that little glass jar go.

"What are you—?" Dillon says.

"Last time we tried to get rid of evidence, bad things happened," Harper tells him, concentrating like doing math.

"So now we've got *two* eyeballs with us?" Meg says.

"From different people," Harper says.

"I don't think that makes it better," Dillon says. "I think maybe that makes it worse, even."

"It's evidence," Harper says. "Jam was right. . . . It was Jam, wasn't it? Or—"

"Why didn't we need proof before?" Dillon says.

"Because we hadn't blown any trucks up," Harper tells him.

"That looks more like one eyeball to me," Dillon says, about the jar Harper's still got pincered up like the worst show and tell.

Harper considers this, considers it some more, then flops over the front seat, bridges her body across the back and stabs her upper body into the bed, her hair whipping her face.

"More, more," she says to herself, and worms forward farther, can finally reach her hand through the centerhole of the spare, grab the only mushy thing there, her chest curling in, her stomach trying to gag those barbecue chips back up.

She collapses down into the backseat, her hair still sucking out the back window, getting a month's worth of split ends. Holding her breath and shielding the baby food jar from the wind, she holds her breath to crack it open, deposit the mostly dry eyeball in. The harsh scent—taste?—of cinnamon swirls through the cab, burns her eyes. She screws the lid back on tight and holds it there. Just in case.

"So now he killed the church lady *too*?" Meg says, turned around backwards in the seat to document this slimy little drama.

"I thought he was a hitchhiker the people from the Thunderbird were *trying* to kill?" Dillon says.

"Because he was trying to kill *them* . . ." Harper completes. "Steal Combover's face or something."

"The face that was on the windshield?" Meg asks, halfway lost, it sounds like. Like Dillon, judging by the way his body's turned to Harper like a radio dish, waiting for her to beam an answer across.

Harper holds the bottle up, considering it. The eye she just dropped in, from the bed of the truck, is blue, is still floating down. The other, already settled, is brown, the white shot through with ruptured blood vessels.

"When—when Bucketmouth is telling the cops he doesn't know what we're talking about—" she starts.

"Just some crazy kids with their crazy stories," Dillon wedges in.

"—remind me we've got this. Proof."

"Because it's got only his fingerprints on it?" Meg says.

Harper makes a show of cleaning every bit of the jar's glass she can, lid too, then she pushes it back into the jacket's weed pocket like closing this discussion. She's nestled down into the backseat, her face just touching the fabric, when Dillon reaches back, grabs her shoulder to haul her up.

"What?" she says. "You the sleep police?"

"Glass," he says, and, her hands so light, Meg brushes the side of Harper's face then holds her palm up, the headlights behind them turning her hand into a rhinestone glove.

"Are we there yet?" Harper whines, and crawls back into the front.

— —

Because Dillon's got his window down again a few miles later, the lit cigarette from the trucker passing them arcs perfectly down into his lap in a puff of sparks.

Like he's supposed to, he stands up as much as he can without even thinking.

"The cherry, the cherry, get the cherry!" he's saying.

The Park truck dives hard to the right, is for sure about to go cartwheeling over the ditch until Harper lunges for the wheel, hauls them off the shoulder at way too steep an angle, which veers them sharply across the lane until Meg grabs the wheel as well, uncorrecting Harper's overcorrection.

As lightly as possible, the side mirror on the driver's side dings into the rig's trailer and comes off, goes under the big tires, is gone. And then they're going shakily straight again.

The camper behind them now flashes its lights at them.

Dillon sweeps the cigarette into the floorboard at last, retakes the wheel with his right hand, holds his left out and up to tell the camper they've got things under control now, thanks.

"They think we're drunk," Meg states. Just a fact.

Harper looks back to the camper people, their faces grim and expectant, their decisions about Harper and Meg and Dillon already made.

Harper waves to them anyway, shakes her head no, isn't sure what exactly she hopes to convey at sixty miles per hour. That all the truckers on this stretch of interstate tonight are waging petty war against the national park system? That maybe they should give her and her sister and her ex a break, since there's a face-changing finger-eating monster of a serial killer on their tail? Probably she should just lob her baby food jar out the back window, let it shatter on the camper people's windshield, hope that at least one of the two eyeballs will stick to the glass for a moment or two, maybe get across some shred—no, some *smear*—of what they're dealing with up here.

She turns back around, says to Dillon, "Maybe windows up?"

"You can handle the smell in here?"

"Better than dying," Harper says.

"Speak for yourself," Dillon says, cranking the stubborn window back up.

"That wasn't your dad, was it?" Harper says with a smile.

Meg looks over to him about this.

Dillon pinches the dead cigarette up from the floorboard, inspects it. "Not a Camel," he says.

"I thought he quit," Harper says.

"That was . . ." Dillon says, thinking back. "April? Think it was all some big April Fool's joke, really."

Harper thinks back as well, realizes she has the perfect image of Dillon's dad at graduation. He's way at the back, hunched behind a small tree, taking one last drag from his Camel before standing up to find his son, grey smoke trailing from his mouth and nose at the same time, like he's on fire inside, like his truck isn't the only thing that runs on internal combustion.

The problem with scratching open the graduation photo album in her head, though, it's that Kissy and Jam are there, Jam's mom and dad even sitting in the same row together for once, Kissy's mom looking more like she should be Kissy's sister, like always, gag. Crossing the stage for his diploma, Jam had stopped to raise his arms, celebrate the moment, his row screaming for him. Harper hopes he got to take that feeling with him. And— and she should read Kissy's Park journal when this is all over. She promises she will. This is the first time the two of them have been apart for summer since third grade. Did Kissy change, working up there? Was she becoming whoever she was going to be? Is it all going to be love poetry? Her writing her front name with Jam's last name?

Harper sucks her lips in, her eyes heating up. Which is when a cup splatters into their windshield, from the next rig passing in the left lane.

This time Dillon doesn't flinch, just clicks the wipers into their slow rhythm.

"Spit cup," he identifies for them, like they can't see all the Copenhagen grains wiggling against the glass like demon sperm.

Meg scooches over to Harper to keep away from the leaky crack.

"It's spit," Dillon says. "I think it's too thick to come through."

Meg looks over to him like is he for real, here.

"But good thinking," he adds.

"Temperature?" Harper asks.

He leans down to get a line on the gauge, says, "Hot but not boiling. Kind of like certain drivers . . ."

He straightens his back, strikes a Marlboro Man pose.

"Certain drivers of other vehicles," Meg adds, not able to contain her laughter.

Dillon playacts being hurt, says, "I mean, we can't all be Omar whoever, right?"

"*Epps!*" the girls say together.

For a moment it's almost like everything's normal. But then cop lights swirl on behind them, the sirens dopplering in.

"What was I doing?" Dillon says, looking down to the speedometer.

"More like what have we done?" Harper says.

CHAPTER
14

Dillon hangs the passenger side of the truck deep in the ditch and the statie pulls in right behind, cocking his wheels sharply to the left at the last moment like they all do, so if their cruiser gets clipped it'll shoot back out into traffic, not plow over the officer writing the ticket.

"What do we say?" Dillon asks.

"Ten and two," Harper instructs, about his hands.

"What?"

"Otherwise he'll think you've got a weapon?"

Dillon places his hands high on the wheel, says again, "So what do we tell him?"

"That it wasn't us?" Meg tries.

"Except it was," Harper says. "It is."

"At least if we go to jail," Meg says, staring straight ahead, "at least Bucketmouth can't get us in there."

"He's dead," Harper says. "Those truckers back there, they— there were so many of them. And he was just . . . he was Jam. Jam couldn't even fight Kissy off, right?"

Nobody answers. Headlights stream past, all jostling into the passing lane to give this bad scene space, and the tension of just sitting there ramps up and up, punctuated by air horns marking the trouble this Park truck is in.

"Band camp," Dillon finally says across to the two of them like it's their rallying cry, their reminder of who they are—that they're *them*—and Harper and Meg repeat it in sequence, confirming that they're still them, and then the statie is shining his Maglite into the cab, all three of them squinting when it's their turn to get lit up.

"What's this about, officer?" Dillon says, both hands still firmly on the steering wheel, in the plainest possible sight.

"Trooper," the statie corrects.

Dillon nods yes, that.

"License, registration, insurance," the statie says.

"That's the thing," Dillon says, not looking over yet.

"You're employees of Yellowstone Park?"

"Well," Dillon says.

"No," Harper says. "It's not our truck."

"Ma'am?" the statie says, directing his light up to her and leaving her in that burning white brightness. "Little far from the reservation, aren't we?"

Harper manages to not say anything smart back, to just swallow all the comebacks and educational opportunities down.

"What were we doing?" Dillon asks, probably trying to draw the statie's attention.

"Whose truck *is* it then?" the statie asks, his light lingering on Meg now, his cop-brain probably calculating the extra time arresting a minor is going to carve out of his night.

"It's Yellowstone's truck," Harper says. Obviously.

"And you're driving it because?"

"Our friends who work at the Park this summer brought it to Laramie for their—for her dad to look at it," Harper says. "He didn't want it."

"What friends?"

"Good ones," Dillon says.

"Dead ones," Harper adds.

In less than a second, the Maglite has a pistol under it.

"We were going to call you about that," Meg says, her voice flat. "The line for the phone was too long."

"It's the truth," Harper says, and holds her left hand up until the statie can settle his light on it. Moving slowly so he can follow, she dips it into the secret pocket of the leather jacket, births the baby food jar up, holds it between her fingers like the specimen it is.

"*Dash, dash!*" the statie commands, pointing there with his light and pistol both.

Still moving slow, Harper deposits the jar on the center of the dash above the radio, her wrist nudging the cassette back in on accident. Gordon Lightfoot swells up from the door panels like a surprise fourth person in the cab. One who nearly gets the other three shot.

Meg darts her hand forward, dials the volume knob down an instant before Harper can catch her hand, slow her down. You don't move fast around bears. It's not an Indian thing, it's a trucker thing, one she learned from making runs with her dad.

In response to Meg's sudden movement, the statie backs off a long step to better keep all three of them in his line of fire. His *potential* line of fire, Harper tells herself. Very, very hopefully.

"Look," she says about the jar, lacing her fingers behind her head, chicken-winging her elbows out. Meg takes her lead, does her hands just the same. Dillon keeps his on the wheel, tighter than tight, like if he doesn't hang on, he's getting sucked out the window, up into the sky. "*Look*," Harper says again.

Before the statie can, the mic clipped to his shoulder crackles open with static.

It's someone back down the road, reporting possible body parts in the westbound, and does anybody out here tonight know the difference in human vertebra and deer vertebra?

"That's our friend," Harper says. "Her name's—it was Kissy."

In response to that the statie works his left hand into his shirt pocket, shakes loose an ID badge, lets it unravel to the end of its forest-green lanyard.

It's Kissy's smiling face and unforgettable name twirling on the end of that string.

"You got called there for the disturbance," she tells the statie.

"We found the male as well," the statie says. "James."

"Was he . . . his face," Harper says. "Does he still look like his picture?"

"Is he still alive, she means," Dillon adds, covering, which is just getting them deeper into this, and not in a good way.

The statie is just watching them.

"We found his *badge*," he finally says.

"He's trying to trick us," Harper says to Dillon and Meg. "They already found him."

"I'm the one asking the questions here, ma'am."

"Was that a question?" Harper says. Then: "You found Jam—*James*, in the pasture by a place where a car punched through the fence. One finger missing. Or a tongue. An eyeball. Doesn't matter. He was dead."

"Save it for after I've Miranda'd you," the statie says. "Not that spontaneous confessions don't carry any weight in a court of law."

Harper shakes her head in defeat, amusement, hopelessness. It's maybe the most Indian gesture there is.

"*Look*," she finally says again, losing her patience. Because what her and Dillon did and didn't do aren't the most important thing right now. What's most important is that Bucketmouth is real, and really out there.

Slowly, moving like he knows this is a trick of some sort, the statie lights the baby food jar up.

Two eyeballs look back at him, sediment swirling all around them.

"They're not ours," Dillon says, like saying it just to be sure there's no misunderstanding. "I mean—*we* didn't do that. We just have them, we didn't, like, get them."

"We got one of them," Harper corrects. Reluctantly.

"I'm going to need the three of you to step out of the cab," the statie says. "*Slow*ly."

"There's someone out here killing people left and right," Harper says. "This is—we found his trophies, his snacks, whatever. This is the last one left. At least until he makes more."

"Why did you even stop us?" Dillon says, and turns over to inspect this statie at last, which gives Harper a line on him as well, through the haze of Meg's flyaways.

"Cut yourself shaving, officer?" she says, about the . . . *is* that razor burn on his jaw? Sunburn? Acne scars inflaming all over again? And, sunglasses at night?

"*Trooper!*" the statie says, his trigger finger twitchy, his upper body angled over to the front, one foot forward like he's setting himself to absorb some recoil.

"Why did you pull us over?" Harper repeats, because that is the pressing question, suddenly.

The statie stares at her with his chrome eyes, stares some more, then comes back with, "We got a report of a truck matching this description. It was leaving the scene of a crime."

"Of a fire?" Harper says.

"I need the three of you *out* of the cab now!" the statie insists.

"You're right," Dillon says to Harper. "What's up with his face?"

Meg's crying now, her hands still behind her head, her whole upper body shuddering in a bad kind of sinuous rhythm like she's about to blow over, not be able to get back up.

The statie leans down to his shoulder-mounted radio rig, says, "All units be advised, I've got the operators of the truck in question—"

"What?" Harper says. "This is—he's talking like a TV cop, isn't he? Did you hear that on *Walker, Texas Ranger*?"

"'Truck in question?'" Dillon says, catching on.

The statie presses his mouth down to the mic, says, "I'm going to need backup at mile-marker, mile-marker—"

"Wait, wait," Dillon says, and takes his left hand off the wheel to open the door, speak to this statue man to man or some macho bullshit like that, and his pinky must be hooked into the handle when the statie takes a step farther back from whatever's happening here, and fires a warning shot over the cab, that report the exact sound of the end of the world.

Harper jumps in her seat, her hands still up, at least until she's pulling Meg close, like there's any way to protect a little sister from bullets, and Dillon rips his hand away from the door, to grab back onto the wheel.

There's no undoing this, though.

Especially since his pinky was already hooked in that handle.

With galloping through the ditch and all the other trauma this Park truck's suffered this night, not counting the hundreds of thousands of times it has to have been opened over the last however-many years, it . . . it—

Opens.

Harper surges over to try to grab it across Dillon, grab it and keep it in place, but it's like it's spring-loaded.

An old trucker trick is, if a state trooper stops you, and presumes to step up onto your running board to get face to face with you, and she or he elects to pull up with the mirror's strut instead of the grab bar, then all you have to do is pull the door handle back, just like Dillon just did on accident. Opening that door the statie's hanging on sends them tumbling, maybe teaches them about where it's okay to put their hands, where it's not okay.

This statie isn't hanging onto the truck's side mirror—this truck isn't that tall, and doesn't have a running board anyway—but still, he's familiar enough with this trick himself, evidently, knows that the driver's door opening means find the ground, set yourself.

He does. Except, already being a step back in order to keep his pistol and the Maglite between him and the cab, stepping back from that position—

His green on brown outfit lights up halogen hot, and before Harper can even breathe in, the ancient flatbed riding the white line clips him, after somehow *missing* the cocked-out nose of his cruiser. It takes Dillon's door with it in a scream of metal and sparks, slaps it and the statie into the front fender, and when that hundredth of a second is over, the statie's upper body is on the hood, his face to the windshield, opening and closing.

"*No!*" Harper screams, her hands still behind her head, Meg's too, so that when Dillon stands on the pedal, the truck fishtailing sideways in the slick grass, they sway over to the side window, Harper's leather elbow shattering it out.

For maybe a hundred feet, the statie's upper body and staring face rides the ditch with the Park truck, the spiral cable of his radio mic in the windshield wiper the only thing keeping him there, but his radio rig finally pulls free of belt and shirt, his body sloughing off, the radio staying with the wiper assembly, bouncing on the side of the truck now, on Harper's door, Dillon either screaming or moaning, it's hard to tell over the sounds she's pretty sure her own mouth is making. That her head is full with, full to spilling.

She sets the heels of her hands against the dash to try to make it through the Park truck fishtailing from side to side in the ditch, galumphing up and down over the dips and swells, eating up reflector poles, its headlights shining uselessly up into the sky when there's no weight on the front tires, then, on landing, showing only yellow grass rushing up under them. Dillon doesn't let up on the gas until Harper manages to reach across Meg, touch his knee.

It wakes him, sort of. He flinches, looks to her, then seems to become aware of where they are, what they're doing, how crazy and wrong and bad this is.

He doesn't brake, which would be disastrous in the ditch,

but keeps the same speed, directs the driver's side tires onto the shoulder of the interstate, gravel spitting up into the wheel wells like machine gun fire, and then, using his blinker—blinkers still exist, the world is still real—he merges back into traffic. The missing sound of the grass brushing the undercarriage is a massive silence. It presses in all around Harper, takes her breath away.

The first vehicle to pass them is the little brown Audi.

The college freshmen in it all look over directly into the cab through the space where there used to be a door, and what they must see are three shattered people in a windstorm, their truck coming apart around them, the dome light on now because the door can't turn it off.

With his left boot Dillon pushes the plunger in that the door used to keep pushed, and the dome light sucks its light back in, giving them the darkness they need for what they're going through right now.

The Audi surges past.

Harper screams in frustration, bangs the sides of her fists into the dash over and over.

Sitting between them, Meg still has her fingers laced behind her head. She's crying, sobbing, too terrified to even process.

Harper reaches over, guides those chicken wings down, holds her hands over her little sister's until she becomes aware of something cold against her wrist.

The baby food jar.

Of course.

CHAPTER
15

The big rigs are more spaced out now, this far from the fire. And the signs coming east out of Utah are probably flashing that the road's closed, so there's less people getting turned around for the night, coming back westbound.

Harper's standing at the front of the truck watching the interstate, her hands in her pockets, her hair still crunchy with glass from the side window.

They're at the Wagonhound rest stop. When she was a kid and her dad would stop here for her she would always think they planted these three brick buildings to commemorate the single windiest spot in all of Wyoming. Compared to riding in the cab of the Park truck now, it feels more like the eye of the storm: still, calm.

But when they leave, it all starts again, doesn't it?

Harper closes her eyes.

"No . . . no," Meg says from the backseat.

She's telling Dillon if the fuse he's popping out of the Park truck is the one for the dome light or not. Which means he has to now put that one he just pulled back in, and all he's using for pliers is two pennies pinched together.

Over the wall in the restroom that didn't go quite all the way up, Harper had been able to hear him next door, sobbing in his stall. And then punching it. Not about Kissy and Jam, she's pretty sure—they were always more competitors for Harper's attention than running buds—but that highway patrolman he didn't *mean* to kill.

He's got his brave face on now, though.

When the dome light casting Meg's blurry shadow onto the sidewalk blacks out like they've been waiting for, she calls "Good" to Dillon and he sits up at last. There are campers and RVs and station wagons and minivans scattered around every few spaces, the rigs farther out in their parking lot. Dillon eases up to the front of the truck, takes the time to balance the little glass fuse on the hood between them.

"Find a better station?" Harper calls over her shoulder to Meg. Moments later Gordon Lightfoot croons on, then becomes AM static going up and down with Meg's dialing.

"There's no good reception in Yellowstone," Dillon tells Harper, about the useless quest she's sent Meg on. "That's why there's cassettes in all the trucks, probably."

Harper looks down at the stained concrete she's standing on.

"They're going to shoot us on sight now, you know that, right?" she says. Obviously.

"Not you," Dillon says. "Me. I'm the one killed him."

"You didn't—"

"I don't open my door, he doesn't get hit. Case closed."

"Was he even really a cop?" Harper says, turning to catch Dillon's eyes, see if he's thinking the same thing.

There's grease on his cheek now, and the right side of his nose. She licks her finger, dabs at it, only succeeds in spreading it. It makes her laugh. The laugh turns into a sob. Dillon pulls her to him, presses her face into his shoulder.

"I miss them too," he lies. It's a lie she could kiss him for. It makes her shake harder. Makes her madder.

"It didn't have to happen!" she says into his shoulder. "They were just—they just wanted to bum around Yellowstone for the summer, maybe see a wolf or two, have some stories to tell their kids someday . . ."

"My dad always says that when your number's up, it doesn't matter where you are, what you do. It's just time."

"It wasn't *their* time."

"It's not ours either," Dillon says.

Harper pushes away from him, tries to compose herself, pretend she's a better, strong person. One who can handle all this bullshit.

"You saw that statie's face too," she says. "Tell me there wasn't something—"

"I was looking in the mirror right before," Dillon cuts in, the argument in his head spilling out into their discussion.

Harper steps around to see him head-on. "What are you—what did you see, Dill?"

Dillon gulps a swallow down, rubs the spot of grease on his nose worse.

"The headlights of that truck that hit him, they came *on*," he says. "They were—they were off when it was barreling down the shoulder, and then . . ." He poofs both hands open, does the soft sound effect: headlights where there were no headlights. "And—then I was looking right at the cop, where he'd been standing, and then, then right after, too. After it happened, the taillights blipped off."

Harper stares over at the interstate, her arms crossed, her brain cooking.

"And how do you hit the cop without hitting his car first?" he adds. "It's like . . . you'd have to *try*, Harp. And even then, you'd have to really know what you're doing, right?"

"What are you saying?"

"First, that I killed him," Dillon says. "Not you, not Meggie. Not Jam, not Kissy. I'm not running from that, understand. It's just a fact. I don't open my door—"

"On *accident*," Harper insists.

"If the door doesn't open, he doesn't die. But, second, I wasn't the *only* one who killed him. Now we just... we wait for the paper tomorrow, if we live til then. He had three kids, a wife, was probably paying for his mom's nursing—"

"If that trucker really took him out on purpose, it'll be on that, that drunk driving camera thing those cruisers have on the dash, won't it?"

"The one pointing over the hood, you mean?" Dillon says, lodging his objection. "But, yeah, it'll for sure have me opening that door." Like caught in that camera's eye, he re-enacts the middle and index fingers of his left hand popping that handle. "Then leaving the scene at a guilty rate of speed. There's even proof," he says, and steps back, unwinds the stretched out mic and radio from where it's hanging by the passenger side front tire, the wiper it's attached to bent out. He balls the radio up like trash, lobs it over the cab into the bed. Then, probably wanting to do good instead of bad, he tries to bend the wiper arm back to functional, but once a wiper's had torsion applied to it, it's never the same wiper. When it snaps off, he loses it for a bad few seconds, whips the hood with it over and over, chipping the paint, the rubber blade slinging out, losing itself in the faded black of the parking lot.

Harper hugs him from the back until he's calm, Meg watching through the windshield, the radio still pushing the same static now because Dillon's outburst has frozen her in her seat. She's not used to being around adult-sized men, Harper realizes. They're bulls in the china shop of her young life, bulls that can go red-eyed for any reason.

Dillon sags down to the ground, his head pushed into the crusty side of the truck, and Harper goes with.

"I would have stopped us too, if I were him," he's saying. "He was just... he was just doing his *job*."

"It's not on you," Harper tells him.

He turns around, careless of the seat of his pants on the asphalt, and stares up into the sky, his face greasy *and* wet now, his eyes blinking fast.

"I should—" he starts, swallows, starts again: "Y'all go on in the truck. Tell my brother you need the white Camaro. I'll, I'll *hitch*, I'll disappear. Or they'll catch me, and I was alone, I did everything, no accomplices. My mom left forever ago, my dad's on the road all the time. They'll believe anything of me."

"I don't give half a fuck what they expect you to be," Harper tells him, standing, looking around. "I know who you *are*. This isn't the end, not for either of us, and not for Meggie either. I won't let it be that. If we disappear, we disappear together, got it?"

Slowly, Dillon looks up to her.

"That doesn't mean we're back together," Harper says, her smile giving her away a bit.

Dillon pulls his lips in so he won't smile either.

"This truck is toast," he says, looking around for other options.

"I'm not becoming a car thief along with everything else," Harper tells him.

"Because that's the tipping point," Dillon says.

"I'm thinking it's more cumulative."

Dillon shrugs, can accept that. He lets her haul him up.

"You've got shit on your face," she tells him, touching her nose to show where.

"You've got shit in your hair," he tells her back, flicking it, her peripheral vision sparkling with glitter for a moment.

"The truckers know us by this stupid arrowhead," she says, nodding down to the passenger door they're standing beside.

"And the cops have our plates," Dillon says. "He had to have read them into the radio before coming up to the cab."

They nod, each knowing what they have to do.

For Harper, it's ducking back into the Ladies', making herself dig in the unmentionable trash until she comes up with a bottle of aerosol hairspray. Then she tears a blank page from the back of Kissy's journal, has Meg light a corner off the truck's lighter—it just takes breathing on it steady, not even really blowing—and then holding that burning paper in front of the faded arrowhead on the passenger side, shaking the aerosol can for one last prayer of a burst, and torching all of that decal off she can in the twenty seconds of hairspray left. The ash that's left smears wonderfully, looks like tar, or fiberglass bodywork in-process.

For Dillon, his part of it means wandering off, pinching a cigarette butt up from beside the trash and fake-smoking it until he can track who's driving alone, who's in the bathroom. That plus a skinny dime for a screwdriver and he's walking back with a license plate tucked in the back of his jeans, under his shirt.

"Texas?" Harper says, fake-smoking that gross cigarette to cover Dillon at the bumper. "I thought we were trying to get people *not* to hate us?"

"Thought it matched the POS truck," Dillon says, and stands to appreciate his work.

"We're going to hell, aren't we?" Harper says, disgusted with how easy it is to flip a switch, be a criminal.

"Better later than now, right?" Dillon says.

"I still can't believe it, really," Harper says.

"That Kissy and Jam are gone?"

"That there are people, things, whatever like him."

"You mean he's not the only—" Dillon starts, but Harper's wide eyes stop him: a big rig's headlights are sweeping across them, the trucker gearing down to swing around but then just pulling through instead, making the circle, like he missed the spot he was aiming for. Like he was just . . . looking for someone?

"Probably just wanted to see if there was anybody here he knew," Dillon says with a smile.

It's what they used to do when they'd come up here to park: scope around for any familiar trucks or hats, then settle in to read the thoughts and lives of all the drivers coming through. Rigs and tourists and businessmen all. Dillon was especially good at the obvious emergency cases—the people hunched over, doing the peepee dance up the sidewalk.

Harper's specialty was making them all into rich snobs, looking down their noses at this grubby unclean place, the only facilities for miles in either direction—only port in a storm.

"Ex NASCAR driver," Harper says about that trucker. "He likes turning left, turning left."

"What is that, anyway?" Dillon says, that circling rig still in their conversational sights. "Rusty old Kenworth?"

"Peterbilt," Harper says. "281."

"Shit, girl," Dillon says, impressed. "Got diesel in your veins, what?"

"Their fronts look like faces," she says, "see? They were my favorite when I was a kid. My dad always pointed them out to me."

The truck's head-on to them again so they can see its headlights like two trembling eyes.

Dillon cocks his head over about that.

"Why is it—?" he says, and Harper finishes it in her head: Why are they seeing it from the front *again*?

Easy answer: because it's made the circle, is in the *car* parking lot now, is coming right at them, pouring smoke from its twin stacks, the asphalt trembling, the whole rest stop shuddering from this fundamental wrongness—from a rig pulling its long, empty flatbed up into the land of dog walkers and picture-takers.

"*Shit!*" Dillon says, diving across the hood, the Park truck already rumbling to life, because, because—Harper's coming around the passenger side fast and desperate—because Meg's behind the wheel, is at the key.

"Go go go!" Harper yells, waving her backwards, just running alongside like Dillon is, and Meg stomps the pedal an instant before pulling the shifter down into reverse.

The tire on Harper's side chirps back and takes the whole truck with it just a hair before the rig turns hard into where they just were, the curb nothing to it, the trash can even less.

"*Stop, stop!*" Dillon's screaming to Meg in some other part of the world, and Harper has the dim awareness of the Park truck crunching into the sloped-down nose of some little Chevy. She's mostly watching this antique Peterbilt slam into and *through* the camper parked three slots over. Almost immediately after that it rams the light blue work pickup parked on the other side, pushing it over until its passenger side tires catch on the curb. The work truck starts to roll over sideways, takes the front of the Peterbilt up with it and they stop together, the pickup dead on its side, the Peterbilt's ugly tough front bumper chocked up on the horizontal driver's side doors of the pickup, front tires hanging down in open air.

"Shit," Harper says.

She's only ever seen big rigs in the ditch, after the wreck, the crushed and broken cars all around. It's completely different, seeing it happen—a tank falling through the roof, from deep in the sky.

And this one's got reverse.

The driver grinds down and around to it and the drive wheels hitch and spin in the camper, pulling the front end back down with a ground-shaking clang, the pickup finding its tires again, its windshield finally blowing out like a soft exhalation of glass.

A man runs out from the bathroom, his pants clutched at his knees, and a woman is hustling two children away from this, and three or four drivers are prairie-dogged up from their front seats to get a better view of just what might be going on here, but more are starting their cars, stabbing their headlights out into a different future than this.

Harper looks across the front seat of the Park truck to Dillon, standing by the steering wheel, his hand to Meg's shoulder, her face bloody from—from backing up into that little Chevy. Her head must have slung back from the impact and then whipped forward from the sudden stop, whipped forward into the steering wheel.

"A flatbed," Dillon says in wonder, and turns to Harper. "That's the same truck, Harp. Ninety percent sure. Hundred percent if there's statie blood on the front bumper."

"There is," Harper says, and eases the passenger door open to stand up onto the rocker panel, tippy-toe for an angle into this Peterbilt's dark cab. Before she can make even a silhouette out the rig bounces back and back, its empty forty-foot flatbed bowed up in the middle from no load, the rear bumper crunching hard into the restroom, shaking dust up from it, its low metal roof finding a new tilt, like the little building has just adjusted its hat.

The Peterbilt granny-gears it forward in a sudden hop, plowing into the work truck again, its drive wheels spinning in the trashed, bisected camper, and then it comes back harder, the flatbed's rear bumper gouging into the brick wall of the restroom now, pulling a section of it forward.

"He's not gonna stop," Harper says to Dillon and Meg. Meg grabs onto Harper's wrist. "We need to see what he looks like now," she says then. "That's—it's his secret power, right? That he can be anybody else?"

"Harp, no—" Dillon says, reaching across Meg for her, but Harper's already down and running.

Not letting herself stop to think about how stupid this is, she crosses the strip of parking lot at a leaning-ahead run, leaps up onto the empty flatbed and lands hard, rolls across that splintery rocking platform and flies halfway off the other side, only just manages to grab a dirty yellow cinch strap.

The Peterbilt stops and she knows she's in its side mirror.

She stands holding that four-inch strap for balance, feels like the smallest bullrider.

"Come out!" she calls to the cab.

The truck guns forward, trying to dislodge her, but she moves with it.

It tries reverse in as jerky a way as it can, knocking her down this time from the hard judder of the rear bumper cutting even deeper into the restroom now.

She gets back up, has that strap wrapped twice around her hand now, a suicide grip.

The truck stops, is in neutral, she can feel. At least until she lets that strap slacken the least bit, she knows. But then the truck, instead of trying to shake her, it turns off, easy as that. Like it knows when it's beat.

Harper lets the strap go, stands there waiting.

The Peterbilt's door opens and a man-shape stands up out of it, looking all around, one hand to the grab bar so he can lean out.

"Harper Harper Harper," he says, face still hidden in shadow. "Got to say, that little stunt back at the gas station, I wasn't expecting that."

"It didn't work, evidently," Harper says back.

"You are leaving quite the pile of bodies behind you, yes," he says. "You're all over the airwaves, did you know that?"

"You will be too," she says, then says his name out loud, like identifying him out in the open will give her some power over him.

He nods, shrugs, repeats it: "'Bucketmouth,' yep. Odd name, isn't it? But you don't get to choose. I don't *feel* like a largemouth bass, I mean. And it's not like this is fishing country, either."

"It's not about fish," Harper says, trying to get a line on Meg, make sure she's good.

"It's about something," Bucketmouth says. "Maybe you could cast some light on that?"

"Maybe you could tell me why you're even after us," Harper tells him. "We're not—we didn't do anything to you."

"Have you seen this face I went to so much trouble to grow?" Bucketmouth says back, turning his head to spit what Harper guesses must be blood, maybe a molar. From John Henry's fists. From all the fists, all the knees, all the boots.

"You had my *sister*," Harper says. "You left me no choice."

"Ah, the backed into a corner defense," Bucketmouth says. "I know it well. You could say it's the one I'm using now. I either take care of you and yours, now that my big secret's out, or . . . well. I'm sure you understand."

"You were doing this long before those holy rollers picked you up," Harper says.

Bucketmouth digests this, says, "Either way, did you or didn't you, aside from using this face all up, burn up all my secret ones too?"

"That was just *me*," Harper says, stepping forward. "You were there, you saw. Let them go, take me, this can be over."

"What, are you some kind of bad-ass hero girl?" Bucketmouth asks. "Seriously, hero girl, why settle for one when all three are just as easy?"

"Try it," Dillon says, swaggering up onto the trailer with all his height, all his shoulders, all his tone.

"Ah, the knight in shining armor arrives to—" Bucketmouth says, but stops from what's got Harper's attention now as well: a motion on the *other* side of the Peterbilt's narrow cab. Something's scrabbling out the open window and tumbling down, falling, crunching and yelping a sharp pitiful little cry out.

A lap dog.

"*Sheba*," Harper says without thinking, the waiting silence making her voice travel more than she means.

This must be that rank trucker from the gas station's rig.

Bucketmouth fought or killed or wormed his way through all the fists and boots pummeling him and found this trucker stepping up into his old Peterbilt, left him lying in the tall grass, didn't realize the dog was already up in the cab until he was out on the interstate feeling for the tall gears, the better to slap a statie with.

The dog flops over on the asphalt and stands trying to scurry away but its front leg is what that crunch was. It chin-dives, rises shaking, is still trying, still mewling.

"Sheba?" Meg says then, in wonder, and Harper realizes Meg's out of the Park truck. That she heard this random nothing-dog's name. That it kind of means everything to her—is why she's on this crazy ride in the first place.

"*Meg, no!*" Harper screams, but this is already happening. All she can do is try to catch up. She grabs hold of Dillon for traction, pushing him back hard so she can launch forward. It sends her off the side of the trailer too fast. She splats but doesn't slow even a little, doesn't need skin on her knees and hands right now, just needs to get to Meg.

Meg is *to* the scrawny hurt dog now, is on her knees cradling it up. Harper slides to a hugging stop, placing herself between Meg and the footsteps she hears behind her.

She looks up through her hair and it's Bucketmouth, still with Jam's beaten-in, split open face. He's holding a tire beater. Not the kind you get off the rack but the kind that's a sawed-off bat wrapped with electrical tape. Because he left his pistol on that shelf in the store, of course.

"Can't say it wasn't a good ride," Bucketmouth says with Jam's voice—the voice *does* change—and raises the tire beater, Harper's hand and arm coming up like they're on a string attached to that tire beater, and, does she close her eyes? Either her eyes or her mind, because what Dillon says, it comes *into* the darkness she's mired in.

"Hey, numbnuts," he's saying from the far side of the flatbed he's just climbing back up onto. "I wasn't done with you."

Bucketmouth halts his swing, looks from Harper and Meg back to the flatbed, then finally nods, says to Harper and Meg, "Just be a minute, ladies. Y'all keep each other company, all right?" With that he turns around, but a couple of steps later he stops, looks back. "Did you already name that dog?" he asks, impressed it seems. "How can anybody name a dog that fast just from seeing it?"

"Dillon!" Harper calls. "*Run!*"

Dillon shakes his head no, is just standing there on the flatbed waiting like it's a canvas mat in the center of an empty arena.

Bucketmouth appraises him, shifts the tire beater to his other hand, then back.

"I would say this is going to be fun," he says, "but . . ."

He turns back to Harper and Meg, then calls out to Dillon, "Y'know? Think I will start over here, if nobody's particular."

"*No!*" Dillon says, coming to the edge of the flatbed.

Bucketmouth raises a hand to keep him there, his eyes still to Harper and Meg.

"Wonder if that dog will lick up anything I splash out of their heads?" he says loud and clear for Dillon. "Dogs don't know, right? It's just—it tastes good, why not eat it, right? That's not a bad way to get through life, you ask me."

"If you want to—" Dillon starts, but Bucketmouth's already going: "I know, I know. Mano to mano, let's beat each other senseless, blah blah, whoever hits the hardest or gets back up the most times wins, all that boring stuff. Know what, though? I've already been a couple of rounds tonight, with gentlemen significantly more, um, stout than you, no offense."

"You don't know," Dillon says.

"You're right," Bucketmouth says. "And I don't think I choose to."

"You don't have a—"

"There's always a choice," Bucketmouth says with a smile.

"And this time, it's yours. Either—either I take two steps forward, bring this down into a skull or two, or . . ." He looks back and Harper takes that chance to lunge up.

She's stopped by the blunt, rounded top of that tire beater pointing right at her forehead, touching it almost, Bucketmouth looking at her down along it with Jam's swollen nearly-shut eyes, Jam's beat-to-crap face.

Still talking loud to Dillon but watching Harper now, he says, "Or . . . you look like you know your way around a load, yes? Like you might have helped secure one at some point in your life? Something about you. I've got an eye for that, see. So, what I want you to do, *Dillon*, is strap yourself down up there."

"How do I know you won't—"

"I give you my word as a weary traveler," Bucketmouth says, still watching Harper, Harper unable to move, as he can flick the tire beater either way, tap her hard on the temple. "The weariest traveler, you might say."

"You'll let them go?" Dillon asks.

"For now," Bucketmouth says, and raises his other hand, doing the Scout's honor fingers.

"Dillon, no!" Harper says, moving as little as possible.

"No, no, stay with us a little yet," Bucketmouth says over Harper to Meg, trying to creep away with the hurt dog. Then, to Harper: "Tell me what your boyfriend's doing back there if you will, Harper."

"You don't get to say my name," Harper says.

"Harper Harper Harper . . ." Bucketmouth says, tasting it and grinning wide. "Do I hear any cams ratcheting down back there?" he calls out to Dillon.

"I don't care what happens to me," Dillon says. "I'm already toast."

"Well that's no fun," Bucketmouth says, then: "If the law

shows up before you're done up there, then all deals are off, you understand."

Dillon holds Harper's eyes for a long moment, then nods once and casts around for the dirty yellow strap. He finds it, pulls it, reseats the buckle onto the rail.

"No," Harper says, her throat awash with hot tears.

"Ah," Bucketmouth says about the defeat on her face. "Yes."

Dillon sits down, squirms his legs under a strap and reaches for the heavy ratchet.

"Across the *mid*section, let's say," Bucketmouth calls back. "But lying on your stomach, of course, facing front. Once we get on the highway it'll feel like you're flying, won't it?"

"Don't," Harper says. "Please."

"I just wanted to get a little further along down the road," Bucketmouth says, shrugging like this is all too bad. "I didn't ask anyone to—"

"You can't do this," Harper tells him.

"What I'm already doing, you mean?" Bucketmouth asks, and chances a look back to the flatbed.

"Please," Harper says.

"Ah, what stage of desperation would this be?" Bucketmouth says. "We start out with denial, then flight, then comes resistance, which you're really better at than I was thinking, then . . . is deal-making next? Are we skipping something here?"

He looks back to the truck, and all around.

"Oh yeah," he says, snapping his fingers by his head. "Next up, for you, is acceptance. Now, say goodbye."

Harper turns her head from Dillon, ratcheting himself down, and senses the tire beater coming for the side of her head.

She flinches back, looks up to Bucketmouth watching her, holding the tire beater just short of where it would have made contact with the eggshell side of her right temple.

"See you soon," he says, and jogs backwards, sits up on the flatbed and swings his legs over.

Harper rushes after, gets there as he's planting his knee into Dillon's back, watching her the whole while.

"Harp, no!" Dillon says, his face sideways against one of the wide wooden slats of the flatbed.

"*Harp, no!*" Bucketmouth falsettos, and cranks the ratchet once, tightening the strap a few clicks, and then again.

Dillon groans, his face going red.

"Stop!" Harper says to Bucketmouth, reaching ahead but not coming closer.

"This would be where I say that's entirely up to you," he says, and cranks the ratchet again, having to put his weight into it now.

Dillon pukes into the boards he's being pressed against, blood vessels in his eyes bursting.

"When I was in elementary school," Bucketmouth says, his tone all about having all the time in the world, "our classrooms and hallways would get infested at a certain time of year with these fuzzy caterpillars. You don't have them up here, but trust me, they were a plague—a beautiful one, but still a bother. Being kids, we made a game of it, of course. We found that you could step on them from back to front, and shoot all their insides out their head. Whoever got the longest spurt won, right? Too, remember this is elementary. All us young boys, we were interested in the opposite sex, but didn't know how to talk to them, exactly. Our solution? We'd wait until we saw them in proximity to a caterpillar, then we'd rush forward, our hearts full of love, and we'd step on that little caterpillar front to back, gushing caterpillar brains and guts onto the girl's shoes, or, if we really liked her, and it was a really juicy caterpillar, her *shins*. It was the only way to show the depth of our affection."

He lets that sit, then raises the ratchet handle one more time, his hand ready to drive it down, this push being the one that forces Dillon's guts up through his mouth.

"All leading to you wondering how much affection I have for you, right, Harper? Harp? Do I love you enough to send the very best? How far do you think his insides will go if I push this down just—"

"No, don't!" Harper says, backing off.

"This doesn't mean I don't love you, of course," he says, standing, his foot to that cam lever now.

"I'm going, I'm going," Harper says, still backing off, coming down to her knees beside Meg and the ratty little dog.

"Nice seeing you again," Bucketmouth says, raising his hand in farewell. "I'm sure we'll be running into each other again somewhere down the road." With that he walks up the long trailer, jumps onto the tractor, pulls around into the cab and fires the engine up first turn, all this destruction just another day at the office for this rusty Peterbilt.

"What's he going to do?" Meg says.

This time, instead of trying to go through the work truck, he backs deeper into the restroom and hauls the wheel to the right, just nudging the work truck to the side, bumping and grinding through the camper, over the curb, the flatbed rattling, Dillon's face loose against the wooden planks, his chunky throw-up stringing from his cheek to the boards over and over, but he's past caring about that now.

Pulling out of the parking lot, Bucketmouth lets the horn go, raises his hand friendly-like from the window, doesn't tap his brakes in response to the clump of blue and red lights screaming eastbound, on perfect intersection with him.

"Yes, yes, yes," Harper says, standing, stepping forward to help this along.

Just like it looked, the Peterbilt hauling Dillon away should cross perfect with all the emergency vehicles . . . except the cops and ambulances and firetrucks are shooting *over* the bridge for the officer down, and Bucketmouth is ducking *under* that bridge. All it would take is one statie to look down past the railing, see Dillon strapped down tight to the trailer. All it would take is one single fireman high in his truck looking idly over to the rest stop, at everybody standing from the rubble.

Instead, the Peterbilt eases under, its left blinker a dot of white now, the red plastic crumbled off in the restroom.

Harper sags down to her knees.

Bucketmouth makes the turn, belches smoke up into the night, and right as he's about to step up onto the interstate, all his lights turn off.

He's gone.

CHAPTER 16

Harper's trying to attend to the diagonal cut—more like a burst—on Meg's forehead when Meg says it in her checked-out voice: "He wants us to follow him, doesn't he?"

Harper dabs at the edge of the torn skin and Meg doesn't even wince. The dog is licking delicately at the blood pooled in the hollow of Meg's throat, its eyes on Harper the whole time. Harper can't tell if the dog's asking permission or if she's making sure Harper's not going to dart in, steal some. It doesn't matter. The dog weighs all of two pounds. Harper pushes it away from Meg's throat, tries to clean that up too.

"I thought he would have a different face by now," Harper says. "He still looks like Jam. Just, Jam all beat up."

Meg settles her eyes on Harper.

"We've got to think," Harper says. "We can't outmuscle him, probably can't outrun him, definitely can't outcrazy him, and he probably already knows every move we think we're coming up with. So, what does it *mean* that he still looks the same?"

"That he can't—can't change too much, or that fast?" Meg says with a shrug.

"Or he's a picky eater," Harper says.

"Both?" Meg tries.

Harper dabs at the blood, nods sure, both, could be. And ten other things besides. The phase of the moon, blood type, rate of human digestion, presence or absence of snacks to burn as fuel. On and on. Maybe it only works at highway speeds, even.

"I need to get you home," she tells Meg.

"The one you're running away from, you mean?" Meg says.

"It's not—that's just me and Mom," Harper says. "Nothing about you."

"It's because you're just the same," Meg says.

"I'm not like her," Harper says. "I won't ever be like her."

"'Watch out for boyfriends like Dillon, Meg,'" Meg parrots with their mom's 'talking while doing the hateful dishes'-delivery. "Is he a movie nobody in our family should rewatch the next night, because we all know how it ends?"

Harper licks her lips, looks back to the truck, crunched into the blue Beretta, and tries to figure out whether that's what that last big blowout was really about or not. And also wondering how little sisters can be so perceptive. But, years hiding in the corner, watching, listening? Maybe they are, yeah. Maybe they can be.

Still, "I thought I was smart when I was twelve, too," Harper says.

"Said Mom to Harper, when she was twelve," Meg says right back, and Harper winces to have to remember *that* big blowout.

"I'm trying to keep your head wound from leaking your brain out, here," Harper says.

"I'm using that brain," Meg says with an evil grin, and brings her hands up, picking another dab of glass from Harper's hair.

"Then use it to help us," Harper says. "Why does he want me to follow him? He could have ended it right here if he wanted."

"Something worse, right?" Meg says. "Isn't that the only reason you drag a thing out? Because there's something better for you at the way end of it?"

"Worse for me is better for him," Harper says, sitting back, Meg's forehead as good as it's going to get without a first-aid kit or an emergency room, a time machine or a magic wand.

"So it's all about you?" Meg says, sucking the dot of blood from the pad of her finger from that last shard she plucked from Harper's hair.

"Like you weren't already losing enough blood?" Harper says.

Meg shrugs, keeps sucking.

"And, it's about *me* because I'm not letting *you* go any further down this road, remember?" Harper says.

"It's my fault he has Dillon," Meg says, the dog back in her lap, favoring its shattered front leg.

"It's not your fault," Harper says.

"Y'all were going to have him up there on that trailer until I . . ." Meg says. "Sorry?"

"He was as surprised by Sheba as we were," Harper says. "It's not like that was some big plan he had. He just, like, took advantage. Anyway, I don't say her name like that, you don't come out to save her."

"Why *did* you call her that?"

"Because that's her name," Harper says, nodding down to the dog's tags. Meg thumbs them up from the fur: QUEEN SHEBA on one side, DON'T TREAD ON ME on the other.

"I'm keeping her," Meg says, roughing the dog up between its alert ears.

"Have to ask Mom," Harper says, flicking her eyes away from the pale Buick one building over that she's only just realizing she's been staring at.

She's been here all along.

Mom.

Shit.

Her car's okay, though. She's not in it now, too, meaning . . . restroom? Not coming out until all the crashing and destruction is for sure over?

More important, she hasn't seen her daughters huddled together in the parking lot.

"What?" Meg says, registering Harper's eyes, but Harper—no time to think of a proper fake-out—hunches forward like in pain. It works: Meg stops cranking her head over to clock the Buick, reaches forward to help.

"Just—glass in my hair," Harper grunts, losing her fingers in her hair, where she's pretty sure there really *is* glass.

"Here," Meg says, and starts threading the larger shards out.

"Why aren't the cops here yet?" she says, completely focused on Harper's hair now.

"Busy night," Harper says, watching the door of the Ladies' so closely, now. "Think they're spread kind of thin. And—" making a show of casing the rest stop, because she can't have Meg seeing that Buick—"no payphone here. If they hear about a trucker losing his shit at Wagonhound, it'll be from another trucker, most likely."

"And they don't rat their own out," Meg completes, citing The Gospel of Dad.

"I don't know if Bucketmouth counts as a trucker," Harper says. "But I guess he was driving a truck, yeah, so how would the other truckers know he wasn't one of them."

"Bucketmouth," Meg repeats, sort of tasting it. "That's like—what is it? Buffalo Bill, yeah. From that movie we rented."

"He's made up, just on video," Harper says. "Bucketmouth's real."

As proof, she nods to the destroyed Men's restroom across from them, which it's completely safe for Meg to look at.

"In the movie version, he'd have driven right through that in slow motion," Harper says. "And it wouldn't even mess his grille up."

"So we know he can drive a truck," Meg says.

Harper nods, hadn't considered that.

"I can too, though," she says. Then, quieter, "Dad was going to teach you too. He told me."

"It's a truck-driving contest?" Meg says back.

"Me and him, maybe," Harper says. "Not you and me."

It's always been an unspoken point of contention or jealousy or something, that Harper, just because she was born first, ended up having more time with Dad. More memories of him.

Guilty as she feels for that, though, she wouldn't trade them.

"He can ride a motorcycle, too," Harper goes on, getting her and Meg over this conversational hump. "If he . . . if he lives out here on the road like this, catching rides and, you know, *eating* people, we have to think there's not anything he can't drive, and there's no cab or car or bike he can't talk his way into, onto, whatever. If we think like that, then he can't surprise us."

"Road graders, harvesters, cop cars," Meg enumerates, narrowing her eyes to try to think of what else could be traveling by interstate.

Harper nods, has to accept this: not only can Bucketmouth change faces on some obscure schedule or mechanism, but every vehicle on the road, it has the potential to have him behind the wheel.

"RVs," Meg adds, still doing that. "School buses. Normal buses."

"Those big things that change the concrete dividers," Harper adds with a grin. Her and Meg have only ever seen those on the news—with Dillon, right?—and this stretch of 80 doesn't have anything like that going on, but still. If you're going to dream, dream big.

That probably goes for nightmares as well.

"Those three-wheeler choppers," Meg says, trying to make this last. "Trains?"

"He's getting away in something right now," Harper says, standing like looking for him. She tips her head to the Ladies', says, "Grab a handful of paper towels for your bleedy head, and we'll hit it."

"We," Meg says, letting Harper haul her up.

"Sisters," Harper says.

"Even though he *wants* us to come out there again?" Meg says.

"He's got Dillon," Harper says back, in defeat. "His game is the only game, for now."

"But he'd come for us, wouldn't he?" Meg says. "If we just . . . *sat* here?"

"Dillon," Harper says, pressing her lips together after saying it, meaning: they have to give chase, can't just sit here.

Meg can't argue with that, just says about the bathroom run Harper's sending her on, "I thought you said there weren't any paper towels in there?"

"I didn't check if there were any pads," Harper says. "We can stick one to your big head."

With that, she nudges Meg off to do this last errand. "I'll extract the truck from your great parking job," she adds, turning back to survey the damage.

"The parking job that saved us all, you mean?" Meg says, leaving for the Ladies' at last, thank you.

"Taking your rat?" Harper says about the dog. "I got a truck to care for, can't be babysitting."

Meg scoops Sheba up—Harper's already calling her that in her head, not "dog."

"She needs to go too, you think?" Meg says with a smile, twirling away with the dog.

"Be safe," Harper calls out, nominally about these paper towels, that restroom, but she means it just generally as well, and for it to last for however many years it's about to be until she sees her little sister again. If ever.

"Bye, girl," she says where Meg can't hear, then makes herself turn away, wipes the tears from her eyes, and steps up through the Park truck's missing door, and then can't help it once she's in the seat—she has to cry, thinking of her mom taking two long steps from the sink to pull Meg to her, hold her and hold her, not let her go all the way back to Laramie.

"You're welcome, Mom," Harper says and fires the truck up, screeches and tears and drags away from the hurt Beretta then pulls out of Wagonhound through the entrance, taillights off. If they even work anymore.

When her dad didn't come back from his Tacoma run her sophomore year, Dillon found Harper on the roof of that same apartment complex. They were broken up that May—Dillon had Jennifer Chalmers's initials in fancy white script on the passenger side back glass of his truck, and Harper was making sure to be seen with Randal Sees Bull—but evidently Harper's mom had been calling around for where her oldest daughter might be, and her oldest daughter's main ex-boyfriend was standing around the kitchen, overheard that call.

"What are you doing up here?" Harper said to him without even looking around.

"Don't worry, I didn't tell her where you'd be," Dillon said back, settling into the gravel beside her but not touching sleeves.

"Her?"

"Your mom."

"Good," Harper said. "It's her fault."

Dillon looked over to her about this. She could feel it.

"Thought you might be hungry," he said at last, and pulled a paper-wrapped burger from his pocket. It was from the cooler at the truckstop.

"You nuke it?" she asked.

"A minute longer," Dillon said, leaning forward to connect the burger with her hand. "Knew it'd cool down, getting here."

"Your defroster's broke in your truck now, what?" Harper asked, tearing into the rubbery bun.

"My defroster?"

"You can turn it on high, set your food up there to warm it," Harper said, blinking fast. "My dad taught it to me, said it's how you can still have a hot meal at sixty miles per hour."

"Got to drive with the windows down, I bet," Dillon said.

"Got to do that anyway," Harper said. "Bunk smells like a locker room."

They were her dad's exact words. They were what made her finally start crying, the kind she couldn't stop. When Dillon edged closer like to maybe touch her shoulder, she pushed away, stayed alone.

"How late is he this time?" he asked.

"It was just *Tacoma*," Harper said. "Electronics. It's not even winter, right? What could happen between Wyoming and fucking Washington? Why wouldn't he have called?"

Dillon just sat there, finally extracting another burger from his pocket, opening it for himself.

"Unless you want it," he said about the burger.

Harper just stared at it.

"If—if nothing happened to him," she said, like there was a jury that could hear this logic, make it so, "and we'd have heard about it if it had, then, then, then what does that *leave*?"

Dillon just squinted and chewed.

"It means he saw his exit is what it means," Harper said, wiping her eyes hard. "He saw a way to get away from my mom and he took it, just left his rig somewhere nobody'd ticket it for a few weeks and walked away. I don't blame him."

"He's probably just hung up somewhere," Dillon said. "Maybe the cops jammed him up about something."

"For delivering electronics he has a bill of lading for?"

"I mean, they're *cops*."

Harper couldn't deny that. "He used to always tell me there were aliens," she said then, quieter. "Maybe that's what happened."

Dillon watched her about this until she looked away. "I don't think aliens would take him," he said, then added, "If they've got UFOs, then they're pretty covered for electronics, think?"

"Mom was always saying he was just like his brothers," Harper said then, just all at once. "That he only cared about making enough to get through this week. That he wasn't thinking big enough thoughts, that he wasn't thinking long-term."

"My mom and dad used to fight too," Dillon said, shrugging.

Harper looked over to him, didn't say the obvious: that his parents divorced five years ago, that his mom lived two floors below where they were sitting now, that his dad took every job he could and hadn't turned in an honest logbook for years, just to stay gone as much as he could.

In the truckstops she always moved through like a dream when making a run with her dad, him having to shake her awake to go inside and hold onto her shoulders for the first few steps to keep her upright, all the blankets and caps always had some version of a trucker or a biker merging with an Old West cowboy or Indian, and going kind of grand and transparent in the process.

Was that what had happened to her dad? Had he zoned out coming down a grade and just shimmered away, gone ghost without even dying, without leaving a fiery wreck behind? Was he still out there haunting the slow lane, finally at peace? Was he Phantom 309 now for hitchhikers? If it meant not having to go home and be reminded what a failure he was, then yeah, that might be him, Harper figured.

Fading into the backdrop was all he had left, his only real option anymore if he wanted to stay the same person he'd always been. But he *could* have come home, that was the thing Harper couldn't let go. Not for Mom, Mom hated him, but for his *daughters*. He could have come home long enough to take them with, anyway, couldn't he have? They could live in the bunk, who cared what it smelled like. It smelled like him, and that had to be better than never seeing him again.

"So . . ." Dillon said then, right when Harper's thoughts were really roiling and churning, about to spill over, make her stand up and sling her hamburger off the edge of the building, "so you're gambling on him driving between here and here?" He held up his right finger to mark where the part of 80 they could see started, then his left finger to show where it ended.

"He has to come through there to get to here," Harper said, obviously, ready to fight about this. Looking forward to it, even.

"But," Dillon said almost meekly, squinching his face up like he didn't want to have to be the one to tell her something this obvious, "have you tried, you know, looking for him on the air?"

"On TV?" Harper said, pretty sure this fight was about to be on.

"My dad's home right now," Dillon said, setting his burger down half-eaten and wincing: "Sorry, I didn't mean that—"

"You said we could find him," Harper said, setting her burger down as well.

"We can try," Dillon said. "We can use my dad's CB—*that* air. I know where his keys are."

Harper stood into this new idea, looked around at all the possibilities: someone out there had to know, had to have seen him, had to have heard something. Going CB to CB, you could leapfrog across states in no time, cast a blanket as wide as you could want.

Her dad would be under that blanket somewhere, she knew. He had to be. There was no trucker out there who wouldn't pass along a message from another trucker's kid.

"Well?" she said, tilting her head to the idea of Dillon's dad's truck only a half-mile walk away, and he stood and they walked to the broken roof door together, and he jogged ahead at the very end to pull it open for her like always, and *that's* the Dillon

Harper's pulling onto the interstate for now, no door on her left side, blood and pee on the windshield, vomit in the floorboard, tears running back from her eyes, into her hair.

The Dillon she's going after, it's the Dillon who jogged ahead to catch that door for her when she was perfectly capable of getting it herself. But it made her feel special. Just like her dad always did when he was home. And, right before stepping through that open door, to sit up all night with Dillon talking to truckers under the dome light of his dad's million-mile Mack, she'd looked back to the interstate one last hopeful time, just on the chance, and what she saw was their two paper-wrapped truckstop burgers side by side in the gravel, which is how she knew he wasn't going to be with Jennifer Chalmers much longer, that her initials were going to be all over his life.

Like they still are, Harper figures.

Only, now they're carved in, and he's bleeding from them.

Which is pie-in-the-sky hopeful, she knows. If he's bleeding, he's still alive.

But if a monster's a real monster, then it has to be able to sit by you on a flatbed trailer and bite your index finger off, chew the meat from each side of it like a chicken wing while your stump burbles blood out onto the wood slats.

Why wouldn't Bucketmouth want to be a tall, strong eighteen-year-old with sure hands, a quick smile, a devil-probably-doesn't-care reckless look to his eyes?

Trick is, though, the first rule of taking someone's face and life, it's got to be erasing the chance of there being two of you in the same aisle at the truckstop at any point.

Harper puts her foot into the pedal, tries to go faster.

CHAPTER 17

The truckers are no longer blowing their air horns down at her when they sweep past, and there's no more spit cups drifting through the air for her windshield, no more cigarettes sparking into the cab. It can't be because of the arrowhead she burned and rubbed off the passenger door—the Park truck's not limping past anybody in the left lane, so the only eyes seeing that smudged arrowhead are the deer and coyotes out in the pasture, and they don't care.

It can't be the Texas plates letting her slip past either, she doesn't think. Texas plates in Wyoming, where the cowboys are *real*, are more an invitation for abuse than a shield. Probably it's that word of her circulating from cab to cab like a joke or a call to brotherhood or an appeal for justice, it went *with* the group of truckers who are now asleep, or in another state. They didn't hand the instructions about what to do with and to this Park truck back to the next set of wheels rolling in, and so now that be-on-the-lookout-for was getting forgotten. Not forgiven, but there were other idiot drivers on the road to deal with. And schedules to keep. That always has to come first: the schedule. And Harper isn't on it anymore, it doesn't feel like.

At first she thinks this is good, but a few miles to the west she decides that really, the truckers not paying her any attention anymore, that just leaves her out here even more alone, where Bucketmouth can do whatever he wants.

If she ever even catches up with him, that is.

When the temperature needle edges close to the red she flips the heater on, feels not even one speck of that warmth. The brown Audi passes her again and the college kids don't look over this time—it's dark in the Park truck's cab now, thanks to Dillon yanking the fuse—and Harper wonders if they were at Wagonhound when it came tumbling down, are still shellshocked. If not, then they're just in a loop, driving west until the turnaround at the fire then hooking it back this way, deciding twenty minutes into it that the interstate has to be open by now, doesn't it? They're the Moth People, Harper decides. They're just battering themselves against that bright light over close to Laramie, getting singed, then drifting away, coming back for more in tighter and more suicidal circles.

It doesn't matter.

She rolls through the AM for a voice—church, politics, sports, weather, whatever—but the statie evidently took the antenna into the ditch with him. She resigns herself to side B of the Gordon Lightfoot.

"Where are you, where are you?" she says to Bucketmouth, leaning forward like being ten inches closer to the windshield is going to be what makes him pop out in the headlights. But this Park truck's about to boil over, too, and if it does, she's back to riding her thumb, and that's no way to save Dillon. She hits the heel of her hand on the top of the steering wheel in frustration and drifts the truck onto exit 260. There's no lights calling her in, no signs talking about services leading up to it, and the ramp is hardly even maintained, might as well have grass growing in the cracks, but still, she slows, looks left and right, comes to a full stop at the intersection.

Nothing. Wyoming at night. A wide spot in the road, and hardly even that.

The gauge is edging up to 230, is in the red now because it doesn't have fast air cooling the radiator.

"Why do you suck so much?" Harper says to the Park truck—and to herself, she guesses—easing back into that cool wind, then feels bad, pats the dash. This stupid unsellable truck *did* keep them from getting steamrolled on that first ramp out of Laramie, she guesses, which probably used up its last gasp of youth, and it's taken some hits meant for them since then, for sure. The windshield is trash, the door is gone, the rear bumper's crunched up into the gas tank, and she doesn't even want to think about all the body fluids splashed around. Including statie blood, which is just blood, she tells herself. From a person who *was* living, isn't anymore. A person who was just doing his job, stopping who his cop radio was telling him to stop.

Shit.

To say nothing of that explosion at the pullout, all the lives and schedules probably left burning there. And what if there was somebody in that restroom when Bucketmouth pulled it down, right?

Is this all fallout from the fight she had with her mom over Omar Epps, or would some version of this be happening anyway, with someone else? The first read on the situation puts her at the center of the world, which she very much knows not to be true, but the second just accepts that all this bad stuff was unstoppable, so why even try.

But at least Meg's on the way back to Laramie, Harper tells herself. With their mom, sure, but Harper survived her high school years in that house, under that regime. Meg can too. And who knows, maybe it really was a Harper and her mom thing all along. Maybe it'll be better with Meg. Or maybe her mom's learned something, has some regrets, will try harder now.

Harper cues fast through that moany shipwreck song, can't handle it right now, thank you, and then she sings along with the next one even though she doesn't like it. It's not about staying awake, it's about trying to keep from thinking and dwelling and wishing, none of which helps.

All that's going to help is seeing that rusty old Peterbilt and turning the steering wheel that way, dealing with whatever comes next.

"The one that's not here, not here . . ." Harper mutters, coasting through this dead exit, taking the sad excuse for a ramp back onto the interstate.

The truck cools down to 220 again with the wind cooling the radiator, but even at just forty-five, that temperature gauge won't let its little arm fall any lower. The gas tank didn't puncture on that Beretta, though, which is a miracle in itself, since these trucks were built to explode, pretty much. Harper tucks her hair down the back of the leather jacket then zips it up tight to her neck. It's not a ponytail holder, but it's better than nothing. She should have got one from Meg, who wears them like bracelets, like she's the Girl Scout of hair bands, but screw it.

"Where are you, where are you?" she says again, to remind herself.

And if she makes Utah before finding Dillon? What then?

Well, first, half a tank won't get her that far. But, even Rawlins, right? If she rolls into Rawlins, hasn't seen Dillon, what then? Keep driving, or follow the Audi's maybe-lead and just start making circles, showing the truck from all sides to draw Bucketmouth out?

"Tell a cop," she says out loud. Obviously. Except this truck is probably on video shaking a torn-in-half statie off its hood.

If she could just cue forward and backwards like this cassette tape in the deck, she thinks. She'd either jump ahead to after this is all over and her and Dillon could lift a sad beer to it, or she'd go back to right after the big storm-out, and this time she'd take the east ramp instead of the west. Then Kissy and Jam never find her on their way back to Yellowstone. Her sister might still be following her, but—so she watches Harper go one way instead of the other? Who cares. Going east like that, too, Harper doesn't tangle up with the Thunderbird people, which has to be where this all started. If she doesn't take their bottle of water and stupid glow bracelet, then she doesn't feel obligated to follow that big red car out into the pasture, Dillon doesn't hike Bucketmouth's lost duffel bag of baby food jars onto his shoulder, Harper doesn't insist they burn it, along with a few trucks and as many acres of BLM as they can. Wagonhound survives the night as well. And Kissy, and Jam, and the statie.

Kissy maybe finishes her journal and tucks it into a drawer for her someday daughter to find, read on the sly, find out that her mom was once young and stupid too. Younger and stupider than anyone ever. And so in love with Jam, who Harper guesses had to have been strangled out in the bushes, Bucketmouth watching his eyes lose their light the whole while.

This is what her dad always told her was the worst part about driving alone: living in the cab with nobody but yourself to talk to. You end up cycling through the same bullshit over and over.

Harper turns "Sundown" up, is kind of actually starting to tolerate that one.

Halfway between exit 255 and where she knows there's a gas station or a truckstop a few minutes ahead, Harper lets her foot off the gas and watches something slip past on a white stripe.

Not a dead animal, not a cup let go from a window.

She checks her rearview, coasts to a stop, backs up in three hitches, between approaching headlights, then pulls up right alongside.

A boot.

"No," she says, rushing to it, looking up at the coming headlights.

The boot's Dillon's, though. She can tell from how the back quarter of the heel is worn down, from that leg-dragging way he walks when he thinks he's bad, when he's got his gunfighter eyes on. Which is most of the time.

Harper blinks her tears away.

She leans over, hooks a finger through the pull-hole, and rolls out of the way of a car-hauler barreling past, horn blasting.

Breathing hard, gravel speckled all over her, calving off, Harper sets the boot on the seat beside her.

Four or five miles later she slows for what turns out to be the camo cap he had on. It's held to the stripe by a heavy bolt laid crosswise over it.

Harper shakes the bolt off, seats the hat on her head, the brim low over her eyes.

At least the boot doesn't have a foot in it, she's telling herself. At least there's no blood on the inside of the cap. Oh, wait: except Dillon didn't have a cap on when he strapped himself down, did he? Even if he did, it would have blown away just on the on-ramp. Meaning—shit—this is that one Bucketmouth stole from Akal, when he said it was *him* who should be wearing the Realtree.

Harper peels out of it, tosses it through the rear window into the bed. She pulls onto the shoulder to let a rig slam past then gets back up to speed, the temperature back up above 230 now from all the reverse action, which is the opposite of putting air against the radiator, she knows.

Passing exit 235, watching the white stripes closer than she ever has, Harper chances a look down the ramp not taken, sees a boot standing up in the middle of it. She cuts hard right, gouges across the long narrow triangle of grass, the Park truck fishtailing like it wants to start rolling but she turns into it as best she can, rides it out until the tires crash up onto the asphalt of the ramp and she can brake.

To the right is a Shell station. She sees it for maybe two seconds before the dust she dragged up catches up, engulfs her. It takes nearly a half minute to settle. A half minute until she can breathe. Two rigs whine by on the interstate but the drivers must be able to tell she's not a wreck, has done this intentionally. Either that or they don't want to get involved, have already heard over the air that Wyoming tonight is haunted as hell, best just keep on truckin'.

Harper coughs and looks around the Shell station. It's what her dad would have called a cigar box—small, square, temporary. Cigar boxes were his generation's comparison for everything. There's truck parking behind it because you've got to cater, but only one rusty old Peterbilt, looking back at her with its headlight eyes. One rusty old Peterbilt 281. Translation: this is mostly just a gas station, doesn't have showers or booths, doesn't keep the deli fired up twenty-four/seven. More like sunup to sundown, for the daylight crowd. No lights are even on now. Could be it's closed down, even. The pumps are still there, though. Just, nobody to take any money for a quarter tank.

Harper sits at the turn, the Park truck's engine loping unevenly, gasping for cool air.

Either that Peterbilt she knows and will never forget isn't idling, or Bucketmouth's got all the lights turned off. There's a house with green trees just past the parking lot, which means somebody lives there, and there's an old rowhouse in the parking lot with all its windows gone, turned into empty eye sockets.

Harper tries to make anything out on the Peterbilt's flatbed, can't in the darkness, even though there's a massive white tank behind it like a sideways silo. For gas, maybe? It's too big for propane or butane anyway, she thinks. Never mind that the go-juice is usually in underground tanks.

"Enough stalling," she says to herself for resolve, but kind of in farewell too. This is some version of a trap, zero doubt about that, but what choice does she have? Bucketmouth led her here, sure, but that's exactly what she was wanting.

She dials the Park truck down to parking lights so as not to wake the sleepers in that house, hauls the wheel over to the right, eases down the blacktop and into the crunchy surface of the truck parking. When she's head-on with the middle of the flatbed trailer, she turns her brights on all at once, throwing a line of shadow onto the big white tank.

Just like she didn't want to have to see, Bucketmouth's sitting there alongside Dillon, still has him strapped down tight. He shields his eyes and in that hand is a little knife, the blade huge in shadow against the tank.

Harper steps on the brights button, brings the headlights down to not-quite-so-blinding.

Bucketmouth waves thanks, and then, like he's been waiting for an audience, for the right spotlight, he brings the knife down to Dillon's hand, hits it once with the heel of his other hand, and snatches a flying front joint of an index finger from the air, easy as anything, like he was born to do this.

Dillon's body shudders, some part of his knocked-out self registering the pain, the loss, but he doesn't wake, quite.

Harper surges the truck forward like that's supposed to be any kind of threat but stops just short of the flatbed. Bucketmouth watches this with bored eyes, doesn't even flinch.

He says something she can't hear over the engine so she kills it.

"Gonna need your lighter," he says, over-enunciating, and holds his hand out for it.

She pulls it, holds it out, but he shakes his head no, says, "Heat it up, please? If you really love him?"

Harper pushes the lighter in, waits the twenty seconds, Dillon's finger blood pooling around his hand—she's standing on the rocker panel, can't help looking. When the lighter pops out she hot-potatoes it up to Bucketmouth. He catches it, juggles it to get the non-burny end, then, before its glowing-red coils can ash over, he presses it onto Dillon's stump, holds it there, the flesh sizzling, smoke rising. He breathes its deliciousness in, closes his eyes, then steps back.

They both watch Dillon's hand.

The blood doesn't come again.

"Call me the Florence Nightingale of the road," he says, blowing on the lighter, turning to toss it off the other side of the flatbed then stopping himself: "Boom," he says about the big white tank, wowing his eyes out. Instead he underhands the lighter over the cab of the Park truck, into the bed.

"Resale's better if all original parts are there," he says with a smile, about the lighter finding the truck it was born with.

"Are you done now?" Harper says back. "I've got half the cops in Wyoming here in five minutes. That's how much headstart you've got."

"Half the cops in Wyoming . . ." Bucketmouth says, still Jam under all that damage, grandstanding on the flatbed like it's his own personal stage. "So, what, six officers? Seven?" He laughs about this. "They've got bigger fish to fry tonight, I'm afraid—or, *un*fry, as it were. And anyway, how are you supposed to have called this particular emergency in before it even happened?"

"Handheld CB in the bed," she says. "That statie you clipped?"

"Clipped in *half*, yeah," Bucketmouth says. "And if that radio's still in the bed, then that means you haven't been using it, doesn't it?"

"How'd you know I'd follow?" Harper says.

"Specimen like this?" Bucketmouth says, pushing the toe of Jam's hiking boot into Dillon's side. "How could you not? Good nineteen-year-old stock—"

"Eighteen."

"—liver's mostly whole, long limbs, kind of rangy but with promise once he settles down. More smalltime rodeo hero than underwear model, but he's definitely a product of this great state, wouldn't you say? None of that matters to you though, does it? You love him, don't you? That's why you're here."

"We're not together," Harper says.

"No single people in a fox hole," Bucketmouth says, turning on his heel like a professor on a television show, lecturing. "Though I do wonder where your precious little sister is, now . . ."

"Gone," Harper says. "You'll never get her."

Bucketmouth shrugs, watching some car or rig pass on the interstate.

"Don't they look like they're just going to launch up into the sky?" he says, and Harper risks a look back at the bridge, at the headlights now on the other side of it, headed west.

She comes back to Bucketmouth, says, "Just give him to me, walk away. I won't say anything to anybody."

"Going back to bargaining?" Bucketmouth says, disappointed. "Thought we were past that?"

"I was already running away," Harper says. "Give him back to me, I just keep on doing that. Nobody even knows I was here for all this. If nobody asks me any questions, then I don't slip up answering."

"Spoken like a true criminal," Bucketmouth says. "You've got potential, Harper. You might actually make it out here—" He holds Dillon's finger over his lips, shushing himself, then adds, "I mean, I mean you probably *would* have made it out here on the mean old road. If you hadn't run into someone who's been doing this longer than you've been alive."

"*Why* are you doing it?" Harper says.

"Because it's *fun*," Bucketmouth says right back, a distinct glitter to his eye, "and because why not," and with that squats down to the other side of Dillon, stands with a flourish, presenting . . . a five-gallon gas can? It's one of the old ones, round, metal, and rusted, its yellow emblem long since faded, its spigot stumpy and connected to the handle in some many-jointed way that probably seemed like a good idea in 1942.

Bucketmouth swirls it down to his feet then props a boot up on it, shakes a cigarette up from the pack in his shirt pocket, flicks a match alight with his thumbnail.

"Could your friend Jam do that?" he says, cupping the cigarette and leaning down to light it. "All that potential, untapped."

"What did you do to him?" Harper says. "If you—if you just have to eat a part to steal somebody's face, then . . ."

"Hopeful, good," Bucketmouth says. "We can use that. We can definitely use that."

He breathes in deep, extracts the cigarette to study the red coal at the end of it, then nods, satisfied, and pulls the gas can up by the handle, so the spigot opens into a gaping mouth.

"Careful," he says, splashing some onto and around Dillon but keeping his own boots dry.

"What—?" Harper says, coming down to the ground to rush up there.

Bucketmouth holds the cigarette up, says, "Don't want me dropping this on accident now, do you?"

Harper stops at the thick metal edge of the flatbed, is looking right into Dillon's face.

She thought he was unconscious. He's not. He's just past being able to care.

She hikes herself up, straightens her arms just as Bucketmouth steps onto the Park truck's hood, still splashing . . . it's not gas? It's sweeter, more oily.

"Kerosene," Bucketmouth says. "Doesn't burn fast as unleaded, but burns longer. And, for our purposes here, I'd say it's fast enough."

Harper, not on the flatbed yet, just glares at him.

He nods like that's not unexpected here and sits down on the hood, slides off, still trickling kerosene out.

"I'm not going to let you do this," Harper says, coming back down to the ground, glaring at him.

"Good," Bucketmouth says. "Because, believe me, I don't want to. Fireball like this will draw more eyes than would be . . . *beneficial*. All I want is for us to have a sit-down, like. This is just insurance." He pats the gas can. The kerosene.

"He needs medical attention *now*," Harper says.

"Won't take but this long," Bucketmouth says, and holds his cigarette out horizontal like a timeline, then stabs it into his mouth, fishes the box of Reds up from his pocket, slings it into the scrub without tracking it.

"Matches too," Harper tells him.

"Smart girl," Bucketmouth says, squinting from his own smoke, grubbing the box of matches up too. Instead of tossing them he shakes one out, pins it in the little paper drawer and holds it to the cherry of his cigarette, waits for it to flare up before tossing the lit box to Harper.

She wants worse than anything to slap it back at him, to make him flinch from the sparks then go for his eyes, his balls, his heart if he has one, but an ember might fall into the kerosene he's pouring. The kerosene that leads up the hood of the truck, right to Dillon.

She catches the box, tosses it clear of them and they both watch it spurt flame out both sides when it lands.

"Here I am," Harper says. "Talk, if that's what this is about."

"Over there," Bucketmouth says, pointing with his lips to the rear of the Shell station. "Got a little picnic all ready for us, and just enough of this"—the kerosene—"to get us there."

"One cigarette," Harper says, falling in, keeping her feet and pants legs clear of the splash.

A crotch rocket on the bridge throttles into the brief climb, trying to make more of the rise than there really is, and Harper looks away right as it crests, doesn't know whether it's going to launch into the sky, become a constellation, or crash and burn.

Bucketmouth works the gas can onto the ratty picnic table sitting bent and ugly behind the Shell station, one of its tubular legs chained to a cinderblock. Not against thieves, but the wind. The tabletop is mounded with salty snacks and candy bars, jerky and peanuts, all evidently carried here by the armful, dumped and spilled. The back door of the Shell station is kicked in, hanging on by the top hinge.

Bucketmouth settles into what's apparently his side of the table, the one that keeps his back to the station, which she guesses he knows is empty. Unlike the parking lot that'll be behind Harper, where people from the house could appear at any moment. She'll see that in his eyes, though, she tells herself.

She sits down opposite him.

"You could have started honking back there, you know," he tells her, like a coach critiquing her game. "Woke the neighbors up, maybe slipped away with your beau while I was talking them down. Or, you know. Getting them *quiet*."

"He's not my boyfriend," Harper says again.

"You just drove a beat to hell truck to a dangerous place with a guy like me at midnight in the middle of nowhere because he's a good friend?"

"It's not midnight."

"More dramatic if it is, c'mon. You got to work with what you got, don't you know."

"That what all this is?" Harper says about the plundered snacks.

"Didn't know what you liked," Bucketmouth says.

"Not hungry."

"That makes one of us," he says, and tears into a bag of Fritos.

"What do I call you? Bucketmouth?"

"*Sir*," he says, then has to laugh. "No, no, sorry. I just always wanted to say that. Um . . . not 'BM' either." He has to stop to chuckle about this as well.

Harper regards him, says, "Are you drunk?"

"On life," he says back with a guilty shrug.

Harper nods to the cigarette he's just holding, not smoking down.

He obligingly takes a drag, angles his mouth up to exhale into the blackness.

"Not often I get to really *talk* with someone," he says. "I mean, without all the buildup on my part, of when am I going to carve a piece of them off. You know."

"I really don't."

He looks back to Dillon like checking on him.

"This your way of telling me you're not going to eat me?" Harper asks. "Because I'm a girl?"

He smiles a tolerant smile, pulls the cover off the gas can's spigot and ashes delicately into it, Harper's fingers spread wide on the table to push away, as if it's possible to outrun the kind of explosion that would be.

"You're Native American," he says, twirling his cigarette hand to indicate her hair, her skin, the whole deal.

"We not good enough for you?"

"Endangered species," he says with a grin. "What can I say? I'm a conservationist."

"More of us than you think," Harper tells him.

"Said the girl who . . . *didn't* want me to take a bite out of her?"

"You just don't want to be a girl," Harper tells him.

"Native Americans—"

"Indians."

"You have natural immunity or something, I don't know," he says. "Your kind is just meat to my kind. And, if it's just about meat, then give me a double cheeseburger at the drive-in, thanks."

"Your *kind*?" Harper asks.

"More of *us* than you'd think," Bucketmouth says, gesturing grandly with his cigarette. "I mean, active and aware, no, okay, not that many. But who knows. It's not like we have a clubhouse. Really, I bet a lot of people can do . . . *this*"—Jam's face—"but they never think to *try*, or it starts to happen and they freak out, wreck into a bridge pylon, fall out a window, choke on a sandwich, hang themself in a closet."

"You mean, they never eat someone's ear, so never know they could have looked like that person?" Harper asks, incredulous.

"I found out in Vietnam," he says, as if Harper might have asked. "It was a . . . you could call it a bad day, I guess. Like every single other day over there. Except, next morning, I slipped through the lines with a face like Charlie, right?"

"From eating someone," Harper says flatly.

"I wasn't even hungry," Bucketmouth says like this is all history, so hardly matters. "I was in a, like, a hamster tunnel I guess you'd call it, Charlie was all over the place in their black PJs and slope hats, and then my tunnel started caving in from the rain, and from them poking sticks down to find where I was. It was a bad situation all around. But then, doing that Army-crawl up out of that tunnel, hoping for the light at the end, y'know, who do I bump faces with but a gook sent down to flush me out? We got all tooth and nail like happens when you meet a body coming through the rye, and then I just, yeah, I bit his lips, pulled them away, and then I was like an animal, I went for the tongue. I think that was what did it. I spit the lips out, I'm pretty sure—lips are chewier than hell, did you know that? Like jerky that's been soaking in Crisco for a week. But that tongue, I swallowed that right on down, didn't even chew it, it fit perfect down my throat hole, and was still twitching like an eel, helping itself along, and then, like probably had to happen, the tunnel collapsed. By the time they dug me out a few hours later—" He uses his fingers to stretch his eyes out.

"I don't want to hear this."

"For a few years after that, I thought tongues were the magic ingredient," he says. "And that I had to swallow them whole like that. I even got superstitious about if the tongue's taste buds rubbed on mine on the way down. But, really, shit, any little bit'll do, long as it's got some meat to it."

"You took Jam's face, though," Harper says. "Not Kissy's."

"That was her name?" Bucketmouth says, slapping the tabletop with his open hand. "Man. I thought I heard it wrong, that it was 'Kris' or 'Chrissy.' That's the hard part about this, you know? Nobody says anybody's name when everybody knows each other. I thought you were Harp at first, didn't know what it was short for."

Harper just stares at him.

"No," he says, "I'm not what you might call equal opportunity with the sexes. How it works is I turn into whoever right as they are when I carve that piece of them off, yeah? Like, this finger, that ear, it's a biological snapshot of them at that exact moment in their life. Make sense? I mean, sprained ankles or an arm in a cast don't matter, but . . . *permanent* situations. Leukemia, diabetes, lupus, spinal shit—all that junk the body can't kick, that's the stuff that can cross over to me, yeah?"

"Leukemia doesn't have to be forever," Harper tells him.

"Whatever, but, with the ladies? I know y'all's time of the month isn't, like, a condition, but it crosses over too, don't ask me why, I didn't make the rules. But, if I'm going to be wearing someone's skirt, I go through the last two or three trash cans she's passed beforehand. Just because I don't need that kind of hassle."

"Like we do?"

Bucketmouth shrugs.

"Still," Harper says, "people on the road are gonna pick a Kissy up off the shoulder long before they stop for a Jam."

"There's trade-offs, sure, sure," Bucketmouth says, pouring

peanuts into his mouth and then gauging the length of his cigarette as he chews.

"Why are you telling me all this?" Harper asks.

"Right to the point, aren't you?" Bucketmouth says back.

"Tick tock."

"Because I never get to unload like this?"

"And because it doesn't matter what I might tell anybody?" Harper says. "Because I don't live through this night?"

"Runaways disappear all the time," Bucketmouth says, just stating sad, general facts.

"Like you'll let me disappear."

He opens his hand to the interstate, offering it to her.

"*With* Dillon," Harper says.

He closes his hand, purses his lips in regretful apology.

"Why do you do all this cat and mouse on the highway bullshit?" Harper asks.

"It's not always the highway," Bucketmouth says, studying the bridge again. "But—you figure it out, I guess. Living like I do, doing what I do, it's good to always have a fast way out. Hundred years ago, maybe I work the rivers, right? I'm the Steamboat Boogeyman, the Canoe Killer. Just, what someone with my . . . my predilections needs is some place where not all the heads are counted. Where every next face you see is anonymous."

"Lonely life," Harper says.

"You can say that again," Bucketmouth says.

"*That's* why you're talking to me."

He doesn't shoot that one down.

"So you just hitch around," Harper goes on, "take a bite out of whoever stops to help you out?"

"Why do you think it's always *me* with my thumb out?" he asks back, leaning forward to look right into her eyes. "Is it because of that movie? Often as not, I'm behind the wheel for these little sorties. Well—" He opens his cigarette hand to the Peterbilt as evidence.

"Sometimes you're the bug, sometimes you're the windshield," Harper says.

"I like that, I like that. Can I use it?"

"That's why you save people in jars," Harper says, figuring this out. "You take a piece when they're in their prime, or . . . when they're how you want them. When they're how you want to *be*."

He looks at his cigarette from the side.

"What does the cinnamon do?" Harper asks.

"It tastes good," Bucketmouth says, obviously. "You should try it, y'know? See if you're like me. Never know until you take that first bite."

"I've eaten chicken," Harper says. "It didn't turn me into one."

"That's cooked," Bucketmouth tells her. "The essential vitamins burn away in that kind of heat. And it doesn't work with animals anyway."

"Happy to go through life ignorant," Harper says.

"For . . ." He makes like peering down at a watch, seeing how much of her life she's got left to be ignorant in.

"Smoke," Harper says, urging him on.

He takes another deep drag, their timeline losing another eighth of an inch.

"Can't believe your friend didn't smoke with this body," Bucketmouth says. "It's glorious, truly."

"So you get new lungs each time around?" Harper says.

"Well . . ." he says. "If I were going to stick with him, they'd be kind of new by the end, yeah."

"The end?"

"It lasts about two weeks," he says, waggling his fingers over his face, "this. Stay any longer, you can get stuck. Just saying this so if, you know, if you do end up going for the lifestyle."

"Stuck?"

"You don't just have to eat a finger or an eye then," he says. "You've got to eat and eat and eat, down to the bone, and crack into the marrow. It's kind of ugly. Guess that's the downside to all this."

"*That's* the only downside?"

"Don't knock it till you've tried it, girlie."

"Harper," Harper says. "It's Harper. We almost done here, or you got more important stuff to be telling me?"

"'Bucketmouth,'" he says, blowing his smoke out in a tight stream this time. "I don't know. Do you like it? Does it fit, you think? I mean, if you're going to be a legend, you want to be a good one, don't you? Have a proper sounding name, all that?"

"Why us?" Harper says, glaring right at him. "Road was full of people tonight. It could have been anybody."

"Would you accept bad luck? On your part, I mean."

Harper shakes her head no, hitching a bag of chips up through the V of her index finger and thumb, flipturning it then starting on the other side. The nerves have to go somewhere.

"Did you not wonder how I had that picture?" Bucketmouth says, not looking away from her.

Harper dials back, back.

Picture?

Photograph. The dead guy. The mummy propped up against the snow fence.

She pushes back from the table, shakes her head no.

"That was *you*?" she says.

In answer he collects Jam's short hair on one side of his head, makes to comb it over to the other side.

The Thunderbird people.

"You were the holy roller," she says. "You—the two of you didn't pick someone up who killed them. You were *already* in the car."

"Sometimes you're the windshield, sometimes—"

"So you knew *then*?" Harper says.

He takes another drag, holds it in, his eyes watering from it.

It makes sense, Harper guesses. The driver, Mr. Combover, that *was* his face that had slapped down onto their windshield, special bird-delivery, but he wasn't stumbling out through the darkness like her and Dillon had thought. He'd been waiting out there without a face, waiting for one of them to be alone. So he could take a bite.

"I should have known," she says.

"*Bam*," Bucketmouth says, pointing his finger right at here. "That's what you all say."

He takes another contemplative drag.

"Want to see something cool?" he asks.

"I just want to be not here," Harper tells him.

Bucketmouth delicately inserts the cigarette between his lips then reaches back to the hinge of his jaw on the right side, his fingers pinching for, for—for a *grip*. Something to grab onto.

He tugs and a flap of skin rips free.

Harper steeples her hands over her mouth, sucks air through her fingers, shaking her head no, please no.

This is happening, though.

Working slowly, breaking it free tug by wet, creaky tug, Bucketmouth peels his cheek off all the way up to the corner of his mouth, showing some molars, then, being careful of the cigarette, guiding it through the lip hole, he keeps going, has peeled the whole lower part of his face off.

"I can usually do it in one piece," he says, Harper watching the words form in his mouth, those words different now, being shaped at the end by lip muscle, not the actual lips. "But your trucker friends at the gas station back there—there was some trauma there."

With that he works his right index finger up under his eyelid and pulls it gently out, pulls the top part of his face off like taking off a domino mask. Now his cheeks and eyebrows and chin and jaw and forehead are muscle and blood shot through with white and yellow.

He reaches into the pile of stolen food, comes out with a little bottle of Visine. He lips the cigarette with raw muscle, the paper sucking up the blood, and tilts his head back, applies two drops to each eye.

When he smiles, Harper gags.

This is hilarious to him.

"I don't mean one piece like whole *body*," he says. "That all comes off too, but that takes a week to get done, usually. Bit by bit." He punctuates it by crumbling a handful of Fritos into his mouth.

Harper can see the chewing in a new and terrible way. She promises then and there to never eat a Frito again.

"What about 'Lockjaw' for a name?" Bucketmouth says then, snapping his mouth open and shut, spilling wet yellow crumbs. "I could learn to like Lockjaw, I think. No, wait. That's tetanus, isn't it? Yeah, I think it is. It is, shit. Okay, I don't want to be tetanus."

"Are we, are we—?" Harper asks through her hands.

"Done?" Bucketmouth says, shrugging, watching more headlights on the interstate. "I've always wanted to do this too, if you've got the—" He eyeballs his cigarette for how much time they've got left in this conversation.

"No," Harper says. "Please."

"Just real quick."

He holds his hands up under his chin, fingers fanned out.

Harper's shaking her head no, no, please.

"How many fingers am I holding up?" he says with a big smile, and—no no no—it's eleven.

Moving slow so she can see every bit of it, he leans forward, takes the eleventh finger, Dillon's, into his mouth, sucks it up.

Harper is throwing up before she's even aware there's anything in her throat.

"Not bad, right?" Bucketmouth says when she's done.

"You're, you're—" Harper says, about the cigarette.

Bucketmouth takes it out, studies it. It is almost to the butt.

"You don't need him anymore now, right?" Harper says, about Dillon on the flatbed.

Bucketmouth looks over there, considers this.

"That's always a quandary," he says. "No, technically, I don't need him to complete this . . . *process*. But?" He inhales the cigarette bright red, holds it up between them. "Problem is, see, there can't be two of us either, can there?"

With that he flicks the cigarette . . . *away* from the line of kerosene he trailed into the parking lot.

Still, Harper dives for it, can't help trying.

Bucketmouth laughs about this.

"I keep my word," he says.

"Now can we—" Harper says, but doesn't get to finish: the cigarette has bloomed into a flickering flame. "No," she says, looking over to the flatbed trailer.

The flame goes wide all at once then, is a line, *another* line of kerosene, one he poured out before she got here. And, kerosene, of course: gas would evaporate. But kerosene's oily, kerosene lasts longer. And she didn't question the harsh scent on the air, since he poured it out while she was watching. Since the can was sitting on the table between them.

The line of orange races in a wide curve towards the trailer . . . and then goes *under* it.

"What?" Harper says, looking to Bucketmouth.

"Wait, wait," he says. "It's just that kind of night, isn't it?"

His face glows orange when the flame ignites the pool he'd evidently poured under the tank. In all that dry grass.

"What's in that tank?" Harper asks.

"Hell," Bucketmouth says, looking for all the world glad that she asked. "But don't worry. It's not the end of the world."

He sweeps away the chips and peanuts and jerky to reveal a fire extinguisher laying on its side. Harper looks from it to the fire to Bucketmouth's anatomy-class face, sees that she can either take that heavy hard fire extinguisher, hold it high and come at his head with it, or she can do exactly as he wants: race with it across the parking lot, try to put that fire out, save Dillon.

"Asshole," she says to him, stabbing her hand down for the dull silver handle of the fire extinguisher.

"That's not how it's pronounced," he says back, watching the fire lick up at the tank. "Think it's more 'Bucketmouth.' You've got to do your mouth where it says 'Buck-et' at first, then, after that, 'mouth.'"

"This isn't over," Harper says, striding away.

"Hope not," he calls after her, and after about three dignified steps, she's running.

Because the flames are surging up under the flatbed, she can't slide under it, and would need both hands to climb over, so she runs around the rear, already turning her head away from the heat.

"Dillon!" she calls out, pulling the pin on the extinguisher, aiming its nozzle down and squeezing the handle.

Nothing.

She looks down to the extinguisher, shakes it, squeezes the handle harder.

A disappointing burp of white foam spurts out, doesn't even have enough pressure behind it to clear the wide nozzle.

"No no no no," Harper says, and drops the extinguisher, sure that exactly what Bucketmouth wants her to do now is clamber up onto the flatbed, try to free Dillon.

What he *doesn't* expect is for her to be able to put the fire out.

Harper runs back around the rear of the trailer, skids to a stop at the passenger-side back door of the Park truck, and hauls out one case of water bottles, then the next. She chocks them under her arms, galumphs back to the tank, empties a bottle each onto her pants legs and sneakers then wades into the flames with the cases, rolls them under the tank one by one like grenades.

For a few seconds there's nothing, but then the fire melts through the plastic and the water splashes out, turns almost instantly to steam. If anything, the water just somehow feeds the fire bigger, send its orange fingers even higher up around the side of the tank.

"*No*," Harper screams, having to back up from the heat. Having to imagine whatever combustible stuff's pressured up in that tank. The explosion is going to take this whole lot out, is going to be visible for miles.

Now she has no choice but to try to get Dillon away from it, whether that's what Bucketmouth planned for her to do or not.

She hops up to see over the flames and tank, make sure the kerosene on the trailer hasn't caught a spark yet, and, and: *Bucketmouth's* up there with Dillon?

"Get him out of there!" she calls to him.

Bucketmouth, just a silhouette, watches her through the flames.

"*Please!*" she screams then, and Bucketmouth finally nods, steps forward with that same knife, only has to touch the blade to the very edge of that dirty yellow strap to snap it, it's ratcheted so tight.

At which point Harper's right pants leg bursts into flame.

She falls down instantly, rolling and patting, and by the time she comes up she's twenty desperate feet out in the pasture. She rubs her calf and shin and ankle, searching for hidden embers. She leans around to see one, threading her hair out of the way, and suddenly her leg goes black. Not from burn or ash, but because— because she *had* been lit up by headlights. And now she's not.

"What?" Harper says, standing, looking through the smoke.

Bucketmouth. He's driving away in the Park truck, Dillon slung over the hood like a gutted mule deer.

"No," Harper says, shaking her head. He's—Bucketmouth, he's supposed to fire the *Peterbilt* up, leave in that, and she's supposed to go after him in the truck he's now driving.

This isn't how it's supposed to work.

Harper runs around the edge of the fire after him but gets there too late, can just grab a handful of gravel, sling it after them, none of it even pinging in the bed.

The Park truck gentles around the turn, taking the ramp slow to the west, so as not to sling Dillon off.

Yet.

"What are you doing?" Harper says, and squats down on her toes to push her fists into her temples, *think*.

What she needs to do first is get the hell out of here, she knows. Before that exploding tank turns this place into *Hell*.

The second is . . . she doesn't get to two.

By the toe of her right sneaker is . . . another finger?

She narrows her eyes to look back to Dillon's hand from before, try to remember how many fingers *he* was holding up. She starts to pick the finger up, save it—for what?—but then can't quite get her own fingers to touch it.

Which is when a window in the house goes yellow.

CHAPTER
18

The old Peterbilt fires up first try, the hoods on each side clattering with all the exhaust leaks. Harper releases the parking brake with her left hand, clutches in, works through the low gears to be sure she has them down.

Sort of? Maybe?

Her dad said learning to shift, it's more about doing it wrong about eight hundred times, until there's only one right way to get it done. And it's not about thinking, it's about instinct, it's about feel, it's about being one with the road, the engine, the grade, the load. At any point in a run, she could ask him what gear was he in *now*, and he could never answer, even in general ranges. He would look down at his right hand like just being reminded that it was part of him, and kind of smile in wonder at it.

Harper eases the clutch out, trying to get a sense of where it breaks over, hands off to the engine, and the Peterbilt jumps forward, almost stalls before she catches it. She checks the mirror on the far side, trying, she guesses, to maybe gauge or guess when that big white tank might finally blow. The flames flickering under its wide belly make her forget everything she just figured out about the gears.

"Calm, calm, it hasn't blown yet," she tells herself, and makes herself slow down, take stock of this cab all over. A faded eight of clubs tucked up into the speedo. Toothpicks lined into a crack in the dash. An old election bumpersticker on the inside of the windshield, probably being used as Band-Aid for a crack or hole in the glass. And, in the passenger floorboard, two dog pans. Instead of a passenger seat there's a wooden box with a dog bed nestled inside.

Meg will need these, Harper thinks, her hand running through the gears again, getting them down without her head running interference.

In the house now, more of the windows are going yellow. Because Harper's had the engine rumbling too long, isn't just someone cruising through to see if this joint's open.

She eases forward again, has enough of a feel that she's pretty sure she can do this, but then she stomps the clutch and brake in when a rotating yellow light cycles in from the east. At the top of the bridge it becomes a bright white tow truck, one of the big-big ones that go fifty thousand pounds—they have to, to pull a semi tractor up from a muddy ditch. Probably every one of these in Wyoming is zeroing in on the burn to drag rigs up from the ashes, try not to cross their cables.

Harper lowers her left hand to the light knob to get this chase started—the Park truck's going to overheat inside five miles—but of course it's a dry pull, since the headlights were trashed back at Wagonhound, are probably still inside that destroyed camper.

It's good the truck stays dark, as it turns out.

A door's just opened in the house, and it filled with shapes for a moment, with people roused from sleep, about to break into emergency mode once the smoke in the air registers for them. The time to decide is *now*, Harper tells herself.

She works through what she can think of: Bucketmouth had this all planned out the whole time. He never intended to give Dillon back to her. He always planned on ditching her with the Peterbilt, taking off in the faster, more nimble vehicle. Or, maybe he's ditching her with the big rig because it just demolished a rest stop, might be on some sort of rampage, just plow through the next traffic slowdown, tossing civilian cars to either side like nothing—which is to say, as far as Wyoming troopers are concerned, shoot to kill.

She's still playing into his hand, isn't she? *Shit*. She's still walking right into where he wants her to be. This must be what he does, to cover up: leave a big mess behind, frame someone else for it. A patsy to take the fall, complete with a story even she would never believe—"I was chasing the *real* bad guy, it's not me, he's still out there, you've got to let me go after him!"

If Harper gets back on the interstate in this Peterbilt, then, because she's not like him, doesn't know how and where and when to hide and probably can't drive as well anyway, she's caught inside of ten miles, will either have to shift to a taller gear, drive for the horizon, damn the roadblocks, which will confirm all the reports on this truck, or she'll have to pull over, step down for the cavalry to take her in. And Indians, never mind if they've never been on a horse, they know better than to let the horse soldiers get them.

Harper turns the truck off and steps down from it, walks immediately off the bright surface of the pale parking lot. Voices are approaching. Footsteps are crashing through the brush. An actually charged-up fire extinguisher is foaming and spraying, making that big hollow sizzling sound. This ugly-ass truck isn't supposed to be there, the people have to be saying. And there's not supposed to be *any* flames around that tank, ever. And, once they get that far, the back door of the Shell station probably isn't supposed to be kicked in either.

Harper ducks deeper into the leather jacket, the collar coming up around her ears like it knows what she needs, and she thrusts her hands in the pockets, keeps to the dark brush until she finds the road, which she crosses for more of that lush darkness, to cut over to the on-ramp.

A hundred, hundred and fifty yards down the interstate, her shadow jumps out in front of her.

Like she meant to be doing in the first place, before all this started, she hikes her thumb out.

— —

The next hour is the best and the worst at the same time. It's the best because the red piles of gore spread out across the asphalt are consistently mule deer and coyotes, never Dillon, like she keeps squinting against. It's worst because car after car, rig after rig, they just keep sweeping past, sucking her hair over into their draft, leaving her to breathe their rancid exhaust. Twice there's been beer bottles whizzing by her head—they don't even shatter in the ditch, just thunk in a way that makes her skull feel like paper—and once some college kids in a Taurus station wagon pull over, make her jog the polite jog up to them only to have them flip her off, peel away, throwing gravel at her.

So this is the life, she tells herself. This is what I wanted.

The jacket's probably not helping her any, she knows, but it's too cold to lose it.

For a half mile or so she gives up, walks deep in the ditch by the sheep fence, her hands balled in the jacket pockets. But then the grass starts getting taller . . . because of the concrete tunnel boring under 80, which is in a low spot, of course. She doesn't know if it's for deer to cross without getting splatted or if someone is really hopeful about how much rain this part of the country is going to get someday, but, just like when she was a girl, she stakes it out for a couple of minutes. Not because she really believes a Bigfoot is going to silhouette its shaggy self at the other end of the tunnel, but because her dad always *thought* that was going to happen. That it happened all the time, just, nobody ever thought to look. It had to be how they avoided the headlights though, right? They can't go over, so they go *under*.

Harper, five years old, had nodded yes, yes yes yes. It made perfect sense.

Now she's not looking for Bigfoot so much anymore, though. Just her dad, please.

She's still that kid in that Alabama song, waiting by the phone. Roll on, Daddy, till you get back home. Sure, your rig did eventually show up, its load long plundered it had been sitting so long, birds living in the cab, but it wasn't the truck she was praying would come back. It was her dad.

She maybe cries a bit here. Not for herself, she doesn't think, and not even for Dillon, really. For her dad. Because it would have been so perfect for him to just appear, a shadowy form at the end of that long white tunnel, his hair long, his clothes ragged, but he'd smile, she knows. From seeing his daughter after all these years. He'd smile and open his arms for her, and as she ran to him she'd be shedding all the bad years, leaving them behind her.

She maybe watches more than a couple of minutes, but when she stands she's what she needs to be: hard, tough, leather. Her eyes are flint and her heart's steel, and her lips are always going to be pressed tight together.

That's the kind of girl who survives a night like this. That's the kind of Indian who makes it out of the twentieth century.

When tires wind up behind her again she dutifully hangs her thumb in the wind, and only looks up when the asphalt in front of her washes red with brakelight.

She ups her pace, isn't going to jog like a fool this time, but then the taillights and cargo doors and stripes register for her: an ambulance.

She veers off, swishes through the grass, steps over the fence, is running hard out in the blackness.

Medics have radios too. They know all the cops, all the firemen, have got all the same alerts and warnings.

From out in the night she watches the ambulance. The medics

are standing against their bright white cargo box, looking for her. Calling, but their voices are lost. Both women, one of them Indian, if Harper's seeing right. Indians make the best medics, everybody knows, because of that old-time medicine. But still.

She shakes her head no like she's having to convince herself to stay hidden here. To not trust anybody with a lightbar. Two, three minutes later the medics finally climb back in, use their blinker to get back on the road even though it's only them.

Harper stands when they're gone enough, angles back over to start this bullshit all over.

Note to self, she says: look before you extend that left arm. Or, better yet, only try to thumb down the tall headlights, the big rigs. Because the angle she's taking is meant to connect with the right swerve the road's taking, she's pulling her boots through the tall grass for longer than she meant, until—

The Park truck.

It's just sitting there.

Harper squats, watches it, then slowly, carefully, circles around it until headlights from the interstate show her its silhouette in snatches.

"Hey!" Harper calls out to it. "You! Bucketmouth!"

No reply, and she's pretty sure it's not like him to keep quiet.

She feels around for a rock, lobs it onto the hood, no response. Just the rock, clattering off.

She approaches from the side, on the chance the truck's going to start up, either drop into low or reverse, to run her over.

It doesn't, "Can't," Harper aloud when she's finally to it.

It's been left behind.

She runs her hand along the bed rail, over the two doors, the cab empty, then pats the front fender.

"You were a good pony, weren't you?" she says.

She pops the hood, touches her palm fast to the radiator cap, and it's still hot like she knew it would be, but it's not scalding hot anymore. Meaning Bucketmouth and Dillon are miles ahead by now. Well, unless they're walking, Bucketmouth carrying Dillon, or dragging him by the foot.

But, no: carrying him.

It's a good way to get a ride.

Harper grits her teeth, nods to herself, and jogs to the shoulder, is ready for this chase again, now that she has the scent.

The chase doesn't agree, though.

The next two rigs just whine past. The second for sure sees her, since he drifts over to the passing lane to give her room, not blow her face-first into the ditch, but he doesn't let any speed off, doesn't even consider stopping.

"What the hell?" Harper says, getting more and more pissed.

She knows taking riders is against the rules for most companies, and that independent drivers have probably been burned enough by hitchhikers to know better. But still. She's not like that. And she won't call to tattle to Dispatch about catching a ride with one of their drivers. Promise.

An hour without a ride, now. Maybe an hour and a half, even. She stops to skirt a splatted antelope, but then goes back to hold her palm to its forehead, to send it on its journey better. If it's an Indian thing, it's one she's making up, but it still counts, she's pretty sure. The next stop is to play detective: the ditch is still torn up, from a *heavy* rig stepping over into the ditch, but then also making it back out. Which doesn't track for a tractor-trailer, as you never risk pulling this far from the road, just set up cones or flares on the shoulder if you need to, but . . .

That big white tow truck that was booking it this way, maybe? It had an eighteen-foot utility bed it looked like, like most of them do, but's still stubby enough to go four-wheeling like this, and's probably got a 12.7-liter turbo driving the wheels, which is torque to burn, practically a drag-truck compared to all the other rigs out here.

Dredging up the specs of this maybe-truck only makes her miss her dad more, though. He drove a wrecker for a season, when she was in kindergarten and he was trying to stay close to Laramie, and he never lost his love for those custom rigs, would walk Harper all through their features when one was nosed into the truckstop, and then keep talking about them all through burgers and chili and cokes, telling tall tales about what-all impossible things he'd seen them do.

Harper finally shrugs about whatever happened here, shrugs past, hands in pockets, only to stop when a passing station wagon lights the toe of a human foot out in the grass.

"No," she says.

But yes.

It's a dead dude. One for some reason wearing flip-flops and gym shorts with a pearl-snap shirt, unsnapped.

Harper takes her hands from her pockets, narrows her eyes at all the darkness around her, then finally edges in, nudges the guy's calf with her toe.

Nothing. Definitely dead, she can't tell how.

She spins away, doesn't need to get involved, but then . . .

She makes herself stop, her back ramrod-straight, lips peeled back from her teeth in frustration.

"Stupid, stupid," she's telling herself. But she does it anyway, goes back, toes the grass aside to count the dead guy's fingers on both sides.

They're all there.

Meaning?

"Nothing," she tells herself.

There's dead people all up and down this road tonight. And all she's concerned with is the living one called Dillon, thanks. The one who's moving away from her miles at a time, while she's just hoofing it.

Another half-hour creeps past, she's pretty sure.

It's so stupid how, before she started thumbing for real, the night had been clicking forward one single second at a time, each minute packed with wrecks and bodies and monsters, and now these last couple of hours have just been a long, never-ending smear of nothing, the clock hands hardly even moving at all, wherever they are.

For maybe a quarter mile, a pair of eyes pace her out in the pasture. The next rig's headlights show it to be a grinning coyote, tail low. The next time Harper thinks to look for it, it's gone.

Is she not getting picked up because she doesn't have a bag, maybe? Does that make her suspicious? Do the drivers think she's some girlfriend or wife who got pissed at her husband or boyfriend, made him let her out so she can stalk the side of the road? It can't be her hair this time, she knows, or her skin. It's night. She's not Indian in the headlights at seventy miles per hour. She's probably barely even female.

Finally, what feels like a lifetime later, she walks onto a rig pulled over onto the shoulder. No taillights, just a line of angled-out cones leading up to it, telling her this *isn't* whoever was four-wheeling back there.

Still, "Great," Harper says. A trucker with engine problems isn't exactly helpful, is it?

She walks out into the grass, on the dark side of the truck, and there's no light from the cab. The fiberglass hood's pulled forward like she was expecting but there's nobody up in that rocking chair. She climbs up, knocks on the window, tries the door almost on accident, to keep from falling. It's open.

"Hello?" she calls in, ready to run.

Nothing. No one.

It smells like cigarette smoke and body odor. And the keys are in the *ignition*? Granted, this eighty-thousand dollar tractor probably doesn't start right at this moment, but there's probably keys to the trailer on that ring, and some sort of cameo picture Harper knows it's none of her business to look at.

She shuts the door, climbs down, walks around the front of the truck, nearly breaks her ankle on the gouges in the ditch: tires. Deep, double. *Here's* that big white tow truck, then. The one this trucker must be riding in now, for whatever reason.

"Good for you," she tells him.

At least someone found help tonight.

Harper keeps walking, then, not quite far enough she can't see the broken-down rig anymore, she stops, looks back to it, a particularly evil thought bubbling up.

In five minutes she's there again, pussyfooting it across the tow truck ruts. She doesn't clamber into the cab again—not that a snack wouldn't be nice, a nap even better—but picks around behind the sleeper. Not for boomers, not for chain, not for shovels or a pry bar. She digs past all those, feels around the air hoses, finally finds what she was hoping for: a little two-gallon gas can, emergency red.

It's full but she pours it out, doesn't need the gas this driver was carrying just to give the hapless unleaded crowd ten or fifteen miles down the road. What she needs is that bright red can.

Before leaving she does haul herself back up into the cab, to paw around for a notepad, a pen, to leave an IOU in front of the gauge cluster. The pen is easy—the visor, always the visor—but she can't find the logbook anywhere. Not even a battered metal clipboard, which you always have to carry for the loading dock to sign on.

"Sorry, sorry," she says, broaching back through the curtain, into the musty bunk.

She finds the light third-try, lucks onto a paperback right off, and tears a mostly blank page from the back, is writing her note on it when she realizes she's being watched.

Slowly, pen still to pulpy paper, she looks up.

It's the driver.

He's staring at her from the hindmost corner, where he's been stuffed.

Harper jumps and pushes, gets nowhere in the blankets.

The driver doesn't move.

Harper gets conscious about her breathing, is still pushing as far away as she can.

"Sir, sir, sir?" she's saying.

Nothing.

Moving jerky, she pulls the paperback to her, lobs it back at the driver. It hits his face and his expression doesn't change. A dark line of blood seeps from his right nostril, though, around his mouth, and hangs onto his chin, waiting to gather enough weight to drip down onto his chest.

He's dead. And hidden.

Shit. Second one of these inside of a mile? But why, what's the gain? *Think*, Harp, she tells herself.

But the dead trucker won't stop watching her with his dry eyes.

She balls her note to him up, doesn't turn her back to him the whole way out of the cab, fully expects him to be coming for her.

She falls to the ground on the passenger side, is immediately looking back up to the open door.

Nothing clambers out after her.

She stands, guides the door shut, not just her hand shaking but her whole body, pretty much.

Fifty yards down the road, her breath hitches and suddenly she's crying.

"I don't even know you!" she screams back at the rig.

It just stares at her with its dark headlights.

She sets the gas can down, throws handfuls of gravel back at the windshield.

The one rig that passes during this episode rides the far left edge of the bumper lane. He blinks his lights in understanding, though. Or apology. Something.

Harper sits down for what feels like ten minutes, and when she finally can, she stands, is walking with purpose now, her steps long, the plastic gas can bumping on her left thigh, to keep it in obvious view of the road.

This time she doesn't even have to stick her thumb out. The third truck that sweeps past, its Jake Brake engages just past her—she's thudding down a slight grade—then it pulls over a quarter mile up to wait for her.

Without a grimy bag over her shoulder, she's become a woman whose car ran dry. Now she's just hiking to the next pump, maybe even has a kid or two back in the car she had to leave behind.

Who wouldn't stop?

CHAPTER
19

The driver is doctoring his swindle sheet when Harper finally steps up to eye level with him.

He looks over his reading glasses, waves her on in but the door won't open. He clicks something on his side and it doesn't just unlock, it pops open.

"Fancy," Harper says, out of breath.

"Takes a while to get her stopped, sorry," the driver says back.

"Thanks for stopping at all," Harper tells him, settling into the passenger seat, taking stock of the cab to make sure there's nothing hinky.

He's bald, sun-faded denim shirt with the sleeves cut off, armful of ink, droopy eyes, gunfighter stache. For a shrieky moment Harper wonders how it works with Bucketmouth—if he changes into the person he was at the moment he got a piece off them, does that mean he gets their facial hair too? Their haircut?

"Saw the colors," he says about the patches on her sleeve.

She looks down to them for the first time, licks her lips, telling herself to lie, that lie already forming in her mouth—her old man's waiting in Rawlins, is probably cooking back this way already—but isn't that the wrong foot to start out on, when he's the one already being cool?

"Not mine," she admits, looking out over his hood so as not to put him in a position. So as not to challenge him.

"Not yours?" he asks.

"Found it," Harper says.

He tucks his logbook away, watching her closer now.

"Where's your car?" he says, his tone a little fake now, like he can feel this all going downhill.

Harper shakes her head, doesn't have a good answer for that either. At which point he looks all around her, mostly on the floorboard.

"Gas can?" he tries, the look on his face showing how ready he is to have been taken, here.

"That was just to get somebody to stop," Harper says, her eyes getting a shine to them, she knows and hates. She's never been one to cry when the cop comes to the window, has never used tears to get what she wants, considers that the cheapest of the cheap, and insulting besides. But her eyes are doing shit without her, here. It's from telling the truth, she thinks. It feels good, even if it trashes her only chance at a ride.

"Guess it worked, yeah?" the driver says about the dummy gas can.

Harper nods, doesn't strap in. It's another thing her dad told her: unless you trust this buckle not to have been messed with, not to need a coat hanger or something to pry open, don't belt yourself down tight. He'd heard some crusty old story about a trucker who would trap hitchhikers like that. Not to do anything bad to them necessarily, but because he thought he was a comedian of the road, and liked to try his bits out on a captive audience for a thousand or two miles. At which point he'd let the hitchhiker out not just in a different state, but in a different state of *mind*: shellshocked from bad and constant standup, blinking in the ditch, finally laughing, but just for that experience to be over.

This guy doesn't seem funny like that—*un*funny like that—but you never can tell.

"I can get out, you want," Harper says, her finger to the door just like Dillon's was, once upon a statie's life.

The driver considers this, considers it some more, then checks his mirrors, says, "Where you headed, then?"

"California eventually," Harper says. "Maybe Seattle. Got some stuff to do on the way, though."

"Always rats to kill," the driver says, setting his shifter, easing them ahead, the whole rig shuddering.

"What you hauling?" Harper asks.

"Tortilla chips!" the driver says with fake cheer. "Unless I pull up alongside some hoss carrying queso, at which point it'll be love at first sight..."

Harper smiles into her chest.

Fifteen or twenty trucks left her standing in the ditch the last hour, hour and a half, and it's the gay driver who actually pulled over to help. But she shouldn't judge, she imagines. Maybe all those other drivers were gay as well, and this guy's just stopped for her because of who he is.

Not that Wyoming is any kind of good place for him to be stopping, of course.

"Just to be sure there's no funny business," the driver says then, and reaches behind the console, comes up with what he evidently keeps clipped in a holster back there: a stubby-thick snub-nose.

Harper rubs the side of her face, trying to hide that pistol from herself.

Is it the same one Bucketmouth left on that shelf back at that Akal place a lifetime ago?

Impossible, she tells herself. The world is full of snub-noses like this. The road's a dangerous place.

"Got any good stories from the ditch, then?" the driver says, leaning over the wheel to stretch his back.

"Just horror ones," Harper says. "What do these patches mean?"

She looks down along the sleeve and the driver looks with her.

"It's like—you know Russian tattoos in their prisons? They

tell a story, are an autobiography you write on yourself, maybe a wall of caution signs too. This is like that."

"This one?" Harper says, touching the red wings.

"You don't want to know," the driver says, and pops a knife out from the left side of his belt. "Couple of those a lady maybe shouldn't be advertising around, though."

He flips the knife around, offers it across to her.

"Probably just shave em all off," the driver says. "Bikers are all twitchy about if you earned them, could get you in a pickle."

"Like Boy Scout badges," Harper says, digging the point of the blade in for the thread, trying not to snag the leather.

"Boy Scouts in Hell, yeah," the driver says with a smile, and watches the road and his mirrors for the few minutes it takes Harper to get the patches off, stack them on the console.

"Got a trash?" she says.

He slides them into the cupholder, says, "Coasters now, yeah?"

"So 80's open back there?" she says, tipping her head behind them—east.

"You know about that?"

"You're not my first ride," Harper lies, wincing inside from it.

"Down to one-lane, but yeah," the driver says. "We were all ducks threaded on a string for a while there, though."

"That like sardines in a can?"

"Lot more quacking," the driver says, giving his horn a perfunctory tug.

Harper grins, leans back in her seat a touch. More mentally than with her body, really. Being in this truck, it's . . . it's not quite like her dad showing up at the other end of that concrete tunnel, but it's got that feel, anyway. Like home.

"Hungry?" the driver asks, reaching back, coming up with a tube of Pringles.

It's another thing Harper's been warned about, of course:

taking food. When she peels the top, though, this tube still has the pressured-up foil at top, just like new tennis balls.

"Thanks," she says.

He nestles a cold beer down into the cupholder for her too, letting one of the patches soak up the water from the cooler.

"You're of age, right?" he says. "I don't mean—I'm not trying to—"

Harper cracks the beer open well below window-level, says, "Old enough, yes."

He studies her and she can tell that *he* can tell she's probably not twenty-one, but he lets it slide, says, "You know how the captain on a ship can marry people, and how, in international waters, there's no drinking age?"

She chews, sips, nods.

"This is my ship," he says, reaching forward to pat the dash.

"Never been in one this new," Harper says, taking it all in.

"Be paying on it for a good twenty years after I'm dead and gone," the driver says.

"I just—you're my second ride, so far," Harper says, barely remembering the other ride she's supposed to have had. And also that she's Ava, from Utah. In a brown Audi. And she was never at Wagonhound, and she didn't start any fires, and she ate an exploding hamburger, and and and . . .

"Sure about this-all?" the driver says. "Being on the road, I mean? The life?"

Harper shakes her head no, fills her mouth with salty goodness.

"I don't have any money to pay you for these," she says, trying to hide her hungry chewing.

The driver doesn't care. He shifts down to pass a slow RV with a shaky wheel, pours on the steam to get around them before they wobble into his lane.

"Can you imagine if they had highways just for freight?" he says, daydreaming out loud.

"Like train tracks, you mean?" Harper says.

"Still got to get those heads of lettuce from the station to the grocery sto—" the driver says, flinching back halfway into it.

It's an empty snack-size bag of Fritos slapped to his windshield from whoever's ahead of them now.

"Classy, dude," the driver says to the big white tow truck in front of them, and does his windshield wipers twice to clear the bag.

"Wait," Harper says, setting her beer down blind, feeling for the cupholder. She tries to crank the window down, can't find the handle.

"Gonna be sick?" the driver asks, thumbing a button on his side double fast. Harper's window glides down and she shimmies up and halfway out, reaches around, just snags the Fritos bag whipping back and forth under the wiper blade, her hair everywhere.

She sits down with it and the driver's watching her for what's next.

"You like a, a anti-litterbug, what do they call them?" he asks. "Conversationalist?"

"No," Harper says about the bag, and looks up to the tow truck ahead of them. "Can you pass him?"

On the silver-foil inside of the bag, just barely, there's a smear of blood. It's from eating one-handed while driving. Shaking the bag straight and then tilting it up, pouring the Fritos down to your waiting mouth.

"Was going to anyway," the driver says, downshifting. "Looks like he's just trolling, waiting for the next call."

"If he was, he'd have picked that rig up a few miles back," Harper says, thinking out loud. "He backed up to it but then just left, did you see?"

Harper can feel the driver watching her while reaching for a lower gear.

Smoke and effort billows up from their stacks and they ease around the bright white tow truck, where Harper can see it's a Freightliner, shiny-new and solid as a battleship, right at eye level with them, hooks and chains and rolled-up tarps all over it, pulleys and winches, tow bars and boom arms, feet it can lower to anchor itself, to do some real lifting. It's so clean it can't be Bucketmouth, Harper's telling herself. Trucks with bad intent, they're—they're like that Peterbilt, they're rusty and evil looking. Not spotless and showroom-floor.

The yellow light on top of its cab is still revolving slow like a prison searchlight, just keeping things safe.

"Got be nice to these guys," the driver says, leaning over to raise a hand in greeting now that the cabs are about to be even with each other. "Never know when they might be pulling your ass up from—"

Bucketmouth looks over from that cab, a toothpick chocked between his lips, his face still raw and bloody as a nightmare. He tips the cap he's now wearing then looks over again, realizes who's watching him, her hair floating all around her.

He nods in greeting.

"Who's he think he is?" the driver says about Bucketmouth's pizza face. "Fred—"

"Where is he!" Harper screams between the two trucks, having to sit sideways to try to get her question all the way over there.

Bucketmouth leans towards her, cups his hand around what's left of Jam's ear.

Harper slings her beer across. Bucketmouth leans back, lets the can zing past into his cab. He leans over, picks it up while it's foaming, tries to get an airy slurp off the top before holding it out the window, dropping it into that rushing space.

"What the fuck are you doing!" the driver says to Harper,

reaching for her and losing his straight line a bit, the tortilla-chip truck veering across the stripes, bringing Harper close enough to Bucketmouth that they could clasp hands if she leaned out a bit, reached.

"Where is he!" Harper screams again.

Bucketmouth swirls his fingers around his head, brings them to a point on his own not-yet-done face, like telling Harper to wait a few, she'll be seeing Dillon here directly.

The driver reseats himself, finds his own lane.

"*Ram him!*" Harper says, coming around to give the driver her full attention.

"What the—?" the driver says, and Harper lunges across, grabs onto the steering wheel, pulling the truck sharply over again, this time enough that its front fender taps into the front bumper of the tow truck. Because it's a new truck, isn't metal, the big blue fender bends in, comes loose, goes under the rig with a terrible and fast crunching, sucked into a vortex.

Bucketmouth's smiling, damn him, his tow truck keeping a straight and steady line.

"Lady, you got to—!" the driver's saying, but Harper's looking for what else she can throw.

She calms when she realizes.

The driver sees it on her face and they both dive for the console, for behind the console.

The tortilla truck slings back and forth, pops out of gear, and when the driver grabs the wheel and the shifter for control, Harper comes up with the snub-nose.

She turns sideways in the seat, aims out the window into the cab of the tow truck. Bucketmouth sees this and locks his rear tires up so her shot goes sailing over his hood.

"Slower!" Harper calls back to the driver, and instead he gives it some pedal.

She turns around in the seat, levels the snub-nose on *him*.

"I'm so sorry," she says. "You don't understand. He's going to kill my boyfriend."

"*He* was your other ride?" the driver says back. "What did he do?"

"He's the one who started that fire!" Harper says. "And—and he destroyed a rest stop back there!"

"Like, the Men's room, you mean?" the driver asks, checking his mirrors.

"Like the walls and the cars and the people!" Harper yells, already turning back, having to hang out to see the nose of the tow truck. "Slower, slower!" she calls back to the driver.

"Holy—" the driver says, a new terror washing over his face, and Harper checks the mirror on her side, sees the tow truck coming across from the far shoulder—it veered away so it could come back in at a sharper angle. She grabs onto the open window and the left arm of her chair right at the moment of impact.

The tow truck slams their trailer, taking out that whole flimsy wall. Tortilla chips everywhere. The snub-nose jounces from Harper's right hand, falls silently to the asphalt, is gone just as fast as the tractor's fender was.

"What the *hell* is going on here!" the driver screams, shifting *up* now, to try to shake this crazy tow truck.

"No, no, slower, we need to—" Harper says, reaching for the wheel again, but the driver pushes her back hard now.

Instead of coming to a stop at the door like she expects to, the driver thumbs a button on his side and the door opens, lets Harper fall through, and out, and down, her hands grabbing for whatever there is: a bracket on the gas tank.

Her hair's brushing the blacktop now, the heat off the stack baking the skin of her face. She pulls her head up, terrified of getting sucked under the blurry wall of double tires chewing up the road right behind her.

"Stop, stop!" she yells up to the driver, but her voice is ripped away as soon as she opens her lips. In front of her is the huge naked front tire, its fender gone, its tread liable to knuckle up a piece of gravel and sling it through her face at any moment, and behind her—she looks—the chrome bumper of the tow truck is coming, headlights off, hood trailing remnants of the tortilla truck's trailer.

Harper shakes her head no, no, that she wants a do-over, that this could have all happened different, and then she feels the rig she's hanging onto shift up, the road passing beneath her even faster now, leaving Bucketmouth behind for a moment. Or at least matching the tow truck's speed.

The tow truck's stacks belch smoke in response.

Harper looks above the tank for something to grab onto. The door she came out is shut from the wind, and its chrome grab bar is so high up there.

Instead, she works back on the long tank, hooks her fingers into some cabinet door of the sleeper she can just grab into, hopes it's locked, that that handle won't flop open, spilling her to the ground.

She pulls up with it, pressing as hard as she can into the side of the sleeper, and, reaching and reaching with the left toe of her sneaker, she *just* manages to get to the diamondplate step she's so thankful for, that a lot of rigs don't have. She slaps her hand around the corner of the sleeper, finally connects with a chain. One she knows is just hanging on a bar, isn't meant to support a person's weight. But there's no other choice. She lets go of the handle, swings out on the chain, is in open air now, flopping back, just holding on, whipping in the eighty-mile-per-hour wind.

She kicks forward against the sleeper hard enough that she swings around, falls into the brake lines and uses them to moor herself but they're slick with grime and she's still falling back, back. What she finds instead of the slick brake lines is the pigtail, pulsing with electricity for the trailer. Because pigtails just have a

Bessie lock or some bullshit to keep them in place, not glad hands like make sense, and because that Bessie lock doesn't always get put back on—who would ever pull the power cord?—the pigtail slips right out of the plug and the trailer behind her goes dark. Harper drops the pigtail, grabs onto a boomer clanging against the back of the sleeper. It holds, lets her hand over hand her way in, out of the worst of the pulling wind. But the tires and the road are still right there under her, a mis-step away—there's no catwalk on this truck, what?

She sits down hard, grabbing onto everything she can, gambling it won't let her down too.

There's bright red alarms going off in the cab now, she knows. Has she dislodged or snagged a brake line, making this a runaway truck, now? One out here in the flats, where there's no sandtraps to try to climb? Think, *think*, she tells herself, trying to remember what the blue and red lines do, what her dad was always narrating, each hookup, each drop-off. One's service, one's parking, and . . . and if she pulls the parking one, the red one she's pretty sure, then the trailer thinks it's in the lot, so it locks up. Which, at highway speed, is instant disaster, a moment of smoke billowing up from the tires and then—she doesn't even know, can't imagine. But she knows that, where she is, she won't have to imagine. She'll be in the teeth of it, the thrashing metal of it.

Up in the tractor, the driver lets off the gas, engages the Jake Brake—it's so *loud*, being right here—but then he surges forward, the tow truck probably filling all his mirrors.

Harper crawls forward to sit against the back wall of the sleeper, her knees to her chest. She knows that if Bucketmouth rear-ends them hard enough to break the kingpin connecting the trailer to the tractor, then the front of the trailer will surge forward, pancake her between. But there's nowhere else to sit, no way else to be.

She collects her hair, wraps it around her left hand to keep it out of her eyes, and, moving steady and intentional, the tow truck pulls up even with her, knows right where she is.

Bucketmouth nods hello to her with his bloody face then keeps easing forward like showing her his new tow truck foot by shiny white foot.

When the shadow of the boom passes—it's the only part painted glossy black—he clicks every light on the beast on. Including all the ones shining on his hooks and chains and tow bar at the end of the boom, still folded up neat, a tarp burrito'd to it.

Bucketmouth eases forward a few more feet and Harper thinks he's getting position to swing over into this lane, end this once and for all, bounce her under the trailer, but then he just holds steady, pacing them, the tortilla truck driver probably not sure whether to try to run or hit the Jake Brake again. It's a standoff at eighty miles per hour, and climbing.

But then Bucketmouth engages something in his cab and the tow arm folds out parallel with the road like the two forks of a forklift, and Harper thinks she gets it: he's going to accelerate in front of them, raise that boom arm, get the tow bar level with the rig's windshield, then slam on the brakes.

She pushes against the sleeper to a standing position, bangs her open hand on the metal, trying to get the driver to understand, but then Bucketmouth isn't accelerating.

Harper holds onto the base of the blue line, her hair whipping out straight horizontal, and tries to see whatever Bucketmouth's showing her.

The boom arm. The tow bar. The tarp-burrito strapped to the underside of the two forks of the tow bar.

What?

Those are—tow bars, they're made to slide under the front of a rig, and sometimes that means maybe a foot clearance, getting past the fancy bumper. So they'll lower all the way to the ground, and usually have to. Why would any tow truck operator mess that up by strapping a tarp *under* those twin forks?

Harper's answer comes a moment later, when Bucketmouth nudges the tow bar lower, low enough that the front lip of the tarp makes contact with the asphalt blurring past.

It's enough to unravel the burrito, show the meat inside: Dillon.

And he's awake.

Harper stands holding on tight to the brake line, shaking her head no, screaming at Bucketmouth.

There's nothing she can do, though.

From the cab, Bucketmouth lowers the tow arm a half foot, then three or four inches more, so Dillon's socked toe is right at the blacktop.

"*No!*" Harper screams, unable to even hear own voice.

Dillon wriggles in his straps but there's nowhere he can go, no way he can hope to stop this.

He's looking right down at the asphalt now.

Bucketmouth kills all his lights again, plunging Dillon into darkness. But Harper hears metal moving over there. The big piston of the boom, relaxing.

A light comes on on the side of the truck, shining down over the wheel, then it goes off and the one Bucketmouth meant comes on, spotlighting Dillon.

He's inches from the asphalt blurring by under his face, is jerking and jerking, trying to get away from it, but even if he could shake free, it would just be to fall.

Harper shakes her head no, no, and then, years before she's ready to say goodbye, the lights go dark again. When they come back on, Dillon's had his whole frontside scraped off. Blood and viscera string back from him, most of it burned black by rushing contact. Even the front half of his feet are gone, the heels still so perfect in their white socks.

Harper lowers her face, lets her hair go, and when she looks up a minute later, not wanting to see, she's alone.

Bucketmouth is gone again.

The truck she's in eases over into that lane, its trailer not trailing chips anymore, just sparks, and Harper looks to her left hand, death-gripped onto the red line, realizes that if she would have thought to crank that glad hand connection up, the trailer that's a wall behind her would have locked up, slowing the tractor she's standing on, and . . . and this tortilla-chip truck would have slowed, taking away Bucketmouth's audience—*her*. And? And maybe Dillon lives a half-minute longer?

Unlike Harper, probably, trying to hold onto that red line, whipping its metal head back and forth.

There's nothing she could have done, no. Nothing except— except not tilt that couch up into the ceiling, scream at her mom, and stalk off into the great unknown, pulling all her friends with her, because if she's trashing her own life, then she's not going down alone, is she?

She almost has to laugh about it, about the futility of it all. She huddles behind the cab, sobbing, screaming, chest hitching, and feels the big truck starting to slow to check the damage.

Check the damage and call in the law, hand her over. It's not like this *isn't* her fault.

And? Why not go to jail for a few years, right? What's left for her out here? May as well ride out the coming nightmares in a cell instead of a ratty motel over a bar. May as well go live with the killers and criminals, since that's what she is now. She can't beat Bucketmouth. He's been out here doing this too long, knows all the ins, every out, and all the shit between, knows it well enough he can have fun with it.

Harper nods to herself that no, she's not running off into the pasture before the truck's all the way stopped, but then she looks over into the passing lane, at the car steadily pacing them, honking one long continuous honk.

It's a pale Buick, Meg hanging out the passenger window.

Harper shakes her head no but her mom surges ahead, is even with the tractor for a half mile, trying to get him to pull over, but the driver up there's been spooked, probably isn't sure who's good, who's not.

The truck gears down to accelerate away from whatever this is starting to be.

Harper pulls herself up with the brake line, the lazy spring up there bouncing her, and leans out into the wind to track the Buick.

Maybe a half mile up, it screeches to a stop, parks itself sideways in the road, across both lanes.

"No, no," Harper says, the Jake Brake so loud and all at once, the tractor's brakes trying, the trailer pitching in, but they're not going to make it, they're not going to stop in time.

"No no no no!" Harper screams, then sees her shadow shoot out in front of her, meaning . . . meaning another truck is coming in, doesn't get why this truck is slowing, up here—but then, no, that's not it, Harper knows. The trailer's brake lights are dead! The truck back there isn't going to see them in time! It's going to jam this trailer behind her up against the sleeper, crushing Harper flat in the process.

She steps out onto the bobtail frame, sees immediately what she needs: the pigtail line, flopping in the deadspace between the wheels, its rubbery head catching the asphalt and bouncing up, bouncing up.

Harper drops to her stomach, holding her hair back with one hand, her other reaching for the line. She gets it, loses it, reaches farther, her hair probably in the tread of the whirring tires now, and then she has it, is pulling back, rolling to safety.

She fights the wind up to the sleeper, lifts the flap to plug the pigtail in, and . . . the rubber's all chipped. It won't fit. Harper tries again, insisting, trying to get all those little brass pins lined up. Same result. She drops to her knees, inspects the rubber plug, finally puts it to her teeth and tears the offending rubber away, then forces it in, having to use all her weight.

The lights come on behind her, and the best sound in the world is the rig back there hauling on its horn, its tires locking up, its trailer probably swinging around to jackknife, Harper doesn't know, is curled against the sleeper with her eyes squeezed shut, her fists by her temples like that's going to stop all this from crushing her flat.

It's weird, she thinks, that she can smell that driver back there's tires, but then of course the tires she's smelling are right here—the tortilla-chip truck's locked up too, to try to keep from slamming through that Buick up there playing chicken.

At what has to be the last moment, the driver, not stopping in time, veers over into the ditch, the truck losing weight on one side, trying to roll over. If it had a real load, it would definitely already be on its side, bulldozing earth and grass before it, but what chips are left, they still weigh nothing.

The truck finds its center again, settles, then coughs once, dies.

"Harper, Harper!" Meg's screaming, the rear passenger door open.

Harper steps down into the ditch and the world under her feet is still rushing past at eighty miles per hour, fast enough that she falls to her knees, the heels of her hands. She's shuddering, can't breathe right, her mouth opening and closing like a carp pulled up onto shore to drown in the air.

"What the everliving fucking—!" the driver's saying through his open door.

And he's coming down after it, isn't the nice guy he was. Who would be.

Harper shakes her head no, no, is already rolling away, scrabbling up onto the blacktop, lunging across the lane and collapsing through the open door of her mom's car.

"I'm sorry, I'm sorry, I'm sorry," she's saying into the bench seat, the Buick already accelerating away from what's about to be the worst pile-up on 80 in years, probably.

"Did you see, did you see?" Meg's saying over the front seat, reaching down to pat Harper's back.

"You good?" their mom asks in her all-business voice, like this was just an everyday thing that just happened.

Harper shakes her head no, she isn't, and when she leans forward, it's into her mom's back, to lay her head there, be safe at last.

CHAPTER 20

Because that big white tow truck can be a couple miles behind as well as it can be waiting up ahead—with headlights off, it's invisible, it's everywhere—Harper doesn't let her mom pull them over to the shoulder.

"But you were—" her mom tries, and Harper understands: she was riding on the non-passenger part of a rig barreling down the interstate, she almost died, she might be hurt somewhere she doesn't even know yet. More important, just to be not moving for a few minutes, to rest, to breathe, to settle and reset, take some bearings, stop shaking, let the tears finally come . . . her mom's right about all of it, doesn't even need to say it, can say it all just with her concerned eyes in the rearview mirror, with her right hand on top of Harper's on the back of the front seat.

Harper can't stop, though.

Waiting in her head for the next quiet moment are all of Dillon's last moments.

She swallows them down as best she can, shakes her head no, waves her mom on, on, go, keep moving.

Her mom looks to Meg, who nods yes about this, so she gets the Buick back up to speed again.

"But the first turnaround," she promises.

"Cops," Harper manages to get out.

"She's saying we need the police," Meg clarifies.

"What is going on, girls?" their mom asks, and the way she skips the contraction says how deadly serious she is. How this is the end of whatever bullshit they're going to try. The end before it even begins.

A sign for the Fort Steele rest area smears by.

"There?" their mom asks before either of them can come up with an answer for what's going on tonight.

Together, they shake their heads no.

"Why?" their mom asks, not liking this.

"Rest stops fall down," Harper says.

Meg nods solemnly, stroking Sheba's head.

"Then I think I will just—" their mom says, slowing again to pull over on the shoulder.

"We can't stop, Mom!" Meg says.

"He'll find us," Harper adds, already looking behind them.

"He?" their mom says, then to Harper: "He where you got the jacket?"

Harper looks down to it, kind of amazed to still be wearing it.

"What were you thinking?" her mom asks the two of them. "Two young girls out on the interstate at night? Did you know there's all manner of danger out here tonight? I was stuck in line for that fire for I don't know how long, and then—some trucker blew his lid at that other rest stop, I guess."

"Wagonhound," Harper says.

"How do you know its name?" their mom asks, watching Harper in the rearview again.

"I used to always have to stop there to pee," Harper says, trying to hide her reflection. "With Dad."

"I'm just lucky to have found you at all."

"You weren't supposed to," Harper says.

"I'll always come after you, Harper," her mom tells her. "I don't care what you say to me, what you break in the house. You're my daughter."

"That driver almost had to hit y'all, Mom," Harper says. "I don't know how he stopped. If it wasn't—"

And then she realizes: it was a new truck, wasn't it? Meaning that pigtail's electricity, it wasn't only for the lights, it was also for the electronic braking system, wasn't it?

Meaning, it was *Harper* who almost killed them.

No surprise.

"But he did stop," her mom says. "It wouldn't have mattered if it was a train either, girlie. I would have stood in front of that for you too, I hope you know that. That's what mothers do."

Harper tries to blink the heat from her eyes.

"Kissy," she says, her voice cracking at last. "And Jam, and—and *Dillon*, Mom."

"Dillon will always be around," her mom tells her. "His kind . . . he's made of Laramie, won't ever be able to leave, not really. And I'm sure Kiss and James will show up just before winter. Yellowstone doesn't need as many workers once tourist season is—"

Harper interrupts by sputtering into tears again. She buries her face into the backseat.

"What's got into the two of you?" she hears her mom asking Meg.

Meg doesn't say anything in reply. Because it's Harper's friends, Harper's news, Harper's secret.

Harper's *fault*, Harper corrects, inside.

"And I don't know if the cops are going to help us, Harp," her mom announces. "I think they take the side of truckers when there's a kid trying to stow away on their truck. Trying to get him in trouble might even get you on their radar, right?"

"It's not him, Mom," Meg says.

"Then who?" their mom asks.

Bucketmouth, Harper doesn't say. This monster of a man who eats parts of people and then tears his own face off, grows another one. He doesn't like Indians, though, Mom, so we're safe from him in that regard, anyway—safe from getting eaten, anyway.

Harper sits up all at once, realizing something.

"What?" Meg says.

"He doesn't . . . he can't do that thing he does with, with *us*," Harper says. "With Indians."

Meg considers this but doesn't fill in any of the blanks for their mom. Not out loud.

And then the Buick's speed sags.

Fort Steele. The rest stop.

"We don't have to stop or anything *scary* like that," their mom says, making fun of the idea. "But this is as good a place as any to turn around."

"Mom, no," Harper says, leaning up to touch her mom's shoulder.

"Harper, if you don't tell me—"

"Straight," Harper says. "Please. Please. Listen, I'm sorry I broke the plates, I won't ever watch that baseball movie again, whatever you want. Just—not here. Keep going."

"Why?" her mom asks again, that easy turnaround still drawing the Buick that direction, her foot already off the gas to ease them over into the exit.

"Rawlins," Harper says. "I promised myself I would get to Rawlins."

"Any promises for after that?" her mom says, turning around, face to face.

Harper shakes her head no, and, in response, her mom re-centers them in the westbound lane.

"So I'm helping you keep a promise to yourself that you made when you were mad at me?" her mom asks, raising her eyebrows in the mirror about it.

"Promises to yourself are the most important, right?" Harper says, settling back into the seat, the Buick gathering speed again.

"It's called discipline," her mom says. "And this isn't exactly what I meant."

"It's a start," Harper says, and watches the dark pasture for a glint of chrome, a flash of white.

"What's in Rawlins?" their mom asks a couple of miles later. "I've been there, you know. It's not exactly a resort destination."

"Isn't there that DPS station or whatever on this side of town?" Harper asks.

"Why are you so interested in the police tonight?"

"We're Indian, Mom," Meg says. "That's rule number one, right? Always know where the cops are?"

"So you can know where *not* to go, yeah," their mom says with a sort of pressed-lip grin, switching hands on the wheel to regard Meg.

"He'll follow us there," Harper says.

"Dillon?" her mom asks. "Are you still hung up on him, Harp? He's just going to . . . never mind. Some things you have to learn for yourself, I guess."

He'll just grow up to be like your father, she was going to say. Hauling just enough loads to pay the bills, never enough to sock anything away.

It's almost comforting to Harper, really, her and her mom falling back into their old arguments.

She breathes in deep, lets it back out.

"How far to Rawlins?" she asks.

"Twenty minutes?" her mom says.

"Staties are at the first exit, right?" Harper says.

"They don't like to be called that," her mom says.

"Troopers," Meg fills in.

Harper leans forward, hangs her arms over the front seat, says to Meg, "Turn that on?"

It's the CB their dad wired under the dash that time they drove to Yellowstone for their big family vacation, so he could ask about the traffic ahead of them. He said it felt weird to be on the road without his ears on.

Their mom had hated it, hated that he could essentially leave the car anytime he clicked the mic open.

It hadn't been the best trip. But they had gotten headsup about a blowover ahead of them, which had felt to Harper like looking into the future, seeing over the horizon.

"It still works?" Meg says, twisting the power on.

The mic hisses static.

"The antenna," Meg says, and is halfway out the window working on it at sixty miles per hour before their mom can stop her.

Meg comes back breathless, windblown.

"What are you two trying to do?" their mom says.

Meg hands the mic back, looks to Harper to answer for them.

"Save our lives, I hope," Harper says, and closes her eyes, speaks into the void.

"Breaker breaker," Harper says on channel after channel, because they don't know where he might be listening in. "Come in, Lockjaw, calling Lockjaw, this is Big Sis. Paging Dr. Tetanus, somebody looking for a shot of conversation, here. Bucketmouth, Bucketmouth, got your ears on, come back."

After which, each time, she holds the handle up, eyes closed in prayer. If this doesn't work, then . . . what? Wait for that white tow truck's grill to fill their rearview? If he gets that close on the open road, though, then it's all over.

Some chatter comes back, but it's just asking questions, and asking if she's on the right channel, and how old she is, and isn't, which her mom scowls about, as it just confirms her estimation of all truckerkind.

Wash, rinse, repeat, channel after channel, mile after mile, until, finally, a mic opens up, sucking in the static. No voice comes through but there's ears on the other end.

"There you are," Harper says.

The mic opens and closes in what feels like grudging hello. The way you acknowledge something when you know there's people who can listen in.

"Guessing you don't look like any certain boyfriends by now, do you?" Harper says.

Meg furrows her brow about this but Harper shakes her head no, she can't explain.

"It's because he's *Indian*," she says, her lips right to the mic. "Did you think Indians can only have dark skin, long hair?"

Bucketmouth opens his end, leaves it open, then closes it.

"Sorry about that," Harper says. "Would have told you, but, you know. Had some other things to be dealing with, you could say."

"Harper, what are you—" their mom says, the mic open, and Harper curls around it, away from her mom.

This time a chuckle comes through the static.

"Rawlins," Harper says to him. "Take the first exit. You'll see me."

"And why would I do that, Big Sister?" Bucketmouth says at last, his voice low and creaky—*not* Dillon's. Not anybody's, the way he's talking.

"Because I've got something you want."

The open air sucks in, holds, goes away.

She's got his attention.

"*Bucketmouth*," she says, not to him but about him. "I know where your name comes from."

"I told you, it—" he starts, then seems to remember he's on open air, here. He clicks back off in what sounds like frustration.

"It's not fish," Harper says.

"Bullshit," he says back. "Over."

"You're either there or I'm gone forever," Harper says. "I don't know what you're going to look like next, but I know how you work, can tell the world. This is your one chance. Take it or leave it."

"Rawlins," he finally comes back.

"First exit," Harper confirms, and lowers her face into the top of the front seat.

"I don't know what this is about," her mom says.

"It's almost over," Harper says back.

It's really a prayer, she supposes.

— —

The next call is from the one working payphone at the truckstop just east of Sinclair.

While it's ringing Harper gets herself breathing hard.

"911, what is the address of your emergency?" the dispatcher says instead of hello.

"He just—he's the one who hit that state policeman!" Harper says in her best practiced shriek. Luckily, she's been practicing all night.

"Ma'am, ma'am, okay, I need your—"

"He's driving this, this big white tow truck, like for eighteen wheelers!"

"Ma'am, if you can just—"

"He's at Rawlins in a few minutes, the first exit westbound."

She cringes, was trying to talk stupid, not good.

"How do you know this, ma'am? Can I get your—"

"You've got to stop him! He said he's coming to get the rest of the cops!"

With that Harper hangs up, holds the phone there long enough for anybody standing close by to keep walking.

She turns to Meg, right beside her.

Meg nods good, good.

Their mom is at the pump, filling up for the drive back to Laramie.

"She's gonna ask," Meg says.

"We'll tell her later," Harper says. "We tell her now, she checks us into the hospital because we're crazy."

"You sure about this?" Meg asks.

"Mom?"

"Him."

Harper studies her mom, working the gas spigot back into the side of the pump, taking two tries to get it to hang then threading her long hair out of her face, just looking out at the interstate like studying it.

For maybe the first time, Harper wonders if her mom's looking for her husband out there the same way Harper and Meg are always still looking for their dad. It's something about the way her body's both turned to the road, but also turned away—it's a posture, a way of being, that somehow means something's missing. Some*one*. Does her heart beat harder when she hears a tractor coupling to a trailer through the thin walls of their house? Did she already know that CB still worked, because she listens to it every time she's alone in the car? Does she see her husband every time she looks into the faces of his daughters? Is that why she's so hard on them, because she's forever mad at him for not coming back?

"She's not going to like this," Harper says to Meg.

"Go," Harper says, and steps into the truckstop behind her little sister, casing every face in the place.

He's not there. All these faces have skin, or are covered in beards. And none of them are tracking her and Meg.

They meet their mom at the register, Meg with an apple and a tall blue Icee, Harper with a microwave burger.

Their mom nods, pays for all that and the gas.

"You girls are going to bankrupt me," she says, her usual line.

Harper smiles, puts her burger in the microwave for two minutes and looks past it, out the window.

A big white tow truck is coasting past the pump island for the cars.

Her heart beats once, hangs there when the truck slows, but then it eases forward again for its own pumps, disappears behind a brown Kenworth W900 at the first island, its forty-eight foot trailer painted up with a stagecoach robbery mural.

Harper lowers her head to hide her face in her hair, and, finally, when her burger dings, she breathes out again, draws in with a gasp.

"You ever going to tell me what this is all about tonight?" her mom says, standing right beside her.

Harper nods yes, yes, says, for her mom and Meg both, "I'll be out. Bathroom."

It's not because she needs it, it's so they won't be a mom and two sisters. Still, she makes hot eyes to Meg, directs them outside so Meg will get it, and then takes Meg's hair, pushes it up.

Meg gets it, wraps her hair into a sloppy bun on top of her head, and, on the way out, peels a pair of stoner shades from the spinning rack, has them on like they were hers all along.

"Good girl," Harper says, already shrugging out of the leather jacket, dropping it down on the newspaper rack.

A solid sixty-count later she's pushing through the door after them, telling herself not not *not* to look over to the left, and someone nudges the back of her left arm.

Harper spins around, ready to run, ready to scream, ready to die, but it's just a biker.

He's holding the leather jacket out to her.

"Think you dropped this," he says, and they both look down to the dark places on the jacket's arm, where the patches just were. Where they most definitely aren't anymore.

"Thanks," Harper says, all eyes in the place on her now.

She turns, pushes through the door at last, and makes her way to the Buick, only looks over to the left about eighty times.

"What?" Meg says when Harper gets in, immediately goes to the rear floorboard.

"*Drive*," Harper says to her mom.

Her mom doesn't give her away by looking over the back of the front seat, just eases away, and Harper, traitor to herself that she is, is more thankful for her than anything in the world.

"We don't have to watch that movie again, Mom," she says from under the leather jacket, in case maybe her mom didn't hear her say that earlier.

"I watched it," her mom says back, checking if she can turn onto the road. "That black player, he's easy on the eyes, isn't he?"

"I hate you, Mom," Harper says, her lips pressing together right after.

"Hate you too, love," her mom says back like they never even fought, like their couch is in the same place it always was, and eases them away.

CHAPTER 21

Because of Harper's call, the line for Rawlins starts about a half mile out.

"No no no," Harper pleads, leaning over the front seat again.

"Seatbelts," her mom says, checking the rearview.

Harper does too.

It's just a normal Mack dumptruck, a woman in an orange vest behind the wheel, drinking from a tall green thermos.

Meg belts in and Harper does as well.

"They're only supposed to have a roadblock for *him*," Harper says. "Not for—not for everybody."

"Because that's how roadblocks work," Meg, ever the little sister, says, looking back to punctuate it with her eyes, her Icee-blue mouth kind of undercutting it all.

Harper flips her off close-range.

"Girls, girls," their mom says, then, half in jest: "Don't make me stop this car . . ."

"We're already stopped," Meg says, obviously.

The headlights pile up behind them.

Meg dials through CB-land, finds news of the parking lot this leg of 80 is now.

"What's a checkpoint charlie?" Meg asks.

Harper opens her mouth to answer but her mom's already there: "What your sister engineered up here, evidently."

Harper looks behind them again. Bucketmouth should be

ten, twenty, maybe thirty vehicles behind them, shouldn't he? It's all just headlights, though. He can't be in front of them anyway, or there'd be no need for the roadblock.

He can bring that big white tow truck around in the passing lane, though, can't he? Just hammer on down past the exit, then circle back? How do roadblocks ever even catch anybody?

"This where Dad used to think Bigfoot lived?" Meg asks then, bringing Harper back.

"Bigfoot?" their mom says, looking between them.

"He—" Meg starts.

"I know, I know," Harper says.

"He said he saw him running into a tunnel just east of Rawlins," Meg recites from their meager store of family lore. "Right?"

Harper unfocuses her eyes enough to dredge that bedtime story up: her dad jamming gears out of Rawlins, everything around him grand and dramatic, just an hour and change from his baby girls and his beautiful wife, but . . . is that *Bigfoot* in his headlights? Was he over on the golf course chasing deer, eating flowers? At which point their dad's fingers would find their ribs—Meg's mostly, since Harper was older—and Meg would scream and laugh, and they'd all get in trouble for not going to sleep, for not being reasonable, for laughing until they were crying.

"Must be," Harper says.

That story always ended with Bigfoot running back to his side of the road, out of their dad's headlights, their dad acting out those large steps in the girls' small bedroom, then diving down into a tunnel that went under the interstate. How her dad played that in the confines of the bedroom was wriggling under their two beds as best he could, coming up between, roaring his Bigfoot roar.

Harper hasn't let herself think of that in years.

"Do you think it's really there?" Meg says.

"Bigfoot's a he not an it," Harper says.

"The tunnel, I mean," Meg says.

Harper looks left and right, can tell . . . maybe? . . . that the grass is a touch taller just behind them. Like water's been going more that way than other ways?

"Why would he make a story up about a tunnel?" their mom says, shutting this down because when they're talking about their dad, she's always way on the outside, the bad guy.

"There are tunnels under the road," Harper says. "I saw one earlier."

"Where?" Meg asks.

Harper shakes her head that it doesn't matter, and then it's their turn to process through the checkpoint.

The city bear leans down, looks in, casing all these Indian faces.

"Little far from the reservation, aren't you, ma'am?" he says to Harper's mom.

"This used to *all* be our land, you know?" her mom says back. Harper and Meg lock eyes and shake their heads: this statie doesn't know what can he just opened, does he?

"Ma'am?"

"This used to *all* be Indian land," their mom repeats, clipping her words more than usual, doing her hand over the dash to show she's talking about all of America.

"Ma'am, we just need to—"

"But then men with hats like yours, guns like that one, they came and they took it all away," their mom goes on. "Far from the reservation? First, the reservation system is broken, and second, this is *all*—"

"Okay, okay," the statie says. "These are your daughters?"

"Oh, so now we're talking about stolen children?" their mom asks right back, ready to go. "Do you know how much it used to cost to adopt an Indian baby when I was a girl?"

The statie looks at her, looks at Harper, looks at Meg, sees the family resemblance, the complete absence of smiles, then stands, waves them past.

"Yay, Mom," Meg says.

"Don't try that," their mom tells them.

"Because they can shoot you?" Meg asks. "What about you?"

"Let him try," their mom says back, and Harper looks over to the brand-new DPS facilities that probably weren't there when her dad was making up his Bigfoot story.

"There," Harper says like just thinking of this. "We can watch from there."

Her mom, close-lipped, playing along with a game her shoulders are telling them she knows is stupid, loops them around, parks out at the edge of that parking lot, turns the Buick off.

"How long till he comes through, you think?" she asks.

"He?" Harper says.

"Your boyfriend."

"Not long enough for us to explain it," Harper says.

Her mom nods like she should have expected that.

Meg crunches into her apple and her mom studies the line of headlights for Dillon, completely unaware that there's probably some of him in the tread of the Buick's tires.

Harper squints her eyes, trying to push that image away.

"What's he in?" her mom asks.

"Big white tow truck," Harper says.

"Kiss and James with him?" her mom asks, blind to the knife their names are. "They were looking for you, you know."

"He went by Jam, I think," Meg offers.

"Before signing on with Yellowstone, you mean?" their mom asks back.

Harper's watching a big tow truck silhouette edge forward, just one vehicle back from the checkpoint now. Twenty seconds later it's there, and the staties converge, pistols drawn.

Harper opens her door to see better, stands behind it.

"Run, run," she whispers across, one-hundred-percent ready

to see Bucketmouth gunned down. Instead, a black driver steps out, hands high. He drops to his knees, places his forehead to the ground without being told to. Because, Harper knows, he doesn't want to get shot.

"That him?" Meg asks.

Her answer is one of the staties shining her light onto the door of the tow truck, showing that the paint's not white but yellow. The statie's noting the company the truck tows for.

"Shit," Harper says.

"Language," her mom calls out.

Harper looks farther down the line, doesn't see any booms silhouetted against the far lane.

"I don't understand," she says.

"I understand this stake-out needs some facilities," her mom says, standing.

Together her and Harper look back to the dark DPS building.

"It's after five," Harper says.

"Cops sleep?" her mom says back.

"Me too," Meg says, coming up through her window to drum on the roof of the Buick.

"Again?" Harper asks.

"Forty-four-ounce Icee?" she says back.

"Go, go," Harper tells them.

"You too?" her mom asks. "Hour and a half home."

"I'll pee in a cup," Harper says.

"Not in my car you won't."

"Seat, then," Harper says, then, about the roadblock, "I've got to *watch*."

"They're not going to let us in," Meg says, down in the parking lot now, carrying her apple core by the stem like it's suddenly radioactive.

"This used to all be Indian land . . ." their mom says back

grandly, tragically, like an elder about to go off for six directionless hours, and Harper shakes her head in wonder, steps aside to let her pass.

"Don't go anywhere," her mom says, then raises the keys to show Harper that isn't really an option anyway.

"Thanks for the trust," Harper says.

"Thanks for the great track record," her mom tells her, and's gone, Meg trailing behind.

Harper settles in behind the wheel to be sure not to let Bucketmouth slip through the checkpoint, but now that the big tow truck's pulled to the side, its driver cuffed in the back of the car, she can tell they're pretty much just waving people through, are only still doing this because they haven't gotten official orders to stop. But their heart's not in it so much anymore.

"Thanks, guys," Harper says, and looks down to the blinking lights of the CB, the volume dialed all the way down, the red wire connected straight to the battery, Harper knows, because that's how her dad always did things.

Three cars later, one of them an ambulance that the staties just wave through, a hunting truck pulls up. Harper can tell it's a hunting truck because it's painted camo, a home job. And because it's missing all four doors.

Harper stands fast from the Buick.

It's the Park truck, stripped down and covered back up. And the driver, he's wearing camo too, and evidently has a face of some sort under that same camo cap, isn't just muscle and bone and teeth.

The statie steps back to study this truck and shakes his head in appreciation, or amusement, like this isn't something he wants to get involved with writing up tonight.

He waves Bucketmouth through.

"*That's him, that's him!*" Harper screams, rattling the chain link fence, kicking it, then going back to the car, honking and honking.

All the staties look over to her and she points ahead to the Park truck, points with both arms, with her whole body.

The staties look to each other, shrug, and turn back around.

The Park truck, though. Bucketmouth went back for it, left the doors in the pasture, went after it with a couple spraycans of paint, and poured water into it for one last ride.

Coming up the ramp now, he slows enough to lift something black and blocky from the seat beside him. Then he unwinds a spiral cable, holds the mic up for her to see.

The dead statie's radio rig. Right there beside him for the stop.

Harper fumbles at her CB, finds him on 19 saying "Big Sis, Big Sister, Harpo Marx, looking for you out here, darling. Big Sis, come in, I'm here wait—"

"I'm going to tell them now," she says back.

"Tell who what?" he says so innocently. "I just want to have a face-to-face sit-down, over. Well, emphasis on *face*, over again."

Harper tracks the Park truck's one good taillight to the intersection.

If she doesn't pull him away somehow, he's coming right to her, she knows. And her mom and Meg have to be almost done inside by now.

"Meet me *under* 80," she says all at once.

"Under?" Bucketmouth says back playfully.

"You just drove over it," Harper tells him. "I'll be there when you figure it out. But not for long."

"Sorry, Big Sis, I don't quite—"

"Turn left *now*," Harper says, watching his one taillight.

His blinker comes on flashing white through the shattered red and the truck eases over to the left.

Good, good. Perfect.

"I'll be there," Harper says.

"Copy that," Bucketmouth says.

Harper sets the mic down, checks the rearview, fully expecting to see her mom and Meg walking up.

Nothing. No one. Yet.

"Shit," she says, and stands up, closes the door quietly, just pressing it shut at the end.

She stalks off, comes back five steps later to pull the leather jacket up through the rear window, wrap herself in it against the cold.

CHAPTER 22

Hunched against the curving west wall of the tunnel under 80, the smell of dead animal and must in every breath, Harper catches herself wondering about the Bigfoot story her dad used to tell her and Meggie.

It was just for fun, of course. They even knew that then.

But can a story become real? Because, right now, there *is* supposed to be a monster ducking into this concrete tunnel with her.

The dead animal she stepped through to situate herself here was a dog, Harper's pretty sure. Maybe a coyote. Probably it caught a bumper in the upper world and dragged its way down here to lick its wounds, die in private.

When Bucketmouth kills her, will anybody find her bones, or will some other dogs drag them off? Will the coyotes pull her apart, snap at each other over the choice bits?

It's better than the other option, though. It's better than Bucketmouth getting his teeth into her mom, or Meg. That's the one thing Harper wants to extract from him before it's all over. A guarantee that he won't come for them, ever. That it can stop with her, here, now.

The other option is to end him, of course. But how? She can't outmuscle him, can't outfight him. She could slap him with a fast-moving bumper like he did with Kissy, like he did that statie, but he's not going to let himself get tricked up onto the blacktop,

Harper knows. If anything, she'd be the one standing in those sudden headlights.

If she had a knife she could use that . . . maybe. But he'll have a knife too, she bets. And maybe another gun. If he stashes little jars of body parts up and down the ditch, then he's probably got weapon caches too. Or, no: he's wearing that camo now. Not just the cap. That has to mean he jumped a real hunter, right? Even though it's not hunting season. Meaning he must have knocked on the door of some small house a mile or three off the highway, and then plundered the closet, the shop, taken his time in the mirror, the bodies of a family sprawled over his shoulder.

It doesn't matter.

Harper feels around for a sharp piece of rebar, a bottle to shatter a jabby edge from, but all she finds is grime and plastic cups and, for some reason, balls of yarn. She turns one of the balls of yarn over and over in her hand, imagines all the kittens of Rawlins, Wyoming gathering here in secret, for some serious play. It makes her smile, and that feels good and then bad, because she can't help but suspect it's the last smile she's going to get.

She cracks the wristband alight at last, shakes it brighter, needs the light to see what color all this yarn is, like she can't get killed without knowing.

Purple, one ball of gold.

With the weak glow of her wrist, she can see a pile of blankets a body length farther down the tunnel. Some hitchhiker's slept here, or waited out the rain. She doesn't shake the ratty blanket, doesn't want to know if bones might spill out. She doesn't need to see any skulls right now, thank you. If she's in a mausoleum already, she'd rather not have to know that.

Finally she extracts the baby food jar from the leather jacket's secret pocket and studies it with her wristband, stares into these two swimming eyeballs, one blue, one brown, like scooped out of a dog's skull with a grapefruit spoon.

Who *is* he now? Not Dillon, he can't be Dillon. But, is there a breakover point, by blood quantum? Are half-bloods safe, quarter-bloods a maybe, just have to bite and see?

Think all you want, she tells herself. It doesn't change one single thing that's happened, or's about to, does it?

She sets the baby food jar between her feet, considers breaking it for the shard of glass it'll give. But that shard wouldn't even go deep enough to nick anything vital, would it? It would just make him mad, which would probably prolong whatever complicated death he's got planned for her. She didn't see into the bed of the Park truck, after all. He could still feasibly have the half of Dillon that didn't scrape away, could make her—just spitballing, down here in Hell—he could make her fold him over, sew his ragged edges together, knit his head together without the face, fold the shoulders across to each other.

Thing is, if it saves Meg and her mom, Harper might just do that if he wants it done, she knows. Whatever it takes.

But, a face-to-face sit-down?

Why did he want that back there, at that gas station? Why is he saying yes to it now? Doesn't he just want her gone so she won't tell anyone about him? Sure, he's a cat playing with his mouse, but it's been ninety miles, a few different trucks, four or five hours, and who knows how many bodies. The cat in him should be tired of the game by now, just want to curl up somewhere, sleep for a day or two.

Harper shoots her wrist out to keep that circle of green light in view, not sit in the absolute deepest darkness with this smell, those bones, that blanket. These two human eyeballs swimming in cloudy cinnamon.

She holds them up again, considers them.

"I'm sorry, Bible lady," she says to the blue one, and shakes the little jar gently like a snowglobe, the powdered cinnamon going cloudy, the brown eye floating around to look out at her now, like just realizing she's out here past the glass. "Who were you?" she asks it.

All she knows for sure, if Bucketmouth was telling it true, is that Brown Eyes was most likely a white guy, and probably a healthy one, at least at the moment his eyeball was scooped out. Otherwise Bucketmouth might be crawling into a body festering with cancer, or trying to heal a broken leg, or—

"Big Sister, Big Sister . . ." a male voice says from the north mouth of the tunnel. "You were listening back there, weren't you? You know I was born in a tunnel. Did you think I could die in one as well? I like your thinking, girl."

"It's Big Sis," Harper says, taking his silhouette in with a glance and then choosing to stare instead at the chipped concrete wall opposite her. "In Arapaho it's Nah Bee."

"Na-bi?" he says.

"My mom was trying to teach my sister to call me that when we were kids," Harper says with a shrug. "It means 'my big sister.' My dad thought it sounded good for a CB handle. White people always think Indian words sound ancient and cool."

"Na-*bi*," Bucketmouth repeats, something familiar to his voice—no, to his mis-pronunciation? "It does sound pretty all right."

"*Nah* Bee," Harper corrects, just like her mom used to do with her dad, but it doesn't matter. Not at this stage of things. She's not her mom, and—

Harper stands all at once, her head thunking into the ceiling, her scalp scraping, hair snagging. She smooths it back, holds it tight to her scalp.

Why in God's green earth is she thinking of her dad now?

Bucketmouth feels his way down, is close enough to smell now. Close enough to smell like blood.

"Who?" Harper says about that blood, resigned.

"I never ate your boyfriend's finger," Bucketmouth confesses. "I didn't like being nineteen even when I *was* nineteen. Remember I was saying how, if I was smart, I'd hide emergency rations up and down the highway?"

Harper shakes her head no, no, please.

"It's three years ago," he says. "Winter, but between snows. 80's open for once, so all the trucks that were stuck in the barn, they're out and galloping, you know how it is. One of them picks up a lonely traveler who has to be cold, limping there on the shoulder like his right foot's frozen in the boot. Call it Christmas spirit."

"No, please," Harper says, her eyes heating up in a way she promised herself she wasn't going to let happen.

Bucketmouth takes her wrist in his big hand to *make* her listen.

"Things go the . . . what I guess you would call the *predictable* way," he says. "At least, predictable if I'm the one thumbing a ride. Is it a crime if a mountain lion kills a pretty deer just to not starve? That's all it was, Big Sister. Never mind if that deer has a spotted fawn or two back at the homestead, all—"

"*No!*" Harper says, trying to pull her arm back.

"What you don't understand," Bucketmouth says, "it's that I either take someone in my signature fashion or I'm Mr. Bloodyface. And nobody picks up hitchhikers with bleeding faces, believe me. And then I really do get frostbite."

"Please, just—"

"Anyway, I still had a few days with the face I was wearing, so I stashed a bit of the old man by a certain utility pole, one just up the road from here. For times of emergency, like tonight. Maybe you knew this gentleman of the road?"

With that he pulls her glowing wrist to his face, and under that green glow is, is: her *dad*, after all these years, all her praying, all the deals she's made with the world, in secret.

Harper jerks and pulls and kicks.

Bucketmouth smiles, drinking this in.

"You wanted to know why I didn't finish it back there when I could have," he says. "It was for this, Big Sister. Little girl. That trucker who picked me up, once he got comfortable enough with his new, ahem, traveling companion, he showed me school photos of his two beautiful daughters. Had them right there on the back of his visor. I recognized you the moment when I stepped up from that big red car, Harper, all the way back in Laramie. You could say I'm what you might call *good with faces*. And, damned if I didn't know exactly where this night could take us, if we did it right. And hasn't it all been worth it, for this reunion you never thought would happen in the real world? It's so rare I get to participate in the little rituals like this. It's always bite this, kill him, kill her too, run here, hide that, burn this place down, drive drive drive. You miss out on the normal parts of life, though. And you start to actually miss them. They're boring, sure, but they make it all complete, like. Without them, it's . . . it's like you lose your tether to the human world, does that make sense?"

"*Fuck you!*" Harper screams, pushing him into the west wall of the tunnel. "You're not him!"

"Of course not, of course not," Bucketmouth says, coming forward to hold her by the shoulders, offer his fake consolation. "Nobody could ever replace a father, and I would never presume to. But I did think to bury his commercial license along with his pinky finger, so, yeah. I might deliver a load or three, these next couple of weeks. Our little interaction, this, you and me here, it's going to last me for a while, I think. Give me a lot to . . . to think about. I'm going to miss you, Big Sister. Or, I mean—former Big Sister?"

"What are you saying?" Harper asks, her face going even colder, her heart pausing between beats to listen.

Bucketmouth holds his right hand out, showing the topside and then the palm, like just seeing them himself.

Slowly, Harper guides her green glow over.

Blood. His hand is black with it, along with long strands of matted hair. The blood and hair go up his sleeve, into the camo.

"Your mom actually hit me," he says, touching a place on his jaw. "*Hard*, I mean. I think she thought I was actually him, coming back at the most random time. Just sitting in the backseat of that eggshell Buick."

"No no no," Harper says, falling to her knees.

"I didn't know what you might have told her," Bucketmouth says with a shrug like he regrets this just as much as she does. "Police will listen to a hysterical mother years before they'll listen to her runaway daughter. You left me no choice there, sorry."

"But, but . . . Meg?"

"Ah, *little* sister, yes," Bucketmouth says. "A dilemma, I agree. Actually, she's hogtied down at the end of the tunnel, gagged pretty tight, too. Out of the way of any headlights. I wasn't sure if she was a problem to be solved or a bargaining chip, so I hedged my bets, figured I could solve her later if I didn't spend her now."

Harper's watching that end of the tunnel now.

"Meg!" she calls.

No answer. She pushes away to go there, see for herself, but Bucketmouth has her by the upper arm already.

"Like I was saying," he says, and makes his non-bloody hand into a blade, holds it tight across his own mouth to show, "I gagged her tight. And you could say I've got some experience there."

"Let me see her!"

"What would I get from lying?" he says back to her. "I didn't lie about your mom just now, when I could have, when it would have made you more . . . *docile*, if you didn't know the truth."

"You want me to keep having hope, so you can crush it."

He shrugs, says, "You've got an evil mind there, Harper. I like it, I like it."

"How would she even have been a bargaining chip?" Harper says. "What could I have that you can't just take?"

"I thought you might have found your way to a gun," he says, and pats his chest with both hands. "I'm charming, kind of wily, know my way around these roads, but I'm not bulletproof."

"You're a monster is what you are."

"Said the deer to the mountain lion. That's not what the mountain lion says to itself, though. The mountain lion just says 'I'm hungry.' Guess I better go do what I do."

"What do you *want*?" Harper says, offering herself. "Take me for her, there's your bargain, your deal. I'm the one you want."

"But you said it yourself," Bucketmouth tells her. "I've already *got* you."

"I—your stupid name," Harper says. "I know where it's from, what it means. You don't have that, do you?"

"Ah yes," Bucketmouth says. "That niggling little mystery."

"If I tell you, Meg's safe?"

"Got to see what I'm buying, I think. Be bad business otherwise."

"It's what truckers call someone who won't shut up on the CB," Harper says. "It means you're someone who loves the sound of their own voice."

Bucketmouth lets this settle, finally looks up to her, nodding appreciation.

"It fits, doesn't it?" he says. "Thank you. I wasn't expecting everything to tie up so neatly tonight. Now if only I could figure out what 'band camp' meant to you and yours."

"How do you know about that?" Harper asks before she can stop herself.

"Your boyfriend was saying it when I was . . . cinching him to that tow truck for the big . . . you know." He scrapes his right hand down over the road of his left. "What does it mean to you?"

"It's where we kissed for the first time," Harper lies, hoping it can become true as well. That Dillon's somehow waiting for her by cabin 6, his clarinet hidden behind—no, drums, he would only ever bang on drums, and never with the music the rest of the band was playing, always to his own irrepressible beat.

But then his face scrapes away, the nasal cavities bare, the sinus cavity open like a mucousy geode.

"I'm sorry," Bucketmouth says, touching her cheek with the fingertips of his right hand. Leaving blood, probably.

"No you're not," Harper tells him. "When you're done with me, you're going to kill Meg. If she's not dead already. You don't make it as long as you have by leaving survivors. I'm not stupid."

He shrugs, guilty as charged, his eyes locked on hers, like drinking this up.

"While we're being honest," he says. "That big white tank I set the fire under back at that podunk gas station? It was empty. Been empty for years."

Translation: she should have hit him in the face with the butt of that fire extinguisher. She *could* have, and maybe ended it right there.

"You know what?" Harper says. "Do what you want. It doesn't matter. You can't take away the—the good parts. You can kill Dillon in front of me like that, but I still remember the first time he held my hand. And my mom, you'll never be as tough as she was. And you don't even deserve to wear that face."

Harper reaches out to scratch it off but he catches her glowing green wrist, stops her.

"I really do regret this," he says, his other hand popping a knife open. "I'll make it quick. You deserve that. You've earned it."

"*Meg, run!*" Harper screams, her voice filling the whole tunnel.

"Don't worry about the ropes!" Bucketmouth calls after in Harper-falsetto. "Just shake them off, they're no big deal, he doesn't even know how to tie knots! Because he's never done anything like this before!"

This is hilarious to him.

While he's laughing, Harper brings her knee up with everything she has, to drive his balls up into the back of his throat, make him choke on them, but he sees it coming, sidesteps, and—

"What is *this*?" he says, holding her in place but squatting down.

The baby food jar. Harper must have tinked it over when she stepped into him.

She tries to kick it away, deny him this last morsel at least, but he sees that coming as well, doesn't even have to look up to keep the eyeballs safe.

"You saved one for me?" he says, letting the cinnamon settle so he can see who it is.

"Not on purpose," Harper tells him.

"*No!*" he says then, for the first time truly offended by something, looking fast from the jar to her. "You're not supposed to mix them! God, no, that—*you don't mix them!*"

Harper considers this, shuffling back through this whole night in an instant, through everything he's said, trying to pick out something she can maybe use. There's nothing about mixing or not mixing body parts, though. Just . . . rule one: no Indians. Rule two: nobody who's in a bad-to-him state. Three: any part'll do, not just tongues. Four: cinnamon because it tastes good. The cinnamon and tongues and Indians don't matter right now, though, do they?

The other one, though . . .

"The other jar cracked," Harper says, "it was leaking that cinnamon toast water all over the seat, so I poured them together. Sorry if I ruined the shit out of them."

She makes another stab at the jar, trying but not trying to slap it down.

"No no no," he's still saying, curling away, protecting the eyeballs. "If they—if they stay like this too long, it ruins them both.

They mix together, and you end up looking all like . . . droopy, melty, hangdog."

"Little Preparation H under the eyes," Harper tells him.

"You laugh," he says, looking up to her, "but that works. But—it doesn't matter. They have to mix together for more than just two or three hours. We're talking days. Seasons. These are still good, if we can get them apart again." He casts around for some other place to stash one of these precious eyeballs.

"You said earlier you thought I could make it out on the road," Harper tells him, watching him close to see if this registers.

He nods, nods, isn't really paying attention, is frantic about preserving these stupid eyeballs, about restarting his precious little stash. But then he hears what she's said, looks up to her.

"I think I can make it out there too," Harper says. "And you also said there's more of your kind than anybody knows, because none of us normals ever . . . ever do what you did in that tunnel. We never have to see what we're really made of. What we can *be*, if we just . . . take that first bite."

He nods again, slower. All she's doing is repeating what he's already told her. Confirming it. Reminding him of it.

"Let Meg go," she says then, "if she's even really alive down there. Let her go, promise you won't do anything to her, and—and I'll try."

She nods to the jar to show what she means.

"*Are* there girl ones of you?" she asks.

"I—I don't know," Bucketmouth says, in wonder.

"How does your kind procreate?" she asks.

"We're cuckoo birds," he says. "We grow up in your houses, your living rooms, your breakfast nooks. And then one day we bite into the right piece of meat and everything changes."

Harper shrugs, smiles, says, "I was running away when you found me. I can keep running away, with you to teach me what's what."

"But you hate me."

"Because I'm not *like* you." Harper looks to one end of the tunnel then the other, and back to Bucketmouth, having to scream and scream in her head that this isn't her dad she's lying to. "But maybe I can be, right?"

Bucketmouth looks at the two eyeballs swimming in their cinnamon water.

"You're trying to . . . I don't know," he says. "Trick me somehow."

"What do you have to lose?" Harper asks. "How can it be a trick? I eat that"—she gags a little, gets it under control—"and I either turn into whoever that is or I don't, and we're back where we are right now."

He nods to himself, thinking this through, it looks like.

"Negotiation phase," he says. "Bargaining."

"Either way, you win," Harper says. "If I'm not like you, then you've tortured me more, made me eat an eyeball."

He kind of likes that.

"You'd turn into a—into a guy," he says.

"Always wanted to pee standing up," Harper says right back. "Maybe not get whistled at trying to walk across the damn parking lot."

"And she goes free?" Bucketmouth says, tipping his head to the idea of Meg.

"Now if she goes to the cops, she's turning them on to *me*," Harper says.

"If you change."

"But you've got to eat with me," she says, stepping in closer. "I don't want to go through this alone my first time."

"This face," he says. "It's—it's not even thirty minutes old."

"You look like my dad," Harper says, and nods to the jar. "Anything's better than that, if we're walking out of here together."

He smiles a bit at last, says, "That was just for shock value.

Guess I've used that up already right?" He raises the jar to eye level again, studies its contents. "And it would be a waste to have these and not use them . . ."

"So do we have a deal?" Harper asks. "I do this, Meg's free."

"If you're *not* like me," Bucketmouth says, watching the end of the tunnel as well, "and—and I have to do what I do to make sure you don't go whispering about me to the state police, then you won't know what happens to her, will you?"

"At least there's a chance this way," Harper says. "At least there's a sliver of hope. I didn't come down here to die. I came down here to figure out how to live."

Bucketmouth paces, studies the eyeballs some more, whips his head back to Harper to say something but doesn't.

"I knew you were different," he says at last, excited about this prospect.

"Let's see how different," Harper says. "Must get lonely out there all by yourself, right?"

"You'll try to kill me, first chance," he says. "I took your mom away. Your dad. Your best boyfriend."

"But I won't come at you before you show me how it all works," Harper says back with a smile. "If I'm going to survive, I need to know what you know."

"If it takes."

"If it takes."

"'Silver-Tongued Devil!'" he says all at once. "*That's* what they should be calling me up there"—the interstate. "It's rude to just . . . do what I do with no pre-amble, isn't it? You can't talk a person to death, no, but you can talk them right up to it."

"Liquid lungs," Harper says.

"What?"

"Motormouth, verbal diarrhea, ratchet jaw, a real rattle trap. Babbles like a brook. Flies in his brainpan—"

"Because his mouth is always open," Bucketmouth completes,

smiling so wide now. "At least word of me's making the rounds, right? Worst thing is to be ignored."

"Are we doing this or not?" Harper asks, stopping the bullshit.

"I shouldn't," Bucketmouth says with her father's mouth. "Three times in one night. It's gonna hurt in the morning, believe you me. But—hell. Yes, deal. Your sister will be safe."

"How long does it take to know?" Harper asks.

"With these, how old they are, 'aged' I should say . . . about ten minutes," he says. "Your face starts to itch, like, on the *back*-side. Like tiny bugs are crawling all around back there. But you can't cough them out, can't scratch them away. That's how you know it's working."

"Guess I'm not just running away from home anymore," Harper says, delicately taking the baby food jar from him. "This is running away from myself, isn't it?"

Bucketmouth nods, his eyes watching hers so close, for the slightest indication of deceit. Moving slow, she twists the top off, the cloying sharp scent of cinnamon infusing their air.

"Preference?" she says, ready to pluck an eyeball up.

"What color are my eyes now?" he asks.

"Didn't you look in the mirror?"

"It was dark."

Harper leans forward, looks into her dad's blue-blue eyes, says, "Brown. Dark. My mom used to call him Brown-Eyed Handsome Man, after that song."

"Give me the other one then," he says, and tilts his head back for her to feed him.

Harper gets the brown eye out first, dollops it back in, fishes the Thunderbird Lady's up, careful not to burst it. It's slimy and it feels somehow uninflated, and is leaving clear slime on her fingertips.

"Sure?" she says.

"Hit me," he says, and tilts his head back farther, opens his mouth, then comes back up, mister paranoid, taking the jar from her, shaking the eye left behind up. It's brown.

He nods, lets his mouth drop open and watches the blue eyeball all the way past his lips, his hand guiding Harper's wrist the whole way to be sure there's no funny business.

"Watch this," he says, talking thick, and ovals his lips, giving Harper a window on his tongue smushing the eyeball forward through his teeth, the blue disc of color coming slow past his left canine.

He slurps it back in, swallows it without chewing.

"Like . . . you know how you can separate an egg white from the yolk?" he says. "This is like doing that to an oyster. All you're left with is the protein, none of the taste."

"Why did you—" Harper says, unable to get her words to follow her thoughts. "With Dillon, why did you cut his finger off, then?"

"And not his eye, you mean?"

Harper nods.

"Are you stalling?" he asks.

"Maybe," Harper says.

"It's your first time," Bucketmouth says. "Maybe . . . this might help."

He takes the jar, shakes it for the remaining eyeball and pinches it out delicately, inserts it into his mouth and bites through it with pornographic slowness, the pupil bulging out like a cartoon. Then he mushes it between his lips, keeping all the juices right there. He takes Harper by the back of her head, pulls her into a forced kiss, passing the jellied eyeball from his lips to hers—from her *dad's* lips to hers.

Because he can probably still throw his eyeball up if he figures this out, Harper lets this happen, her mind screaming, her fingers straightening hard, her throat trying to gag, her soul shriveling up in the corner.

She comes down, her saliva rushing.

"Swallow, swallow," Bucketmouth says, and massages her throat with both his thumbs, his long fingers cradling her head.

Harper counts to three in her head, closes her eyes and swallows hard, trying not to think about egg yolks or oysters or that clear sac she saw a kitten born dead in once, and never told anyone about.

They sit down facing each other, their legs parallel but opposite, their backs against different sides of the tunnel.

"Ten minutes," Harper says.

Bucketmouth wipes his lips, nods, watching her.

"About one good cigarette," he says, patting his chest, not finding his pack.

"I can go get one?" Harper says, setting her hands to push up.

He applauds the effort, shakes his head no.

"Was that a dog I walked over back there?" he leans forward to ask, like he doesn't want the dog to hear.

"I think it was a coyote maybe," Harper says. "Is Meg really out there?"

"Scout's honor," Bucketmouth says.

Harper nods, feels her gorge rising. Bucketmouth leans forward to pat her back but she waves him off, gets through it herself, keeping her lips pressed tight together.

"It'll—it'll be better being someone else," she says when she can. "The girl I was, her mother was killed by this mad dog killer on the road."

"Her dad too!" Bucketmouth adds, so chipper about it.

"And her best boyfriend."

"Zhzhzhzh," Bucketmouth says, trying to make the sound of Dillon rubbing away on the asphalt, and then miming it out again with his hands.

"That was pretty fucking brutal," Harper says.

"Life on the road is hard," Bucketmouth says with a shrug. "Especially *on* the road like that . . ."

He tries not to laugh but it spurts through anyway.

"So why fingers?" she asks.

"Not always," Bucketmouth says. "Don't know where they might have been."

"I found his in the parking lot."

"And you didn't figure it out then?"

"That you had an *extra* human finger on you, that you'd dug up on the way there? That you would get some big rush from eating my dead dad's finger across the table from me?" Harper says. "No, I didn't jump to that obvious conclusion."

He laughs, is loving this.

"Fingers, eyes, ears, it doesn't matter," he says. "Nipples are good, kind of rubbery like octopus, but I never go below the belt. This one guy I—in Kansas. He had *milk* in his"—he touches his chest—"Can you believe that? It was sweet, and tasted sort of . . . *blue*, I guess."

Harper breathes deep, trying not to start the gag cycle again.

"But, you're smart," Bucketmouth says, nudging her knee with his. "You should have figured it out already."

"I'm not thinking too well right now," Harper says.

"Maybe it's working, then?" he says, leaning in to look into her face. "I take the fingers because I like them to watch me eat a piece of them. If I take one of their eyes, well. Then they can't watch so well."

"Figured it'd be something like that," Harper says.

"I am as the good Lord made me," Bucketmouth says.

"Got any beef jerky on you?" Harper asks back, trying not to sound like she's stretching this out. "We're going to need the calories, right?"

"The highway's full of snackfood items," he says in a corny PSA voice.

Harper smiles a drunk smile, leans her head back, counts to a hundred and eighty in her head, which is three minutes more. When she looks again, he's just watching her.

"You really are glorious," he says. "You're—if this works out, then you're the perfect one for me. I could never change into you."

"Even if you did women."

He nods.

"Why are Indians immune?" she asks.

"Not immune," he says. "Just . . . they're kind of like indigestion."

"But why?"

"I've thought about that," Bucketmouth says, eyes closed. "The ones of you still around, you made it through smallpox, right? When I got that vaccination as a kid, my mom says I nearly died."

"Your mom?"

"I don't know if she was like this or not," he says. "She never . . ." He opens his hand over the jar.

"It didn't even taste like anything," Harper says. "Just cinnamon."

"People taste the idea, I think," Bucketmouth says. "I mean, they don't actually *try*, but when they think about it, it's the idea that grosses them out. They judge without having any basis to judge."

"How long?"

"Four, five more minutes? It's not exact."

"I think I can feel something," Harper says, holding her hand out, spreading her fingers.

"It's in your face," Bucketmouth says, touching his own.

"You can feel it already?"

He nods.

"So it's started?"

"Started," he says, lost in the painful pleasure of it.

Harper touches her own face, is terrified of any tingling. Which of course makes her skin come alive.

She jerks forward, all ten of her fingers to her face now.

"Really?" Bucketmouth says.

Harper looks to him, her eyes heating up, and honestly doesn't know.

"It has been a lonely existence," he says, leaning back to luxuriate in this moment.

"Will I remember who I am?" Harper says.

"Can't forget," he says, flourishing his fingers over his own face like magic. "You've seen this before," he adds then, "but it kind of . . . accelerates the process, I don't know why. Making room, I guess. Like a snake shedding its skin."

He angles his head over to tighten his neck skin and feels around for a grip on the hinge of his jaw, peel this face off like the last one, and the one before that. But . . . his fingers aren't working? He looks at them like they're traitors, and then tries to snap, manages it once, can't get it to happen a second time.

"What is it?" Harper asks.

"My . . . I don't know," Bucketmouth says, trying to stand up against the curved concrete wall, his legs weak as well. Not his own anymore. He pinches at his thigh, pinches and twists, evidently isn't getting any pain fed up to his nerve centers.

He slumps back down, can't even get his hands up to his face now.

"What did you do?" he asks, his words slurring.

Harper stands, crosses to him, kneels down face to face.

"Breaker, breaker," she says into her right hand, her left cupped over the side of his head. "Anybody out there with ears on, maybe knows what would happen if certain mad dog killers were to, say, eat a part from someone who was paralyzed, come back? Anybody know what eating the meat from a person with a spinal injury might do to someone like him, over?"

His head flops over weakly, drool leaking from the corner of his mouth.

"Over," Harper adds, and does the dead key sound herself, drops that imaginary mic.

"Who, who?" he says.

"You've got some time," Harper says, looking on the ground to his left. "Figure it out. You're smart."

She finally finds the knife.

She pushes the point into the flesh of his forearm, blood welling up all around it. He doesn't jerk from the pain. He can't jerk. There isn't any pain.

She turns the knife over so the edge is down, drags it along his arm all the way to the hand, leaving a long line that opens like a lipless mouth.

"That's so the dogs will smell you," she says. "Or the coyotes. I don't know. Did you know a turtle will scavenge? They do. It's fucking weird, man."

His eyes are cloudy now.

"But maybe you just lie here for a few days," she says, angling her face over to line theirs up. "Sun won't get to you down here, dry you up. And if you figure out how to make a noise—are you trying right now?—who knows, if you figure out how, maybe all the truckers up there will stop, turn their engines off, stick their heads out the window, figure out where you are."

She squats down right before him, says, "But probably not, yeah."

His breath quickens.

"I'm just going to go down there"—the mouth of the tunnel—"see if my sister's really there or not, cool?"

His breath gets even more frantic, his eyes wet.

She watches him, drinking every drop of this up. "She better be there, too," she says at last. "I've . . . I never told you about when I was fifteen, did I? This was when my dad didn't come back from his Tacoma run. And then he kept on not coming back. I went up to the top of this one apartment building, told myself I could close my eyes and listen hard enough to hear through all the other trucks. But I never did, right? And when I came home the next morning, my mom made me waffles, and her hands were shaking." Harper wipes her eyes, doesn't let that stop this from happening all over again. "I think—I think she'd been sitting in the car all night, talking to him on the radio. To the idea of him. And, and *he* was the one who made waffles for us. But now Mom was doing it. And, and she remembered. When she put the syrup on, she did it like—like clock hands, with little dots for all the numbers, the same as he always did, and two lines for what time it was. We sat there and we ate those waffles and we didn't say one goddamn thing, and ever since that morning, it was . . . I don't know if you know what this is like or not. But you can't, can you? You were never a little girl. Wait, were you?"

He doesn't answer, just wheels his eyes all around.

"Until then, *I* was, anyway," Harper goes on. "I thought the world was . . . fair, I guess you'd say. That daddies always came home. But, know what? That day, that morning, part of me hid inside, I think. The little girl part. The me that still hoped, that still knew he was out there somewhere, that he had amnesia, that he'd tried to save somebody from bad people and was all caught up in that, was just trying to fight his way back."

Harper stares up into the curved top of the tunnel, says, "I came up with so many scenarios of what could have happened, what could *be* happening. I couldn't even watch movies at the theater in a normal way anymore. I always knew that rig I was hearing rumble past outside, that it was him, that I was missing my chance."

She settles her eyes back on Bucketmouth.

"I need to thank you now," she says, staring right into his soul. "Until now, I haven't been able to—to move forward? To keep growing up like I should have, I guess. Because I wanted to still be the girl he would recognize when he came back. You can't understand this, I know. But I've got to say it." She leans forward, his head in both her hands, and she puts her lips right to his forehead, says, crying now, "Goodbye, Daddy. I'm sorry you didn't ever make it home. I waited and I waited for you, but now I don't have to anymore. I know you're somewhere with Mom now, if Indians and white guys get to go to the same place."

With that she kisses her dad's forehead, keeps her lips there, trying to make this last and last, and at the end of it she wrenches his head around hard, snapping the neck.

"That's just in case," she says, standing, and, walking toward the mouth of the tunnel then—it's not quite a light, but it's better than this—she stops, the sole of her sneaker not all the way down. There's a caterpillar under it, stopped too, waiting.

Harper considers, considers, then swallows hard, puts her foot down somewhere else.

Two steps later she's running, her sister's name on her lips.

ACKNOWLEDGMENTS

I know Interstate 80 going across Wyoming better than I really want to. In 2015, when Lance Olsen was teaching somewhere else, or maybe galavanting around the world, I taught a semester for him at the University of Utah in Salt Lake City. My kids were still sort of young, but one of them was just old enough to drive—by a few days, I think? Maybe a month. Anyway, we loaded our whole little house into a storage unit, into my office on campus at CU Boulder, and the essentials we were going to need for the fall we loaded into a 1972 Cheyenne, into a 1969 C-10 four-speed, and into our Subaru. The two pickups had their beds mounded and tarped over, and, being just half-tons, they were sitting down on their frames, about. I have a photograph somewhere of our little convoy. Neither truck looks that road-worthy, and the new driver of us was driving the Subaru—the one that kept between the lines the best. This wasn't the first time I was shooting west on 80—the first time had been in the blowing snow in a rental car, with my sister Jenny in the passenger seat, trusting me, still a Texas driver then, to be able to do this—but this was the first time I could see this Wyoming over the ditches.

It's the one I tried to write into *Killer on the Road*.

Over that fall, I ended up driving back and forth between Salt Lake City, Utah and Boulder, Colorado more than I intended, and then, in the snow again, probably about February, my son and I came back to Utah to get the Cheyenne I'd had to leave there. It was a beautiful truck, even had those sport mirrors, all the original trim, stock wheels and hubcaps, but man was it contrary: fuel lines rotted from sitting too long, carburetor that had come from the factory with the wrong jets, and on and on. It wasn't really the best idea to try to shoot 80 between storms in a halfway working truck, but we did it all the same, my son following in the trusty Subaru. A few hundred miles shy of home, the transmission started to slip, then grind. I'd pull over, let it cool, get a few more miles out of it, and like this we got to Cheyenne. Seemed fitting, being in the truck I was in. Had to pull it the rest of the way home, then pay more for a rebuilt transmission than I'd paid for the whole truck. So it goes, right? So it always goes, with the trucks you keep your heart in.

All that time sitting in the ditch waiting for the transmission to cool, though, I could feel this novel uncoiling inside me. I didn't have Bucketmouth yet, but I sort of had Harper, I think, in that I'd already written Nona in *Demon Theory*, Izzy in *The Last Final Girl*, Denorah in *Good Indians*, Char from *Babysitter*, and I was soon to write Jade Daniels. Harper, to me, she fits right in with them. Get her into a corner, I mean, she'll show her teeth, fight her way out, and then fight the whole world while she's at it, just because.

These are the kind of people I prefer to believe in. They're also where I keep my heart.

As for where Bucketmouth finally came from, it's all the rest stops along 80, it's the big rigs slamming past, it's the gas stations out there like they're fading in from 1982. Bucketmouth comes from the loneliness and wind, the cold and the vastness. He comes from "Wyoming" is what I'm saying. Seriously, go drive 80 if it's not closed for wind and snow. 70 down here in Colorado's a gamey proposition most of the time, but 80, it'll plain eat you.

That's where I get Bucketmouth from—that feeling, standing alongside the road, that I could just disappear into all of this.

80 wasn't done with me, either. My son ended up at the University of Utah a few years later, so I was making that drive again, and again, but it was charged differently, now. When you're going to a kid of yours, that changes everything, doesn't it? It did for me. And it made coming back east so much more difficult. I felt like I was in some weird space between two homes, and the result was that 80 became a sort of liminal, weird space for me.

I haven't been all the way up and down it now for probably five years now, I guess? It tracks; I think I wrote *Killer* in . . . 2018? Ellen Datlow had asked me for a novella after *Mapping the Interior* did what it did, and since it only took four days to pull together, I figured, sure, yeah, I've got four days, why not do another novella right fast? Easier said than done. Next time I looked up, it was four weeks later, and I had either this novel or *The Babysitter Lives*. So I sat down to write a novella, please, and . . . four weeks later, it was either this one or *Babysitter*. So, I guess because of that "third time's a charm" lie, I tried one more time, and, bam: *The Only Good Indians* at the end of the next month. I was failing hard to write a novella. But then, finally, I managed to do one: *Night of the Mannequins*. Phew. Sawyer Grimes saved me. I mean, in the good way, not the way he tries to "save" his friends.

So, no, I haven't been back down 80 lately, but neither has 80 left me. I've been down a lot of bad-idea roads, done some pure-stupid drives—on the reservation once, deep in a whiteout in November, my dad drove him and me around the barrier keeping people concerned with living off of Looking Glass, easily the most dangerous blacktop on the rez, and we left our tire tracks on all that deep snowpack for the next hour, just creeping along, somehow never sliding off the mountain like we were supposed to—but there's something meaner about 80. If you've tried it when it's angry and indifferent, you'll know. It's always better to get a motel room, wait it out. Or maybe just go up to 90, or down to 70. Or just go home, keep living.

In Tony Earley's story "The Prophet from Jupiter," he says that "in North Carolina, even in the mountains, it takes more than a month of your life to live through August." That's how 80 is: white-knuckling it through a storm, it takes years off your life that you can never get back. But you're happy just to still have a life, too. Many don't.

This is the interstate where Dark Mill South left his victims propped behind snow fences, facing north.

Chances are I'll go back there again, in story. 80's got its hooks in me, for better or for worse. And, in November 2019, it nearly kept me, when I slid off the road just north of Casper, had some unpleasant adventures in the ditch at sixty miles per hour—wild enough that a lot of truckers stopped in wonder, all aghast and laughing and looking at me from different angles, because this wasn't the kind of thing people live through. I very nearly didn't. I don't think I should have, really, and I don't know why I did.

I miss the truck that happened in. It was a 2004—the first one of mine with a CD player. I felt so modern having one at last, never mind that all the rich high schoolers in Midland, Texas already had CD players in the late eighties. Not me. I had to wait until I sold those two old Chevrolets, got that 2004 FX4 off an old man, and cleaned all his shell casings out from under the seat.

So, 80, it's a drive I know.

As for all the trucking stuff in *Killer*, though, man, where to even start with that. One of my stepdads was a trucker, some months—Darren in *Mongrels* drinks his same strawberry wine coolers—and I'd go tooling around with him on short runs, get to know the road from a rocking chair like I'd need to, for this book. Only longer run I ever went on was with my granddad on my dad's side's twin brother, out in . . . Sacramento, California I think it was? Somewhere close to Yosemite. We were hanging out there one summer when I was fourteen, and it was so weird for me, this great uncle's face matching the pictures of my granddad, which was pretty much all I had to go on for him. This great uncle's job was making runs into Yosemite every night, to resupply their concessions, I think? I went with him this time, high up in the cab, him telling me stories about mountain lions he'd seen, me just soaking all this in. I was wearing a choker that summer, so I could be a real Indian. A choker and a headband, and I tried hard to not smile very much, so everyone would know I was tough. I was probably really too old—and way too tough—to have to try not to cry when my great uncle handed me a ham sandwich he'd brought for me that had surprise-mustard on it, but . . . well, I'm not proud. I'll probably still cry if I get mustard in my mouth.

Darren would too.

But, talking trucking stuff, I'd grown up on *Smokey and the Bandit*, *B.J. and the Bear*, *Convoy*, C. W. McCall, Red Sovine, so . . . isn't that all the research you really need to write a novel like this?

Turns out, no.

After *The Buffalo Hunter Hunter*, this is probably the novel I had to do the most digging to write. Just because all the trucking stuff, it had to be at least close to right. While writing it, I did find a place I could ride my bike to that was stacked with tractors and trailers, anyway. I'd pedal there, crawl all over them, trying to understand how this and that worked, always ready to run if anyone saw me out there. And the videos I watched, man. So, so many. Probably the most helpful text was Finn Murphy's excellent and fascinating *The Long Haul: A Trucker's Tales of Life on the Road*. I think about that one a lot, still. There's a dude in there who never sleeps. He's maybe the most interesting person I've ever chanced across on the page. Well, him and Tom Bombadil.

Anyway, though I wrote *Good Indians* the last of *Killer* and *Babysitter* and *Mannequins*, it came out first of all of them. And then suddenly I was on this publishing waterslide: a trilogy, a standalone slasher, *Babysitter*, and a historical, epistolary vampire novel three months ago. Along the way, though, my heart sort of broke for *Killer*. It was because King's *The Outsider* came out. Even worse? *The Outsider* is flat-out amazing, is easily my favorite of his over the last . . . twenty years, say? I could live in this novel about, yes, a monster-of-legend who can taste the blood of someone and then, you know, become them.

It's good that all those other books of mine hit the shelves before *Killer*, I think. Who can compete with King? And, if people think I'm just aping *The Outsider* here, well . . . at least I had a good model, yes?

But I should also thank all the road movies I'm such a fool for. *Forsaken*, *Joy Ride*, *Road Games*, *Roadside Prophets*, even *Cannonball Run*. *The Hitcher* of course. And I consider the two *Reekers* to be road movies too. And there's so many more I keep close to my heart. I think why I'm so forever smitten with road movies, horror or not, it's that the cars and trucks and rigs and motorcycles always get some good camera time, some good—on the page—description. That's maybe my favorite thing with writing: getting to talk cars and trucks. One of the publications I'm proudest of, I mean, it's in *Street Trucks*.

Too, though, and I'm not exactly sure the how of this, but . . . back in, I don't know, 2015, maybe? My son and me are up on the rez hunting with my dad, and there's just been this huge snowfall, so hardly anybody's able to get up the logging roads into the high timber, where the elk might be. This year, though, I had this stupid-tall Jeep Wrangler with monster tires on it, so of course I figured we could crawl our way up the mountain.

Maybe a half-mile up, those oversized tires turned out to be balloons floating on top of the snow, pretty much. They threw pretty white roostertails everywhere, but we were stuck, deep. We got out, dug under this and that tire, jammed branches and logs everywhere, and, finally, my dad said he would stand in front

ACKNOWLEDGMENTS

of the Jeep's aftermarket bumper, rock it while I went back and forth from first gear to reverse, and maybe we'd get lucky.

It wasn't a bad idea, exactly. Or, it wasn't bad until, just like we were hoping for, the Jeep's spinning tires finally caught enough to launch it forward. Great, wonderful. Except my dad was standing right there. That big ugly bumper launched him back into the trees, like off his feet and cartoon-flying through the air, and I thought for sure he had to be broken—he wasn't, but he wasn't particularly pleased with me, either. Watching that bumper hit him, though, fold him over, throw him up and back, that was so clear in my head, writing *Killer*, here. You can imagine what it's like to pop someone with thousands of pounds of moving metal like that, but until you've actually done it, and to someone you care about it, I'm not sure you really understand it.

Sorry, Dad?

We did winch ourselves out, finally, didn't have to sleep on the mountain that night, which was good, and I'm not trying to say here that I'm glad it happened, hitting you like that. But, too, I'm not sure I write this novel if it doesn't happen?

Thanks also to James Andrew Cowell here at CU, for the one little bit of Arapaho in here. Thanks to Court Merrigan, one of my little brothers' friends, for some indirect help. Thanks to Paisley Rekdal, for the same thing I thanked her for in *The Buffalo Hunter Hunter*. Thanks also to Jim Shooter, for having Captain America and Wolverine going into this falling-down compound in *Secret Wars*, to free the prisoner bad guys, keep this huge building from killing them. When Harper went back for all those truckers after she'd accidentally lit their parking area on fire . . . she was Cap, she was Wolvie. I don't have that moment without Jim Shooter.

Thanks also, as ever, to BJ Robbins, for getting this to Joe Monti, who, as usual, identified the weak parts, didn't tell me how to fix them, just that they needed some fixing. Thanks to Caroline

THE BABYSITTER LIVES

THE BABYSITTER LIVES

STEPHEN GRAHAM JONES

SAGA PRESS

LONDON · NEW YORK · TORONTO
AMSTERDAM/ANTWERP · NEW DELHI · SYDNEY/MELBOURNE

AN IMPRINT OF SIMON & SCHUSTER, LLC

1230 AVENUE OF THE AMERICAS, NEW YORK, NEW YORK 10020

For more than 100 years, Simon & Schuster has championed authors and the stories they create. By respecting the copyright of an author's intellectual property, you enable Simon & Schuster and the author to continue publishing exceptional books for years to come. We thank you for supporting the author's copyright by purchasing an authorized edition of this book.

No amount of this book may be reproduced or stored in any format, nor may it be uploaded to any website, database, language-learning model, or other repository, retrieval, or artificial intelligence system without express permission. All rights reserved. Inquiries may be directed to Simon & Schuster, 1230 Avenue of the Americas, New York, NY 10020 or permissions@simonandschuster.com.

This book is a work of fiction. Any references to historical events, real people, or real places are used fictitiously. Other names, characters, places, and events are products of the author's imagination, and any resemblance to actual events or places or persons, living or dead, is entirely coincidental.

The Babysitter Lives copyright © 2022 by Stephen Graham Jones
This title was previously published in 2022 in audio format by Simon & Schuster Audio
Killer on the Road copyright © 2025 by Stephen Graham Jones

All rights reserved, including the right to reproduce this book or portions thereof in any form whatsoever. For information, address Saga Press Subsidiary Rights Department, 1230 Avenue of the Americas, New York, NY 10020.

First Saga Press trade paperback edition July 2025

SAGA PRESS and colophon are trademarks of Simon & Schuster, LLC

Simon & Schuster strongly believes in freedom of expression and stands against censorship in all its forms. For more information, visit BooksBelong.com.

For information about special discounts for bulk purchases, please contact Simon & Schuster Special Sales at 1-866-506-1949 or business@simonandschuster.com.

The Simon & Schuster Speakers Bureau can bring authors to your live event. For more information or to book an event, contact the Simon & Schuster Speakers Bureau at 1-866-248-3049 or visit our website at www.simonspeakers.com.

Interior design by Lewelin Polanco

Manufactured in the United States of America

1 3 5 7 9 10 8 6 4 2

Library of Congress Cataloging-in-Publication Data is available.

ISBN 978-1-9821-6767-7
ISBN 978-1-9821-6768-4 (ebook)

For Josephine "Tiny" Calflooking Jones, my grandmom. You were born in 1929 and you made it all the way to 2021.

A mother carries her six-year-old daughter into the tiled bathroom where the bathtub is already running, is still running, is overflowing, and for a moment the girl calms, seeing her little brother floating facedown in the water, his hair a golden halo around him, but then this mother is guiding her face-first down *into* that water, that, as it turns out, isn't just water but scalding water, and eleven years later her scream is the drawer screeching out of the counter by the sink.

Charlotte turns away from the sound and Mrs. Wilbanks does too, even sucks some air in about it.

"Sorry," Mrs. Wilbanks says, tilting her head to the side to guide her earring in. "I need to get Rog to call somebody about that."

"I can—" Charlotte starts, but Mrs. Wilbanks is already moving away from the toothbrush drawer to her daughter's pink and turquoise bedroom, to explain how the inhaler works. Like every other inhaler in the history of inhalers, surprise. The daughter, Desi, six, cute as a button, is sitting up in the middle of the huge pink beanbag in the corner, watching the stranger Charlotte is, her eyes big with wonder. Charlotte sneaks a wave to her, and Desi's dimples appear right when she's shying away.

"Mom, Mom!" Desi says to Mrs. Wilbanks in a whisper that's louder than her real voice can possibly be. "Your dress is—"

"I know, I know," Mrs. Wilbanks says about the zipper up her back that's flapping open. "I've written everything down in the kitchen," she goes on, walking and talking again, leading Charlotte down the hall into the master bedroom, neatly stepping around the lamp table, which is pretty much asking to be tipped over. "But you'll be fine, they're good kids, never steal cookies or draw on the walls or play hide-and-seek in the freezer, any of that. We don't even let them in the garage. They do think they're funny, so expect some big joke, I guess, wearing each other's clothes or saying they only drink milk with ice or who knows. At worst they might try to fudge when lights-out eyes-closed usually is, but—"

"One hour from now," Charlotte fills in.

"Is it eight *already*?" Mrs. Wilbanks says, her eyebrows coming up in panic. "Shit. Shit-shit-shit. Okay, um, if we're not back by midnight, Roger says we'll add twenty dollars, does that work?"

Charlotte nods yes, yes, that will most definitely work, thank you, her brain defaulting to the test mode it's been locked in for the past month: *If babysitter X earns thirteen dollars an hour for four hours and gets a twenty-dollar bonus, then that babysitter's smile will increase by a factor of Y plus what?*

She rubs her forehead with the pad of her finger, trying to smush that kind of thinking away for just five minutes, please.

"I just want the two of you to have a good time," she says, stepping in to work that zipper up. Mrs. Wilbanks stills at the touch and draws her breath in, holds it, is suddenly this tall perfect porcelain doll, ready to shatter.

"Thank you," she says, her eyes clocking the depths of the mirror, Charlotte's pretty sure. Clocking it to see if her husband happened to have stepped in, seen this unasked-for intimacy, this dark girl lightly touching his milky-white wife.

"Full-service babysitter," Charlotte says, taking a long step back into her own space like the help she is.

"And if the doorbell rings—" Mrs. Wilbanks starts, leaving the blank for Charlotte to fill.

"There shouldn't be any trick 'r treaters until tomorrow night," Charlotte says.

"But if someone's got their calendar flipped to the wrong day..." Mrs. Wilbanks says, leaning in to unsmudge her eyeliner.

"Then nobody's home," Charlotte says with the right amount of perk, straight out of the handbook she's always imagining. Specifically, the chapter on dealing with paranoid parents who haven't been out on a date since their kids were born.

"And if that homeless man comes back?" Mrs. Wilbanks prompts, widening her eyes to get her line straight.

"Homeless who?" Charlotte asks.

"His calendar is flipped to the wrong *decade*," Mrs. Wilbanks says. "Neighborhood Watch will call the police on him if he comes back, don't worry."

"Is he... hungry, you think?" Charlotte asks.

Mrs. Wilbanks refocuses her eyes about this, no longer looking at her makeup in the reflection but at Charlotte.

"Don't engage," Charlotte says, on cue—what Mrs. Wilbanks wants to hear. "Nobody's home."

"And you know the security code," Mrs. Wilbanks prompts, her tone leading Charlotte to the proper answer.

"The *temporary* code," Mr. Wilbanks says from the doorway of the master bedroom, then—for his wife—"I thought some rooms were going to be off-limits, dear?"

His hands are pulling on the hanging ends of the plaid scarf looped around the back of his neck, and there's a diagonal red crease pressed into his forehead, like he's been leaning in the doorway for a little bit, just watching, and listening.

"Yes, yes," Mrs. Wilbanks says, sketching a fleck of black onto the white of her eyeball and, instead of flinching away from it,

Charlotte can clearly see that she's making herself feel that burn. "Our room's out of bounds, of course"—now she's dabbing the eyeliner away ever so gently with the very corner of a tissue—"no reason to be in here. And Roger's office, naturally."

"It's already locked," Mr. Wilbanks says from his station in the doorway, and shrugs his office at the end of the long upstairs hall into the non-issue he most definitely wants it to be for Charlotte.

"All I need is Desi's and Ronald's bedrooms to tuck them in nice and tight, the bathroom to make sure they brush their teeth—"

"Bathrooms," Mr. Wilbanks corrects, since each kid has their own.

"Bath*rooms*," Charlotte repeats, no insult in her voice at all, thank you, "the kitchen, where the lasagne should just about be done, and the kitchen table, so I can study for my SATs after lights-out eyes-shut."

She shrugs one shoulder at the end of this and practically kinks one knee up enough to twirl her toes into the hardwood floor, her hands clasped at her lower back like she's in some pervy anime.

"Lights-out eyes-*closed*," Mrs. Wilbanks says into the mirror.

"I know we probably sound . . ." Mr. Wilbanks starts in with a self-deprecating smile, "it's just, the off-limits rooms—we've heard, and they're probably the urban legends of our, our age group, but you hear things like—"

"Sex parties, drugs, rifling through personal belongings, absconding with passwords," Mrs. Wilbanks says, ticking through them. "Unmentionable things done to silverware. Intimate photography that, well, compromises home values and probably leaves emotional damage besides."

Charlotte blinks once, trying to gauge whether this is an accusation or not.

"You checked up on me, of course?" she says to each of them, not in a challenging way but a reassuring way—no, a *reminding* way. Because of course they did: 3.96 GPA, Honor Society, Mathlete, president and pioneer of the high school's Premed Club, on the volleyball team that went to State last year, certified in both adult and infant CPR, and no brushes with the law. In short, babysitter extraordinaire, and then some. Like she was grown in a vat to watch their kids, or ordered up from a menu. Plucked from a daydream.

"The Lopezes were very confident in your performance, yes," Mr. Wilbanks says—which is an odd word, right? "Actually, we considered whether or not you might be blackmailing them into being so positive."

For a moment after delivering this he doesn't smile, but when he does, Charlotte can too.

"I love their little Arthur," she says. "My main regret about going off to college is not getting to see him grow up. The next few years will be so formative for him."

"But surely you'll miss your—your parents?" Mrs. Wilbanks asks, her eyeliner pencil held in suspension until Charlotte delivers the next correct answer. "When you go off to college?"

"My mom's working overtime to pay for the applications," Charlotte says, a hint of challenge rising in her voice in spite of her trying to play it so neutral here.

"Speaking of sons," Mr. Wilbanks says, leaning back to look down the hall then speaking to his wife again, as if Charlotte isn't there at all: "Has she met Ronbo?"

Charlotte tucks this nickname away for later.

"I'd love to," she says, skipping forward without waiting for permission from Mrs. Wilbanks.

Mr. Wilbanks backs out of the doorway, presents the hallway to her, and all Charlotte can think for the two doors down to the far bedroom is that her ass is probably going to catch fire here, with all this laser-focused attention she can feel it's getting.

But that's part of it too, she knows: the husbands—that's how she thinks of them, not "fathers," because yuck—they want and need her to be a good girl for this babysitting gig, but at the same time they'd trade anything to be the boyfriend they know is hiding in the bushes, waiting for a romp on the dining room table, the curtains not even drawn.

Charlotte stops by the closed door and raises her hand to knock but holds it, looking back to him for confirmation. He gets his eyes up just in time and brushes past her, his top-heavy bulk somehow sinuous, his hand finding the knob perfectly. "Kids don't have privacy at this age," he says, and swings the door in.

Like Desi, Ronald is six—twins—but unlike Desi, he's not in pajamas yet, just tighty-whities that are pretty much a match for what Charlotte is guessing must be the signature Wilbanks pallor.

His back is to them. He's hunched over something, is skinny enough that his individual vertebra are pushing up through his skin in a knobby ridge.

"Ronald?" Charlotte says, an inviting smile to her tone, a safe look prepped and ready on her face.

Ronald doesn't turn around to the new voice. His right arm moves the littlest bit.

"*Ronnie*," Mr. Wilbanks says.

Neither he nor Charlotte exist for this six-year-old. Only whatever he's working on.

"Maybe we should just let him—" Charlotte tries, making peace before it's even all the way broken, but Mr. Wilbanks is already crossing the room to his son.

Charlotte presses her lips together for the arm-grab and sudden haul-up she knows she's about to have to witness and, against all her training, not report, but at the last moment—maybe *because* she's there?—Mr. Wilbanks steps around Ronald, brings his laser eyes to bear on what's got all his son's attention.

"He's usually not this rude," he says. "I apologize, Charley."

"No, no," Charlotte says, stepping in but keeping to the side, to see what's got Ronald so fascinated. She's not a Charley, is a "Charl" at best, but this forced familiarity hardly even registers. Instead, she's focused on what Ronald's working on so intently.

A . . . an antique *jack-in-the-box*?

He's turning the red metal crank a fraction at a time, like trying to draw out the moment before release. Like trying to make it last—no, Charlotte decides: like a safecracker in a movie, right? Like he's unlocking something he's not supposed to be getting into.

"It's a playground story," Mr. Wilbanks says, dismissing it even as he says it, his hands still gripping the ends of his scarf like a gym towel. "When the cafeteria flooded, all the grades ended up taking recess together, I don't know. The older kids pulled some of the younger ones under the equipment where the teachers couldn't see, and they—I guess they tried to scare them, you know how it is."

"Ronald?" Charlotte says, taking a knee to be on his level, which she knows might be giving a certain husband a leery angle down the too-big flannel shirt she's got tied at her waist, but screw it. It's not a preview if he's never getting to the main attraction.

"Shh," Ronald says, not looking over to Charlotte even a little. He's still turning the crank one single plastic tooth at a time.

"This sixth grader evidently told the first graders that everybody stops when the clown pops up because they think that's the end," Mr. Wilbanks explains. "But there's supposed to be a certain spot *later* in the turn that—"

"Where did he find that again?" Mrs. Wilbanks says from the doorway, already bustling in, snatching the jack-in-the-box up. It jostles it enough that the clown pops up all at once, its black diamond eyes and painted-red smile startling Charlotte back into some rattly action-figure case, then the wall. A huge press-on vinyl poster or banner of the night sky billows down around her—the oversize kind of thing you have made for your kid when your company's got an account with the printer. Instinctively she fights out of it back to the light. Instinctively and a little more desperately than she would have liked, since she's supposed to be the one in control, the one they can trust *not* to panic.

Ronald draws his breath in in the most satisfied way about the jack-in-the-box, his eyes tracking the little clown up and away.

"*Clothes*," Mr. Wilbanks tells him—orders him—then, to Charlotte: "This isn't in any of the parenting manuals, but having to teach them shame? That's the part I never expected."

"Shame is societal, not biological," Charlotte hears herself saying, trying to stand up from the poster without ruining it, then padding her hand into the rug for the tacks that must have been holding it up.

"You really are an honor student, aren't you?" Mr. Wilbanks says, the words themselves harmless, but there's something behind them that's pretty much the opposite.

"1460 on the PSATs," Charlotte says. "But tomorrow I ace it."

"They do tests on Halloween?" he asks.

"Scarier that way," Charlotte says with a shrug.

"I think I hear the lasagne," Mrs. Wilbanks cuts in with all due impatience, the jack-in-the-box tucked behind her back as if Ronald isn't staring straight through her at it, waiting for that crank to turn one delicious click more.

"What time is the reservation for?" Mr. Wilbanks says in a fake and formal way to Mrs. Wilbanks, which is their cue to flutter down the stairs, start the goodbye process.

"He'll be okay with his pajamas?" Charlotte asks on the landing, about Ronald.

"He's a big boy," Mr. Wilbanks says, and, before hauling his own overcoat out of the closet by the front door he flourishes Mrs. Wilbanks's red one out, holds it open for her. It's cute; they haven't been out on the town since that overcoat was in style, Charlotte would bet.

"The numbers are all on the fridge," Mrs. Wilbanks says, straightening her husband's collar, which is really just her nerves keeping her hands busy.

"Our thing's over at eleven, eleven thirty," Mr. Wilbanks says for maybe the third time so far. "We're here by quarter til. Not even that."

"They'll be fine," Charlotte says, making a show of ferreting the key from its high basket in the closet, using it to twist the deadbolt back, punching the *temporary* code into the alarm pad—pure chipper performance, but that's part of it. She opens the door, presents the outer world to these two nervous fledglings.

"Of course they will," Mrs. Wilbanks says, and leans forward to give Charlotte a quick, awkward hug, her right hand, the one closest to her husband, to Charlotte's shoulder, her left to Charlotte's opposite hip, the fingers of that hand tucking something into the waistband of Charlotte's mom jeans, like repaying Charlotte in kind for zipping her dress up—intimacy for intimacy.

Charlotte stiffens, wonders if she's just been tipped or propositioned or what, and nods a courteous bye to Mr. Wilbanks, who, instead of some suggestive goodbye, calls out that Ronald needs to pee like a big boy before bedtime.

"Like a big boy," Charlotte confirms, which is maybe the first time she's ever said this out loud, or at all, and the moment the door's shut she's sliding the key in and turning that deadbolt over so they can clearly hear the *click*.

Standing with her back to the door, the alarm's green light blinking steady, she can finally breathe. Let the muscles of her face go normal and slack. She pulls the scrunchy from her hair, shakes it loose, luxuriates in this small but so-necessary freedom. Next she palms her phone, sends the text she's been working on in her head all day: *sory, do over?* Autocorrect doesn't want to let her misspell like that, but the misspelling's the whole thing. Will Murphy be able to resist texting back to correct?

Fifty-fifty, Charlotte figures, and makes herself pocket her phone instead of staring into it, waiting for Murphy's typing ellipses to burble back. Now to just get the twins fed and asleep, which, if they're anything else like every other six-year-old Charlotte's worked with, should be cake. That should be her next book, even, for new moms: *How to Reclaim Your Life by 9 p.m.* But that's all later, after food and games and brushed teeth.

Now . . . she curls her right side in, extracts the scratchy paper from the waistband of her jeans.

It's not a ten or a twenty but a Post-it folded over twice, the adhesive keeping it shut enough that she has to apply some serious fingernail. Written inside in hasty blue ink, probably upstairs at Mrs. Wilbanks's vanity while Charlotte was getting the Ronald intro, is . . . a *book title*?

Charlotte looks upstairs for any small faces watching her through the jail bars of the wooden railing. When there aren't any she crosses the living room, finds the dark bookshelves built into the wall behind the television. The book Mrs. Wilbanks wrote down is *Plutarch's Lives*, which Charlotte suspects will be about zero-point-zero help on tomorrow morning's SATs.

She starts to haul the heavy volume down, not sure what Mrs. Wilbanks intends here—will there be a quiz? another note folded into the pages?—but then she sees: on the book *beside* the Plutarch is an eight-inch rubber lizard, blue on top, paler blue on bottom. The kind you find tucked in every place in any house with kids, even places as moneyed-up as this.

Only, instead of a hollow throat, this lizard has the iridescent eye of a nanny cam. Motion-activated, surely. Meaning it's recording now. If its rubber tail could switch back and forth like a predator watching its prey, then that's exactly what it would be doing, Charlotte knows.

She holds her face normal, unfocused, and keeps moving as if just scanning this library for something to read for the night, book-girl that she is, and knows now not to change her shirt on the couch this lizard is so interested in. Good to know. Also good to know: Mrs. Wilbanks didn't tell her about this lizard because she wanted to keep Charlotte in line, she told her about it to keep her safe. From *Mr.* Wilbanks.

Great. Wonderful. Just the kind of stress Charlotte needs before the biggest most life-deciding test of her whole life. Checking the Native American/Alaskan Native box on all the forms doesn't mean jack if you choke on test day.

But at least there won't be more cameras, Charlotte tells herself. If there were, Mrs. Wilbanks would have polite-hugged her longer—long enough to tuck Post-it notes all over Charlotte, effectively going ahead and doing the sexual assault she was trying to warn her about.

"You can do this, you can do this," Charlotte tells herself, licking her lips for resolve, then nodding to herself when that doesn't quite take.

Not only *can* she do this, but she's been doing it every Friday night for the past two years, pretty much, all over town—she's the dependable girl, the one sure not to have weekend plans, the one who gets *paid* to hit the books for an hour or two after her charges are safely tucked in. Take that, everybody else from senior class who has to flip fryer baskets until end of shift and then pay taxes to the Great White Stepfather. If she's lucky tonight, the Wilbankses' big important "second first date" will even cross into Halloween by a few minutes, for an easy twenty dollars. Just, she reminds herself, be careful when Mr. Wilbanks offers that lift home. And remember that his eyes are cameras too.

On the way upstairs, already trying to twitch her lips into the smile the twins need, Charlotte caches the jack-in-the-box in the top of the closet by the front door and angles her head over so her face can be at the same jaunty angle as the clown's.

"Yeah . . . I don't think so," she says, and closes that door, rattles the knob to be sure it caught. Behind her the key to the deadbolt is still *in* the deadbolt, exactly as she was warned not to do. But it's their house, she reminds herself. Their paranoid rules. She reaches down for the key but stops at the last moment, narrows her eyes at the closet door.

Was there just a click in there?

Surely not.

— —

After turning the oven off per handwritten instructions and sliding the lasagne onto the kitchen island to set, peeking under the foil tent to make sure things turned out all right, Charlotte leans against the counter and checks for the text she already knows isn't there.

She shakes her phone like that might help, then checks the signal—strong enough—but, just to be sure, she tries to tap into the Wi-Fi. When she needs a password she peels up the night's instructions, turns the sheet over for some cryptic string of numbers and letters.

This was one of their concerns, though, right? That she would snake access then sit outside their house for all the nights to come, using their network to upload terrorist plans and traffic kiddie porn and read all their secret emails?

More like she'd be submitting college applications.

Screw it.

She's got some kids to tire out for bed.

"Fee-fi-fo-fum," she calls up the staircase, less pulling herself up with the handrail than *bouncing* up the steps, "here I come . . ."

There's no giggling in response, no hurried footsteps.

Don't kids know this game from birth? When the teenager goes into monster mode, spreads her fingers wide like claws, you giggle and look around, hide if you can, shriek when the jig's up and there's nowhere to go.

Charlotte crests up onto the second-floor landing and considers which kid to fake-attack first. Desi, she decides. Because she'll need the fun one on her side if she's going to pull the serious one into some make-believe run-and-chase game.

Charlotte galumphs into the doorway of Desi's room, throws an arm up onto the jamb like she's been running for miles, but . . . no Desi?

"Dez?" Charlotte tries in her own voice.

She checks the bathroom, the shallow closet, the hot-pink beanbag, then, smiling, she pulls the frilly pink bed skirt up all at once, her face right there for the little girl who's got to be hiding.

She's not.

"What the hell?" Charlotte mutters.

Instead of flouncing dramatically into Ronald's room, she walks right in, casing every nook that could hide a skinny six-year-old, her hands opening and closing by her thighs.

"Ronald?" she tries, then, getting desperate, "Ronbo?"

Charlotte ties her hair into a sloppy bun—playtime's over—mentally backs off this situation to see what she could be missing.

Twin one: missing.

Twin the other one: just as gone.

She flashes on the key she left in the deadbolt, has a sudden vision of what she's already warned herself never to think of again, ever: two weekends ago, the last time she babysat Arthur for the Lopezes. Arthur, who had never until that night sleepwalked. Charlotte with Murphy in the dining room, perhaps in a somewhat compromising position, hadn't heard him slip out the front door, hadn't even known he was gone until her mom—her ride, not supposed to be there for twenty more minutes—rang the doorbell, a bleary-eyed five-year-old on her hip.

Where she'd found him: in her headlights.

Instead of what he should have been: a lump in the rearview mirror.

Charlotte had fallen to her knees, had made such an empty sound that Murphy had come out of hiding to see what was wrong, and Charlotte's mom had just shaken her head, wordlessly exiled Murphy to her car, then carried Arthur upstairs herself, stayed to talk with the Lopezes about their date, her every utterance about to be the one that told on Charlotte, that revealed what had almost, almost happened there that night.

But she never did say it. And Arthur must not have been checked-in enough to remember. So they drove home in complete silence that night, Murphy in the backseat to be dropped off on the way.

The one question Charlotte's mom finally asked was, "You learned your lesson?"

It had made Charlotte burst into tears.

It's what's about to happen now, too.

"Be serious," she tells herself.

This isn't a repeat of that. It can't be. First, twins might share a birthday, but that doesn't mean they sleepwalk together. Second, she was only in the kitchen long enough to pull a lasagne from the oven, not nearly long enough for a couple of *awake* six-year-olds to have manipulated the stiff deadbolt, slipped out into the night. Anyway, their mom said they don't do that kind of stuff, right? No, there's no way they could have gotten downstairs without passing her. They're not ninjas, and invisibility cloaks aren't real, and they can't—they can't crawl on walls and ceilings, or tunnel under the carpet. There's no carpet anyway, just rugs everywhere on this pricey hardwood.

Charlotte makes herself go Sherlock then, and looks all the

way down the hall, to the only possibility now that everything else is pretty much eliminated: Mr. Wilbanks's office. Mr. Wilbanks's *locked* office.

"No way," she says, and shakes her head, balls her hands into fists, makes herself go down there. Just on the chance.

It's just as locked as Mr. Wilbanks said it was. She bangs her open hand on it all the same, calls for the kids, and . . . *are* they in there? Is this the game? The big joke Mrs. Wilbanks warned about?

Charlotte stills, listens harder, closer, eyes closed, more trying to feel the space on the other side of the door than actually hear it.

Is that breathing?

"Desi?" Charlotte says, more alarmed now, and, if asked why she thought it was Desi more than Ronald, there's nothing she can put her finger on, exactly. Just, for some reason, she got *girl* from what she was or wasn't hearing more than *boy*.

She claps on the door again, listens again, then, mouth a thin line, she turns, goes full-on Terminator, gridding her visual field into sections and processing them each with scrolling text: door one, the hall entrance to Ronald's bathroom, locked; door two, Ronald's bedroom; after that, Desi's bedroom door; and, at the far end around the corner, right past where the stairs spit her up here, the master bedroom. The *off-limits* master bedroom, but screw it, that's the only place left, right?

On the way to it Charlotte realizes there's another door, on the left: a linen closet flush with the wall and not going all the way to the floor. Making it actually a cabinet, she guesses? She grips her hands into the inset handle groove and pulls it open, fully expecting two giggling kids to spill out.

What comes down at her instead is tall and fast and . . . an electric dust broom thing. The upstairs vacuum cleaner, "Featherweight" model, bright red with grey accents. She guides it back, eyes the space behind it. Linens and board games, every shelf stuffed to spilling.

"I'm going to kill them," she says, shutting the door fast to keep the vacuum from tipping out again.

It feels transgressive, twisting the knob on the master bedroom door that Mr. Wilbanks was sure to pull shut behind them, but there's no other choice.

She walks in, can't find the light at first. When she does it brings the ceiling fan on as well, rustles some papers on Mrs. Wilbanks's antique vanity.

"Desi?" Charlotte says tentatively. "Ronald? Don't make me call your parents . . ."

If there's a camera in here, then the Lopezes are hearing about this, she knows. And everybody else as well. But forget all that. She's really getting nervous about the kids. For all she knows they're hiding in the closet right now, playing scuba diver with dry-cleaning bags. Which would be exactly what she deserves, would just be the world calling in its markers after she pulled the lucky card of it being her own *mom* who found Arthur toddling down the road.

Charlotte rushes across the room, pulls the closet door open, rattling the louvres, some sensor glowing the light on automatically—the *lights*: not just a single overhead, but an LED strip tracing the cubbies of shoes, the racks of dresses and blouses and slacks.

"Shit," Charlotte says, legit impressed, and kind of humbled. She's heard of other babysitters playing dress-up while the parents are away, but playing dress-up here would take all night.

No kids, either.

And they're not huddled together in the shower stall, or under the California king bed, or tucked into the leg space of Mrs. Wilbanks's vanity. Charlotte pushes the heavy stool back under, ruffles the edge of the Post-it note pad like there's going to be some secret written on one of the hidden pages.

"Don't cry," she tells herself, trying to get the pad back exactly where it was. "That's not who you are."

All the same, she can feel it building.

She slumps back out into the hall, knows she's about to have to do the Thing she's never done—make the dreaded call, ruin a couple's first date in years, burn them on going out altogether—but then she hears something . . . downstairs?

She gives one last look to the office door at the other end of the hall then, committing to this, she steps out of her shoes, picks her way down the stairs two and three timid steps at a time, hand tight to the rail.

"Desi?" she says. "Ronald?"

The living room is just as she left it. She checks the deadbolt—still locked—pockets the key for safety. Almost into the nanny cam's field of view, she backpedals to the closet, has to look in.

The jack-in-the-box clown is still there, same jaunty angle. Not even moving on its spring or anything.

Charlotte presses that door shut, turns around, and doesn't even have time to gasp, really: she's not alone.

Standing side by side in the middle of the living room, one in My Little Pony pajamas, one still in tighty-whities, are Desi and Ronald. They each have a saucer with lasagne on it. Ronald's mouth is sloppy with tomato sauce.

When Charlotte flinches back like she has to—her body does it with or without her say-so—her heels catch on the step up to the entryway and, like that, she goes down, the back of her head catching the closet doorknob hard enough to rattle her teeth, rush the taste of blood into her mouth.

She pulls her knees up in pain and rocks forward, holding her head with both hands.

"Charlotte?" Desi says, from the distant end of some long dark tunnel.

Charlotte holds her right hand up, keeping them back, back, just until she can get this pain to stop.

Don't pass out, don't pass out, she says inside.

Good babysitters stay awake. Good babysitters don't let the world grey at the edges. They hold on to the light. They, they—

"I'm okay," she says, wincing from her own voice.

When she can open her eyes again, the twins are spooning lasagne in and studying her.

"You're supposed to . . . to use *forks*," Charlotte says, pressing her back against the closet door and sliding up to stand again, still cupping the back of her head with her palm. "And, do your parents let you eat in the living room? Really?" When they don't answer—which *is* an answer—she collects their dripping saucers of lasagne, leads them back into the kitchen, walking confidently for the lizard with the hungry eye.

Instead of eating the lasagne ("Indians didn't come up milking buffalo" is her mom's embarrassing go-to for lactose intolerance), Charlotte asks the kids where their snacks are, goes elbow-deep into that big plastic bin in the pantry, and makes herself a dinner from two boxes of animal crackers, some gummy worms that somehow aren't sugar but protein, and a green apple that's small enough to probably be organic.

"So," she says, standing by the island in the kitchen, surveying the damage two kids can do to a perfectly good lasagne. Instead of cutting it into squares, they've . . . she's not sure: either clumped hunks out with their tiny hands or maybe stuck their faces directly in, used their mouths like crane buckets to deliver bites across to the saucers Mrs. Wilbanks had left out. Though Charlotte shouldn't disallow the possibility of using the saucers themselves as scoops, she supposes. Whatever the case, this lasagne looks like it had a firecracker planted right in its center. One that left a ragged crater.

Without meaning to—unable *not* to—Charlotte imagines Mrs. Wilbanks at midnight, alone in her kitchen, trying to imagine what kind of babysitter lets this kind of damage happen on her thirteen-dollars-per-hour watch. The idea of a lasagne this big has to be leftovers, right? As in, her and her husband each having a piece for lunch tomorrow, while congratulating themselves on having selected the right girl to watch the twins last night.

"Are you really from Thanksgiving?" Desi asks, pulling Charlotte from her deliberations. Charlotte turns, her face pleasant—they're just kids, raised in a pasty-white dream—and focuses in on Desi, then Ronald.

"Is that how your parents explained me?" she asks back.

Desi looks to Ronald and Ronald looks to Desi, and Charlotte's pretty sure they've each been coached that it's not "Indian," it's "Native American."

"We like cranberry sauce," Ronald finally says for both of them.

"Who doesn't?" Charlotte says, opening cabinets now to salvage this lasagne situation. "Have you two figured out what you're being for trick 'r treating tomorrow night?"

"I'm going to be from Thanksgiving too!" Desi says, her excitement bubbling over.

Charlotte selects the right spatula for the job, manages a wooden "Oh, wow," the pleasant look on her face more a mask now. Not for Halloween so much as for life. But college will be different, she knows. Nobody on campus will assume she's the designated expert on *One Flew Over the Cuckoo's Nest*. Nobody will ask if her relatives live in tipis. No one will be elected to ask her if this or that spirit ribbon is offensive or not. The worst thing about being Indian, it's being the only Indian.

She balances a neat square of lasagne across to the first container, leaving room for two more.

"*All* Native American, though," Desi adds, using her whisper-voice again. "Not half-and-half."

Ronald leans into her like shutting her up but she rolls with it, her eyes transfixed on Charlotte.

"Half-and-half?" Charlotte asks, trying to get the lid to seal.

"Like for coffee," Ronald says, saving Desi from having to.

The scene builds itself in Charlotte's head: Mrs. Wilbanks explaining the new babysitter over breakfast and using what she has at hand: her morning coffee. *Your new babysitter, kids? Come here, come here now, listen*, at which point she swirls her cup and explains how a walnut-colored mother and a creamy-white father can have a daughter who looks just like . . . *this*. Except of course Charlotte's father's not really white. More like invisible since the night-of, as her mom refers to it, pretty uncryptically.

"Come here, I'll let you in on a secret," Charlotte says, kneeling down and pulling the twins in. "You either are or you aren't Indian, did you know that?"

"Like this," Desi says, and holds her pudgy cute little hands up like a field goal, like butterfly wings, like moose antlers, having to concentrate to get it just perfect. She leans forward, waggles the tip of her tongue over where her thumbs touch, says—*recites*, Charlotte can tell—"In the middle."

It's good that Charlotte's mom isn't here for this.

"Sure," Charlotte says, swallowing the rest down, and then Ronald's pulling on her hand.

"I'm a nurse!" he says around the bite he's trying to get down.

Part of the babysitter certification process is choking hazards and how to clear airways. The big choking hazards are supposed to be peanuts and cut-up wieners, grapes and hard candy. But lasagne isn't exactly porous.

"Smaller bites, Ronald?" Charlotte says, standing but not losing his hand.

He moves his body back and forth like he's embarrassed.

"Veronica," Desi primly corrects.

This brings Charlotte around, first to Desi again, then Ronald—*Veronica*.

Hmm.

"A nurse, you say?" she asks, starting on the second container, carefully carving around the center of the lasagne, which looks more like Hamburger Helper now. Which is something they probably don't even know about in this house.

"I'll show!" Ronald says, and drops from his stool, scurries the other direction. Not to the living room but . . . Charlotte thinks he's headed for the garage at first, which is supposed to be off-limits, but then he veers around the island and into the utility room, not stopping to turn the light on.

"He didn't even say excuse me," Desi says, trying to make her spoon work in the curvy folds of cheese and big flat noodles.

"Here," Charlotte says, and passes across one of the forks Mrs. Wilbanks had left out.

Desi pokes into the heart of the flat noodles, opens wide to balance this sloppiness in.

"I guess I am from Thanksgiving, yeah," Charlotte says, the three containers stacked on the island now, the tin lasagne pan beside them, still with what probably amounts to two pieces of ragged mess in it. Which will be how much Mrs. Wilbanks will assume their new babysitter ate, once it's crumpled into the trash can.

"So do I call him Veronica?" Charlotte says to Desi—not in a serious, defenses-up way. Just normal voice, for this everyday thing.

"It's Halloween," Desi says with a thrill, and Charlotte hears . . . but it can't be. Was that a footstep *upstairs*? Like a kid, running.

"*Almost* Halloween," Charlotte corrects, not one hundred percent involved with this anymore, then turns to Ronald/Veronica bustling back in, holding his nurse outfit proudly in front of him like a shield.

He wasn't lying: it's nurse whites, the old-fashioned polyester skirt-uniform kind, white hose and Florence Nightingale tiara cap and all. There's even, according to the label on the packaging, a collapsible medical bag that can be used for candy. The tiara cap and the bag both have a big red plus sign on them, and there's a name sewn on the chest in black thread: VERONICA.

"Beautiful," Charlotte says, and means it.

"Mom says he has to wear sensible shoes with it," Desi says with adult eyes, which mostly means leaning her face forward, leading with her forehead.

"What about you?" Charlotte asks. "Where is *your* costume?"

Ronald looks up to them like *oops*, then he's off to the utility again, is opening . . . is that the dryer door? Is that the secret hiding place for Halloween outfits?

Charlotte starts to step over, make sure Ronald isn't endangering himself in any way, but then Desi drips her next bite onto the floor, which needs immediate attending to.

"Moccasins," Desi says out of nowhere, swishing her feet back and forth.

Charlotte looks up at her like to ask about this, but then Ronald's bursting back in all out of breath. He's got the Authentic Squaw costume Charlotte's dreading. Beaded headband, fake buckskin full-body dress. Shoe covers that have the necessary fringe, and of course, the jet-black wig, braids and all.

"Nice, nice," Charlotte says, inspecting the packaging, the model, the price.

"Like your hair!" Ronald says.

Charlotte looks across the island to the utility.

"Are there stairs back there?" she asks.

Both kids try to suppress their laughter, fail pretty miserably.

"Show me?" Charlotte says, standing, holding her hands out for each of them to take one.

"We're not supposed to," Desi says.

Charlotte considers this.

"If there's a fire," she says, "it's important I know every exit, to keep you safe."

"Will you get us out if there's a fire?" Ronald asks, his eyes widening with concern.

"There won't be a fire," Charlotte assures him. "Is it a secret stairway?"

They both nod eagerly, seriously.

"Those are the *best*," Charlotte says, taking both their hands in hers.

"We're not supposed to show you," Ronald says sadly.

Why would the Wilbankses care? And how was it not part of the tour anyway? Charlotte mentally rushes back through that tour: first floor, second floor, one central stairway connecting them. No basement, no loft or attic. Just the garage.

"Maybe . . . what if it wasn't you showing me?" Charlotte says to the twins. "What if it was a nurse and a . . . an . . ."—she can't seem to physically say "squaw," but neither can she call that costume Indian, quite—"a Native *princess*?"

The twins' eyes go as round as the saucers they were eating from.

"Not until tomorrow night," Desi scare-whispers.

"We can fold them back in perfect," Charlotte tells her, eyebrows raised, allowing room for this one wonderful possibility to sneak through.

The twins look over at each other, hardly able to contain themselves, and when Ronald bursts ahead for his costume and tries to follow through to the living room to change, Charlotte snags him by the arm, pulls him around, says, thinking lizard-with-the-glass-throat thoughts, "In here, 'kay?"

Charlotte stacks the three lasagne containers alongside the milk on the main shelf of the refrigerator so the Wilbanks will have to see them, and by the time she gets back to the twins, Ronald has both legs in one side of the white stockings like some nightmare mermaid and Desi's wearing the headband like a choker.

Charlotte wrestles Ronald into shape first, since he can actually ruin the hose if left to himself, and then, instead of the wig, Charlotte works Desi's own hair into two careful braids, her hair finger-parted in the middle.

"But I'm a *Native American*," Desi says, her eyes filling.

"It's not about hair," Charlotte says, tying the second braid off, "it's about here," and she touches her own chest with her palm.

"But that's not how—" Desi says.

"We wear our hair *all* kinds of ways," Charlotte says, "but like that too," and tilts her head over to separate her hair, get three strands ducking under each other on the right side, pulling them tight as she goes. By the left braid, Desi's got a reluctant smile.

"How are we doing, Nurse Veronica?" Charlotte says over to Ronald.

"Ronnie," Ronald says. "Mom says both names work like that."

"They do, they do," Charlotte says, letting the second braid flop down.

Ronald's nurse costume has a toy stethoscope, as it turns out. He's trying to listen to his own heart with it. Charlotte takes the end, says into it, thumping her voice down into *beat-beat*, "You're so cute, you're so cute."

He laughs and pushes her in that way kids have where it's really a hug.

"This all of us?" Charlotte asks, playing the teacher on the field trip.

"Yes!" Desi says back, thrilled with it all, her beaded headband actually not that bad, at least with real braids.

"Well then," Charlotte says, holding their hands to take the first step of this big adventure. Except . . . at the door to the dark utility room, Desi lowers her chin into her chest for six-year-old seriousness, stops them.

"What is it?" Charlotte asks, barely clipping the *now* off the end of that in time.

"He has to go first," she says, nodding across to Ronald.

Ronald nods solemnly, lets his hand slip from Charlotte's.

"This isn't . . . *dangerous*, is it?" Charlotte asks, a nervous smile ghosting the corners of her mouth up.

This time the twins don't volunteer anything.

Ronald looks up to Charlotte and steps into the darkness. Charlotte reaches in to feel for the light but Desi pulls her back, says, "That's not how it works."

"It?" Charlotte says.

"Shh," Desi says. "Native Americans are quiet."

"I mean, some are," Charlotte says as gently as she can, trying to see into the utility but the room's stupid—you walk in and there's an immediate right turn to get to the washer and dryer and everything.

Still, "What is that?" she says louder than she means to—fear is infectious.

"Shh," Desi says again.

Is Ronald talking to someone in there? Whispering?

"Ronald?" Charlotte calls, tentatively.

"Veronica," Desi corrects, her voice defensive.

"We're going in," Charlotte decides out loud for both of them, and, not letting Desi's forty-odd pounds stop her, she steps right in, finds the light immediately.

Ronald's just standing there, almost facing them.

"There," he says to Desi, about the bifold closet doors on the wall right of the dryer—what she must have thought was the sound of the dryer opening, right? The louvres in the doors mean it's probably the water heater closet.

"The stairs are there?" Charlotte says, looking around at all the—the nothing. Just a normal everyday utility room: washer, dryer, both top-dollar, up on pedestals or something, and a wide laundry cart on wheels that's probably nice even if the hanging part's tall enough that it had to be assembled in here. Cabinets up high all around, probably built to order, another cabinet that's probably got a foldout ironing board in it, and two industrial-looking storage containers sturdy enough for the garage. The only thing different from when Mrs. Wilbanks swept through here on the big tour is that now there's kid clothes trailing out of the open dryer, meaning she heard *right*, earlier. That doesn't make it make sense, though.

"I don't like that one," Desi says to Ronald, toeing the floor with her fake moccasin.

Ronald holds his hand out to her just the same.

"You have to keep your eyes closed," he says to Charlotte, his mouth serious so Charlotte can get how important this is.

"Excuse me?" Charlotte asks.

"You can't look," Desi says, just a fact.

"O-*kay* . . ." Charlotte says, waiting for the punch line that has to be coming.

Ronald picks through the clothes on the floor in front of the dryer, comes up with a pair of black tights, probably Desi's. He hands them to Charlotte, says, "They're clean."

"For your eyes," Desi explains.

"What kind of game is this?" Charlotte asks.

"*You* promised to show her," Desi says to Ronald.

"I didn't promise," he says back.

"Show me," Charlotte says.

At best she was expecting secret stairs for, she doesn't know, a maid? Never mind that this McMansion can't be more than twenty years old. At worst there was supposed to be a dumbwaiter back here, probably with an electric motor because kid arms aren't that strong.

What she's getting is a blindfold and no answers.

"Does your mom know about this?" Charlotte asks, working the upside-down tights onto her head like a stocking cap but not pulling the too-tight waistband over her eyes yet.

"Which one?" Ronald asks back, which is when Desi, at the light switch somehow, darkens the room all at once.

"It works better like this," she says, serious now.

Charlotte's heart is beating in her throat. Even Ronald's toy stethoscope could pick it up, she bets.

Desi's strong little hand finds Charlotte's. Ronald folds one of the doors open.

"How can we all—?" Charlotte starts, but Desi's already pulling her in.

The water heater is dusty, and Ronald, skinny as he is, has already pushed in past it, to the corner Charlotte would never willingly lean into, not in a thousand years. Desi turns sideways, slips through as well, right behind him.

"Your eyes," Ronald calls back from the darkness ahead, and Charlotte shakes her head no but pulls the waistband over her eyes, hooks it under her nose. It unbalances her for a moment and she reaches out, finds the cold side of the water heater, jerks back not because it's hot, not because it's coursing with electricity, but because she doesn't know exactly how water heaters work, tucked away in the musty dark places all the time, so it *could* have been boiling hot or coursing with raw electricity or worse.

"The door," Desi says to her, as if the world's upside down all of the sudden and she and Ronald are the adults. Charlotte feels back for the knob that isn't there—bifold doors don't work like that—but she's able to grab the edge, close the three of them in. She isn't sure exactly what changes the moment that door flattens out—not temperature, and the concrete floor under her feet stays solid—but she . . . there's the sense of *space* around her. Like, were she to say anything, it wouldn't echo back to her for seconds and seconds, if ever. The air around her would slurp it up, digest it for centuries. But at the same time, there's a pressure, like . . . like the *opposite* of going up over twelve or fourteen thousand feet. Like going down *deep* deep, where gravity pulls harder, where the air's pushing on you from every side, where your chest feels the kind of tight like you might not be able to breathe so easy, next breath.

Charlotte gasps, reaches forward for the anchor the water heater can be—anything, please, even that—but the water heater's not there. She sucks a mouthful of this thick air in, screams it back out, sure she's falling, sure she's drowning, sure there's nothing real to breathe here, and, reaching up for the tights covering her eyes, she realizes she's not holding Desi's hand anymore.

Spider eggs.

That's what Charlotte thinks before she even realizes she's thinking.

The waistband of the tights is chocked on her forehead now, she can definitely feel that, but it's . . . not dark, exactly. It's *white*, but a fabric-y, light, nothing kind of white. Like spider eggs.

Charlotte opens her mouth and the eggs find their way in, are dry on her tongue, on the roof of her mouth, and she's immediately coughing and retching, pushing her arm all around to find her way up, out, through.

Is she thinking spider eggs because this is a water heater closet? Yes, but there's more. Spider eggs are pretty much web spun powdery and gossamer, she doesn't know exactly what's up with them really, just knows one hundred percent what they feel like when her fingers find them under furniture, or high up in corners.

And when they burst, there's thousands of tiny desperate legs there.

She fights harder, pushing, feeling, trying—

There's something there, something almost solid. Not hard like the water heater . . . it resists her fingers but it gives some too, shifting all the spider eggs around her so they cascade with a hiss, chitter into the empty spaces under her back and legs.

Charlotte slows, makes herself process, her head dialing down to SAT mode: *If a thousand spider eggs hatch at once, and all those newborn spiders are both healthy and hungry, then, never mind how many sharp little legs that will be crawling across babysitter X's face and lips and eyeballs, but how long will it be before babysitter X retreats so deep into herself that nobody ever finds her again?*

Not much longer, she answers.

She feels with her hand for that resistance again, follows it around, around, making herself go slow and rational, and what she finally finds is a seam, a cold, notched line her fingers can trace. It leads her to a metal tab.

She pulls it—*zipper!* zipper zipper zipper!—stands up from the big pink beanbag in Desi's room, the white beans or puffy beads or whatever the hell they are raining down all around her, and static-clinging to everything they can. She spits the ones in her mouth away, looks around the My Little Pony bedroom.

The twins are on their knees on the bed, laughing and laughing, their eyes hopeful that this is as funny to Charlotte as it is to them.

"What the—?" Charlotte says, cutting herself off just in time and stepping fast away from this impossibility, looking back to it just to be sure it maybe really actually might have happened. Because, really, there's no fucking way. Did she hit her head on a pipe in that closet downstairs, and they somehow dragged her up here? But . . . not that they could have . . . but why hide her in—

"The beanbag, the beanbag!" Desi's saying, like this is the best most exciting thing ever in the whole world. "It's never the *beanbag* anymore!"

Ronald is more contrite, it seems, his eyebrows up, waiting to see if he's in trouble. It was his trick, after all. His game. His joke.

Charlotte flips the beanbag over for the trapdoor that has to be under it. That *isn't* under it.

"What just happened?" she says to the twins, trying to keep her voice from rising into a shriek.

"She only shows Ronald," Desi says, stepping down from the bed, her tone all about the essential unfairness of Ronald being the only who knows whatever *this* is. "Ask him."

"Ronald?" Charlotte says, trying to get across that he's not in trouble, that nothing he says here will get him in trouble. "Who shows you what? And why?"

He's bouncing up and down on his knees now.

"Because he's a miracle," Desi says, proudly.

Charlotte translates this, rewinds back to the walking and talking tour of the house, the out-loud biographies of the twins: Desi was born first, showed up with asthma before she was one, will probably outgrow it, and Ronald was born minutes later, not breathing at all. Not until the doctors got him to, minutes after other doctors would've given up: a legit miracle.

"That's . . . that's why *what*?" Charlotte says, not following.

"Why she tells me where they are," Ronald says, his chin pruning up, face tilting down. "Because I'm the only one who can see her sometimes."

"Where what are?" Charlotte says in her kindest, gentlest voice.

"The funny places," he says, obviously, like that's the most boring part of all this.

"She's not our real mom," Desi adds in, then, quieter, in secret, her eyes widening to deliver it, "*She's better.*"

"She's not," Ronald says, as if afraid.

"Is she here now?" Charlotte says, playacting a look around the room, which, it turns out, is exactly like a real look around the room. "Can I—can I meet her?" Charlotte asks, brushing fuzzy white beads from her peripheral vision.

Ronald shakes his head no, no.

"Was she in the closet?" Charlotte asks.

Both twins shake their head vigorously no, definitely no. No way no way.

"She can't go," Ronald says. "She can only use normal doors."

"Or the stairs," Desi adds.

"Does your mom know about her?" Charlotte asks.

"She says she's not real," Desi says with a shrug of one shoulder, dancing from foot to foot on her rug in some game only she's playing.

"We've got to—" Charlotte says, not at all sure how she's going to finish, "I've got to call—"

"*You can't tell*," Ronald says, delivering fully half of that with his eyes and eyebrows.

"It would make her mad," Desi says. "She would probably cry again."

"Again?"

"She doesn't like to do bad things," Ronald says.

"Like bubbles," Desi adds quietly.

Charlotte nods, writing this down in her head, milking it for every iota of possibility.

"This can't—" she finally says, or tries to. "What just happened. It's not right. It's wrong. I don't understand how it can even—"

Ronald's lower lip thrusts out and his eyes get shiny.

Charlotte plunks down beside him, pulls him to her.

"I'll come back, sage the living hell out of this place," she says.

"Is that Native Indian?" Desi says, blinking large and innocent.

Charlotte straightens her arm out to her, opens and closes her hand, telling Desi to come up here too.

"You can help," she says, pulling her to her other side. "I'll teach you. But I've got to tell your mom and dad. I wouldn't be a good babysitter if I didn't."

Now Ronald's full-on quiet-crying. Then Desi is too, just because.

"I'm sorry," Charlotte says to them both. "My job is to keep you safe. Make sure you grow up to be an amazing nurse and the best—the best Native Indian ever. A lot better than me."

Ronald nods *okay, okay okay okay*, and the way he's doing it, Charlotte can tell he's scared too, that he knows this is wrong, even if it's fun and secret.

She pulls him tighter, kisses the top of his head.

"How do your parents not know about this?" she asks.

"She won't talk to him when they're here," Desi says, sobbing.

"But she will when I am?" Charlotte says, just out loud, which is when the doorbell rings.

Charlotte's first reaction is terror: Mrs. Wilbanks told her about the one camera *she* knew about, but maybe the whole house has been keeping tabs on her. Cameras in every room. Meaning Mr. Wilbanks has been watching his phone in his lap all through dinner, keeping track of her . . . oh shit: of her letting the kids dress up in and possibly ruin their Halloween costumes; of her losing the kids long enough that they could trash the lasagne. And now, when the babysitter has for some reason decided to bury herself in the beanbag—he can't watch every moment, there has to be some jumps in time—now the adults have had to cut their fancy dinner short, come home with thin lips and grim eyes.

Good, Charlotte wants to say. There's impossible wrong shit happening here, shit that was not in the initial job description, shit not in any of the babysitter manuals, shit none of the other girls posting fliers up ever even whisper. Either that or she hit her head on that doorknob harder than she thought, in which case she doesn't need to be in charge of little ones, probably needs some medical care, never mind if her mom makes a federal case out of it at the ER.

Right on the heels of that, though, she realizes that there's zero reason for the Wilbankses to ring their own doorbell. Not just because they'll probably park in the garage when they come back for the night, but because parents are duty bound to never give you that kind of warning. Exhibit one: Mr. Wilbanks walking right into Ronald's room. Kids don't have privacy. Neither do the babysitters in charge of those kids.

It's not them, then.

Who, then? That homeless guy Mrs. Wilbanks was all stranger-danger about? Or was that a setup—has Mr. Wilbanks dressed up in layers of castoff jeans and jackets to test her? But nobody's that paranoid, are they? They wanted a date, not a game of catch-the-babysitter.

It's not them, Charlotte tells herself. Don't be stupid.

But it is somebody.

Most other jobs, most other normal Friday nights, a ringing doorbell means already-paid-for pizza. But you don't order pizza when there's perfectly good lasagne. And packages don't come this late. And Charlotte's car isn't parked in some wrong place. She knows that for sure because she doesn't *have* a car.

"Go, go!" Desi says, kneeling to pull the edge of her Pinkie Pie rug up, wriggle under like it's . . . a blanket?

Ronald slides off the bed, runs to the hall fast enough that he has to catch himself on the railing, bounce off the other way, toward his room.

"What are you—?" Charlotte says, following him but keeping

a hand up, like for spiderwebs. She reaches the hall just as Ronald is stepping up into the linen closet, having to hold the door open and the little vacuum cleaner back.

"You've got to go in the *beanbag*," he tells her, which isn't even close to being on the list of Things She Never Thought She'd Have Told to Her, but that's only because it's so left field that it wouldn't have been in the running.

Still standing in front of Desi's bedroom, Charlotte looks back to the exploded beanbag, to the lump Desi is under the rug, then to Ronald, still holding the door of that high linen closet open exactly like it's the top hatch of a submarine, one about to dive.

"Why?" Charlotte asks.

"*Because that's the way it works*," he says, heating his eyes up to show her how important this is. "You have to go back the way you came through. And don't open your eyes. That's the only two rules."

"And don't tell Mom or Dad!" Desi calls from somewhere behind.

"Okay, three rules!" Ronald says, exasperated in his six-years-old way.

"I'm not doing that again," Charlotte says, looking back to—not to Desi, to the lump she is under the rug, but to that lump flattening *out*.

She rushes across the room, jerks the rug away and there's not a secret tunnel there, there's not a hole, not a slide, not a stairway, not a pole. There's just hardwood. She touches it to be sure then slams her hand on it, shuts her eyes against all of this.

"You have to go *now*," Ronald says from the doorway.

Charlotte looks up to him, is trying hard to process all this but keeps hitting snag after snag, all of which are some version of *No, this is crazy, stop*.

She stands on unsteady legs, braces herself on the side of the bed, then nods that she can do this, that she's the closest thing to a grown-up here, that—that reason and rationality have to push everything else down. They do, don't they? The rules have to hold. They have to.

She walks past Ronald to the railing in the hall that balconies down over the living room for about as far as she can reach with both arms.

"Desiree!" she calls.

Desi laughs from what's got to be the utility room, and now the doorbell's ringing *again*. Because sometimes, Charlotte knows from experience—why wasn't this the first thing she considered?—sometimes the parents will be nervous enough that all the neighbors will be tasked with stepping over to check on things throughout the night. Never mind that this babysitter's already been told not to answer the door. Shit. Shit shit *shit*.

"I can't handle this," she tells Ronald, her only confessor here. "I've—I've got the SATs in the morning, this was just supposed to be a chance to brush up on some of the practice questions and get paid for it, nobody said anything about, about . . ."

About whatever this is.

"What happens if I don't, if I just—" she says to Ronald, not even able to form the thought into proper words.

"You get stuck?" he says, shrugging his shoulders and his eyebrows both.

"I get—" Charlotte says, looking around, none of this tracking. So then. Focus on what you *know*, she tells herself. On your training, your duties, your responsibilities here. Because they can't be wrong. "Your sister can't be down there alone," she says, less for Ronald, more just to hear it out loud, like reminding herself. Like faking rationality but making herself accountable to it. She makes for the stairs but now Ronald has her by the wrist with both hands, is leaning back with all of his weight, his feet set as hard as he can get them, his face more serious than any kid's should be.

"You've got to go in *there*," he says, tilting his head at Desi's room. "It'll shut!"

"The beanbag, you mean?" Charlotte says, about to collapse into laughter. "The magic beanbag will shut?"

In response, Ronald's eyes well up.

"I don't—" Charlotte says, and stops because . . . the hallway light is dimming? No, *all* the lights in the house are dimming.

"That's the warning," he says, pulling her harder. "You've got to go back the way you came!"

Charlotte can see the intensity on his face, the plea in his whole desperate little body.

"You mean," she says, "you mean you and your sister didn't come up through the beanbag like I did?"

It was zipped, some other part of her remembers, minutes too late. It was zipped and the kids didn't have those spider eggs stuck all over them. And—and he was climbing into the linen closet, and Desi slipped under the rug.

Meaning . . . the water heater closet, it must have spit them all out in different places. One way in, at least three ways out. And if this woman the twins call their other mother has to tell them where the funny places are each time—each time no adults are around—then, then that must mean it's not the water heater closet every time, is it? Of course it isn't. When Ronald went into the utility room by himself the first time, to get his costume from upstairs, he must have gone into the dryer, just like it sounded. Meaning he also came *out* of the dryer, dragging those clothes out along with him.

Is the rule that it has to be a dark, tight place?

To keep it secret, Charlotte tells herself. Rule three: don't tell the parents. If Ronald or Desi ever get caught, then they were just playing hide-and-seek, shh.

It's kind of perfect.

"*Now, now!*" Ronald is saying, the lights dialing down even lower, and then he can't wait any longer, he's racing back to the linen closet, the tiniest nurse on the most urgent mission.

He climbs in and that stupid useless little vacuum tilts out so he can't get the door shut, and he can't figure out how to pull it *and* the door in at the same time, and he's crying and breathing too fast, is almost having a panic attack.

Charlotte steps in, guides the tall handle of the vacuum in, pushes the door shut, holding his big eyes until the last moment, and she wants worse than anything right now to rip that door back open, see him treading back through some great blackness, or fizzling into static, or sucking down to a pinprick of himself, but what if it works layer by layer, taking the skin first, then the fascia, then the muscle, then—

If babysitter X has to see the boy she's in charge of stripped of his skin, then it's going to be like it wasn't her mom who found Arthur in the street, but the front bumper of some sophomore's new car, one that drags Arthur for Y feet, which makes the question: how long does Arthur get dragged on the asphalt before he's mercifully dead, and is this what he looks like?

The lights dip even lower and the doorbell rings again and this is all too much, this is all so wrong. Charlotte retreats into herself, clings to the only thing she for sure knows: how to think like a babysitter.

Desi is alone downstairs, isn't she? And now Ronald should be too.

That cinches it, then. She's supposed to be watching them, and she can't do that from up here. No taking the beanbag express down, either, only stairs, normal-normal stairs.

Right when Charlotte is three steps down, the lights flicker down to absolute black for a blink and there's a distinct *click* in the hall behind her.

She shakes her head, knows that ridiculous antique fucking haunted jack-in-the-box is going to be sitting there, ready to give her the heart attack to end all heart attacks. But it's probably just that linen closet door swinging back open, she tells herself. From that vacuum cleaner leaning drunkenly against it, now that Ronald isn't there to hold it.

Except . . . it's not the linen closet, is it? And it's not that jack-in-the-box either.

It's Mr. Wilbanks's office door, creaking back.

Charlotte swallows, shakes her head no, *please please no*, and then the doorbell rings *again*, more insistent if that's possible, like there's a depth a finger can press that makes the chime louder, that makes it hang at the top of its sound for too long.

"Okay, okay," Charlotte says, keeping her eyes on that open office door until it's gone from view, her hand gripped hard to the handrail like that can save her. By the time she steps down onto the slick white tile of the entryway, the lights are back to normal, are bright enough that nothing could have really been wrong, right?

"We're not supposed to answer the door," Ronald says from right behind her, and the first and maybe most wrong thing about him is that there's dried tomato sauce all down the front of his nurse whites, sending Charlotte immediately into a vision of her running all over town tomorrow to find this exact "Veronica" Halloween costume, and then faking like she left a book here, so she can sneak around, smuggle the stained one out in her purse, replace it with the one that doesn't make her the worst babysitter.

That's hours and hours away, though. This is now. And . . . it's not making sense, is it?

"How did you—did you eat the rest of the lasagne?" Charlotte says to him incredulously.

"I told him you would come back," Desi says, her beaded headband a choker again, her braids both let go, just hanging pigtails now.

"Come back?" Charlotte says, "I was just—" but then it registers: where they're standing. Right in the lizard's eye.

The doorbell chimes again.

"Just . . . stay, stay," Charlotte tells them, keeping her hand up and out while she steps across to the peephole. As if whoever's out there didn't hear her coming down the stairs, yes. As if whoever it is can't see the lights in the windows going up and down. But just because they know you're in there doesn't mean you have to answer. Really, this many dings in, the polite thing to do would be to back off, come back another time.

Charlotte leans in to see who could be this rude.

At first there's no shape through the thick little fisheye lens, just the porch and the lawn and the street and the night, but then, right as Charlotte's about to give up, a fool's cap jumps up into the fisheye lens like it's on a spring. The cap is a happy mass of three red and black tentacles going every which way, but then, in the image Charlotte takes with her when she jerks back, they taper into stubby-funny arms that end with . . . not bells, like she's pretty sure she's seen on harlequins and jester costumes, but pom-poms, red on the black arms, black on the red one, the skullcap black too, all of it stretched and wrong in the peephole.

"What?" Ronald says.

"Trick 'r treater," Charlotte says, trying to get her breath, trying to push the jack-in-the-box from her mind. The one she was just thinking about. The one she was just expecting upstairs.

That can't be connected to this, though. That was just in her head.

"But it's not even Hallo*ween*," Desi says, loving this, coming up onto her toes like that'll get her a glimpse.

The doorbell rings again and Charlotte leans back into the peephole, this jester stepping back enough so she can see the bone-white, kind-of-peeling face, the stretched-out black diamonds painted over the eyes, the lips bright red and sharp at the corners. The . . . pale yellow contact lenses?

The eyes are the worst part, easy.

The jester rocks back on its heels, hands behind its back so innocently, and then it tries on what looks to be a practice smile. One that shows its dull yellow fangs.

"We don't have any candy," Desi says.

Charlotte smiles, says, "We *are* the candy," and digs for the key in her pocket, guides it into the deadbolt.

"No," Ronald says, eyes wide, but Charlotte hauls the door open grandly all the same, exposing this visitor all at once, because you have to take charge. Most bullies run when they see that you're not going to cringe and cry.

The jester looks from face to face, finally settling its pale eyes on Charlotte.

"Premature, um . . ." Charlotte says, little ears behind her funneling in every word, "costumification?"

The jester does a quick soft-shoe that ends with her right leg curtsying forward, her face down, arms out like thrown-back wings.

"I'm . . . sorry?" Charlotte says, to the jaunty top of this fool's cap.

The peeling white face comes up. And the eyes soft behind those yellowy lenses.

"No," Murphy says, standing into her usual slack posture, her left hand bringing her phone up, screen out, "I think you were *so-ry*."

"You fall for that every time," Charlotte says. "I didn't tell you where I was, though. You didn't—did you locate me with your phone? We promised never to check up on each other like that, didn't we? Did you get your dad to use some cop trick to find me?"

Murphy rubs her gloved fingertip uselessly across her phone screen, says, "Swung by the ER, told your mom you'd left a study book at my place, that you would probably flame out at the SATs tomorrow if you didn't have it right now, *stat*!"

One of Murphy's favorite things is saying *stat* all emergency like that.

"You could have asked *me*," Charlotte says.

"And you would have put me off until tomorrow," Murphy says with a shrug, because this is so obviously true. "You've got work tonight."

"I do have work tonight."

"Anyway," Murphy goes on, "these gloves are too much trouble to peel out of, they go all the way to the elbow." She holds her billowy costumed arms up like that proves her case. "They're from when I was the Grimy Reaper last year, remember? Dirty fingernails and a rusty scythe?"

"Nice eyes," Charlotte tells her.

"The better to drink you up with," Murphy says back, and angles her whole body over to see the nurse and the Indian princess.

"We're not supposed to let anybody in," Ronald says.

"What *are* you?" Desi asks, her face flush with wonder.

"She's my . . . friend," Charlotte answers, and holds both hands out for Murphy's. Murphy takes them, their fingertips catching together, pulling into each other, and at the last moment Murphy whispers, "On the cheek, you don't want this lipstick on you."

Charlotte kisses her on the lips anyway, lingering a smidge longer than would be acceptable on Murphy's front porch.

"Ronald, Desi, this is Murph," Charlotte says, wiping her lips with the back of her arm. "The . . . vampire jester?"

"Dracula harlequin," Murphy says, with full-on mock disappointment. "But vampire jester, I like that. That's like the generic version of Dracula harlequin."

"She's not coming in, don't worry," Charlotte says to the twins but *for* Murphy. "She's just wishing me luck. That test I've got in the morning? Murphy took it last year. She's here to make sure I do great in the morning."

"She's your boyfriend!" Desi says, loving it.

"Yeah, *boy*friend . . ." Murphy says, asking the question to

Charlotte with her eyes. "Not coming in, you say?" she adds, using more than just one question mark.

"It's my first night here," Charlotte hisses back, keeping her face pleasant but her eyes insistent. "What use are the SATs if I don't get enough repeat work to pay for tuition?"

Murphy looks away, down the long porch, and Charlotte winces: that's what the fight was about—Charlotte leaving for good, forever, for always.

"What's wrong with your eyes?" Desi asks Murphy, coming closer by a timid step or two.

"Drank too much lemonade," Murphy says with what sounds to Charlotte like forced cheer, then she gets into it, mimes the pee-pee dance, which her jester costume amplifies by a factor of at least ten. "Speaking of?" she says to Charlotte.

"She needs to use the bathroom!" Desi says at celebration volume. Because: six years old.

Charlotte looks over at Ronald, his face cupping his worried eyes.

"Just for a quick squa—" she says, and bites it off, comes out with "Just for a minute" instead. "Okay?"

"Thank you thank you," Murphy says, and makes to squeeze through the doorway past them but stops, her lead foot comically held up. "Can I enter these premises, ladies of the house?" she asks both the Indian princess and the skirted nurse.

"Because you're a vampire . . ." Charlotte drolls, her shoulders slumping with how little this surprises her.

"Hey, my kind needs permission," Murphy says, like the good girl she most definitely isn't. "I don't make the rules, do I?"

"*Yes* you can come in!" Desi says.

"Thank you, thank you, says my bladder," Murphy says, and takes an overexaggerated step across the threshold.

"We're not supposed to let anybody in," Ronald repeats.

"You're not supposed to be wearing your costumes either, are you?" Charlotte says, hating herself for blackmailing a first grader like that. But she *does* need this job.

"Thing One, Thing Two," Murphy enumerates, pointing to Desi and Ronald in turn, like activating them.

"Why are you already . . . this," Charlotte says, waggling her fingers over Murphy's whole getup.

"Test run for tomorrow night," Murphy says, primping the arms of her cap, luxuriating a bit too pornographically on the plush resistance of one of the pom-poms. "Your mom's big Halloween blowout after you jam on those wimpy SATs?"

"If this house doesn't eat me first," Charlotte mutters back.

Murphy gives Charlotte a look about this, reaches out to tug on one leg of the tights Charlotte is still wearing on her head.

"Thought you had to pee," Charlotte tells her flatly.

"Vampire bladders are surprisingly—"

"Just past the shelves," Charlotte says, but then, before Murphy can actually *go* there, Charlotte has her by the wrist.

Murphy looks down at this, tracks up Charlotte's arm to her face.

"Um, emergency situation?" she says, shifting her weight from foot to foot. "This is a one-piece, you know?"

"Just, here," Charlotte says, doing her eyes big and words packed to bursting with code, so Murphy will fall in without asking questions in front of the kids, "*let—me—reshelve—this—book—over—here.*"

Murphy digests this, looks to the kids, says, "Your parents bought you a robot babysitter? How do you like her so far?"

"She doesn't always talk like that!" Desi nearly screams, loving it.

"She should have gone in the beanbag," Ronald says, his dejection pretty much palpable.

"Like, gone *pee-pee* in the beanbag, you mean?" Murphy asks back, which explodes Desi into laughter.

Ronald just watches Charlotte, his eyes about to cry again.

"Don't worry," Charlotte says, passing him, threading his bangs out of his eyes. "She's not a stranger, it's okay. We'll keep her secret, and we also won't tell about any stains on any nurse costumes, cool?"

Ronald looks away from this.

Charlotte, to *Plutarch's Lives* now, reaches up to pull a random book out from a higher shelf, saying "Now" back to Murphy in a loud whisper, and, while taking a solid ten seconds to get that book down, the lizard's mouth open against her flannel shirt, she hears Murphy and the two six-year-olds tiptoe across the living room behind her, then realizes she can see them in the television's dead screen as well, like ghosts of themselves.

Before joining them in the kitchen, she goes back to that closet door one more time, counts to three, and pulls it open all at once.

The jack-in-the-box is still there. Not in the downstairs bathroom.

"Thank you," Charlotte says, just to the world, and shuts that door again, crossing the living room without looking upstairs even once.

— —

"Let me guess," Murphy says, squatted down in front of Desi and Ronald, "twinsies?"

Ronald flicks his eyes up to Charlotte, somehow making that eye contact into a plea.

"You didn't even bring any books," Charlotte says to Murphy. "What if my mom shows up?"

"Books have boring answers and boring knowledge in them," Murphy says, adjusting Ronald's nurse cap for him, getting it just so. "The SAT isn't that kind of test. You know this, C. It's about how well you can *think*. It's testing your mind, not your data banks."

"It's testing how well I *test*," Charlotte corrects.

"Which is an intelligence thing," Murphy says, standing, taking this posh kitchen in appliance by appliance. "Eliminate multiple choices by assuming that no test with any self-respect, or with a decent randomizer engine, is going to have C be the right answer three times in a row. So, if you have four to choose from, now you've got three. And the first answer, nine times out of ten, is the one they want you to pick, which can poison your read of the rest of the options, just like they want. So, now you're down to two. At which point it's just a matter of—"

"Plugging one of them in, seeing if it works, blah blah blah," Charlotte says. "We've covered all this, haven't we?"

Murphy fixes Charlotte right in her stare.

"Is this pre-test jitters I'm sensing?" she says. "Is this a defeatist attitude from the girl who's going to score so well that she escapes this town, and"—melodramatic blinking—"everyone in it?"

"Your eyes do look weird," Charlotte tells her.

"Classic non-answer with a side helping of deflection," Murphy says, and takes a long step back to clap ponderously with her gloved hands.

"I don't want to leave you," Charlotte says. "I'm not doing this because I'm trying to get away from you."

"And I won't let you hold yourself back *because* of me. See? We're on the same side."

"Are we really doing this again?" Charlotte says, then, about the twins, gulping all of this in, "have we practiced this argument enough that we're finally ready for an audience?"

"I'm sure Mommy and Daddy have adult discussions from time to time," Murphy says, studying Desi and Ronald as well.

"But Mommy and *Mommy* don't," Charlotte says.

"They're not old enough to . . . have those prejudices," Murphy says. "Are they?"

"They're perfect and wonderful," Charlotte says, kneeling to redo Ronald's nurse cap the way *she* likes it. "And in thirty minutes they need to be tucked in and sleeping."

"Wow," Murphy says. "We never got to stay up that late, did we?"

Charlotte doesn't follow, casts around for a digital clock—clocks, *plural*: they're blinking green on every appliance, even the refrigerator.

10:15?

She starts to lodge an objection about this but can't even form the words. She pulls her phone out. 10:16, now.

"No," she says, looking around for an anchor, for anything that can tie her back to half past eight. "The lasagne," she eurekas, biting her lower lip in about this victory.

She brushes past Murphy, yanks the refrigerator door open, and pulls out the top container, sets it importantly on the island, exhibit one.

"Okay . . ." Murphy says.

"It's still warm," Charlotte says, nodding for Murphy to prove her wrong. "I pulled it out of the top oven almost right at eight. Not even thirty minutes ago. No refrigerator works that fast, not even rich people's."

Murphy looks from Charlotte to Ronald and Desi.

"It's okay," she says to them. "The adults are just having a breakdown the night before the big test."

"Touch it," Charlotte says, nodding to the container again.

Murphy shrugs, pinches a plastic corner up, holds the body of the container with her other hand, and pulls, slips, grabs again, pulls harder, and—the lid comes off all at once, flies behind all of them.

"It's warm, isn't it?" Charlotte says, about the lasagne.

"I've kind of got gloves on . . ." Murphy says.

"Here," Charlotte says, and rips the container away, jams her index finger down, undoing one of her neat spatula cuts.

Instead of smushing all the way through into a dark Italian heart, her finger stops at the top layer of cheesy pasta.

It's cold.

Charlotte rushes to the refrigerator, grabs the next container, has no choice but to register that it's the *last* container. Of what was three.

"Ronald?" she says about this.

He looks away, right to the sink, where the other container, what was the top container, is balanced. Where he was standing, eating.

"He *likes* it cold," Desi says. "Dad says that makes him a weirdo."

"If it's anything like cold pizza . . ." Murphy says, and holds a fist out for Ronald to bump. He doesn't.

Charlotte touches the top of the last container.

It's not just cold, it's fogged.

She covers her face with her right hand, leans back against the counter shaking her head no, no.

"How long did it take me to get downstairs?" she asks, weakly.

"I was considering using the bushes, if that's any indication," Murphy says.

Charlotte doesn't want to cry but can't help it either.

It changes the tone of the room. She's supposed to be the one in charge, she knows. But Murphy's here, Murphy's here. Charlotte hears her asking the kids if any of their favorite shows are recorded, maybe? Do they know how to work the remote?

Two minutes later, after a toilet flush that sounds like a jet engine, Murphy jesters back from the living room alone, takes Charlotte's wrists and guides her hands down from her face.

"You were going to tell me something," she says.

"It's not—this can't be happening," Charlotte says.

"Of course it can't," Murphy says, picking a spider egg from

Charlotte's hair and inspecting it on the end of her red finger. "But, what? *What* is it that can't be happening?"

After the painful tedious apologetic blow-by-blow of the night so far, which Murphy dutifully soaks in, missing time and all, her painted-white eyebrows V'ing higher and higher with concern, Charlotte pulls the bifold door open in the utility to prove it.

They stand there hand in hand.

"So it's an enchanted water heater?" Murphy finally has to say, unable not to grin about it.

Charlotte hip-checks her softly.

"You said you wouldn't laugh," she says.

"That's just the face paint," Murphy says, leaning in to inspect the walls. "There's probably just a hollow wall they can shimmy up, think? They're skinny little rats."

"*I* didn't shimmy," Charlotte tells her.

"So sayeth Concussion Girl."

"Try it, then."

Murphy looks at her with her black-diamond, yellow-iris eyes.

"You've noticed I wore my *good* Dracula vampire outfit?" she says, straightening her arms out to show it off.

"Thought it was Dracula harlequin?" Charlotte says.

"It is," Murphy says, turning back to the darkness of the closet. "I was testing your recall. That was practice for tomorrow morning."

"Then I'll go again," Charlotte decides out loud.

"Is there even a light in there?"

"You can't have lights on for it to work."

"These are rules the *kids* told you?" Murphy asks, to show the obvious flaw in Charlotte's thinking.

"I'm figuring them out," Charlotte says.

"The kids?"

"The rules."

Murphy steps back, giving this demonstration over to Charlotte. Charlotte shakes her head no, starts to step in but then goes to Murphy instead, holds her face in her hands and kisses her long on the red-red lips.

When Charlotte draws back, the insides of all her fingers are pale with white paint, and she's sure her mouth looks bloody.

"That wasn't goodbye," she says.

"Where I'm from, we call that kind of action foreplay . . ." Murphy says back, holding tight onto both of Charlotte's wrists.

"We're kind of from the same street," Charlotte tells her, stepping in, her fingers trailing out of Murphy's hands.

"Then it *was* a promise of things to come," Murphy says.

"Just count to, I don't know, count to ten," Charlotte says, her hand set to pull the door shut.

Murphy holds Charlotte's eyes in hers, says, "If you start screaming—"

"Get your clown ass in here," Charlotte finishes.

"Dracula harlequin, thank you very much," Murphy says, and gently pushes the door from her side, using both hands.

The blackness is sudden.

Charlotte sucks her breath in sharp, nearly throws up from inhaling what she's ninety percent sure is a cobweb. That is, something that came from a spider's ass. Something that has sucked-dry gnats and flies gummed up in it.

She bats her arms around her face, manages to clang her left elbow into the water heater tank, and that must trip something in there because it whooshes on, a blue glow casting out at knee level.

Charlotte pushes back into the corner, knows there has to be all manner of unspeakable detritus and husks there, but she can't help it.

And: there *is* a corner. Not a whole world of empty space

pressing in around her. She grunts a sound out, testing the closet, and the darkness doesn't drink those sound waves up.

It's not working. This isn't a funny place anymore. She waited too long.

The door cracks open and Murphy's jester face is tilting in, a floating white visage with pale eyes.

Charlotte edges out past the heating-up water heater.

"That's not how it works," Ronald says, suddenly there, Desi tagging along.

"She has to point where to go," Desi says, her voice small like she thinks she's going to get in trouble.

"She *who*?" Murphy says to Charlotte.

Charlotte shakes her head no but Murphy seems to hear through that.

"*She* . . ." Murphy repeats all the same, tasting it with her clown mouth as if she almost has it identified.

"What are you—?" Charlotte starts to ask.

"*No*," Murphy is saying now, backing off Charlotte, and away from the twins as well, her black-diamond eyes looking at the ceiling of this utility, at the walls, at all of it in a new and not-good way, like she doesn't trust it anymore. "This isn't *that* house, is it?" she asks. "The . . . what was their name?"

"What house? Who?" Charlotte says, cutting her eyes to the twins in an attempt to censor whatever Murphy, the retired homicide detective's daughter, is about to say.

"It was Halloween . . ." Murphy's saying, her face somehow even paler now. "Oh shit, C. It was Halloween then too, wasn't it? Don't you remember? Second grade? First for you?"

It was the year they didn't get to go trick 'r treating, the year the church started its "*trunk* 'r treating" blasphemy: the whole parking lot lined with cars, trunks and hatches and tailgates open, bags of candy mounded in, a parent stationed there to hand it out, assembly-line fashion.

The take was good—the parents were all trying to buy their kids' lives with taffy and chocolate—but Charlotte and Murphy, just best friends then, came to realize that Halloween wasn't just about the candy, was it? It was about running through the darkness from house to house, your costume falling apart all around you, skeletons and ghouls and ghosts on every sidewalk, coffins and zombies stationed on the lawns, spring-loaded to stop their hearts for a moment, so they could restart them with shrieks and laughter.

Halloween in the church parking lot Charlotte's first-grade year pretty much sucked. But they didn't die, their parents reminded them, so there was that, right?

It wasn't until probably third and fourth grade that they even learned *why* their Halloween had been ruined, and even then, what they got was the legend, whispered behind the open doors of lockers, smuggled from stall to stall in the bathrooms.

The homeschool kids, Tad and . . . and something like "Tad." *Tia*. Tad and Tia *Spinell*. A brother and sister Charlotte and Murphy had never seen, names they only learned when they slipped into school legend. Not because their parents were homeschooling them, but because they'd been killed. And not just that, but killed *by* their mother, and the night before Halloween, which pretty much canceled Halloween.

There were a lot of different versions of it in circulation. The facts were that this Spinell mother . . . was it "Nia," to go with Tia? No: *Nora*. She had, for her own reasons, no note left behind or anything, drowned her six-year-old and her four-year-old in the bathtub, and then tied a rope to the railing of the upstairs hallway and stepped off into the open space of the living room. Her husband, busy with all the other dads building the haunted house in the park, had found her.

Those were the facts.

But the story got a lot juicier than that in the retelling.

The part that thrilled all the kids in elementary was that Nora Spinell had hung herself naked, and that her head had popped off, and also that—kind of a combo deal—she'd jumped off that balcony in her nightgown, actually, but her head had still popped off, letting her body slip down out of it to the floor, the nightgown up there for the husband when he got home late that night, the head rolling around everywhere.

The embellishments didn't stop there, either.

Tad and Tia got involved, of course.

The part that finally started giving some of the third graders nightmares, which is when the principal had to step in, was that the water in that bathtub had been boiling, and that Tad and Tia had risen from it after they were dead and run barefoot all through the house playing hide-and-seek, their skin peeling off. The proof that they'd done this was that when the cops got there to carry the husband into the white van that would take him away, there were little footprints all over the house, still with white tufts of bubble popping in them.

Of course the husband, this dad, had gone crazy, never got a name, just got carted off into a white van.

How this killed Halloween was that the murders happened the night *before* Halloween, meaning, by Halloween morning, it still wasn't clear if Nora Spinell had done this, if the dad had done this, or if somebody still out there had done it.

So, last-minute trunk 'r treating in the church parking lot, maybe because hallowed ground was less prone to horror. Each costumed kid carrying two or three bags of candy to sell back to the dentist next week.

Charlotte was a hippie that year—round glasses, homemade bell-bottoms, her fingers always saying *Peace, man*—and Murphy was her favorite animal, a chipmunk, which was mostly face paint and the way she acted, always sniffing everything.

Yes, Charlotte remembers.

"That was *this* house?" she says to Murphy, being vague because the twins are still right there.

Murphy keeps her Dracula harlequin face pleasant, as if they're just talking about nothing.

"We drove by here once a few years ago for the community garage sale," Murphy says, "and my dad wouldn't come to this driveway, even though we'd been looking for a canoe and there was a canoe right here."

"Canoe?" Desi asks.

Charlotte blinks the heat from her eyes.

Murphy's dad, the homicide detective. The one, they found out later, who had been first on-scene that night. Which maybe had something to do with the sea of vodka he was swimming through these last few years?

"So you're not sure," Charlotte says, trying to find a ray of maybe.

Murphy steps neatly to the twins and then behind them, cups her hands over Ronald's ears.

Charlotte steps in, covers Desi's ears from the front.

"Who is this 'she' they're talking about, then?" Murphy asks, boring her eyes right into Charlotte's.

"That mom was, she was disturbed or something," Charlotte says, insists, "not—not evil. Not still *here*."

"Then why are they seeing a woman, not a man?" Murphy asks. "If they're just trying to scare themselves, don't they conjure up a tall scary *man* to do that? And if they wanted a playmate, it'd be a kid, wouldn't it? Or a—a *dinosaur*?"

Charlotte looks past them, to the part of the kitchen she can see.

"I can't do this," she says, Desi's little hands wrapped around her wrists, her big eyes turned up, waiting for the babysitter to make everything right.

"This?" Murphy says.

"Here," Charlotte says. "I'm going to—I'm going to call them. The parents."

"Smart," Murphy says, releasing Ronald's ears. Instead of letting him go, though, she hikes him up onto her hip, which gets Desi reaching up. Charlotte pulls her up as well.

"It's nothing, nothing," Charlotte coos to her, and to Ronald too. "Just, I'm going to call your mommy and daddy, okay? I have to ask them a question."

Ronald nods yes to this. *Yes yes yes, thank you.*

"They're going to say you're scaring yourself," Murphy says. "That it's the season, that it's a big house."

"I don't care," Charlotte tells her. "Long as they come right the fuck home," then, to the twins, "Excuse my bad mouth."

The four of them trail back into the kitchen and Charlotte dials the number on the notepad into her cell. No answer. Then the next number. It rings and rings, and finally the line opens.

"Mr. Wilbanks?" Charlotte says.

He's not the one she wanted to have to explain this all to, but he's who she's got.

Or not.

"Is this a good time?" she asks when he doesn't say hello.

But there is something.

"Shh, shh," she says to Murphy and Ronald, rattling and crackling through the contents of the pantry. Murphy looks up and Charlotte steps over, switches Desi across to Murphy's free arm. Murphy, a trouper, takes the weight.

Charlotte steps into the living room and squats down, covering her other ear, because there *is* something coming through the cell, isn't there?

It's . . . it's other kids?

But they're far from that receiver. They're laughing and—and *splashing*.

Charlotte stands, shaking her head no, looking all around for Murphy, just so she doesn't have to be hearing all of this alone.

There's just the lizard, watching her.

She's hearing back into the past. Into . . . into eleven years ago. Tad and Tia, bath time. Eleven years ago a mom, on her way upstairs to check on the kids—to *drown* the kids—has stopped to pick up the phone ringing on the wall.

The reason she's not saying anything is that she's listening. To Charlotte.

Charlotte drops her cell, backs fast enough away from it that she catches the couch with the bends of her knees and falls down into it, then jerks forward when she's sure a shadowy form is about to rise up *behind* the couch, catch her in its wet arms.

Murphy's right: she's let herself get spooked. Also—of course—Murphy's standing in the doorway for this performance, Desi still on her hip, Ronald beside her, trying to open a mini candy bar.

"We broke into the Halloween candy," Murphy confesses, shrugging one shoulder like she does.

"What does she look like?" Charlotte says to Ronald. "This—the woman who tells you where the funny places are?"

"The Grey Mommy?" Ronald asks back.

Charlotte's stomach drops.

"You can't go again," Desi says, and Charlotte tracks up to her.

"Why not, love?" Charlotte says.

"Go where?" Murphy asks.

"Because you're already there," Ronald says, and bites into the candy bar.

"So they didn't answer?" Murphy says maybe thirty seconds later, about the Wilbankses.

The twins are parked in front of the medieval episode of *SpongeBob*, which Desi volunteered was off-limits because of name-calling but Murphy said was a special treat for the night before Halloween, like the candy.

Charlotte and Murphy are in the kitchen, the water in the sink running to hide their voices.

"*She* answered," Charlotte says.

"'She' as in—" Murphy says, throttling an imaginary kid in her hands.

"I'm serious, Murph," Charlotte says, licking her dry lips. "And, the boy, Ronald, he said I was 'already there,' whatever that means."

Murphy reaches across, touches Charlotte's shoulder like confirming she's not anywhere else.

"I don't know what he meant," Charlotte says. "It creeps me the hell out, though."

"Okay," Murphy says, messing with the faucet's handle, going from hot to cold and back again. "But, but this . . . this whatever-she-is, she only talks to the boy, right? And when nobody's around?"

"He was born dead," Charlotte whispers. "I think that's the connection."

Murphy holds Charlotte's eyes about this, leans back to reconsider Ronald on the couch. "But he's all right now?" she asks.

"It's not his fault, obviously."

"So we just, what?" Murphy says. "Stay in the same room with him until the parental units are back, right? Problem solved? If he's the only one she talks to, and if she only talks to him when he's alone . . . ?"

"She's getting them to, to take *shortcuts* through the house," Charlotte says. "I think she wants to trap them between places or something. That's got to be what it's building towards."

"You know how out there this sounds."

"I wouldn't believe me either."

"I believe *you* believe it," Murphy volunteers.

"That really helps," Charlotte says back. "Thanks. Humor the crazy girlfriend."

"If it's real to you, then it's real to me," Murphy continues. "So, evil killer mom-lady—the, the Grey Mother or whatever."

"Nora. Nora Spinell."

"So, Lady Spinell is coming for the little angels busy getting brainwashed by Sir SpongeBob in there. But . . ." Murphy draws it out until Charlotte has to look up for her big delivery: "But not on *our* watch, right?"

"It's my watch," Charlotte says. "I just—I can't leave knowing she's still here."

"Because you're that good of a babysitter."

"Because I can't let her do it again."

She looks to the water steaming in the sink.

"She can't hold them under though, right?" Murphy finally says. "Ghosts can't do that, can they?"

"She can lock them in the dryer, or a cabinet nobody ever opens, or a cardboard box under a car in the garage, I don't know."

Murphy considers this, gauges Charlotte, then nods, finally says, "So, what's plan B, then?"

"We leave."

"That's really next in line for solving this, SAT girl?" Murphy asks.

"We can't call the cops," Charlotte says. "I mean, we can, but it'll be a shitshow."

"A shitshow with authorities here," Murphy says. "With guns."

"Would your dad help?" Charlotte eurekas, ramping off Murphy's "guns."

Murphy eyeballs around for a clock—10:38—says, "For this place, yeah. He might call in a favor or two."

"But?"

"But it's after three o'clock in the afternoon," Murphy says, crossing the kitchen for the landline on the wall. "I'll try, cool?"

She stops with her hand to the phone, Charlotte's eyes boring into the back of that hand.

"What are you—what are you *doing*?" Charlotte asks.

Murphy comes around, her face blank, her eyes moving from Charlotte's to the twins, watching her from the couch as well, everybody sort of holding their breath.

"Oh yeah," Murphy says, her face cracking into a guilty smile, her other hand palming her cell up, "my cell's almost dead, yeah?"

She pulls it back to her, thumbs into it, and reads the number aloud as she punches it into the landline's clunky buttons.

She turns around, holds the phone sideways from her ear so Charlotte can hear. It rings and rings, and when it shunts to voice mail she hangs up softly, shrugs apology to Charlotte.

In reply, Charlotte recites Murphy's home number. The same one they've had since forever. The one Murphy just had to look up.

"That's because you just heard me say it," Murphy says, fundamentally offended. "Nobody knows phone numbers anymore, doll. Here"—she swipes higher through her contacts, stops at one only she can see—"tell me yours."

She lays her phone facedown on the island like hiding Charlotte's own number from her.

"This is stupid," Charlotte says. "Did your dad ever say anything about that night?"

"Because he wanted me to become a raging alcoholic too?" Murphy says. "He probably told my mom, I guess. They used to be all hunky-dory and share-bear like that. Not good to keep stuff inside. Unless, you know, your big secret is that you like girls, gasp!"

Charlotte squeezes the side of Murphy's gloved hand, says, "I know I ruined your life."

Murphy squeezes back, says, "You saved my life."

"Don't blame your mom," Charlotte says. "She just—she wants grandkids."

"So do I," Murphy says. "I mean, someday. But kids first. That's the right order, isn't it? You can't just jump to the good part, can you?"

"Can't have your pudding if you don't eat your meat," Charlotte recites, their joke since elementary, when they found that record in her mom's closet.

"I wish my mom was cool like your mom, though," Murphy adds. "They could have coffee, talk about their carpet-muncher daughters."

"*Shh*," Charlotte says, tilting her head to the idea of the twins. "Anyway, you think it's easy being the family's official two-spirit, whatever the hell that even is? You should see the way she trots me out at pow-wows. I mean, no, you shouldn't."

"*She'd* come get us, wouldn't she?" Murphy asks. "Your mom? No questions asked, isn't that her policy?"

It is, yes.

"I told her this was an easy night, though," Charlotte says, "a nothing night. That it wouldn't interfere with the SATs tomorrow morning." She shrugs, adds, "And . . . she's at work, too."

"You can always put it in the scales," Murphy says. "Let them decide for you."

"Scales?"

"How mad she'll be about messing her shift up weighed against how happy she'll be that you're not freaked out, which—"

"Messes up my SATs," Charlotte finishes, not able to resist this logic. "But," she says, feeling it out as she goes, "she'd see Desi's costume, wouldn't she? And then she'd park on the couch, wait to give her big lecture to the Wilbankses when they get back. Cultural appropriation, misrepresentation, training the next generation of colonizers, Manifest Destiny never really stopped, blah blah whatever, you know how she can be."

"Oh, yeah," Murphy deadpans. "*That* old speech. I tell you

about the crime-scene photos my dad tried to scare me back into the closet with?"

"I'm sorry," Charlotte says.

Murphy waves it off, says, "So, my dad's zero help, as usual, your mom's *too* much help—"

"As usual."

"And we still have one hour before the parents get back," Murphy says. "Where's that leave us?"

"Not here," Charlotte says. "That's the main part. I'll figure out the rest later. Along with my new job."

"Your what?"

"Nobody's going to hire the spooky babysitter. The one who doesn't have any proof. The one who freaked out for no reason. The one who took two six-year-olds out into the cold until midnight and fed them sugar to keep them awake."

"Good point," Murphy says. "Where do we go when we leave?" she asks then. "I mean, where isn't going to freak the kids out, make them think we're kidnappers? Do we just sit on the lawn until the parents get back, say the house smelled like it had a gas leak or something?"

"I want to be all the way off the property."

"You bussed here?"

Charlotte nods, says, "You?"

Murphy presents her velvet shoes, curled up at the toe, one red, one black.

"So we're hoofing it," she says.

"The park?" Charlotte tries. "We can sit in the rocket, right? That's safe. Like a jail cell."

"Kind of cold," Murphy says.

"We'll make it fun," Charlotte says. "I'll bundle them up, you'll make hot chocolate. I'm sure there's a thermos in here somewhere."

"Marshmallows?"

"Bring the whole bag," Charlotte tells her, and lets Murphy's hand slip out of hers.

―――

When the kids are still zoned out on *SpongeBob*, jaws slack, legs not even swinging, Charlotte ducks into the bathroom, since the one at the park is probably locked, this late. The toilet is still a jet engine, one you don't want to be sitting anywhere near. Washing her hands, she looks up, draws her breath in sharp: she's still got Desi's tights on her head somehow, the two black legs almost matching up with Murphy's fool's cap. Raising her hand to touch one of the hanging-down, empty legs, she remembers Murphy running her hand down along that slackness as well, only—she pauses the sensation as well as she can—only: feeling the oh-so-seductive texture of a pair of tights while wearing *gloves*?

Charlotte dials back in her head to be sure Murphy actually *did* have those stupid gloves on, and: yes, for certain, for sure, one hundred percent, zero doubt. In this slice of a memory, too, Murphy's mouth is right to Charlotte's left ear, the lips moving in what should be the most secret secret, but there's no whisper, there's just her lips, moving, like, like—

Charlotte peels the tights off all at once, hangs them on the towel rack and pets them smooth with her *bare* hands, watches them until the feet stop swinging.

"You're losing it," she says to herself, her voice creaky, and finds herself getting lost again, this time in the tights' *stillness*. Because, because if she just stays right here, stays right in this moment, then nothing bad can happen, right? Or, nothing she has to know about. Everything bad, that's the stuff that's going on outside this bathroom door. Not in here with her.

But she's the babysitter, isn't she? She says it out loud, to make it true: "I'm the babysitter." It's an hourly job, sure, but it's a responsibility, too. And if she can save Desi and Ronald from whatever's going on here, that'll prove that Arthur sleepwalking into the street was a fluke, just a one-in-a-million spot of bad luck, of the almost-worst luck. If she can save Desi and Ronald, though, it'll be like Arthur never sleepwalked out into the street at all, and then she can go off to college because she *wants* to, not because she's running away from a scene she shouldn't have been able to walk away from.

She does her best to wipe all the tension from her face, blinks her eyes twice fast, holds her chin high, and opens the door, steps back out into the living room, SpongeBob's machine-gun laughter going off right beside her, and . . . and—

The twins are gone?

No, they're hiding.

Under the couch cushions.

She just catches Desi's faux moccasin sliding under a couch cushion, and for a slipping-away moment she can make out Ronald's face sideways under that same cushion, like this is the big trick their mom warned about, like the couch is the one hiding place nobody ever finds them, because nobody but a skinny six-year-old could ever fit there.

Charlotte shakes her head no to Ronald, that this isn't funny, and steps ahead to stop this game before it starts, but then Ronald pulls the couch cushion down over his face, is gone, and it's less like he's having to scrunch under, more like he's . . . stepping down *into* a different space. A hidden stairway, a tunnel, the top of a slide.

Charlotte's running now, sliding to her knees on the thick rug, banging her hip on the coffee table, shoving her arm as deep into the couch as she can.

All she comes back with is a nurse's cap.

She peels the cushion back. There's only the box-spring part— the bottom of the couch, a thin silver bracelet with a single charm on it about to slip down into the crack. The charm is a megaphone, for the cheerleader Mrs. Wilbanks must have been once upon a time.

"No!" Charlotte screams. "No no no fucking *no*!"

She stands, her fingers hooked under the front of the couch, and tips it onto its back. Maybe she can catch the kids sliding down or up whatever tunnel they're in.

It doesn't work like that, though.

The couch tumps back halfway, catching on an end table or decorative footstool or whatever, and there's just dust bunnies and hardwood underneath, and one lone Cheerio.

"*Ronald!*" Charlotte yells, aiming her voice upstairs, her hands balled into fists. "*Desiree!*"

They don't answer, but she's pretty sure there's a rattle up there, metal on metal, a loose sound . . . yes: that night-sky shower curtain that matches the vinyl poster in Ronald's bedroom. Meaning they're in his shower. Or, one of them got spit up there, anyway.

Charlotte steps over the coffee table to run up there but stops, turns slowly to the kitchen.

Shouldn't Murphy have burst out to see what's wrong?

Charlotte counts to three, trying to make this make sense.

"Murph?" she finally says.

No answer.

Charlotte tries to watch the kitchen doorway while at the same time checking every shadow and corner of the living room, not sure if seeing a Dracula harlequin standing alongside the curtains is what she wants or the last thing she needs.

The bathroom, then? Already. No. Okay. The utility, then? The garage? The—the walk-in pantry? Yes. Murphy's looking for marshmallows, of course. And the sink's still running anyway, because that's how Murphy makes hot chocolate: from the tap, not from water heated up on the stove or in the microwave. Maybe she didn't even hear Charlotte calling for the kids. Maybe all the canned goods and bags of noodles in that pantry are muffling the rest of the house. And she's got that stupid cap on anyway.

"Murph?" Charlotte says again, crossing the living room now, giving the television and the coffee table wide berth. When she draws even with the swung-back bathroom door she nearly dies right there, but that's only her own reflection in the mirror.

The doorway into the kitchen, though, there's no way to both step through *and* watch behind her. Not without walking into who knows what. She does it anyway, latching onto the doorframe and pivoting in less like a soldier, more like a fraidy cat.

The water is still running, billowing up steam that's fogging the glass-fronted cabinets.

"Murphy?" Charlotte says with less confidence, stepping into the heat to quiet the water, the heat from the sink instantly clinging to her wrist.

The pantry light isn't even on. Because the marshmallows were right there, just past the doorway, on a high enough rack to keep them away from grubby six-year-old fingers. But now they're hanging half off the rack, the bag torn open, spilling white down onto the tile floor, the quietest, sweetest avalanche.

"*Murphy?*" Charlotte says again, with all the control she has left.

She can see that the utility doorway is dark, that the window in the door to the garage isn't lit up, and—and where else can Murphy even be?

Back in the box, some part of her says before she can stop it.

The jack-in-the-box.

In the same instant, Charlotte asks herself how long *did* it take to make her way down the stairs when the lights blinked?

The question makes her slap at her left ear like Murphy's lips are still there. Not whispering but gulping. And—Charlotte can feel this now too, can remember that her left hand was wrapped around to Murphy's right shoulder blade—Murphy was shorter than her for this, wasn't she? Just like she most definitely *isn't*?

It doesn't make sense. Not even a little.

Charlotte turns, runs across the living room, swaying her back in because she knows there's going to be something behind her, that it's been shadowing her all night. She slams into the closet door by the entry, holds onto the doorknob like something's about to drag her away.

In this new quiet she hears it as distinct as her own slamming heart: *click*.

In one motion she turns, flings that closet door open, not remotely ready for anything but having to face it anyway.

It's still just the same jackets and overcoats as before. The jack-in-the-box on the high shelf.

"Fuck you!" Charlotte screams up at it, and hauls it down, shoves the stupid clown back in as deep as she can and jams the flap down over it. Then she collapses to her knees, hugging that box, muttering apologies to it. Her chest and breath are crying but her eyes are dry, her mind blank.

"Charlotte?" a small voice asks, bringing her back.

She cranks her head up, looks through her hair.

It's Desi and Ronald, holding hands at the top of the stairs. Both of them are crying, scared, the high schooler in charge of them losing all control.

Charlotte opens her arms, meets them halfway, goes to her knees to hug them to her.

"Don't be scared, don't be scared," she tells them, her left hand finding a right shoulder blade again in a way that slows her thinking down. "We're—we've got to go down to the park. Or next door, okay? Can you do that for me?"

"What about Murph?" Ronald asks.

"She'll be okay," Charlotte says, looking around at where they are on the stairs. If it did take her two hours or whatever to get down here when the lights blinked, then this is where she would have been, right?

"We have to put on our warmies," Desi says, standing like a brave little adventurer, ready to do this.

"Just," Charlotte says, letting Ronald go as well when he stands. "Do you have sleeping bags? Just bring those, I can wrap you in those. Or blankets. We don't have time, I'm sorry."

"Is something wrong with the house?" Desi says, looking around.

"Nothing," Charlotte lies, checking all around for a flicker of motion.

"My sleeping bag's in his room," Desi says, afraid of messing up.

"I was building a fort," Ronald adds, standing up for her like a brother should.

"Go, go," Charlotte says, ushering them the rest of the way up the stairs. "I've just got to—to write your mom a note, okay? Fast, I'm counting to ten, *go*."

They scurry down to Ronald's room, the nurse and the Indian princess, and right when they duck in, Charlotte steps into the off-limits master bedroom for the second time, beelines to Mrs. Wilbanks's vanity.

@ the park, just call! she writes in loopy blue ink, then tags a jaunty happy face on the end of it like code, like whispering that everything's fine, it's all all right, don't worry that I've taken your two young children out to a dark place late at night without permission.

"Five . . . six!" she calls out, and steps back into the hall holding the Post-it, ready to stick it to the front door—the *outside* of the front door. "Eight . . . nine . . . nine and a half!" she says around the corner, not quite as loud, and on what would have been *ten*, Desi and Ronald burst out trailing blankets and sleeping bags, two perfect little kids.

Two perfect kids framed by an open office door at the other end of the hall.

"Here, here," Charlotte says, spreading her arms for them to come to her, and their little legs and little arms and intense eyes are all focused on exactly that. Until Ronald steps on Desi's trailing sleeping bag and they go down in a pile.

Charlotte smiles—this is a live-action *Saturday Evening Post* cover, pretty much—but then, just when they're untangling, banging into this wall then that one, one of those walls turns out to be the linen closet door. It swings open, just needed a touch, the red Featherweight vacuum cleaner's long handle tipping out against the opposite wall like a crossbar in front of them.

"Charlotte!" either Ronald or Desi screams.

"It's okay!" Charlotte yells back, already wrestling with the stupid little vacuum, but when she lifts it, the business end hooks under one of the shelves and all the board games and sheets avalanche down.

Charlotte kicks and pushes, can fucking *do* this, but: "You came in through the bathtub, didn't you?" she says, awareness washing down her face.

Ronald's eyes go big.

"I was under his bed," Desi says.

"Go back that way," Charlotte tells them. "You've got to anyway, right?"

The silence from the other side of the linen closet door means . . . it means that this stupid vacuum cleaner, it just saved them from—from whatever hell Charlotte's already in, from only coming through one way, not taking the return trip.

"I'll meet you down there!" she says under the linen closet door, and the twins scamper away, either with or without their sleeping bags, who cares anymore. Getting out is more important than hypothermia.

Charlotte stands, slams the linen closet door, and then checks it hard with her hip, telling it she's had about enough from it tonight. It stays shut.

She runs to the railing, sees the twins crawling up from the half-overturned couch, their hair even more mussed and cute, somehow.

"Stay there!" she says to them, and they look up to her.

"Where are you going?" Ronald asks.

"The way I should have before," Charlotte says, and is already turning, already walking into the inky darkness of Desi's My Little Pony room.

Instead of turning the light on, she just stands over the burst-open oversize pink beanbag.

She knows what has to have happened to Murphy: there was what Ronald and Desi call a funny place in the kitchen, probably right in the pantry doorway—it's dark, secret enough—and Murphy stepped right into it, only had that bag of marshmallows to hold on to. Meaning she's still in there, is falling through the hidden spaces of this wrong house. And she didn't have anybody to hold her hand, tell her not to open her eyes.

"This will work," Charlotte tells herself, about the beanbag.

It has to. It can't have shut yet. Please.

She drops to her knees, scoops as many of the spider eggs back into the beanbag as she can, because maybe they're part of it, maybe they're fuel pellets for the door to open under her.

"I'll be right down!" she calls to the twins, her voice not faltering. Then, to herself, adds *with Murphy*. She'll tumble out of the water heater closet or the dryer or the couch cushions holding Murphy's gloved hand, and then the four of them will run and run and run.

She steps in, works her feet down through the spider eggs to the solid ground, the floor of Desi's bedroom, and then she sees herself doubled in the dresser mirror—just a silhouette flecked with white dots. She nods to her reflection and sits down, working herself in until she has to lie back in it like a body bag.

This is stupid, the traitorous, sane part of her mind is telling her.

But this is the only way, she says back with all necessary curtness, and reaches down for the zipper, pulls it up all at once. She covers her lips with her hand before drawing a breath in, and then, because this is part of it, she makes herself close her eyes.

The darkness is a crawling darkness.

In it, she again feels Murphy's lips brushing her ear, Murphy not even having to lean over or bend down to do this, the lights around them dialed down to almost nothing, Charlotte's left hand nosing through the white interior of the beanbag on instinct, like wrapping around Murphy's back to pull her in, hold her there—

Charlotte stiffens, bucks, the memory of Murphy's mouth being forced away, but . . . but pushing Murphy away wrenches Charlotte's jaw up. The whole side of her head. Because Murphy isn't whispering or kissing, these aren't sweet nothings at intimate range. Her mouth is going up and down because she's *suckling*. She's drinking Charlotte in, taking her out through the ear, or the porous bone right behind the ear, and the reason she's not having to lean over to do this is she's standing a step lower on the stairs, and *not* in a fool's cap, Charlotte would have fabric tentacles in her face if Murphy had that on, meaning, meaning this had to have happened during that hour or whatever when the lights blinked— Charlotte sucks air in and the spun dryness of beanbag beads lodges in her throat. She gags, coughs, sits up on reflex against the backside of her soft pink coffin but can only writhe against it.

And then, moving slowly like it wants her to feel this, one of those beads, beans, whatever, one of them still on her lip, it crackles open. Sharp tiny legs feel out, and all around her, her arms, her stomach, her neck, her ankles—the spider eggs are hatching all over her, all around her, the inside of the beanbag skittering into a thousand-thousand desperate legs.

Charlotte rolls hard to the right in a complete panic, thunks into the dresser, and then she shoulders and kicks back the other way, screaming, hitting, convulsing, gagging, spitting—dying, she knows it.

The tiny spiders crawl into her ears, across her eyeballs, are in her hair right by her scalp, are between her fingers, are up her pants leg, are, are—

She forces her hands up to her face, covers it like that matters, and makes herself breathe, breathe.

At the end she's sobbing. At the end she's lying in a beanbag she zipped shut over herself in a dark room in a house she doesn't really know, with two scared kids listening downstairs.

"Charlotte?" Desi's saying from the living room, her voice so far away.

Charlotte latches onto it, uses it to pull herself back, her fingers finally pinching the zipper tab up from the darkness.

She stands, the unhatched and weightless spider eggs raining down off her.

For a bad moment she's sure her reflection isn't waiting for her in the mirror, but her vision settles. She's really here.

"I'm okay!" she calls to the twins. "Turn *SpongeBob* back on!"

Dutifully, Bikini Bottom washes up the stairs.

Charlotte steps free of the beanbag, looks back to it for the baby spiders she knows aren't going to be there.

But they were. It wasn't just in her head.

That's a dead entrance now, or for the moment, but that doesn't mean a little of the other side doesn't leak through all the same.

Okay, she tells herself.

Murphy's in here somewhere, in the house, but so are the twins. She can do this in stages: kids out the door first, then come back, dig into every dark corner for her girlfriend.

"I'm coming!" she calls down from the top of the stairs, and—no: when she latches onto the handrail, it's slick with . . . bubbles?

Charlotte pulls her hand back, crashes down three steps at a time, holding her arms close.

Desi is on the couch, hypnotized by Sir SpongeBob, and Ronald, he's doing what he's been wanting to do all night: sitting hunched over that jack-in-the-box again, his head turned to hear every click he's cranking up.

"No!" Charlotte says, sweeping him up, away from that, then holding her hand out for Desi too. "We're going down to the park," she tells them, trying to sound more confident than she is. Less shaken.

"What about—?" Ronald says.

"*We're going!*" Charlotte says, hauling their light little selves across the living room to the front door.

Which is, of course, deadbolted.

"Shit!" Charlotte says, about to collapse. She sets Ronald down gently, parks him by Desi, and she digs in her pockets for the key, the key, the key, knows it's going to be upstairs in the spider nest beanbag.

She comes up with it. It's the single most glorious key in the whole history of keys.

And it fits, and it turns.

Before she hauls the door open, though, she enters the temporary code on the security keypad thing. It swallows those four numbers, blinks green twice.

"We're, we're going to the—" she says, taking Desi's hand, already holding Ronald's, and she steps them over the threshold feeling . . . not heroic, but like a survivor. Like they're the lucky ones, getting out when they shouldn't have. Maybe because of that, because it doesn't feel like she earned this, the sky looks phony somehow, like there's no depth.

Or?

Is it phony?

There's not usually a ringed planet hanging up there so close, is there? And now there's more . . . not texture, but *contour*, like empty space itself has ripples.

Charlotte, still pulling Desi and Ronald ahead, brushes her face into that ringed planet.

It's painted on. It's painted on some, some layer or—

Charlotte holds tight to Desi's hand, even tighter than she was, and brings her other hand up to this sky her forehead is most definitely pushing against.

Plastic? Vinyl?

What?

This isn't the sky, it isn't space, it's the nighttime sky printed *on* something. On an oversized wall poster, on a shower curtain hung all around the house, hemming it in.

Charlotte grabs it to pull it away, but, while it will wrinkle and fold, it won't pinch up quite enough for her to *grab*. She pushes against it and it gives, but only so far.

"What is happening?" she says.

Ronald reaches his hand out like to touch it, but Charlotte guides his hand back down.

"I don't, this doesn't—" she says, looking back into the living room, which, bubbles on the handrail aside, and not taking into account all the secret passageways and the beanbag filled with spiders, is still a functional *house*. Unlike everything outside the house, evidently.

"Are you still in it?" Ronald says up to her, and Charlotte looks down at him, trying to let his words make sense.

"I want to watch *SpongeBob*," Desi says, her lower lip trembling.

Charlotte steps back, closes the door gently, twists the key in the deadbolt and leaves it there, then uses her temporary code to tell the alarm not to worry, they're fine. It's a lie, of course. Maybe the worst she's ever told.

Desi scampers back to the couch they must have rolled back forward—twins working together—and Ronald is already looking around for the jack-in-the-box.

Charlotte lifts him up, settles him down on the couch with Desi.

"Count to twenty," she tells them. "It's a slow race. Whoever can do it the slowest gets a marshmallow, okay?"

"Are you playing?" Ronald asks.

"I've got to check something in the kitchen," Charlotte says, standing, the television casting her shadow down over the couch.

"Onnnne . . . two-woo . . ." she starts, stretching the numbers out to show how slow they're supposed to go.

"*Three*-eee . . ." Desi says, picking this game up instantly.

Ronald is looking around her to the television in that blank, hungry way kids have. Good enough.

Charlotte gathers her hair, ties it into a one-minute bun at the back of her head, and steps into the kitchen. Not for the marshmallows, but the garage door.

She steps out into that concrete coolness, flicks the light on and makes sure the chest freezer's just the chest freezer, the Audi just another rich-people second car. Maybe all the dangerous tools are on their pegboard, maybe not, but she can't get caught up thinking about that.

She feels the wall beside her for the big button and the door grinds up on its loose chain, the whole garage shuddering. When it's done Charlotte steps down into the empty space.

Through the two-car-wide garage door space is . . . either

the nighttime sky or a print of it. She steps gingerly around the kitty-littered oil stain, walks purposefully into the garage door's sensor, making the light above and behind her blink with danger, strobing her shadow onto the slick concrete at her feet.

"Please," she says, and pushes her hand out into what she wants to be coolness, emptiness, nothingness.

It's slick, taut vinyl.

The whole nightscape wavers and stretches, would look good as the backdrop of a high school play, probably. But it sucks as the outside she wants to blast into.

"Are they home?" Ronald says from the doorway behind her. "I heard the garage."

Charlotte shakes her head no and looks around the garage, around the garage . . . *yes*: the high window on the other side of the Audi.

"She said this is what can happen," Ronald says, quietly.

"She?" Charlotte asks, trying not to scare him.

"The Grey Mommy. If you don't go back through before it—before it shuts again, then you're stuck between the houses."

"I don't—" Charlotte says, her plea to a six-year-old. "If, if this is happening," she says, "how did she say you get out?"

Ronald's lower lip comes out a bit and he blinks fast.

"It's okay, it's okay," she tells him. "I'm figuring it out. Just—just stay right there, 'kay?"

She hauls a blue and white cooler down from its wire shelf, plunks it down against the wall as a stepping stool and comes up to the window's level in one shaky step. The window opens easy, wasn't even locked. Dried wasp bodies hiss down and she flinches back, looks up to the nest she just crunched the top of the window into.

"I'm just seeing if it's cold," she calls back to Ronald—it's the worst explanation ever—and forces her hand through fast, punching right through the screen.

More vinyl.

"*No!*" she screams, and scrambles down, goes straight to the pegboard, comes down with a pruning saw with a bowed-up back like a witch's index finger. She looks back to Ronald, who has Desi beside and kind of behind him, now that the babysitter's suddenly got weapons in play.

"I got to twenty," Desi says.

"Good," Charlotte says, "you're amazing, both of you are. Now I've just got to—"

She runs at the vinyl print hanging over the garage doorway and slashes down with the saw, tearing a gash open.

"Yes!" she says, and drops the saw, finds the flap she tore, pulls at it with all her weight, ripping the sky open all the way down to the concrete.

Behind it is the same thing. More vinyl. More ringed planets and cartoon stars.

She falls to her knees, her hands in her hair, her bun already falling out.

"Do you want me to close it?" Ronald asks.

Charlotte nods and the door grinds down, burps to a stop when she's still in the sensor. She scooches back and Ronald presses the button again, then one more time. The door comes down right in front of her, like severing her from anything outside the house. Like being sure she knows that.

Breathe in, breathe out.

"You *both* get marshmallows," she says to the twins, and walks purposefully back to them, taking them both by the hand. When Ronald isn't fast enough she hauls him up onto her hip. She deposits him by the pantry, reaches up for the bag.

Desi squats to pinch up one of the spilled marshmallows but it strings out. She yelps, tries to shake it off.

"Yeah, we only want the good ones," Charlotte says, and steps over for a paper towel, cleans Desi's fingers one by one.

"I'm sorry," Desi says.

"You're not going to cut us with the saw, are you?" Ronald asks, his chin pruning up again.

Charlotte's lips tighten the same as his. She shakes her head *no, never*, pulls them both to her, says, "Your babysitter's not being a very good babysitter, is she?"

Neither of them know what to answer but they both flinch in Charlotte's arms when the phone on the counter rings. It's Murphy's guitar-carnival ringtone. Murphy's left-behind cell.

"It's for you," Ronald says.

Charlotte shakes her head no but picks it up all the same, thumbing the line open, drawing the screen up to her ear and then shaking her bun loose over it like that can keep this private.

At first there's nothing, then . . . muttering. Clinking. Silverware? No. Glasses.

"What did you say she was?" a man is asking, his voice breathy. "Was it dots, or, you know, bows and arrows?"

"They don't do dots *plural*," a woman says back. "Just one, right here."

"Like a bullseye for an arrow," the man says with a chuckle.

"You're not supposed to ask that anyway," the woman says back to him, and now Charlotte makes that voice: Mrs. Wilbanks. This is them at . . . at some bar, maybe? They're getting drinks after whatever their date was. They're discussing their new babysitter's skin color.

"I'm not supposed to ask *her*," Mr. Wilbanks says. "I'm asking you. She's not Mexican, is she?"

"Because Alfred and Maria are?" Mrs. Wilbanks says back—the Lopezes, Arthur's parents.

"I mean, maybe that's why they gave her such a good recommendation."

"*Seventeen* is what she is," Mrs. Wilbanks says.

"Should we check on her?"

"It would probably wake the kids," Mrs. Wilbanks says, stopping to take a drink it sounds like. "And if we call we'll just sound paranoid."

"Because we are paranoid," Mr. Wilbanks says. "We can be paranoid. It's our kids. We can be anything we want."

"*I'm right here!*" Charlotte screams into the phone, startling the twins. Charlotte turns away from them, says into Murphy's phone, "Come home now! We need you! There's something going on!"

"I told her about your little lizard," Mrs. Wilbanks says, oblivious.

"Little?" Mr. Wilbanks purrs back, his lips probably close to his wife's neck.

"*Come home!*" Charlotte screams louder into the phone, one of the kids actively blubbering now, but this is more important.

"Is that Mommy?" Desi asks, reaching up, her arm straightening out she's so short.

"Bad connection," Charlotte says, then, one last try: "Mrs. Wilbanks! Mr. Wilbanks! This is Charlotte, the babysitter!"

"How about we find a place to pull over on the way home," Mr. Wilbanks is saying. "It'll only cost us twenty dollars. I'd pay a lot more than that to . . ."

"*No!*" Charlotte screams to them. "Come straight home! Please! I don't want the money, just get here fast!"

"Second stall at the car wash?" Mrs. Wilbanks says back, her voice dialed down just for her husband, not the whole bar. "Is that lightbulb still out, you think?"

"It can be," Mr. Wilbanks says, and then the phone's dead.

Charlotte holds it out in front of her to make sense of this and there's a thin line of bubbles coming up through the mic, the speaker.

She drops it in the sink, which Murphy must have had the plug in when the water was on. The phone plunks in, swims sharply to the side, comes to a rest faceup, the screen flickering once then shorting out.

"Murph isn't going to like that," Ronald says, wiping his right eye—*he* was the one crying.

"Murphy," Charlotte corrects before she can stop herself. "I'm the only one who calls her Murph."

She looks down, hates herself a little more, even: Ronald's eyes are about to spill over again, even more.

"Is that Squidward I hear?" she says in her most cheery voice, and pushes on her nose, drooping it down, making her eyes all hangdog. It gets Desi to smile a bashful smile, Ronald to look away like maybe he *wants* to smile. She'll take it.

She leads them back into the living room, parks them on the couch, deposits the marshmallow bag between them.

"Now don't go crazy on these," she says, eyebrows serious.

They both nod, little liars.

"And, and," she says, kneeling down in front of them for all their attention, "this is going to be a *new* game, now."

Desi's dull eyes and Ronald's suspicious ones lock on hers.

"*The floor is lava*," Charlotte tells them in hushed confidence, reaching down to the rug with her palm, making the hissing sound herself and drawing her hand back up fast. "This means stay on the couch, right? Do you know how to play this one?"

"You're already burning!" Desi screams with delight, standing, pointing.

"Ah, you're right!" Charlotte squeals, and comes up fast, steps up onto the very edge of the coffee table, looks around for what's next: the overstuffed chair.

From there, with both kids watching, she's just able to jump across to the entryway. She hops on one socked foot while holding the other, like she got a bit singed.

"This is water," she calls back to them about the tile, lowering her fake-burned foot to it. "It feels so good."

Desi laughs and laughs. Ronald is still considering this.

"Now, I don't want your parents to get back in thirty minutes and ask me how did the kids' clothes get all black and ashy, okay? We don't want it to smell like a barbecue in here, do we?"

"Barbecue!" Desi says.

In spite of himself, Ronald smiles.

"And no going in any funny places anymore, okay? Promise? No listening to any—anyone who tells you where they are?"

"It wasn't the Grey Mommy this time," Desi says, and Ronald claps his hand across her mouth.

"You . . . just *knew*?" Charlotte says.

Desi, after checking with Ronald, nods contritely.

"No more funny places at all, cool?" Charlotte says.

Ronald finally nods as well.

"Can we roast the marshmallows on the lava?" Desi asks half in secret, already giggling.

"Just don't burn your fingernails," Charlotte says, and takes a mental picture of the two of them there, then reaches out for the jack-in-the-box, floating in the lava.

It goes back into the top of the closet, and she closes the door on it again.

"Where are you going?" Ronald asks her, his voice ramping up into the scared register.

"Nowhere," Charlotte assures him. "Just—just upstairs. I lost that note I wrote your mom, need to write another one, don't want her to be scared when she gets back and we're not here."

When Ronald can't poke any logic holes in this, he nods *sure*.

Charlotte pastes a smile on her face and turns, makes herself go up these stairs one last time.

She can't get them out of the house, no, but she *can* go deeper into it. There's still one place Murphy could be. One room left.

Charlotte doesn't expect the hallway light upstairs to work, but it does. She even flips it on and off to be sure. She leaves it on, pulls the red Featherweight vacuum from the linen closet, holds it in both hands in front of her like a rifle, like she's a soldier going to war.

Backing up to be sure, or because she doesn't want to do this, she sights down through the balcony railing, gets a line on the twins' feet dangling off the couch. One of them, probably Desi, is holding her marshmallow out over the heat she's imagining.

"Everything good down there?" Charlotte calls through the railing.

Ronald leans forward, peers up at her, says, "What are you doing?"

"Cleaning," Charlotte says, and steps ahead, out of his view.

A small black spider darts up from the doorframe of the master bedroom then must see her in its cluster of eyes. It freezes, waiting for her to make the next move, and she can practically hear its sharp feet gripping the wall, ready to go any which way, including straight out at her. Maybe it's just a normal spider, she tells herself, but knows it could also be that the—the membrane between the house and whatever's under the house is thinning, is punctured, is leaking across.

Through the master bedroom doorway Charlotte can see the monstrous closet's accent lights are on, for no reason she can come up with. She's not up here to investigate lights, though. She pulls that door shut, doesn't need to think about a shadowy figure stepping out when her back's turned.

What she's thinking is that when she stepped into the water heater closet and took the back way upstairs, then didn't shut that door by going back through the beanbag, something else was able to come through, after her. Some*one*.

It's a babysitter's worst nightmare: a stranger in the house. Not just any rando, either, but the one person she knows has killed before and died here. The mother who has a history of drowning young children in the bathtub. The mother who wants the rest of the children as well. The mother who's been earning the trust of Desi and Ronald by playing harmless fun games with them.

But she only comes out for them. Meaning she must be going back somewhere else the rest of the time, right? And Ronald said she can't use the funny places, didn't he? At this point in the night, Charlotte's been in every room of the house, she's pretty sure. Except the room that's locked. Except the room whose locked door she *saw* opening.

That's got to be when Nora Spinell came out. It has to be. Meaning—meaning there's something a*bout* that room. If that's where things start, then that's where they can end. Maybe all Charlotte needs to do, even, is shut that door again, right?

Or maybe Murphy will be in there taped to a chair, stuck to the ceiling, tied in the closet, bleeding out on the floor, trapped behind a mirror, suffocated in a shopping bag, trapped in a giant jack-in-the-box—*Don't think about it,* Charlotte tells herself, and rolls her grip tighter on the vacuum, which is *not* "featherweight."

"Murph?" she calls down the hall.

She's not even sure if she wants a voice to answer back. Even Murphy's, since what she'll see, she knows, is Nora Spinell standing dead center in the office, speaking with Murphy's voice, her arms dripping bubbles down onto the rug. She might even have Murphy's pale eyes, her sharp teeth. Just, they'll be real.

Charlotte's heart is battering at the walls of her chest, trying to get away.

At the doorway to Desi's room she reaches in without looking deeper, pulls the door shut. She does the same at Ronald's room, and his bathroom door is already shut. She looks behind her for any straggle-haired dead women slithering up the stairs or crawling along the wall—movies have poisoned her—but it's only her, and all the shadows are hers too.

She places her palm to Ronald's bathroom door just for the solid feeling, for something to push off, and right when she pulls her hand away a bathtub faucet roars on behind her. From Desi's room—Desi's *bath*room.

So that's where it happened. That's where Tad and Tia Spinell died. That's where they were held under the water, that's where they probably looked up *through* that scummy surface at their mom, holding them there.

Charlotte doesn't want to have to know this.

The head of the vacuum cleaner scrapes the wall and she jumps to the other side of the hall, swinging down at the noise her head knows she just made. Tell that to her body, though. To her hands, her arms.

Desi erupts in giggles that straighten Charlotte's spine even more.

Do I even have to be doing this? Charlotte asks herself. Can't she just plant herself on the couch with the kids, wait for the garage door to groan up, pretend not to notice the Wilbankses' wrong-buttoned shirt and mussed hair from their car-wash rendezvous, accept the twenty they slide her then slope out into the *non*-vinyl night, wait for the last bus home?

Yes, she could, she should.

Except for Murphy.

Murphy's trapped somewhere in this house.

"Hello in there?" Charlotte calls ahead of her, through the office's open door.

She edges closer, can see that the light is off in there, but there's a blue glow all the same.

Charlotte shakes her head no but does it anyway: switches the vacuum to her other hand, having to balance its awkward weight while her right hand feels around inside the office for the light switch, her wrist turned the wrong way, her hand blind.

Which is when the worst sucking noise she's ever heard reels up right by her head.

The vacuum. Her left hand's blundered into the power switch, and evidently this model is battery-charged.

Charlotte screams and jerks and drops it, but, but—

It's pulled her hair in.

Her head goes down with the vacuum, both hands pawing for the stupid power switch, that spinning roller whirring closer and closer to her face.

The vacuum finally winds down, its open mouth right up to her forehead, half her hair deep in its dusty guts. She's sobbing, not breathing right, the office sideways to her eyes. But there's no feet standing there, thank you. No bubbles.

Charlotte extracts her hair as well as she can. But there's tearing, for sure. And the smell of burnt keratin. Finally, when there's just a few tens of strands left, she pulls the vacuum steadily away, gritting her teeth against the sound, against all those years of growth ripping away.

She's free, though.

She drops the vacuum, stands from that wreckage, inspects the office from a normal angle.

It's just what she imagined it would be: three lateral file cabinets, degrees and family photos on the wall, bifold closet doors folded flat, a shuttered window, and, below that window, Mr. Wilbanks's desk and computer, the screensaver a digital clock batting around from side to side on the monitor, corner to corner.

11:36.

Charlotte turns the light on, scrunches her fingers through her hair on the left side, feeling out the damage. The office looks the same lit up, just more detail.

Just to be sure—no surprises—she crosses to the closet doors, rips them open, ready for whatever.

Legal-file boxes, stacked and leaning. A closet that hasn't been opened in a while.

"So?" she says to the office, to this last room she had to work up so much nerve for.

She steps over to the window, wonders if, past those shutters, it's the same vinyl nightscape. She wonders what if one of the funny places downstairs would have spit the twins up in here one time. The door, if it locks—and it does, it was, Mr. Wilbanks said it was—has to lock from the inside, doesn't it? They wouldn't be trapped. And surely they come in here anyway, when their dad's working.

She leans over on the desk to survey the office one more time, and her spread fingers nudge the mousepad, which moves the mouse, wakes the screen, lights the room up a different way.

Even in the new reflections in the glass over the multiple degrees, though, there's nothing. Just her own shadowy form, and the square of light Mr. Wilbanks's computer screen is now.

At least now she can lock the door back when she leaves, she thinks. Make it look like she followed *this* rule anyway, never mind the rest.

She feels through her hair again—it's ratted out on one side—crosses back to the door, turns the light off, looks back one time, and . . .

The computer screen?

It's just Mr. Wilbanks's desktop background, some pale office building he probably either designed or works in, but down at the right corner there's something darker, something moving, or playing.

Charlotte looks behind her, then to both sides of the office, and steps hesitantly over, settles herself into his tall chair with arms higher than she needs.

What's moving in the lower right corner of the screen is the feed from the living room. The nanny cam.

That's why he didn't want her in here, the perv.

Charlotte maximizes that little window, fills the screen with it.

The kids are sitting there, their high-stakes life-or-death game mostly over, the lava floor cooled down to imaginary black. Desi is tranced out, staring right into the lizard's mouth—into *SpongeBob*—and Ronald is at the other end of the couch, hanging over the arm to reach onto the end table, turn the crank on the jack-in-the-box he can't stay away from, the jack-in-the-box that has a shimmer or something to it through the lizard's mouth, probably because of its antique paint.

Charlotte touches the screen lightly with her fingertips, shocking herself enough that she jerks back, has to laugh at how stupid she's being.

This is just another Friday night gig. Murphy's probably just playing a joke. Charlotte's spooking herself. It's the curse of any babysitter around Halloween, isn't it? In the morning she'll take her SATs, and in the fall she'll blast off for somewhere else, Murphy right there with her. They'll live together, and Murphy will be her secret study weapon, quizzing her deep into the morning hours, rigging up flashcards on all the biology and chemistry Charlotte will be loading up on, to get ready for med school proper. Charlotte smiles, minimizes the window again just like Mr. Wilbanks had it, and is standing to go downstairs, open the front door, tear through however many layers of vinyl she has to in order to climb back to the real world, when—

What?

Something in the nanny-cam window.

Instead of enlarging it again, Charlotte leans right down to it.

It's . . . *Murphy*?

She's—she's climbing up over the back of the couch. Like . . . like she was there all along?

Charlotte turns to the open office door as if she can look downstairs, into a few minutes ago, when the kids had disappeared under the couch cushion and she'd flipped the couch back, looking for them.

It hadn't tipped all the way over, had it?

It had caught on something. Charlotte had assumed there was a footstool or ottoman or some decorative doodad back there for the couch to kickstand back on. But it had been *Murphy*? Murphy who hadn't said anything? And she'd stayed there until the twins rolled the couch back forward? She listened in on Charlotte starting the lava game? She hadn't answered when Charlotte had been desperate for her to?

Charlotte maximizes the screen, sits back fast from how close the living room is now.

Desi looks over to Murphy, settling between the twins, and Ronald turns to her as well, his lips a thin line.

Murphy's eyes are still pale.

She smiles wide, her vampire teeth lapping over her bottom lip.

Desi pushes away, her eyes widening, but then Murphy's shoulders move in silent chuckle and she reaches her gloved fingers into her mouth, pulls the fangs out, sets them down on the coffee table.

The twins watch those teeth in wonder, then come back to Murphy.

She takes one of their marshmallows, pops it in, says something the lizard can't hear. The twins smile, even Ronald, and she peels out of her gloves, gives one to each of them. Desi immediately runs her arm into the black one she has, pulls it all the way up to her shoulder. Ronald just holds his, watching Murphy.

Next, moving carefully, Murphy leans her head back, applies her bare right fingertip to her right eyeball, and pulls the contact up.

"What the hell?" Charlotte says, standing to go downstairs, stop this . . . this whatever-it-is. But—but she has to know how it ends without her interfering, too, doesn't she? She sits back down, has to watch.

Murphy leans to the side to dig inside her jester costume for her contact lens case. She deposits the right contact into its side, then extracts the left, puts it in as well. She blinks fast and big, shakes her head like trying to unblur her eyes.

Ronald and Desi step down onto the crust of lava, come around to see her face. She looks from one to the other, pops another marshmallow in, says something that makes the kids laugh again.

Now she's . . . she giving Desi instructions? Yes. Desi scampers off, is back a few shakes later with the hand towel from the bathroom, wet.

Murphy runs her finger up into it, dabs at her white makeup.

It comes off agonizingly slow, in deliberate circles, and—and it's *not Murphy*?

"You did come back," Charlotte says to the screen. To the dead mother she knows is going to be under that makeup. Because— because the Grey Mother killed Murphy, stripped her down, took her fangs, her contacts, her costume, and, and . . .

It's worse.

Charlotte stands again, shaking her head no.

The resolution on Mr. Wilbanks's camera isn't high-def, but—

"No," Charlotte says, shaking her head. She's not insisting. It's a plea.

It's—but it can't be—it's *Charlotte*. Her face is still pale from the face paint, and the black diamonds are dull shadows bisecting her eyes, but . . .

Charlotte feels her own face. It's partially to be sure of the contours and planes and angles she's seeing through the nanny cam—like watching security footage of herself—but it's also to be sure that she's still *her*, that she's just been . . . been *copied*, not replaced. Like that makes anything even close to sense.

It does to the twins, anyway.

They're jumping up and down from this wonderful excellent joke. From Murphy disappearing long enough that Charlotte could go upstairs, dress like her, then sneak down for a Halloween trick. The best one ever.

The Charlotte downstairs points to the Charlotte upstairs—no, no, to the television—and pushes her nose down and downer with her right finger, miming Squidward just like Charlotte had done for them in the kitchen.

"That's not me!" Charlotte screams, pushing away from this, the chair clattering over behind her.

She bangs on the desk like that can do anything, and is about to turn away, race downstairs, when . . . when the recording changes?

The webcam is too slow to keep up with whatever's happing. Walls and rugs, darkness and light.

"What?" Charlotte says.

When the recording settles again, it's her, from the side, and she's giant. No, the camera is *low*.

She turns to the doorway, one hundred percent expects Murphy to be there, ready to laugh about whatever impossible joke this is, but the doorway's empty. No, *not* empty.

She tracks down to the blue lizard looking up at her, its mouth open.

She falls back against the desk and tries to climb up on it, tipping the monitor over and down. The lizard turns, zips away, leaves Charlotte breathing deep, her knees up to her chest, her breath fast and shallow, her head shaking *no, no, this can't be happening, this isn't real.*

"Call me Charley," the Charlotte downstairs says clearly to the twins, and louder than she needs to, like she wants to be sure her voice makes its way upstairs.

It brings Charlotte back to herself. She feels her eyebrows come down, her lips set.

She steps down onto the plastic mat Mr. Wilbanks's chair rolls on.

It accepts her weight, lets her cross slowly to the door. She grabs onto the doorframe, finally convinces herself to pull through.

She stops when there's a nightgowned woman walking away from her. Nora Spinell. Her arms are wet and bubbly, and she's crying so hard she can barely stay upright, her whole body shuddering with each sob.

She's just done it, Charlotte knows. She's just killed her children. And, and there's a yellow nylon rope trailing from her hand, probably from the closet of this office when it was a different room.

Nora Spinell doubles it, loops it over the balcony railing and then has to stop, collapse into even worse sobs. She shakes her head no, though, *no*, and stands, raises her chin to tie the other end of the rope around her neck. She pulls it tight-tight, then looks back to Desi's room, and . . . does she see Charlotte?

She sort of does. Charlotte shrinks back, her hands over her mouth, and this child-killing mother doesn't look away, keeps Charlotte in her eyes the whole time she's stepping up onto the balcony, having to duck and hunch to keep her head from scraping the ceiling.

And then, both too fast and in the slowest possible motion, she plummets down, her arms out to the side.

The railing creaks and shudders and splinters, looks like it's going over as well, but it holds her.

An instant later the rope pops back up, slack, the body it was holding gone.

There's no sound of it hitting downstairs.

The twins don't scream.

Charlotte tries to process this, their nonreaction, and then—no.

She hears Ronald again, telling her she has to go back through the beanbag. Ronald asking her if she's still there. It hadn't made sense when he said it, but . . . he was right, wasn't he?

She's on the wrong side of the house. She's *in* the wrong house. And she somehow left enough of herself behind that Nora

Spinell was able to step into it, occupy her, *be* her, as far as the twins can tell.

Now *Charlotte's* the shadow who can tell Ronald and Desi where the funny places are. Except she also told them not to listen to that woman anymore.

And, and Murphy, she was never even really here, was she? When the lights went down earlier, what Charlotte thought was a blink but had to be more like an hour, that was long enough for... for Nora Spinell to body up to Charlotte on the stairs, put her lips up to Charlotte's ear, and drink enough of her memories out to sneak away, dress up as Murphy, wait out the transition that was already happening to them, between them, whatever.

All so she can take a couple more kids.

Charlotte closes her eyes, shakes her head no, and steps forward, knows that at any instant a headless nightgowned body is going to be trudging up the stairs, her hand to the rail because she doesn't have eyes to gauge the next step.

But a good babysitter doesn't hide upstairs, either.

Charlotte steps forward, forward, her hand to the wall like that can prove she's still real, that she's at least still *connected* to something real, and when she passes Desi's room, her fingertips skating across the door, the water shuts off in there. And now, bubbling under that door—the laughter of kids at bath time? Not the twins, right? It can't be.

Charlotte twists the knob and steps in, feels for the light but... she has to look to be sure: the light switch is just a blank slate.

Because she's where she is—on the wrong side of the house.

She makes herself breathe in, breathe out, and steps to the side, just far enough to see through the open door of the bathroom—which is how you leave it when kids are bathing: open, so they don't get up to anything dangerous; open, so everybody in there stays alive, including them if they're splashing water out onto the floor one more time.

The tub is empty. No twins, and no other kids either. Because Tad and Tia Spinell died forever ago.

Charlotte turns to leave this place, just catches that laughter of bath time again. The tub is still empty when she turns around, though.

"Stop, *please*," she says, and then she *sees* that bath time. In the mirror.

Both Spinell kids are alive. She assumes that's who the blond girl and her little brother are. The bubbles are mounded everywhere, are floating up in tufts like a unicorn daydream.

Charlotte steps forward, keeping the angle of the reflection right, and touches the mirror.

It's just glass, isn't wet or anything.

"She's coming," she warns the kids in that reflection.

They can't hear her.

Charlotte looks behind her all at once, for the headless mom in the doorway, too close all at once, but she's not there. Yet.

Back to the kids. Back to this movie still running all these years later.

Tad slips under and Tia reaches in instantly for him, guides him back up, clears the bubbles from his face, taking care like big sisters do. He starts to cry but she covers his mouth, her scared eyes looking around for their mom, probably. Because she doesn't want to get in trouble.

Tad calms, laughs through his sister's fingers, and comes up with a bright green turtle he can squeeze to shoot a jet at Tia.

She sputters the water away, her lips thin with surprise and anger, but then, still playing, she piles bubbles into her hand and sculpts it into hair for him, scolding him to sit still for this. When she's done he stands to try to see this in the bathroom mirror, which is out of Charlotte's view, and then Tia stands by him, both of them slathered in bubbles, trying to see their reflections.

Which is when Tia turns her head just enough to see Charlotte in the bedroom mirror. Charlotte's chest hollows out and she staggers back from this, loses her angle into the bathroom for a moment. By the time she comes back, the corners of Tia's mouth are twitching up into an almost smile, and then she turns to her brother to sculpt his hair again, fix the left side, which is calving off in the slow way of bubbles. He stands still for it, and at the end Tia calmly guides the turtle down from his hands, away, then brings her own hands to his cheeks to fix his dripping beard. Right after she's got it perfect, she rotates her hands on his cheeks and jams her sharp little thumbs through his eyeballs, having to change the angle of her arms to get all the way in, and through. The fluid in his eyes spatters her face, and then the red comes, slathers down Tad's cheeks and Tia's hands, and still she pushes deeper, moving her sharp little thumbs around in his head, making his shoulders and arms puppet helplessly.

Tad starts to scream so she falls forward, driving him into the water, holding him there and holding him there until a line of drool comes down from her mouth, disappears into the white bubbles. Tad's not shaking anymore. The water sloshes over the edge of the bathtub once and then finds its level, and by the end of it Charlotte's face is cold, her hands over her open mouth.

If—if Nora Spinell had come in and found Tad just *drowned*, then it could have been an accident. Even with just one eye pushed in, still, that could have been the plastic tail of a toy dinosaur. But with *both* his eyes punched in like this, then, then: a mother knows, doesn't she? She knew it was her daughter. And . . . that was why she was being homeschooled probably, wasn't it? Because she was displaying violent tendencies? Because she did something to the class guinea pig in kindergarten? Because naptime always ended in disaster when she was lying there on her mat, her lips moving with whatever she was dreaming, whatever she was muttering into the heads of all the other sleeping kids? Because she had this in her and her parents knew it, Charlotte knows. They knew it but thought they could love her enough to fix it. Like you do. Like anybody *would*.

But they couldn't get her to stop being her.

Charlotte turns to the doorway again for this mom who killed herself not out of guilt but a grief so massive she couldn't contain it, but she's still not there, and when Charlotte comes back to the mirror, the reflection of the bathtub looks the same as it does straight on: just dark, empty, nobody there.

But now she knows.

"Tia," she says, intones.

It's not Nora Spinell downstairs in Charlotte's left-behind body, is it? It's her dead daughter Tia, grown up in this dark house, in this house under the real house.

She's been waiting for years for someone her age to show up, so she could crawl across, sneak out for the night. It wasn't some sixth grader who told Ronald about that jack-in-the-box, either, Charlotte knows. It was the shadowy woman only he can see. The one who smuggled that antique jack-in-the-box across somehow, to use like an anchor, like a grappling hook set in the real world, one she could pull herself through with, if some kid would just put enough heart into cranking it, each slow turn pulling her closer. But now that the Wilbankses finally got brave enough to call a babysitter in, Tia doesn't need that anymore, can just step into that babysitter's body, if only that babysitter can be stupid enough to leave her body behind, empty.

Tia's been waiting for this perfect . . . not storm, but winning lotto number.

Charlotte shakes her head no, walks out to the railing to scream to the kids that that's not her, to run, but they're . . . not on the couch anymore?

Charlotte slides her hands wide on the railing to lean over the stairs, see more of the living room, and the railing, splintered from Nora Spinell's suicide, snags her right palm, tears it open.

She draws her hand up without looking, brings it to the side of her mouth, and then, finally, has to look down to her cut when her lips and tongue aren't finding the warmth of blood.

The cut's not red, it's not bleeding. It's just open, with dry, springy white inside, like . . . like *tofu*? Like the spackle her mom made her use to fill all the tack holes in her bedroom wall when she finally took her junior high posters down. Like . . . it's like she's nothing, now. Like what's under her skin isn't supposed to be seen, is just a form keeping her looking like herself. For . . . for as long as she remembers what she looks like?

She shakes her head no, pushes back, and turns to race down the stairs but now the headless mom *is* walking up them, following the handrail just like Charlotte knew she would.

Charlotte backs off, cringes down, her hand finding the floor to balance her and, just like all the stories in her elementary halls said, her palm finds a wet footprint, a wisp of bubbles.

And now the headless mom is to the top of the stairs, is about to walk right into Charlotte.

Charlotte does the only thing she can: she clamps her hands onto the railing and climbs up, is going to balance there or hang there as long as it takes. Except this railing can't take anymore.

It cracks over, falls with Charlotte to the first floor.

She lands in the Lopezes' kitchen two weeks ago, her mouth filled with taste: Murphy's new coconut lip gloss.

Murphy has her pressed up against the Lopezes' wide refrigerator, Charlotte's shirt hiking up from Murphy's hands.

It was supposed to be a study session, but, well. The kid's asleep, the house is empty, Mr. and Mrs. Lopez—"Call me *Maria*"—aren't due back for another hour, and if Charlotte has to run through one more practice question, the rest of everything she knows is going to start leaking out her head.

"When the brain is full, the body must play," Murphy told her about ninety seconds ago. It didn't track, exactly, and wasn't really a saying either, Charlotte doesn't think, but this isn't exactly the time for thinking.

Charlotte presses her body out, against Murphy's probing hands.

If this goes any further, as in all the way, Charlotte wonders if the world will look different from that new place. Her mom told her not really—it's just sex, not a brain swap—but all the same she thinks colors might be more vibrant, something like that.

Right here in the kitchen, though? It is a nice kitchen, Charlotte guesses. With granite-cold counters, yeah, but their bodies are radiating heat, are practically glowing.

There are other considerations too, of course, the first of which would be Arthur suddenly standing in the kitchen doorway clutching his blankie, trying to figure out which of these naked tangled bodies is his babysitter (hint, kid: the dark one), and can she read him the story about the choo-choo and the horse again.

"Wait, what if he—" Charlotte says, this visualization all too real, but Murphy's mouth is there again, hungry.

"He won't," she says, working the snap of Charlotte's jeans now.

"In here," Charlotte says anyway, and breaks away hand by hand, lip by lip, grabs Murphy's waistband to pull her through the kitchen and into the formal dining room, the one Mrs. Lopez vacuums so intentionally that all the carpet nap is facing the same way. It means Arthur's footprints show if he goes in there where he's not supposed to be.

If he knows not to go there *already*, Charlotte figures, then surely he won't go in there at night when it's dark and scary, right? Not unless he hears sounds.

"We've got to be shhh," Charlotte says, her hands finding their way up along Murphy's sides, her thin shirt hiking up against Charlotte's wrists, the pads of Charlotte's fingertips somehow hungry.

"Shhh," Murphy says back.

"Do you, you know," Charlotte says right into Murphy's neck, "*have* something?"

It's their running joke, kind of from Charlotte's mom: when Charlotte came out to her (commercial break during a *Next Generation* rerun, no eye contact), her mom had gotten up from her wingback chair, gone to the pantry where the clear plastic jug of gimme condoms from the hospital were, that she'd already said were just going to be there, uncounted, and carried them to the trash can, poured them in with a shrug, and told Charlotte that being into women wasn't going to make Charlotte's life drama-free, it was just, now, going to be a different kind of drama. It wasn't until the internet and friends over the next couple of months that she decided Charlotte was all special and two-spirit. But Charlotte doesn't want to be thinking about all that at this precise moment. She isn't even sure if she's shimmying out of her jeans or if they're actually melting off.

This is good, she tells herself. This is what it's supposed to be like: someone you love, dimmed lights, exotic place, just enough danger.

She tries to slow her head down so she can take every last detail in, since this only happens once. There's the wavery depression glass set in the front of Mrs. Lopez's china hutch, which is the main reason Arthur can't play with his little cars in here anymore. Murphy's back is in each frame in a different way. There's the Etsy chandelier or hanging light fixture or whatever—salvaged wood, hand-worked metal—running nearly the length of the long dark dining room table, all its Edison bulbs showing off their glowing-hot filaments. There's Charlotte's own hand curled around the top of one of the high-backed chairs, all her veins standing at attention, like they have front-row seats for this big event. And—and there's more and more clothes on the directionally vacuumed carpet, the carpet Charlotte is going to have to rake back into place when this is all over, since the vacuum might wake Arthur, and would probably leave its exhaust smell in the air anyway.

But that's all later.

Right now it's Murphy's mouth, Murphy's hands, Murphy's breathing and her own with it, over it, under it, inside it.

"Like this?" she says to Murphy, a few minutes in.

Murphy's groan is answer enough.

Their next joke, when it's over and Charlotte is back in her shirt in case the front door opens, is Murphy saying she wishes one of them smoked.

"Here," Charlotte says, miming a cigarette to pass over. She blows fake smoke out, her eyes slit to watch it slip away.

Murphy takes the idea of this cigarette and draws deep, looks at it in her hand while holding the pretend smoke in, and Charlotte, not even on purpose, takes a mental picture of her doing that, knows that's what she's going to remember best about all this: the cigarette they didn't smoke, in this elegant dining room they're not even supposed to be in, the carpet going every which way.

It's when Murphy blows that smoke back out and Charlotte tracks it up, imagining the paisley patterns, that she sees the blue and red lights in the depression glass of the china hutch.

"Huh," she says, directing Murphy to the window, to the street out front, where the police car evidently is.

Murphy stands naked but for her retro socks and makes her way to the huge window in the dining room, scrunching her hair up in back, completely comfortable with herself.

"Something's going on," she says back to Charlotte, and Charlotte comes up on alert, the blood rushing to her head and unbalancing her so that she tips over, nearly falls *into* that delicate treasure of a china hutch, and this lurching feeling in her gut, this sense of falling . . .

"What is it?" Charlotte says.

Murphy turns back to her, but Charlotte was just saying it to herself, not actually asking.

"This already happened," Charlotte says. "But . . . not like this."

Murphy turns back to the window, maybe can't hear, or process, and Charlotte steps into her jeans, hops to get them snapped.

"I'm going—" she says needlessly, tilting her head at the front door.

The blue and red lights pull her out the front door, over the lawn, into the street.

It's not just one police car, like she guesses she was expecting. There's three of them, and a fire truck, and an ambulance, and other cars besides, all the porch lights up and down the street on, people in house robes and glasses standing in their open front doors like they're completely ready to be ordered back inside.

"No, no," Charlotte says, drifting to the center of the lights, "this isn't the way it happened . . ."

Still, in the center of the street, a stretcher alongside, there's a small form under a sheet. Charlotte tracks up from it to, to the bumper of—

She falls away, shaking her head no.

Her mom's blue Pontiac.

Someone puts a hand on her shoulder and Charlotte looks around, follows this arm up to a fireman.

"You knew him?" the fireman asks. "The Lopez boy?"

"Arthur," Charlotte sputters. "Where's the—who hit him?"

The fireman points with his chin to the second cop car, and, behind that glass, her shoulders forward like her hands are cuffed behind her, is Charlotte's mom in her scrubs. The ones with little birthday gifts floating all over them.

"Why is she—?" Charlotte starts, shaking her head like this doesn't track. "Is she arrested?"

"Refused to take the breathalyzer," the fireman says.

"That's—she says to never take those!" Charlotte tells him, getting light on the balls of her feet to fix this, to save this, to . . . she doesn't know.

The reason her mom says to never take them is that cops always stop you for Driving While Indian, which is where you weren't doing anything wrong, but maybe they can find something under the seat, or you've got a bench warrant, or your registration's expired, or it *looked* like you were about to pull a weapon. All because of that eagle feather hanging from the rearview mirror.

This isn't like that, though, Charlotte wants to tell her mom. Who would no way have stopped for a drink between the hospital and picking her daughter up. She hasn't even been in a bar for years, so far as Charlotte knows.

Take the breathalyzer, she wants to tell her mom. *Prove it's not your fault.*

But then she sees it like her mom has to be seeing it, her mom who probably recognized Arthur Lopez the moment before he went under the car: him being out there is her daughter's fault. But if she can make it her own fault, then her daughter can get out of this town, maybe. Have a life.

Charlotte shakes her head no, no, this isn't real, this isn't the way it happened, her mom *saw* Arthur in her headlights, she *stopped*, he's right now up in his bed asleep, where Charlotte tucked him in.

"I've got to—" she says to the fireman, who's not even listening, and like that she's gone, her bare feet barely touching the grass between the street and the Lopezes' front door, their stairs, the second floor. Arthur's room, his nightlight the only glow, giving all the toys tall shadows.

There's a small form under the covers, just like there's supposed to be.

"He's here!" Charlotte calls back down the stairs, out the open door, and she covers her mouth because it doesn't seem like the right time to giggle. But she can't help it.

She steps forward and then remembers, stops.

"Murph?" she says, loud enough that Murphy should hear if she's still here, and—and this is just like before, isn't it? Wasn't she calling for Murphy earlier? In some *other* "earlier," or a "later" that somehow happened before?

Murphy wouldn't be in Arthur's bedroom, though.

"Artie?" Charlotte says softly to the sleeping form under the covers, not wanting to jar him awake.

The covers don't stir, don't rustle.

Because he's a hard sleeper, a deep sleeper. Because she got him double tired, since she knew Murphy was coming over, because she knew tonight was The Night.

Still, "Arthur?" she says, louder.

She touches the covers and he's really there, is solid, not just wishful thinking or a memory.

"Art, listen, I'm sorry, I just need to—" Charlotte says, pulling the covers down.

At first she must be seeing wrong, it must be the nightlight's weird angle. But then she's not seeing wrong.

His eyes are gone.

Charlotte jerks back, her hands steepled over her mouth.

It's not Arthur Lopez, either.

This is Tad Spinell.

The glow from the nightlight intensifies and Charlotte looks over to it like she has to, and it's not the nightlight. It's that big pink beanbag, incandescent, its shadow crawling with legs.

Desi's My Little Pony Room.

Did—did Nora Spinell, after drowning her daughter in the bathtub, carry her murdered son to bed and lay him to rest before stepping off the balcony? None of the stories in elementary ever said anything about that.

"I'm so sorry," Charlotte says, and reaches down to pull the covers back over him.

His little hand comes up, his fingers circling her wrist. Then his other hand.

He starts writhing and convulsing then, like trying to work something up from deep inside. Charlotte pulls but he's got her. He's . . . he's pulling her hand now, guiding it to his face?

Is he trying to show her that his eyes are gone?

"I can—" Charlotte starts, almost saying she can *see*. "I know, I'm so sorry, I don't know why your sister would—"

She doesn't finish because this is when her index finger slips into the wet cavity that was Tad Spinell's right eye.

She tries to pull back but he holds on tight, his head coming up with her hand, driving itself deeper onto her finger, deep enough that—

When she looks to the sound in the hall, she sees what Tad must have: his dad rushing past. Meaning . . . if Tad *saw* this, then this was when he still had eyes, wasn't it? It has to be. Charlotte, looking through Tad Spinell's *memory*, steps out into the hall after him, but all she sees of him is his behind-leg, stepping into the master bedroom.

The other direction down the hall, Tia is standing there in her pajamas, not drowned yet.

This is before all that, Charlotte can tell. No bubbles whatsoever.

"Shh," she says to Charlotte. To Charlotte in Tad's head.

Charlotte shakes her head no, is sniffle-crying.

Tia, the big sister, sterns her face down, stares her little brother into submission. Dutifully, Charlotte trudges down. Together they step into her bedroom—*Ronald's* bedroom, some part of Charlotte registers—pull up the bed skirt, reveal the plate of scrambled eggs that are congealed over.

Tia squats down, pulls the plate out. The eggs are writhing with maggots.

"Where?" she says to Tad.

"I don't want to," Charlotte hears herself saying in Tad's small voice.

"You promised," Tia says. "I'll scream if you don't do it."

Charlotte can feel Tad's slow tears on her cheek.

She closes her eyes and a, a *sense* opens in her, like hearing but deeper, somehow thrumming through the muscles under her jaw. She can feel what Tia wants. It's down the hall.

"Mommy and Daddy's closet," she-as-Tad says, still crying.

Tia nods, takes his hand in hers and stands, balances the writhing eggs before them.

"Shh," she says at the open doorway to the master bedroom. They cross hand in hand, their mom and dad just mounds of sleep.

"There?" Tia says.

The big closet's light is on. It's just clothes and shoes and belts and, up top, hats.

Charlotte-as-Tad nods to the outlet on the wall, nothing plugged into it.

Tia goes to her knees before it, looks up to be sure her little brother isn't crying too loud, and then, moving delicately, she pinches a maggot up, holds it before one of the upright slots of the outlet.

It falls in, is *sucked* in.

Charlotte steps back, falls into the clothes, two empty hangers rattling.

Tia looks back, her eyes slits, and then she looks back to the outlet.

From the mouth part of the outlet now, the hole under the

two slits, there's . . . skinny black legs? A fly crawls out, buzzes into the air.

Tia smiles, nods, and says back to Charlotte, her voice a whisper, "Here?"

Charlotte nods *yes, yes yes yes*, and Tia's fingers find the seam of wallpaper, follow it down to a corner, and she peels it up and back.

Instead of wall behind there, it's a yawning blackness.

"Where does it go?" Charlotte hears and feels herself asking.

"Tia?" their mom says from the bed, her voice creaky with sleep. "Are you two in my closet again? Do you know what *time* it is?"

Tia smiles, her eyes wet with happiness, and holds her hand back for Charlotte, to pull her into this blackness with her.

Charlotte shakes her head no.

Footsteps are approaching across the bedroom now.

"*Thaddeus*," Tia says, and Charlotte hears and feels herself calling for Mommy and Daddy, which is exactly like telling on Tia.

Tia peels her lips back, showing her teeth, then shrugs *so what*, turns back to the wall, ducks down and in just as their mom steps through into the closet doorway, her scream already starting.

Charlotte—Tad—pushes back deeper into the clothes and boots and hanging scarves, feels more than sees Mr. Spinell crashing into the closet, his voice a boom of desperation, his knees hitting the floor, his long arm stabbing into the wall for his daughter, and this father's son tries to hide deeper in the hanging clothes, is fighting for space in there, pulling away scarf after scarf, hangers rattling down over him, over her. Slowly, Charlotte realizes that there's muted, kind-of-golden accent lighting all around her now.

Mrs. Wilbanks's closet.

She surges through the open door, falls into the bedroom, looks immediately to the king bed. It's made, empty.

"Desi!" she yells. "Ronald!"

And—is that their voices in the living room? It is. It has to be.

Charlotte smiles, stands, is dizzy again but she can stagger anyway. To the bed, then pushing off the bed to the doorway but the headless body of Nora Spinell is *still* coming up the stairs, using the handrail.

Charlotte falls back against the railing, which creaks behind her, gives way, sending her falling.

Again.

Still.

She wakes to the soft chiming of midnight, the right side of her face pressed into the living room rug.

The broken railing is on her legs and hips. Charlotte pushes it off, sits up, her eyes finding the clock on the mantel striking the hour.

It's officially Halloween, then. Just thinking this makes her look to the stairway, for that headless body. Or for Tad Spinell, his face pressed between two posts of the balcony, his bloody eye sockets watching her.

Her fingers feel around to the sharp pain on the back of her head and dig in through the split or crack in her scalp, touch the springy whiteness in there, making her gag so fast the impulse doesn't really come up from her stomach. It's more like it's a tight, humming line between that spot in her head and the sudden bulge in her throat.

She draws her hand back fast, pulls her knees to her chest.

The railing is broken on the floor beside her but it's still up at the balcony as well, like she's both here and not here. Charlotte touches the railing there on the floor with her and it's solid, real. Still touching it, she focuses hard on the balcony—the other railing. It's definitely there as well, unbroken. Which doesn't make any sense. *You're still there, aren't you?* Ronald had said to her. She must be, yeah. When you come through a funny place but don't go back through, then you're stranded, a foot on each side. Sort of? Something like that? But you're losing ground with every step, too. You're slipping into oblivion. Into this. That's why she can see Nora Spinell walking around. It's why she can see the kids in the bathtub. It's why she's made of nothing.

"This is such bullshit," she says, pushing away from the broken railing.

At which point she remembers she's not the only one lost in this. "Desi?" she says, swinging around to the couch, which leaves her dizzy. "Ronbo?" Where has Tia taken them? No, not Tia. "Charley." Where has *Charley* taken Desi and Ronald?

Charlotte plants her hands to push herself up but draws her right back up. It's not bleeding, it can't bleed, there's nothing *to* bleed, but it definitely hurts. And now it's torn open even wider, more of the white showing.

She uses her other hand to stand and immediately balances wrong, is falling across the room, into the television screen. It crackles and blues where she touches it, would probably just be a bump in the signal for anyone watching.

And, what's wrong with her? Why can't she stand without tipping sideways?

Her head stings, reminds her: *that*, yeah.

She feels up and some of the white is protruding in its dry way. This is why she can't balance, isn't it? She needs to hold it in somehow, with something. And bandage her hand to keep it from splitting open any wider, peeling back like a glove.

She takes a step and finds herself falling across the room again, over the coffee table, into the couch.

She comes up with the fool's cap Charley left behind. Murphy's fool's cap.

Charlotte works it down over her head delicately but it's too big, won't hold anything in. She sloughs it off, lets it drop. Her hand, then. She pulls up the red glove—the only one left—works it over her right hand all the way up to the elbow. Perfect.

For her head, she wheels and finally crawls across to the bathroom, pulls the tights down from the rack, works the waist down as low as she can onto her forehead and feels the thin fabric stretched over where her head is trying to spill out at the back. It's still bulging. When she touches it she reels into the wall, leans forward to puke nothing into the sink. Which she's thankful for. If she were to throw up, it would be dry white paste, she knows—if a babysitter's nightmare is a stranger in the house, then an Indian's biggest fear is being white on the inside.

"One, two," she says, and on what would have been *three* she uses two fingers to shove that bulging white back into her skull.

Her world spins, tilts, goes grey then black then shiny purple like videotape, her whole life in frames on it, blurring past, but thirty, forty seconds later it settles.

Still gripping onto the counter around the sink, she straightens her arms, looks at herself in the mirror, just sees the open doorway behind her—*through* where she should be. Because she's not really here. The tights on her head are even still hanging on the towel rack.

Charlotte huffs a sick laugh out, turns to find the kids.

Walking is the same as it's ever been, now. Or: *again*. Her feet don't sink down through the floorboards, and she can't step up onto some pad of magical air either. She wonders if every house is like this—if there are people always walking among and around, a shade away, a blink to the side.

She lifts Mrs. Wilbanks's note from the island just to see if she can. She reads the first two bullet points—lasagne, TV time—but can, at the same time, still see the note where it was on the island.

"So this is death," she says, and knows that just because she heard her own voice doesn't mean it actually went anywhere real.

Her reflection isn't smearing from shiny surface to shiny surface of the stainless-steel appliances, and she tries to imagine ten-plus years of this. If Tia Spinell hadn't already been whatever she was, then walking around like this, nobody to talk to, never seeing herself reflected back, that would have turned her into something else, wouldn't it have? Something worse. As it is, it probably just ratcheted whatever was inside her up higher and higher, to a permanent screech, an always-there hiss, a whisper that never goes away. Especially if her headless mom was always walking around blind, groping through the dark with her long wet fingers. And there would be Tad floating in the bathtub, or maybe running around without eyes.

But maybe Tia would like that, too. Maybe her mom and her brother were trophies to her, right?

Charlotte shakes her head, decides it's time to either choose the utility or the garage. Charley and the twins have to be in one or the other—but wait: they can be outside too, can't they? And that's where they already thought they were going.

"Shit," Charlotte says, and pulls around the island for the garage, but then . . . what is that?

In the utility.

She slows, leans in.

It's a—a bright shadow? That doesn't track, not really, but that's for sure what it is: a shadow that's not being cast, but that's *casting*, like from a source. Not from some dark bulb but shining through from someplace so much darker.

Charlotte steps all the way into the utility, her fingertips to the wall. The bright shadow is coming from the open door of the dryer.

"It's the funny place again," Charlotte says, getting it. Because there's only so many enclosed places downstairs, probably.

She looks all around the utility to make sure she's alone, then steps hesitantly across to the dryer, jumps back when her left leg brushes into the shadow leaking from its open mouth.

It's cold, burning cold.

She pulls her pants leg up and more pores than not are weeping white, like she's being boiled. She rolls her pants leg back down, and her next step—back from the dryer—she nearly falls *into* the shadow when her hurt leg gives under her.

"Wonderful," she says.

She backs carefully away from the dryer, her eye on it long enough that she catches the bright shadow flickering, then fading. In a few moments the inside of the dryer is just the inside of a dryer again.

"Desi?" she calls, knowing it's useless. "Ronald?"

She steps back out into the kitchen. There's only the garage left now. She nods to herself, crosses to that door, and on the way realizes that she's not thinking right, that her insistence that the kids have to be either in the utility or the garage or outside since they're not in the living room or kitchen is wrong, since it's not taking into account the ten or twenty minutes she was conked on the living room floor after falling over the railing, *with* the railing, whatever.

If Charley's really going to steal her life from here on out, then the thing to do would be to tuck the twins in and get them asleep, right? Collect her handful of cash and walk right out of this house at last, or maybe accept a certain ride from a certain husband, already ready for round two of the night.

Still: the garage. To be thorough.

Charlotte steps down into it gingerly, like she doesn't trust the smooth concrete to hold her new self.

It's the same as it was last time. Just a normal garage with an Audi in it, cabinets and a pegboard for tools and the freezer and coolers and camping chairs, a high window with a punched-through screen that nobody will probably even find until spring.

She taps the button to raise the door, see if the vinyl's still there, but the door stays put. She punches it again, watching her finger to be sure the click happens, but the door doesn't move.

She steps down to where one of the Wilbankses parks, stands under the garage door's hanging motor, and finally reaches up, takes the plastic handle on its barber shop rope—braided red and white—and pulls down, disengaging the heavy garage door from the chain. Then she goes to the door itself, finds the handle, sets her feet, pulls, and: nothing.

It doesn't even creak, doesn't even acknowledge that she's there, doing this to it.

The door shakes in a satisfying way when she kicks it, so she turns around to kick it with her heel, and again, only stops when she sees white seeping out through the weave of her sock.

It can't have been this way for Tia, can it have? Maybe since—since she came across dead, not alive, she got a different kind of body. Or a more durable one. One that keeps its white in better. If not, then there's no way she makes it through eleven years of damage, when even the slightest hurt is massive, and doesn't heal.

Charlotte limps to the doorway, washes up in the kitchen breathing hard, her heart pulsing in her shin, her other foot throbbing.

"You're falling apart," she tells herself, holding her left leg out to see if her pants leg is dark down there, from leakage. The whiteness she's made of isn't damp, though. It just crumbles from her cuff. And on her other foot, the white that was seeping up through her sock is dry powder now, like large confectioner's sugar. Especially small spider eggs.

"You're not going to cry," she insists out loud, for whatever it's worth.

She takes a painful step, using the island as a crutch, but she can't take the island with her.

No way can she make it across two days like this, she knows. She's not going to make it another thirty minutes, even.

But—but if she doesn't, then Charley's going to go home tonight as her, isn't she? She's going to be in Charlotte's house and

Charlotte's life, is going to be living with her mom, is going to have Murphy showing up on her phone at all hours. And she's probably skipping the SATs in a few hours, because who would want to sit in a classroom after being locked in the same house for so long?

But what can Charlotte *do* about any of that? She's over here on the wrong side.

She pushes off from the island, staggers back into the empty living room, stops to try to locate the . . . plastic clattering? What?

And then she sees: there's a jester squatted down in front of the television, before the open cabinet doors of the built-in entertainment center.

Tia. Charley.

She's . . . she's tossing something into the avalanche of DVDs and videogames?

Beads, from Desi's beanbag? No, these are harder.

Charlotte zeroes in on the heavy little jug on the floor by Charley's left foot: BBs, for a BB gun. A solid little pound or two of copper-coated balls.

Charley's tossing them one by one into the cabinet and then turning her head to the side to listen.

One BB bounces, comes to a rest, and Charley nods, stands, surveys the living room, decides on the couch. She steps up to it and pulls the end-seat cushion up like a lid, exposing the boxspring part that must not have been there when Desi and Ronald went through earlier. Or, it was there but also not there, Charlotte doesn't completely understand. It was there and not there the same way the back corner of the water heater closet was sometimes there, sometimes not.

Charley holds a single BB out, drops it.

It careens off, pings onto the glass part of the coffee table.

"You want to go through again," Charlotte says, nodding with realization. "But you can't see the funny places anymore, can you?"

Charley steps away from the couch, hissing disappointment.

"Babysitter?" she says to the room, the house.

Charlotte cringes back, exposed in the middle of the room. She's not really there, though. Not in a way people in the real house can see.

Charley looks anyway, then shrugs, studies the coffee table for that rogue BB, finally has to kneel down to pinch it up from the carpet.

"Mrs. Wilbanks," she says, testing it out, "you—you might find BBs around. The kids got into them, spilled them, tracked them all over the house."

She nods, likes that.

"And I'll see them again next Friday, and the Friday after that?" she adds, batting her—Charlotte's—eyelashes in a *poor* way, a *pity me* way. "If Mr. Wilbanks's car is, you know, *dirty*, I'm sure the two of you could go down to the car wash . . ."

By the end of it her laughter is spurting out.

"You don't ever see these kids again," Charlotte tells her, stepping in.

"I've got the rest of senior year left," Charley says aloud, looking around and rattling the jug of BBs.

"Why do you want to go back through?" Charlotte asks, squinting to try to make this make sense.

Charley doesn't answer, has the remote now, is studying it like seeing it for the first time.

She points it at the television, unpauses medieval *SpongeBob*.

On-screen—it's either still the medieval one, or the twins restarted it—Squidward is the jester.

Charley huffs a laugh out, falls back into the couch exactly like every babysitter ever, once the kids are down. Never letting her eyes leave the screen, she peels out of her jester costume, and Murphy—"Murphy"—was right: it's one-piece, a pain. Under it she has Charlotte's mom jeans, her same too-big flannel shirt tied at the belly.

Charley hangs the empty jester getup over the far arm of the couch, and on the way back to her chosen place she collects the buckskin dress and the stained nurse whites.

They make Charlotte take a step back.

The kids left the living room without their *clothes*?

"Where the fuck are they?" Charlotte says to Charley. "What have you done with them? Tia, Tia, can you hear me?"

The real name doesn't work, though.

"This is such bullshit," Charlotte says again.

Charley shakes her—*Charlotte's*—hair out behind her, leans forward to tie it into a high messy bun.

"I don't wear it like that," Charlotte tells her. "I haven't worn it like that since elementary."

At Charley's jaw on the right side, kind of under, there's still a crumbly streak of leftover white face paint. And there's some in both her eyebrows too.

"Why a jester?" Charlotte asks her, cocking her head over like trying to shake the good answer up. Was it because of that stupid jack-in-the-box? The one Ronald was supposed to . . . do *what* with, exactly?

Charley brings her eyes back up from the hair-tying operation and studies the living room, says, not in Charlotte's direction, and not that loud either, but kind of sly and knowing and almost playful, "Are you here yet, babysitter?"

Charlotte doesn't move.

"You know what I'm waiting for the most?" Charley goes on, just generally, out loud. "A *bath*." She has to chuckle about this. "Seriously. I know, right?"

Charley stands up between the couch and the coffee table, trying out the arms and legs of this new body.

"Look, Mom," she says all around, "I dressed up for Halloween this year! I'm an Indian, can you believe it!" She claps whoops from her mouth, brings her knees up in dance, spins around with it.

"That's not your body," Charlotte tells her. "That's not your life."

"Or maybe you're not here," Charley goes on, giving up the Indian act.

"Just tell me where the kids are," Charlotte steps in to say, standing right between Charley and *SpongeBob*.

"But no trick 'r treating until all messes are cleaned up," Charley tells herself, and steps into the kitchen, comes out humming to herself, carrying the rest of the twins' costumes in her arms. And the packaging.

She plunks down onto the couch with it all, loses herself in *SpongeBob* for a solid thirty seconds, long enough that Charlotte finally has to watch some as well, to see what's so interesting. It's just the same Bikini Bottom, dialed back a few hundred years.

Her eyes still glued to the screen, Charley starts picking at the tomato sauce dried on Ronald's nurse whites, then sneers when crumbling that dryness off doesn't make the red underneath go away. Instead of taking them to the sink, then—it's hopeless, but you have to try—she folds them this way and that, trying to hide the stain. When it's good enough, she works it back into the plastic sleeve—just what Charlotte would have done, if she were a crap babysitter.

What this means, though? Tomorrow night, when it's dress-up time, Mrs. Wilbanks is going to shake the folds from these nurse whites, see what's obviously lasagne dripped down the front, and then look over the top of that costume to her guilty son, who has some explaining to do.

Halloweens have been ruined by less, haven't they?

Charlotte looks up to the second floor, trying to see past the posts, hoping to see Ronald at the railing, sneaked up from bed, and then she thins her lips, pissed at herself: when she went up there, it wasn't to find the kids—the kids were right there on the couch already, didn't need to be found. She'd been all about the office, and when she came *out* of the office she'd . . . she'd walked right past Ronald's room, hadn't she? She had, yes. And she'd only stopped at Desi's because the water turned off, never falling back to that night at the Lopezes'. What's important to her now about it all is that she never once looked into *Ronald's* room, just, sort of, Desi's. These kids are twins, though, and six years old, aren't they? They probably still sleep in the same bed more often than not.

"Found you," Charlotte says.

That has to be where Charley put them: to bed. Not because she's a good babysitter, but just to get them out of the way, so she could find the funny places. Charlotte's been having a panic attack about them for nothing. And now it's time for that panic attack to wind down, thank you.

She lurches across the living room on her bad foot and worse leg, pulls herself upstairs with the handrail, and, halfway up, SpongeBob's machine-gun laughter straightens her back. She looks back to the couch and Charley is still just folding and refolding Halloween, isn't fiddling with the remote, isn't thumbing the volume higher just to screw with the babysitter.

"Don't go anywhere," Charlotte tells her, climbing up, up, each step torture.

The master bedroom closet is dark now, the office door at the end of the hall closed again. Because Charley, Tia, whatever, because she's getting the house back in order for the Wilbankses' return, right? Because she wants to be here Friday after Friday, tossing single BBs into all the dark places, waiting for one not to bounce back.

Charlotte pulls herself into Desi's doorway, looks in again just to cross this bed off the list, and sees the little lump of her under her covers. "Shit yeah," Charlotte says. At last, something good, something right.

Except, some evil part of her whispers, what if it's really Tad again, eyeless, wanting to pull her into the memory he can't stop living. What if it's a roiling pile of maggots, or—or what if it's Desi, but it's Desi with scissors shoved down her throat deep enough to pin her to the mattress?

Charlotte hates her mind sometimes. All the time.

"Des?" she says timidly, not quite letting go of the doorframe yet.

The pink beanbag isn't glowing from the inside, at least. But all the My Little Ponies are most definitely watching.

Charlotte lowers her head, staggers forward, comes down on the edge of the bed. Enough to wake a sleeper, but she's not shaking the real mattress, probably.

"Desi?" she says again, and touches Desi's hip lightly.

Nothing.

Not Tad, not Tad, she says to herself, trying to make it true, and pulls the covers back gently, an inch at a time, exposing Desi's blond hair. Her blond hair that's absolutely perfect, even sort of styled, a kind of flip-turn at the bottom.

What?

Charlotte runs her hand along that hair, and it's . . . it's not right.

She grips her hand into it, pulls gently in case this *is* Desi, and an oversized My Little Pony turns to face her. One with an expensive blond mane.

Charlotte pulls the covers lower and Desi's body is all pillows and ponies, puzzled together into the shape of a six-year-old.

"No," Charlotte says, standing before she remembers her leg isn't into that.

She collapses into the beanbag and it envelops her, is a giant pink slug trying to suffocate her, disappear her. She fights, kicks, finally manages to spill out onto the little rug. On her hands and knees, her hair in her face, she just breathes, breathes.

When she looks to the side, to check the beanbag, it's just a kid's pink beanbag, one Desi will outgrow in T-minus five or ten minutes, and when Charlotte checks her other side, to be sure the bed is there acting like a wall for her, a coolness presses into the wet of her eyes, a harsh oily tang assaults her nostrils, and then she tracks reluctantly to the source, almost hidden in shadow: Tad, under the bed. Not watching her, he can't—no eyes, and also he's *dead*—but tracking the sounds she's making. Sniffing the air for her.

He draws back, deeper into the dark, and Charlotte pushes away as fast as she can, scrabbles across the floor for the door, and the moment she pulls into the safety of the hall, Desi's bathroom door slaps open, startling Charlotte up onto her bad leg, leaving her grabbing for whatever she can find—the railing again.

She pulls hard to it, is about to trust it to take her weight, to keep her safe, but—

"That's what you want," she says, opening her hand, hovering it above that smooth lacquered blonde wood.

She was supposed to go over a second—no, a *third* time—wasn't she? Or through. Down. Because that's when this house that's not the house has her: when she's falling, when she's between places. That's when it can land her wherever. It can nudge her into this version of itself, into that fear, this memory, into some other ready-made nightmare mined up from Charlotte's own head.

Charlotte pushes her back into the wall, makes her way to the linen closet and stands up beside it, the wall still supporting her. The little vacuum doesn't come out to play. Charlotte taps the linen closet door with her palm, nods thank you, then stops, remembers, pulls the door open slowly.

All the board games are back on their shelves. All the sheets are folded and arranged.

She closes the door, holds it there until she's sure it's not springing open.

Ronald's room, right around the corner.

Charlotte stands in the doorway long enough for her eyes to

adjust to the darkness. Long enough to see the headless woman in a nightgown standing by Ronald's bed, her chest black with blood.

"This was her room, wasn't it?" Charlotte says. "Tia's."

Nora Spinell's hand is opening and closing, bubbles sliding down to the fingertips, dripping onto Ronald's blankets.

Charlotte backs out, knows that if she were to creep in, pull Ronald's covers down, it wouldn't be him. Worse, Nora Spinell might look up at her with—with the stump of her neck, and Charlotte would fall into that bloody hole, that open windpipe, or that windpipe would try to whisper some secret to her, something that would scream from side to side of her skull, never stop.

So, the twins *aren't* up here.

That's what you came up here to find out, she reminds herself. Nothing else. *That's how you get lost in here. Don't investigate sounds, don't follow shadows, don't open doors you don't need to open. Have a mission and stick to it.* Charlotte's mission right now, it's the twins. And, if they're not tucked into their beds—lights-out eyes-closed or -shut, whatever—then . . . what would Charley have done with them? Where could she have stashed them?

Also: why? If there's no kids to babysit, if the twins are out of the picture, then there's no coming back next Friday. Really, there's probably just going to jail.

And Charley couldn't have stashed them in a funny place, Charlotte knows. Charley doesn't know where the funny places are anymore. Only Charlotte does, now that she's on this side of things.

But—but Charlotte can't *tell* her, can she? Isn't it only Ronald who can see the shadow people? And anyway, if Charley goes back into a funny place with Charlotte's body . . . Charlotte doesn't know. Are they both stuck here forever?

She wishes her mom were here, to help run all this down. She has that step-by-step way of thinking, doesn't allow any nonsense into it, is all about—

Charlotte stops, feels her eyes narrowing with possibility.

Why not call her, then? It's the obvious solution.

She palms her phone up from her pocket and the screen comes alive from being raised.

She puts her thumb on the home button to let it read her print, but, instead, it kicks up the number pad.

"Huh," Charlotte says, but swipes through the four numbers—her initials plus Murphy's, so cute. The screen goes black before she can finish.

She shakes the phone awake, goes through it all again, entering her code faster this time. The numbers aren't glowing from her touch, though. Because she's not really touching them, even though she brought the phone across with her. It should be made of whatever she is, shouldn't it? Can't a shadow make contact with a shadow, at least?

"Shit," Charlotte says, and shoves the phone back in her pocket, turns to clock the hall behind her, make sure no headless women are shambling her way, and then the wall beside her explodes into her head.

The doorbell.

She reaches up, touches her ear canal on that side with the pad of her index finger. It comes back powdery white. She snaps by that side of her head, has to look at her fingers to be sure they're snapping.

So, no more sound on that side now.

Wonderful.

With her other ear, though, she can still hear the after-chime of the doorbell. Charlotte reaches up, touches that high-up box with her whole hand, letting it vibrate down her arm, the tone filling her for a moment before she realizes what this sound actually maybe might mean.

Someone's here.

It doesn't matter who it is, who it might be, Charlotte has to be there before Charley. That's the only important thing. Never mind that, like with the garage door, she probably can't haul this one open anymore. Never mind that she can't sneak past whoever it is, *not* run into a hanging vinyl nightscape.

It's not about thinking, it's about getting there. Down the stairs. Which Charlotte takes two at a time, also not thinking about them, or herself.

Her bad leg gives on her second long step and she falls grasping for the handrail, goes head over feet into the second half of the wooden stairway, her mouth filling with dry white when her face slams into a step. She sputters it out in a dull white spout, keeps rolling, and instead of coming down in a jagged pile on the hard tile floor of the entryway, or in some scene still happening in the past, or in what could have been, instead of all that she splashes into *water*.

Because that's what she told the kids the entryway was.

She gulps it in and it's soapy, so when she tries to gag it out the bubbles remain, are still choking her, and it's deep under her feet, and—she's only just registering this—it's *hot*.

Charlotte thrashes, kicks, clamps onto what's supposed to be the hardwood floor of the living room but is a slick bathtub shelf of shampoo and bubble bath bottles, and one squeeze turtle.

She throws herself the other way, just manages to grab the last upright post of the stairway railing. At which point the surface of the water around her gets soupy and thick, starts to get regular lines. It's gridding up, it's—it's turning back into the tile entryway, shit.

Charlotte grabs the railing with her other hand and pulls, fights up onto the hard-enough surface, makes it all the way out except for . . . the last half of her right foot? It's embedded in the tile?

She pulls gently at first, the doorbell ringing above her again, filling her head with sound even though it can only be coming in through one ear, and then, when Charley is hustling up from the couch, Charlotte just jerks with everything she's got.

The front part of her foot breaks off, stays there.

She drags herself up onto the first step, inspects her foot. It's—it's like one of those Fun Dip candy sticks, one you just dipped into the colored sugar, so it's all blue on the outside, but, if you bite it in half, then it's shockingly white and dry on the inside.

She touches this white candy center and feels a nerve twinge in her calf, but otherwise there's nothing. Just the feel of the pad of her finger pushing against that springy tofu.

She looks up from this to Charley, standing by the couch and saying, "Wait, wait," trying to pause *SpongeBob*. She bustles up onto the entryway to answer the door exactly like Charlotte was told not to do, but then at the last moment she stops, turns back to the living room, holding her hand out, fingers spread as if she's checking things one last time, to make sure there's nothing left out to give her away.

When it's clear—just two costumes on the coffee table, folded and packaged away like new, and one jester costume on the arm of the couch—she shakes her head, getting limber for whatever interaction this is going to be, collects her hair behind one shoulder, and shoves her hand into her pocket for the key.

Charlotte touches her own pocket for that same key. It's not there. Not in the other pocket either.

Charley pulls the door back just enough to see out, like you do at night.

"Yes?" she says, her voice neither inviting nor standoffish. Just polite.

Whoever's out there doesn't say anything.

Charlotte leans over to try to see but now the alarm is giving its little reminder chirrup, the keypad blinking some countdown.

"Oh, oh," Charley says, going from foot to foot to remember

the code. "Hold on," she says to whoever's out there, and, choosing each glowing number at the last moment, she gets it right first try. The keypad relaxes back into peaceful green.

"Now," she says, her attention coming back to this caller, her body still blocking the doorway, her nervous left foot digging into the still-tacky tile. Charlotte fixes on that, waits to see if the sock will stick. It's close, she thinks, but it doesn't quite grab onto the tile. Or the other way around, she guesses. Charley doesn't seem to feel the slick of bubbles at the edges of the entryway either. The entryway's just an entryway again.

When Charley's left hand drops to the knob on the house side, like to open the door farther, Charlotte pushes back across the tile, stands fast against the closet door, catching the back of her head on the knob again.

Her hands find this new pain without her having to tell them to and the world spins and tilts, her eyes the shaky center of that ride. She holds on as best she can, one hand flat to the closet door, the other exploring this new injury. If it looks like it feels, then it's shrimp meat puffing up from its thin shell. When she pushes it back in, slower this time to keep from having to scream, it rewinds her back to years ago then fast-forwards her all at once, through playing in the sprinklers on Murphy's lawn in first grade, getting gum stuck in her hair the morning of a sleepover, sitting in the ER waiting for her mom's shift to be over, her legs not long enough to reach the ground, and then before she's even close to ready she's rushing through the PSATs, her heart beating in her throat, only, when everybody in that classroom with her turns around to the disturbance she's being, they all have black diamonds painted over their yellow eyes, and—

Charlotte opens her eyes to a murmured response from the porch, the question already gone.

"Excuse me?" Charley says, her hand still to the door like any girl knows to do, even if she's been shuttered in the ghost-half of a house for more than half her life. Meaning it's a *man* out there, not early trick 'r treaters, not a neighbor-mom informing the babysitter that the parents are going to be later than they meant.

Cop, cop, cop, Charlotte prays, not at all sure how a police officer could make this situation better, then she gets a glimpse.

It's the homeless man. The one Neighborhood Watch was supposed to have already called about. Which is maybe even better than a cop, right? People living on the street aren't fitted with society's blinders, can see what's really happening—who's *really* answering this door.

At least Charlotte wants this to be true.

She reaches across for the round newel at the head of the stairway rail, pulls herself around to see more of her savior.

His clothes are grimy and layered, his face bristly with beard, his eyes dull under the brim of his crooked cap. It's the kind of look you can smell, the kind that stings your eyes.

"Who are you?" he's saying to Charley, like he doesn't understand who knocked on whose door, here.

"Who are you looking for?" Charley asks back.

The man considers this question for an awkwardly long moment, and Charlotte realizes it's not the actual question that's gumming up his thoughts, it's that it's a response at all. Someone's talking to him like a person.

He looks like he might be about to cry.

"My—I'm looking for my daughter," he finally says, trying to peer around Charley, and when she steps to the side to let him, letting the door swing back all the way, Charlotte can see how she's now *watching* this man. Not like he might be the threat Mrs. Wilbanks was sure he was, but like . . . she recognizes him?

There's wonder on her face. A kind of waiting excitement. Charlotte can feel it radiating off her.

"Tia, you mean?" Charley says to him.

It brings the man's eyes back to her.

"Do you live here now?" he asks, measuring his words, his tone, and maybe—yes—trying to reel his kerosene breath in, too.

"I'm the babysitter," Charley says primly.

"Have you seen her?" the man asks.

Charley turns back to study the living room with him, says, "I don't—do you want to look for yourself, maybe?"

"*No!*" Charlotte screams right over Charley's shoulder, but she can't stop the homeless man from stepping in, and she can't stop the door from closing behind him, the alarm pad on the wall blipping once. Charley twists the deadbolt over, pockets the key.

"You've seen her, haven't you?" the man says.

"You must be . . . *Mr. Spinell*," Charley says, sitting on the couch, patting the cushion beside her for him.

He's just watching her, but a breath or two later he's sitting where she offered, is looking around this living room.

"That wall used to be . . . Nora liked green," he says.

Charlotte turns to a rustling up the stairs and there at the railing, both her hands curled around that smooth wood, is Nora Spinell, bib of dried blood on her nightgown, neck stump still and forever seeping. Maybe you always know the vibration of your husband's voice, though. Maybe you can feel it in the gasping hole of your windpipe, after this many years.

"Why do you think she would still be here?" Charley asks, the cheer in her voice sick to Charlotte's ears—Charlotte's *ear*.

"I told that detective," Mr. Spinell says, blinking away tears, his nervous fingers clamping onto the jug of BBs at his knees, tilting them right then left, the little copper balls avalanching back and forth.

"Murphy's dad . . ." Charlotte hears herself saying, trying to make sense of Mr. Spinell's response.

"You must be starving," Charley says to him, standing in that way that means she's been forgetting her manners.

"No, I—"

She's already making for the kitchen.

Charlotte reaches forward with her half-foot, gives it her timid weight. It doesn't hurt to touch its blunt edge, but it's searing agony to put weight on it. Trying to keep her weight in her arms—like that works—she limps and hitches into the center of the living room, planning to . . . she doesn't know . . . get Mr. Spinell's attention somehow?

Instead, trying to stand on her heel, she loses her balance, tilts backward into the entertainment center, the television.

A book or two spills, a vase tilts over on its shelf without breaking, but not a thing shifts in the real living room.

Charlotte stays leaning against the bright television screen, is slight enough on this side that she can feel its warmth like a space heater. It's not just warmth, though. It's almost like . . . gravity? No: static cling.

Mr. Spinell looks up, grins . . . right at Charlotte? He can *see* her?

She waves wildly, desperately, and his eyes track away.

"What?" she says, and leans back, away from the pain in her foot. Into the pleasant warm television screen.

Mr. Spinell grins again. Or—Charlotte looks down to her hand on the screen—he's not smiling about *her*, but the television. Her hand is distorting the paused picture.

She pulls her fingers away and it's like trying to get free from suction. The light from the screen goes with her for an inch or two, then drips back into *SpongeBob*. At least to her eyes, on this side.

Mr. Spinell can probably only see some version of the ripples, an interruption of the screen or the colors, some pebbly imperfection the picture's finding its way around.

"Yes, yes!" Charlotte says, and touches the screen with her other hand, dragging iridescent swirls down across Patrick's starfish face.

Mr. Spinell looks away, up to Charley, mincing back in with a plate.

"I don't walk like that," Charlotte tells her.

It's the second container of lasagne, dumped out and warmed up, a fork chocked into it at exactly the right angle for that first bite, like Charley's primed this lifesaving meal.

"What are these for?" Mr. Spinell says, setting the jug of BBs down to take the plate.

"They were just there," Charley says, taking her place on the couch and tucking her feet up under her. "Maybe the dad who lives here now . . . maybe he doesn't like squirrels?"

Mr. Spinell looks over to the idea of the backyard, says, as if connecting this word to the concept, to the animal, "Squirrels."

"Tree rats with bushy tails?" Charley says with what Charlotte can tell is a fake smile—is *her* fake smile.

"Squirrels hibernate, don't they?" Mr. Spinell says.

Charley watches him like the holy oracle he isn't, and shrugs, playing along.

"You bitch," Charlotte says.

It falls on no ears.

"*Look, look!*" she screams, and rakes all her fingernails across the screen, nearly dragging sparks.

Patrick wavers and undulates, almost dances, but nobody's watching him.

"I used to live here," Mr. Spinell says around his first bite—*through* the bite, really.

"It's a good house," Charley says, blinking twice like to make it true. "Lots of . . . *room*."

"I found my daughter in the wall once," he adds, like it's the natural next thing to say, like this is something any father might say about his kid.

"In the . . ." Charley says, ever so politely, then abandons the question, opts for another: "What did you—what did you *do*?"

"I think she's there again," he says. "This house . . . I don't know. I think it's like a Venus flytrap. Do you know what that is?"

"It's for flies?"

"It waits for a fly to stumble in, and then it traps it inside, digests it for . . ."

Charlotte looks high on the wall to whatever Mr. Spinell's tracking.

"For years?" Charley completes for him.

"She was in the master bedroom closet," he goes on, chinning upstairs. "She was . . . the house was already eating her. But I pulled her back. I think it got a taste for her then, though. I think it found a way to—to get her back inside."

"Or something," Charley adds.

This quiets Mr. Spinell. He studies his lasagne.

"I have to save her," he says at last. "That's what . . . I'm her dad, I mean. I'm supposed to. She's been waiting for me all these years."

"I don't know if the people who live here want a—you know," Charley says. "Like, a hole in their wall?"

"I can pay," Mr. Spinell says, looking upstairs and forking another bite in, chewing contentedly until his eyes find the jack-in-the-box.

He stops chewing, rattles the plate onto the coffee table, his hands jerky and unmedicated all of the sudden.

"Yes?" Charley says, so hopefully.

He looks from the jack-in-the-box to her, then back to the jack-in-the-box.

He's breathing deep now. Like afraid.

"That was my—my son's," he says, taking it into his lap reverently.

"Your son?" Charley says, eyes open wide to drink every last drop of this deliciousness in.

"Shut up," Charlotte tells her.

"Thaddeus. Tad."

"You left it behind when you moved out?" Charley prompts.

Mr. Spinell doesn't answer.

Moving slow and deliberate, Charley reaches across, removes the jack-in-the-box from his hands and places it like a ritual object on the coffee table.

Charlotte studies it, looking for that sheen she could see through the nanny cam.

"Mrs. Wilbanks told me not to let the kids play with that," Charley says. "I think she's trying to restore it or something?"

Mr. Spinell nods but Charlotte can tell this isn't quite registering with him. That finally being back in his old house is overloading him.

"Wilbanks?" he finally asks.

"They live here now."

He keeps nodding. He's looking up at the balcony now, pressing his lips together.

"If I can just," he says, "they won't mind if I just go up there and feel around inside there. She's been there for ten years."

"Ten?"

"Eleven."

"Wouldn't that make her . . . about my age now?" Charley asks.

Mr. Spinell keeps staring at the balcony. Finally, he brings that stare down to Charley.

"What's your name?" he asks. "I mean, not to be—"

"Charley," Charley says. "Short for Charlotte."

"Chucky and Charlemagne," Mr. Spinell says right back.

"Um, what?" Charley asks.

"Charley starts like Chucky, with a hard *ch*, and Charlotte is—"

"Charlemagne," Charley completes. "You're not all there anymore, are you?"

"When are they home, these Wilbankses?"

Charley shrugs, says as if she couldn't be less concerned, "Any minute?"

Mr. Spinell gets his lasagne plate again, slurps a big bite in, some of it hanging up in his matted beard.

"There's more in the fridge," Charley offers.

"I know she's still here," Mr. Spinell says back.

"Why do you want to find her?" Charley asks, boring her eyes into the side of Mr. Spinell's face.

He doesn't look over, just says, "When I walked in that night—when I came home, my wife, Nora, she was, she was . . ."

He points to the balcony fast with his fork, cheese trailing behind, hanging between, and then he buries the tines back in the lasagne like he doesn't want to get caught pointing.

"She was waiting for you, wasn't she?" Charley says.

"Tia too," Mr. Spinell adds.

"What do you mean?" Charley asks, turning her whole body to him, her right arm cushioning her head.

"I only saw her for a—a flash," he says, squinting like looking into the past. "I told the detective, even showed him where and everything."

Charlotte leans in about this.

"But she was dead in the bath upstairs, wasn't she?" Charley says. "That's what we all heard at school, I mean."

"She was . . . just out of the bath, I guess," Mr. Spinell says. "She was running through the living room, right over there. I heard her feet on the kitchen floor, slap slap slap, but when I ran in there . . ."

"No," Charlotte says, steepling her hands over her mouth. "No no no."

The stories were *true*?

"They told me I—that it was wishful thinking," Mr. Spinell says. "But there were, the detective found them before they all went away, there were bubbles on the carpet. They wouldn't be there if she hadn't really ran through just then, would they?"

Charley shakes her head no, they probably wouldn't.

"But her skin was all coming off," Mr. Spinell adds, holding back tears now.

"Was that why she didn't like baths?" Charley asks. "Because of the hot water?"

Charlotte studies her about this leading question.

"Kids don't like bath time until they're in the bath," Mr. Spinell says, the skin around his eyes crinkling with the memory.

"Was it that bathroom she didn't like, maybe?" Charley asks, so earnest. "Was it that it only had one door, and is maybe six feet by eight feet, counting the bathtub?"

He looks over to her.

"She didn't like enclosed spaces," he says, like slow-motion agreeing with Charley. "The—the doctor said she would grow out of it, probably."

"So," Charley says, digging into this, "so as she got bigger and the world around her got comparatively smaller, this feeling of being closed in would somehow go away? Interesting."

"But she didn't like going outside either," Mr. Spinell says.

"Because it felt like she might fall up into the sky?"

"How do you—?"

"I've studied this," Charley says. "Agoraphobia at one end of a fragile, incomplete, still-maturing psyche, claustrophobia at the other end, no real happy place between the two."

"Studied it where?" Charlotte asks.

"We had to take her out of school," Mr. Spinell says, buying Charley's sincere understanding.

"Classrooms are so small for a girl with her . . . *issues*."

"We'd have to sedate her to get from the front door to the—to the car," Mr. Spinell says, his eyes getting a shine to them.

"What are you saying?" Charlotte asks him. And her.

"I wonder what kind of space would have been perfect for a little girl like her, then?" Charley says all dreamily, and Charlotte can't help but flash on Ronald and Desi's injunction to her, stepping into the water heater closet: Don't open your eyes. And that vast feeling in there, that was also pressing on her at the same time. It was a cloying muggy closeness combined with the distinct sense of unlimited space. Perfect for a little girl afraid of the sky *and* of closets.

"You don't want to go through," Charlotte says aloud. "You want to go *back*. You want to *stay* there. You opened your eyes when you were in there, didn't you? There was nobody to warn you not to."

"Maybe she would have liked a, a huge cavern underground or something, I guess," Mr. Spinell is saying. "But, she would have gotten better. The doctors said."

"If your wife hadn't killed her, you mean?" Charley says, and Mr. Spinell looks over to be sure he heard right.

"I don't—" he starts.

"Did your wife's head really pop off?" Charley asks with a thrill. "Like a"—she takes the jack-in-the-box, turns the crank slowly ahead—"like one of these, right?"

She smiles about this, holding her breath for that next vital click.

"They never found it," Mr. Spinell says. "Her head. They thought I, that I had—but I wouldn't."

"*Leave, leave, go!*" Charlotte screams to him, and turns to the television screen, hitting it with her shoulder now.

Mr. Spinell doesn't notice, but Charley does.

"Oh," she says. "You're here, then."

"Don't do this," Charlotte says to Charley, and steps ahead like she can actually stop this from happening.

"Look, Dad, it's your daughter," Charley says, pointing to . . . not *SpongeBob*, Charlotte knows. To her own dim outline in the television. "I think you're right. She is still here. She's trying to talk to you."

Charlotte looks back to the screen, still rippling, and shakes her head no, no.

"There's a reason they never found your wife's head," Charley says then, cranking the jack-in-the-box one more quarter-turn. She stops, looks up to be sure she has all of her dad's attention to say it: "When I ran into the kitchen, I was carrying it."

He looks over to her like to confirm she's really saying what he's hearing.

"I didn't get to go to—to any underground cavern, though," Charley says, shrugging that whole ordeal off. "I was stuck . . . I guess you could say 'between,' right? I was stuck between. All I had for eleven years that was real was—you guessed it—my mother's head. But things don't rot away the same over there, when you're between. And, if you've got enough time, and you really really want to, if your parents taught you to never give up, if they told you that you can do anything if you try, then you can take that hair, those bones, those teeth, that white putty on the inside, and you can lick them all together like a baby pearl, shape them into something new. Something better. Something you can *use*."

She holds the jack-in-the-box up for show-and-tell, and now Charlotte can see that that sheen the paint has, it's dried blood.

"N-*Nora*?" Mr. Spinell says in mounting awareness—the scrollwork in the kind of armored-up corners of the box are teeth, pushed in root-first—and then, maybe a breath later but still years too late, he straightens his arms against the couch cushion he's sitting on, pushes away from Charley.

"You're—you're not her!" he says. "She's in the walls, I know. I can—I can still save her!"

"Funny thing about walls," Charley says. "Feel along them long enough, say, eleven *years*, and you find a doorway. One you can step through."

She presents herself with a flourish, and some style.

Mr. Spinell shakes his head no, no.

"Your eyes were, they weren't—" he tries.

"They weren't like Taddie's, you got that right," Charley says, and rolls over to straddle him, her hands caressing his rough face. "Remember?" she says, "his were more like—"

She punches her thumbs through his eyeballs, one of them spurting up onto her throat so she has to stretch her chin up and away, straighten her elbows to drive her thumbnails deeper and deeper in.

"No!" Charlotte screams.

Charley drives her thumbs in up to her hand, and she, she—no.

She's pulling to the *side*, and smiling as she does it, not just not looking away, but drinking this in, not wanting to miss a single moment of it.

Her dad's hands come up to wrap around her wrist but he can't stop this.

The skin over the bridge of his nose tightens, stretches white, and then the bone in there, his skull, it fractures down the center of his face. Charlotte can't see it, but she can almost feel Charley's hands suddenly pushing a half-inch over in each direction, like she was trying to work a giant walnut open and it just gave.

Mr. Spinell goes limp, his left hand spasming down, the ring finger and pinky curling up right at the end. Blood wells up in his mouth but doesn't quite spill.

Charley leans down to him, whispers in his ear, "You were right, Daddy. I was in the walls. I never left." She kisses him on the forehead and straightens her arms against his chest. "But I'm getting back, don't worry," she adds, standing away from him. "And this time I'm going all the way in, and you can't save me anymore. It's where I need to be."

Charlotte turns away, throws up into her hand.

It's dry white crumbles, like flash-dried cottage cheese.

"You can't stop me either," Charley says without turning around, her shoulders rising and falling, her hands dark with blood, the fingers opening and closing. "Oh, babysitter?"

"I'm not helping you," Charlotte tells her.

"No, no, you're going to bleed on the rug . . ." Charley says about Mr. Spinell's body. To keep his mouth from spilling red out, she props his head up with a pillow. His head immediately rolls to the side, though. Only Charley's fast reflexes and cupped hand keep his mouthful of blood from the rug. Holding his head on her knee, she looks around for where to wipe her hand, finally thrusts her hand under the end cushion. "There," she says, and props the pillow under his head again. Just like before, his face turns immediately to the side. "Very funny," she says, then to the idea of Charlotte: "Enjoying this, babysitter?" She hauls her father's body up to a sitting position, holding him up from the back, looking around. "Where, where . . ." she's saying, then she shrugs like *whatever*, uses one shoulder to pry up the couch cushion with the bloody underside. With her outstretched foot, she tilts the other two back. Then, having to practically wedge under him, she scooches him up onto the box-spring part of the couch, being sure to jam his face into the rear cushion to keep it from rolling to the side again.

She stands, appreciates her work.

"See, babysitter?" she says. "No blood. And—" she steps forward, arranges the three cushions over him in lumpy, joking fashion—"nobody can even tell he's there, right?"

This is hilarious to her.

"Just temporary," she says to Charlotte, looking around, to the kitchen. No: the garage. "Didn't I have to put a saw back on the wall for you?" she says. "This may be more of a garbage disposal situation, I guess. With trash bags. Unless you want to tell me where any dark light is shining through . . . ?"

"Don't do this," Charlotte tells her.

"You will tell me, don't worry," Charley says, and strides out. Charlotte hears the garage door swing back, the pegboard of tools rattle.

It's just her and dead Mr. Spinell now.

"I'm sorry, sir," she says, and then steps back in wonder, and fear: the couch cushions are sighing down into their place, flattening out.

Charley walks back in right when Mr. Spinell's hand is slipping into the crack between the cushion and the couch. She drops the saw, dives forward, just touches his fingers as they're slipping away.

On her knees now she rips the cushions up and flings them away, jumps up onto the box-spring part but it's too late.

"You could have fucking told me!" she screams all around to Charlotte. "This could all be over right now already! I could already be over there . . ."

She collapses onto the couch, screamcrying with frustration. With loss.

"I know you're still here," Charley says after maybe a minute.

She melts down off the couch and leans back against it, spent, her knees up before her, forearms on her knees, hands hanging.

Looking at her is like looking into a mirror.

Charlotte draws a temporary X on the television screen.

Charley registers it, lets her head fall backward, her eyes watching the ceiling, Charlotte guesses.

"Tad was the one who found the way in, did you know?" she says, just talking out loud. "I guess you wouldn't. He was a cute boy, I'll give him that. But he was a scab picker, too. Mom used to joke that he needed a funnel thing on his head when he had a cut, to keep him from pulling at it."

"Cone of shame," Charlotte says.

"He was—he got in trouble for picking scabs," Charley says,

"so he started, like, *hiding* them. That and his eye crust. He was weird, I don't know. Maybe he would have grown out of it too, right?" This is sickly funny to her. "Anyway, he knew about electricity, but he thought it was blue fire, that it would burn up anything he shoved into the light socket. The plugs on the walls."

Charlotte scans the living room wall, finds an electrical outlet right by the front door.

"Some of the plugs he hid his scabs in, though, they'd kick . . . *other* stuff back out, yeah. It was like a kid-secret, the best thing ever. He didn't know what he had. I don't need to tell you that. When I went through up in their closet, though"—she flings her arm at the couch, at the idea of Mr. Spinell—"*he* reached in, pulled me back." She laughs with the memory, adds, "Screaming all the way, believe you me. Screaming and fucking clawing, babysitter."

She brings her head back, is facing the television now.

Charlotte taps the screen twice, two iridescent ripples.

"She kept—" Charley starts, then does it better: "Mom, I mean. She kept asking why I did it, why I . . . Tad. In the bath." Charley shrugs. "He kept saying my eyes looked different, since I'd, well. You know. Since I'd looked around in there. He said he was going to tell Mom that I needed glasses. But it was just because he was scared. Of what I'd seen. That blackness in there, it's . . . I don't know how to explain it. It's not empty. It's like velvet, really big velvet, but it's also like ash pressing in all around you, or really thin smoke, smoke you can breathe so deep and it doesn't hurt, it's cold, like, and alive, it moves around in your chest, and . . . you didn't look, did you? I don't think you did, no."

"He was four years old," Charlotte says, her hand in place on the television screen, ripples wavering out from her touch.

"But now you're him," Charley says, clipping it off like pulling the two of them into a new chapter. "Now *you* can tell me where they are, the funny places. No, what I mean is, you *will*."

Charlotte knocks twice on the television screen.

Charley nods, gets it immediately, maybe because she has Charlotte's actual brain in her head.

"You *can* see them?" Charley asks.

Charlotte knocks once.

"You'll tell me where they are?"

Charlotte knocks twice.

"That's not just 'yes' two times in a row, is it?" Charley says with a chuckle.

Charlotte flips her middle finger up, presses her hand like that into the screen.

"How about I give you something for free," Charley says. "Took me a while to figure it out. When you're—when you're between like you are, and you're all bleeding white everywhere, leaving powdery tracks like the fucking Easter Bunny, there's something that kind of . . . cauterizes you shut, like."

Charlotte taps once on the screen with the back of her index finger knuckle.

"Brass," Charley says. "When you're between, brass is so cold it's kind of like hot, I guess, I don't know."

"*Brass?*" Charlotte says, incredulous.

She's already looking around the living room.

All the fixtures are brushed aluminum. All the bookends are marble. All the appliances in the kitchen are cast iron or stainless steel.

"The pans hanging above the island are copper," Charley says. "Copper isn't the same. Copper can suck it."

Charlotte knocks once on the screen.

"Somewhere in this house there's a doorstop," Charley says grandly, mysteriously. "It's a dachshund, but kind of like, stretched out long, for a joke. I think it's sentimental. It weighs like five pounds—you can't pick it up. But you can rub what ails ya on it."

Charlotte knocks on the screen again.

"Okay, okay, it's in the *office*," Charley says, pointing up there with her chin. "That's a freebie. A trust builder."

Charley lays her head back on the couch again.

"Hurry," she says. "They're here any minute, I bet."

Charlotte pushes across to the stairs, hangs onto the rail, still not trusting the entryway, and hauls herself up onto the first step.

"But then I *could* be sending you up there so you won't see where I've stashed the kidlings, of course," Charley says with a smile, still staring straight up.

Charlotte stops trying to pull herself to that impossible second step.

"You bitch," she says again.

Charley laughs to herself, her whole body shaking with it.

"I'm not lying about the brass," Charley says, standing now, stretching one shoulder then the other. "And I'm not lying about little Ronnie and oh-so-adorable Desi, either. What does their mother say? 'Lights-out, eyes-closed?' I kind of like that. I mean, it applies not just to going to sleep, doesn't it?"

"Tell me what you did with them," Charlotte says, stepping back down.

"I can tell you right where they are," Charley says, looking for an accidental moment right into Charlotte's soul. "You might even still be able to save them, I don't know. What time is it anyway?"

They both look to the clock on the mantel.

12:12.

"Car wash is getting *steamy* tonight, isn't it?" Charley says, walking around the coffee table, extending the tip of her middle finger to the television screen. It doesn't waver, doesn't ripple, doesn't care that she's touching it. "All these years," she says, shaking her head with wonder, "I never knew I could be jacking with their shows."

Charlotte lunges forward, plants her hand in the middle of the screen. It ripples with color.

Charley nods, likes that.

They're standing right in each other's faces now.

"So I'm going to give you . . . three minutes," Charley says, stepping back, hands held high to show that this is a Charlotte task, not a Charley thing. "You find where that dark light's shining through, and if it's on *this* side of the house"—the kitchen—"you tap on *that* side of the screen. If it's over by the front door, that side of the screen. If it's upstairs, the top. It'll be like . . . what's that game where you tell somebody they're getting hotter or colder? The funny places don't last long, though. Which you should know by now. We do this right, and this is all over right now, I don't ever have to come back to babysit. Believe me, you don't want me to be the new babysitter. I don't just put the kidlings to bed, I put them to *bed*."

Charlotte stares hard at Charley.

"Tap once in the center of Patrick's forehead if you understand."

Charlotte touches where she's supposed to, and it's like a slow-motion realization is rippling across Patrick's thoughts.

"Three minutes," Charley says then, and turns, falls back into the couch, counting aloud: "One, two, three . . ."

Charlotte stands there until the count of ten—long enough to accept that this is really happening, that this is really what she's about to have to do—and then she grits her teeth and stiff-legs it as best she can across the living room, into the kitchen.

The dryer is just the dryer again, not a major appliance vomiting bright shadow out its stupid round mouth.

How do you even *find* the funny places? Tad Spinell—she knows from being inside his memory—could open his senses, sort of, and "feel" them.

Not Charlotte.

She pulls the door to the water heater closet open, takes a broom from its holder on the wall and reaches in with the plastic bristles, meets resistance right where she expects to.

She doesn't put the broom back. It's her crutch, her cane, what she's using now to pole herself forward. Holding tight to it with both hands, one high, one tight at the middle, the bristles up by her face, feels better than teetering around, always about to fall.

She eyeballs the utility for where else a tunnel could be. That's what they are to her, that's what this stupid house is: a demented game of chutes and ladders. Well, it's that with some haunted carnival ride mixed in. And a whole maze of unwanted trips down every memory lane she has that might hurt. And she's the clown in all of this, just, she's wearing her white paint on the inside. But don't worry, it's leaking out.

She crutches back into the kitchen, forgetting for a moment that this crutch is a broom, meaning she gets an armpit full of sharp bristles stabbing dirty holes into her.

"*Three minutes?*" she groans uselessly.

There's no way.

First, finding a tunnel has got to be like trying to stomp on the head of a firehose someone's turned on, let whoosh around everywhere from the pressure. And all she has to go on are the rules she can back-figure from what she's seen—rule *singular*: it'll be some tight, dark place.

Well, there might be an upstairs-downstairs component to it too. She's seen nothing to prove that you *can't* duck into the linen closet upstairs, come out just down the hall in Ronald's bathroom, or under Desi's rug, but so far it's only been an upstairs-downstairs thing, anyway.

But, that rug, and the couch: it's not always even an actual *place*, is it? Sometimes a tunnel just opens up where there shouldn't be any space at all.

Shit.

And Charlotte's the shadow lady who's supposed to know where that is? Seriously?

Charley—Tia—had eleven years to get all chummy with the tunnels, to plot them out, keep charts in invisible ink on all the walls, to figure out the pattern, the tendencies, *anticipate* them instead of just luck onto them.

It can even be behind wallpaper, can't it? That's where it was that first time for Tia. For Tad.

"Fuck this," Charlotte says, and crutches into the doorway of the kitchen.

Charley has *SpongeBob* unpaused, is smiling with it—from Squidward's squeaktacular clarinet playing, it looks like.

For eleven years she hasn't had the remote, Charlotte guesses. It must feel good.

"Ninety seconds!" Charley calls out arbitrarily, without looking away from the screen.

Charlotte makes her painful way out into the living room.

Different plan.

Studying for the SATs, Murphy clued Charlotte in that sometimes it's not about getting the *exact* right answer, it's about sketching out what should be the general shape of that right answer. Like, this proposed angle will probably be obtuse, not acute. That polyhedron will have at least this many sides, not below that many sides. Doing it like that, you can usually get down to a couple of likelies, so if you're jammed for time and have to guess, you can do Murphy's trick of looking back to the previous question, seeing if it was A or B or C or D. Chances are this answer won't be the same, just because of odds. According to her. But, even though she's not going to college, she did flat-out ace the SATs, just to show she could, like she wanted to step over to a life she could have had, leave her own little tag.

Charlotte tries to map out what might be the general area of the right answer to her current problem: either the twins, the brass dachshund, or her body. Those are the three things she needs. And hopefully, of course, the right answer can be all of the above, and all at once. Failing that, though, she itemizes what she's got to solve this problem with: ninety seconds. Probably more like one minute, now. To be specific, one minute to knock on either this or that side of the television screen, right? Which is a little different than actually solving the problem.

What she *can* do is direct Charley back this way, direct her over to the front-door side of the living room, or send her upstairs generally. And . . . if they're all bullshit, then which bullshit gets her closest to the three things she needs?

If babysitter X has no real options, how can she change the question to eke a few more minutes out, maybe get lucky?

Answer: lie, girl. Lie hard. Lie in a way that benefits you.

"I need that brass dog," Charlotte mutters. Meaning, she doesn't need Charley tromping around upstairs, maybe remembering that she told Charlotte where the dachshund is.

Once Charlotte cauterizes her various cuts shut and sears the pain from the blunt front edge of her foot—once she's keeping her insides from crumbling out—then she can get around better, find the twins, can't she? She won't be able to physically save them, but she's hoping Ronald can at least see her, or some version of her. Maybe. Please. And then she'll find a magic wand that'll get her body back from Tia, yeah. This and other impossible fantasies, coming soon to a venue near Charlotte.

But, possible or not, that's the proper order to come at the first two things anyway: dog, then twins. Dog, then twins.

Say it enough times in a row and it's almost like a plan.

Charlotte nods to herself and crutches forward, slams her palm onto the left side of the screen hard enough that all of Bikini Bottom wavers and ripples.

Charley sits forward, dials her eyes over to the kitchen doorway—what the left side of the screen means.

"Okay, o-kaaayy . . ." she says, standing, pausing the show and then dropping the remote. She's breathing deep, not breaking eye contact with the kitchen doorway, like if she does it might stop being real.

This is everything she's wanted, Charlotte knows. Just to get back to that dark limitless closed-in hug of a place. To step into a tunnel and just camp there forever, infinite space all around in the most pressing, wonderful way.

"It's not the garage," Charley says, thinking out loud. "So . . . kitchen, utility?"

Why not *the garage?* Charlotte wonders. She was counting on the time it would take for Charley to comb three big spaces—the kitchen, the utility, the garage—not just two.

Charlotte touches the left side of the screen again, that warmth suffusing her hand, bleeding up her arm.

"It does like the smell of laundry detergent, I think . . ." Charley says, and disappears into the kitchen, stopping on the way, it sounds like, to check the double oven, the refrigerator, the dishwasher, the trash can that pulls out on smooth rollers from the island.

Charlotte is only just to the entryway when Charley's back, scraping the jug of BBs off the coffee table.

"You can do this," Charlotte tells herself out loud, climbing, not looking back. She's halfway up the stairs with her broom-crutch when she hears the first BB ting off either the washer or the dryer. She stops, considers: What if a tunnel *does* open up in there? If it likes out-of-the-way places, then the utility has to be the default setting for downstairs, doesn't it? And, assuming there's always at least one active tunnel—Charlotte has no real reason to think this—and that they are upstairs-downstairs affairs, then Charley's next BB might *not* be tinging back, right?

And . . . if she does find her happy place?

Then she takes babysitter X's body in there with her, and

Charlotte's trapped in this between place for however long she can hold herself together.

She tries to go faster, crutching with the broom, pulling on the handrail.

This can all work, she's telling herself. And wasn't the master bedroom's closet light *off*, earlier, when Charlotte had left it on? Could *that* be where Charley stashed the twins?

But first the office. That brass dog.

This is going to work, she knows. It has to.

She gathers herself for the last push—pull, really—crests up the second half of the stairway, her face level with the floorway of the long hall of the second floor, and—

No.

It's the blue lizard again, but it's the size of a Komodo dragon, is big enough to fill the hall from side to side, and almost end to end as well.

It brings its sluggish head over to fix its black eyes on her, and then, moving languorously, it opens its mouth like to lick her taste off the air, but what it's really doing is exposing the huge black camera lens in its throat, shining it on her like a spotlight. Just, one that's drinking her in.

Charlotte sees the fisheye version of her face in there, flinches from the simultaneous crash of the jug of BBs exploding against the wall in the utility, and then, impossibly, stupidly, she's *seeing* the feed from that camera in the lizard's throat, seeing it on a *screen*.

She looks down to her right hand on the mouse, no red glove on that hand anymore, and then she turns up to the computer monitor in front of her.

Mr. Wilbanks's office.

Charlotte stands so fast from the chair that it rattles over on its back like a roach, one of its lifted casters still spinning in its plastic way.

Don't hyperventilate, don't hyperventilate.

But she does have to breathe, too. Somehow.

She spreads her hand over her upper chest, gasps air in through the spasming constriction she used to call her throat. Then she spins around to the office door, for the giant lizard.

The door's closed. No lizard.

Charlotte takes a step back, feels down for the desk, finds it with her fingertips.

"This is such bullshit," she says at last.

She cases the office again, this time looking for any shadow-people lurking, any spiders darting for cover, any jack-in-the-boxes cranking their little clowns up.

It's the same exact office.

Except . . . she turns back to the monitor, like to interrogate it. She could be wrong, but didn't she knock it over when she ran out earlier? Is this house a videogame? Does each room reset after she leaves?

Charlotte crosses to the door but stops midstep, fascinated with her painless right foot. Her *whole* right foot. She waggles her toes in her sock, says with an almost-smile, "Hey, you." She opens her hand for the cut and her palm is just smooth skin again. She guides it to the back of her head, feels gingerly for the shrimp-meat bulges that make her gag, that send her into random images from her life. They're not there either. She presses her fingers all around through her hair, desperate for at least a bump, a knot, but there's no evidence that the last couple of hours have even happened. Even the tights she was wearing are gone, are probably still on their towel rack in the downstairs bathroom, or maybe even further back than that—in the dryer?

When she brings her hand back, her hair is tangled in the

fingers, trails into her vision, is as healthy as ever, doesn't show any signs of having been wrapped twenty times around the hungry roller of a small vacuum cleaner. She brings it to her nose to smell for evidence. Just her same usual shampoo.

"What the hell?" she says, looking around in wonder. It wasn't just the computer monitor that reset, was it? She reset too. Is that how Tia made it across all those years? Do you go back to Go every two or three hours, collect your old body, no harm no foul?

That would be one way to make this last, she knows. And last, and last.

"Then use it," she says to herself, and steps forward with resolve, jerks the doorknob hard, to blast out into the house proper.

It nearly pulls her arm from her shoulder. Because the pull has to go somewhere, she stumbles forward, her face almost making contact with the door. She looks down to be sure her hand's on the knob like it feels like. She turns the knob like insisting that this work, only . . . the knob stays still?

"Hey!" Charlotte barks into the door, kicking it once with her left foot, sure Charley's standing on the other side, holding the knob in place.

No answer. She looks down to her socked foot to see if the stinging she feels was enough to push some dry whiteness up through the fabric's tight weave.

Not quite. Or, not yet. But it does smart.

"Watch yourself," she tells herself, like saying it out loud will make it stick, then ducks down to eye level with the crack at the bottom of the door—houses with hardwood don't have doors flush with the floor—presses her sideways head down to see into the hall.

No feet. Nobody holding the knob. Not that she wouldn't have freaked out if there were, but she had to know, right? She stands, tries to twist the doorknob with *both* hands now, then she spreads her feet wide for a solid base, puts her shoulders and weight into it.

Nothing.

Her left foot, though, it's nudging into something, isn't it? Something both cold and hot through her sock.

Charlotte tracks down, leans over to be sure.

The dachshund. The brass dog. The . . . the supposedly "healing" doorstop.

"You're real," Charlotte says down to it, not looking away, like if she keeps eye contact it maybe won't wag its tail and blip away.

She doesn't know how she missed it before. It's right there behind the swing of the door, its brass muzzle long and pointed and somehow polite, its tail a perfect upturned apostrophe.

She falls to her knees before it, shoves her hands under its long stomach, and . . . nothing. Instead of lifting it up to take it with her, to apply it to her open parts, it's like it's curled its little claws into the hardwood, is standing fast, not budging.

And Charley was right: it's the kind of freezing that burns, that would hiss and sting if she had any white showing through, probably.

Charlotte runs her other hand under the dog's belly as well, gets her feet flat on the ground, and pulls and strains.

Nothing, just a pop in her shoulder that doesn't make sense if she's undifferentiated white through and through.

Is it things in general she can't budge, or is this something new with her?

She raps on the wall to be sure she's solid, and both hears it and—in the bones of her hand and wrist and arm—feels it.

She reaches over to nudge a diploma on its nail. It rocks back and forth.

It's not her, then. She's still here. Here enough. Is this part of some trade-off? Does she get a fixed body, just, she can't do certain things with it?

And—stand still, don't breathe—are those *voices* out in the hall, now?

Charlotte steps right up to the door again, turns her head sideways to press her ear to it, only right then remembering that her eardrum is supposed to be ruptured. But sound's coming in just fine, thanks.

"—and up here is where all the kids' stuff probably needs to stay," Mrs. Wilbanks is saying.

Charlotte's stomach surges and churns and her face washes cold then hot then she doesn't know what. Just numb.

This is the big walk 'n talk tour through the house. It's . . . almost eight o'clock again?

"This is Desi's room on the right," Mrs. Wilbanks is saying, half-muted and distant.

"That short for Desiree?" the Charlotte taking this tour asks, trying to show how smart and capable she is, how tuned in to the twins she's going to be.

"She doesn't like the accent mark," Mrs. Wilbanks says, and Charlotte looks down to her forearm, remembering that Mrs. Wilbanks punctuated *accent* by touching Charlotte there, like to get across how silly children can be, and how Charlotte must surely understand.

Moments later, Charlotte holding her breath in the office to hear better, that drawer in Desi's bathroom screeches open and Charlotte screams with it to try to get their attention, bangs on the door with the sides of her fists, too.

Now the sides of her hands split open. Two or three little bursts on each, a swarm of paper cuts yawning open, her insides that sickly dry white that nearly makes her gag again.

She holds her right hand up and rotates it before her face, gauging these cuts. And then she steps back to see this brass dog again.

It just stares straight ahead, ignoring her in a way that feels elite, like this is a class distinction between it and Charlotte.

"Let's see what you can do, then," Charlotte says to it, and lowers herself to her knees, tries again just on instinct to rotate the heavy little dog around to her. When it still won't budge, she reorients herself to *it*.

"Okay, okay," she says, and nods fast, holds the unhurt side of her right hand with her left to be sure it makes contact, and pushes down all at once.

The white hisses and almost steams and her right hand tries to jerk back but the left is cruel, won't let it.

Charlotte keeps her teeth together, angles her head back, and screams, the cold heat from the brass solidifying tendrils of the whiteness inside, like crystalizing them. After maybe five seconds of this she breaks contact, cradles her hand to her chest and curls forward over it, apologizing. Five seconds after *that*, she gets the nerve to look at it.

The cuts are . . . melted shut? The skin the color of—of *ash*?

It's not pretty, but it's functional. She waggles her fingers to be sure the congealed tofu in her doesn't get in the way. She can waggle fine, but now it's like each finger has a sort of stalk or root in her palm that she wasn't aware of before.

"The Grey Mother," Charlotte says, trying to focus in on which twin said that.

Ronald, it was Ronald.

And it was Grey *Mommy*, but it was really Tia. Just, a Tia who'd lived in this house long enough to have to have grown up, and cauterized her whole body with this brass. Leaving her the color of ash, of shadow.

"You're not like her, you're not like her," Charlotte tells herself, and scooches over to the other side of the dog to press her *left* hand into that healing brass.

It cauterizes the two little ruptures shut, leaves the skin mottled and grey, wrinkled and dead, the shrimp meat on the inside somehow fuller, less giving. Charlotte touches it to her lips and the skin is still warm. It leaves her tongue a pleasant sort of numb, that kind of numb with the sting of returning sensation right under it.

More important: this is really the only brass in the whole house? Are the Wilbankses that well-off, that moneyed-up? When the Spinells lived here, every fixture probably would have been a triage center for any ghost girls caught between houses.

Charlotte stands from the dog, studies the office again.

"Brads," she says, excavating the word up from junior-high art class—from final portfolios. They'd all had to hole-punch their art, then bind it together with "brads." It was the first time she's seen them. Bendy, light—she could lift one of *those*, couldn't she? Even halfway not-here like she is? It wouldn't be as freezing hot, as healing, but it would be portable. She wouldn't be having to clump her way up here for each scratch. She wouldn't have to lie down backward on the hardwood to touch the back of her head to the prissy little dog that's so insulted by this contact that it just keeps staring straight ahead, its back ramrod straight.

"Thanks," Charlotte says to it, and pulls open the top middle drawer of Mr. Wilbanks's desk.

Just like there's supposed to be, it's all binder clips and plastic rulers with price tags still on, staples and paper clips, pens and pencils and snap-rings and one cork coaster with some business logo stamped in raised white on it. And way in the back, a box of BRADS, BRASS, #6, which must be the size or gauge or who cares.

She flicks the top of the thin box open, exposing some fifteen or twenty unbent brads. When she reaches down to pluck one out, though, the cold heat from it already warming her fingertips, there's a sudden and huge bark from *right* fucking behind her. She jerks forward, away from it, driving her right thigh hard into the edge of the desk.

She keeps going, climbs up onto the desk, pulls her feet up.

The dog is still just standing there. Same place.

She stares at it and stares at it, finally says, "Seriously, dog?"

Without lowering her feet again, and watching the dog close now, she works the drawer back open, feels down for the box.

It doesn't budge when the back of her fingers knock into it. Like it's superglued to the bottom of the drawer. The top is still flapped back, though.

She crawls her index and middle finger up and in, and this time, instead of a bark, there's a sharp snarl and a *bite*. Not from the open space past the desktop, where that brass dog could conceivably *be*, but . . . from inside the box?

Charlotte jerks her hand back and her index finger is a stump with a white core. She pulls it to her mouth to staunch the blood that's not coming and there's not even any taste, just dryness. She pulls her knees up to her and shudders with sobs, her finger stump still in her mouth, her head shaking no, no, that this can't be happening, no way is this real.

Her index finger is definitely half gone, though. Bitten off by a little brass dog that thinks it's a god. Being digested by a house that's worse than a god. Being digested just like Charlotte is.

"Please, please," she says, and moves over to the corner, farther away from the dog, nudging the mouse enough to wake the monitor again, throw her blurry shadow onto the glass fronts of the degrees on the opposite wall.

She works her way around to see what this is going to be.

It's . . . tweed-brown fabric rushing past too fast for the camera to capture.

And then it's the couch in the living room.

Mr. Wilbanks steps into that field of view and leans down to look into the lizard's mouth.

Of course. This must be what he was getting done while Mrs. Wilbanks was walking the new babysitter around.

He steps back almost to the coffee table, calls upstairs, quiet enough that he doesn't want an actual response, is just kind of checking, "Dear? Hun?"

Because this lizard doesn't have ears, Charlotte has to read it from his lips, and from the hopeful, not-hopeful tilt of his face.

He waits, ready for Mrs. Wilbanks to call down over the balcony, ask him what he wants.

She doesn't.

He flicks his eyes to the lizard again then, and, moving somehow fast and casual at the same time—a motion he doesn't have to think to accomplish anymore—he pulls *his* lizard out.

"Oh, no, no," Charlotte says, turning her face away but not her eyes. Not quite. Not enough.

He's already half-hard.

In two, maybe three strokes, he's all the way there, probably just from the thrill of about to maybe get caught.

"Dear?" he says again, his lips so clear, his eyes so puppy-dog, and then, looking right into the camera, right into his office, "*Charlotte?*"

Charlotte pushes back, away from this, and falls off the desk in a pile of limbs, is scrabbling on the plastic mat his chair rolls on.

It was like he was looking right at her. Like he knew she was watching.

Or, like he had her in his head, anyway.

"Don't don't don't, please," Charlotte says, coming up to her knees to see over the edge of the desk, though she doesn't want to.

She's lost count of his strokes, and probably wouldn't have wanted to count them anyway, but either way he's already hunching forward, about to go off, and then he lunges forward, his other hand pulling the camera down to his crotch, the camera shaking out, spinning to the rug.

It spins to a rest with him in the corner of the frame, sideways, tilted.

He's pulling the blue lizard down, is shooting into its throat, his throat bulging with spasms of pleasure, the lizard swallowing it all, plastic eyes open the whole while.

Mr. Wilbanks nearly falls forward, has to lean his head out of frame, into the shelf or something.

After, spent, he's breathing deep, his eyes kind of dull. He's still with it enough to keep the lizard's mouth tilted up, though. Like a champagne flute he doesn't want to slosh anything thick and white out of. Then he comes back by degrees, finally looks around like just settling down into a living room completely alien to him: his own. One with two women upstairs, two kids who could come crashing to the railing at any moment, to spy on their daddy.

He darts his eyes upstairs, and when he's evidently still alone, he collects the camera again and the feed goes smeary, finally settles back on the couch tableau. On Mr. Wilbanks, wiping his hands on his long plaid scarf then looking at his right palm, smelling it, and rubbing it on the scarf again and then working the scarf ends high and low, brushing it across the back of his neck like anchoring himself in the here and now.

Charlotte looks down to herself, can't remember if he's about to touch her on the shoulder, pat her on the hip, shake her hand.

Mr. Wilbanks walks to the left, his right, and is gone upstairs to remind his wife and the babysitter about certain rooms being off-limits for the night, unaware there's still a red indent pressed into his forehead.

Charlotte shakes her head no, can feel herself crying, she can't even say exactly why. She dabs the wetness from her face and the undersides of her fingers come back white, which is the last color she wants to see right now. Or feel. Or think about.

She rubs it onto the thighs of her jeans and keeps rubbing long after it has to be gone, just to be sure.

Charlotte sweeps all of Mr. Wilbanks's shit off the desk, left to right: the stapler, the lamp, the calendar, the mouse, the mouse pad, the coffee cup of pens and pencils.

They explode against the wall, rattle into the corner.

All that's left is the monitor. She leans forward to hoist it up but its power cord jerks it down, out of her arms. She leaves it lying there on its back, pulls the drawers out instead, throws their papers in the air and walks through them to the wall, tears down the degrees, their thin glass faces shattering at her feet. Then she's face-to-face with the family photographs. Desi and Ronald, growing up. Mrs. Wilbanks looking the same ten years ago as she still looks.

Charlotte turns back to inspect the damage.

The office is the same as it was before.

The only difference is . . . Desi, in the recording?

Charlotte leans over, looks down into the screen, flickering unhappily now.

Desi's standing in the right edge of the lizard's field of view, and her mouth—

It's lasagne.

The twins have already tunneled downstairs to sneak into the kitchen, but Desi just heard Charlotte calling for her from the upstairs hall, and can't help drifting out here in response.

"Desi! Desiree!" Charlotte yells into the recording, lifting the monitor and shaking it.

Desi looks back to the kitchen, maybe to Ronald saying something to her, and walks out of the frame.

Charlotte lowers her face in defeat then stands fast, is to the door in two steps, her left hand twisting the knob because she's missing half a finger on her right.

The knob still won't give.

"C'mon, c'mon," she hisses, turning the knob harder even though she knows it's a lost cause. She opens her hand, pushes away like telling the house she's done with this, she's not playing this stupid game anymore. Except that she has to. It's the only way out.

So, she makes herself think, trying to dial down to the *basic* basics. In this room, this office, she A) can't open the door, B) can't lift a box of brads, and C) can't lift the brass doorstop.

She *can* sweep everything off the desk, she guesses. It doesn't matter, it just resets, like erasing how pissed off she was, but she can have that moment of satisfaction all over again, anyway. For whatever that's worth.

This is what it means to be a ghost, she knows. You can see and hear and know, you can drift through and among, but that's pretty much it. All cause, no effect. The only consequences are on herself.

Yeah, if you're Tia, if you're anybody locked in here for ten, eleven years, you're scrabbling at the exit. At any whisper of an exit that presents itself.

That doesn't make Tia a good person, though. She's still stealing a body, a life. She's still dooming someone else to what she endured. She's still holding two little kids hostage to get what she wants. She still killed her little brother in the bathtub one night, and then ran away with her mother's severed head, her little feet leaving bubble footprints that pretty much killed her dad too.

"How do I do it?" Charlotte says, looking up to the backside of the door right at the moment when the her that was in the hall earlier—which is *now*—bangs her open hand on it and lets that settle, like she can echolocate through the wood. Like she can stand still enough, focus every fiber of her being into the office.

"Desi?" the her out there is asking.

Charlotte slaps her hand into the door from *this* side but there's no response, no step back, no immediate "Who's there?" Meaning there was no sound, no actual contact. Just a shadow brushing a shadow. Less than that.

Charlotte leans forward, presses her forehead into the wood of the door, her breath neither hot nor cold in that small space, just there.

"Desi?" the Charlotte in the hall then says again, so close, tuning in to a feminine presence in this office, but not able to register anything more precise than that.

In the office, Charlotte is crying again, snuffling with the hopelessness of it all.

The her in the hall bangs on the door again, losing her patience, and Charlotte jerks back from the feel and the sound, can feel herself standing on the other side of the door, listening with her whole body.

"They're in the kitchen," she tells the her who's about to figure that wrongness out.

A breath or two later, Charlotte's alone upstairs again. She turns around to slide down the door, sit by the stupid dog. Is the office where she lives now? Is this even living?

Charlotte pushes her fingers through her hair, only remembers a moment too late that she's using her injured right hand.

She brings it down, extracts the strands of hair from the blunt white stump of her index finger, blinking away tears.

Where does Charley think she is? Doesn't she need Charlotte to show her the next tunnel?

Charlotte nods yes, yes, it's *Charley* who will come save her, whenever time catches up and puts them in the same house again. The same-*ish* house. Unless Charlotte will now forever be four hours behind Charley, always playing catchup, never able to run the stairs fast enough to be in the same moment.

But if she came here through . . . through the lizard's throat, or recording, whatever . . . then there must be a way *back*, too. When the things you're interacting with are only half-real, the usual rules can't hold, can they? Not if Charlotte wants to have any hope about this situation.

And: you can fast-forward, can't you? You can, can—she *did*. It was after the doorbell rang, from when Murphy got here. Coming down the stairs, the lights had dimmed and . . . and by the time she got to the bottom, it was an hour later. Long enough for the lasagne in the fridge to be thoroughly chilled.

Never mind that, that time, she's pretty sure she'd been not just stopped for a syrupy-long moment on the stairs by Tia, but had her memories or self or whatever sucked out her ear, but still, forget that if you can, what matters is that an hour had slipped by in what at least *felt* like a snap, a blink, a breath.

Meaning she can still catch up to whatever moment the twins are in.

It's not hopeless. Well, not completely.

Think that, anyway.

Charlotte reaches back blindly for the doorknob to pull herself up with it, and, again, only realizes a moment after she's doing it that she's using her right hand, which is the wrong hand.

But maybe not.

The doorknob gives, slightly.

Charlotte looks down to it, up to the door, then grabs the knob again fast, turns hard.

Nothing.

"Just when I'm not looking?" she says, and tries that, making a stupid show of peering behind her while she turns the knob. Same nothing.

Was somebody from the other side trying the door, and she just happened to be touching it? But the other her and the twins, they're both downstairs, aren't they? Soon, maybe now, Ronald will be up here, scurrying around for his and Desi's costumes, but—the costumes aren't in *here*, are they?

Charlotte looks behind with purpose now, studying every place a dad might stash a couple of unopened costumes. Nothing.

She lowers herself to the floor again, the side of her head flat to the hardwood, and looks under.

No feet, no shoes.

She stands, tries the knob one more time—what else is there?—still can't turn it.

"What the hell?" she says, and then, just to test, she goes to the bifold closet door, pulls on the little dummy knob.

The door folds to the side just as it's supposed to, and Charlotte pulls her knee back from whatever's suddenly burning it.

It's a bright shadow, back behind a tower of stacked boxes.

"Found it!" she calls out uselessly behind her.

The thigh and knee of her jeans are smoking or steaming, she can't tell. There's no smell. She pats the heat away, reaches over the dark leakage from the tunnel, pulls the boxes down, still checking for costumes.

Unshuttered now, the bright shadow blasts up like it wants to, so Charlotte has to fall back to keep from getting singed.

This is a big one. The mother of them all, maybe. Is this where the funny places return to? Where they come to hang out when they're not blipping from cabinet to dryer to closet? If so, then why did Tia never find it, all those years she had been here alone, up here rubbing her injuries on the brass dog?

Maybe it's not big. Maybe it's just the angle, or the aperture. Can you judge a tunnel's size by the shadow it casts, or bleeds, leaks, whatever?

Charlotte tiptoes around, giving the ray of darkness a lot of room, and folds the door shut, the bright shadow only showing through the louvres now but not really coming out to slice her into sections.

Wouldn't that be about perfect.

"No thanks," Charlotte says, and goes back to the door she *can't* open. Coming upstairs was supposed to get her whole enough to find the twins, somehow communicate with them, but all she's accomplished so far is watching Mr. Wilbanks perv out in the living room.

Using her right hand very intentionally, since it sorta kinda worked once, a little, she grasps onto the doorknob again, just squeezing normal-tight. Trying to think successful thoughts, she turns, fully expecting it to roll over.

No such luck.

But there is a . . . click?

Charlotte spins around, one-hundred-percent expects a tiny floppy clown arm to be sneaking out through the lid of the jack-in-the-box, its hand turning its own crank so it can burst up, stop Charlotte's heart.

She's still alone.

And, anyway: she *felt* this click the same as she heard it, didn't she?

She steps to the side, still holding the knob, and sees what she can't feel: the nub of her finger, the white front of it, when her hand turned around the unmoving knob, it jammed into the little button lock.

It *pressed* that lock, made it click.

Charlotte pushes again with her finger stump. The button lock clicks in and then comes back out, unlocking the door. Was that it the whole time? Excited, Charlotte turns the knob again, not hard, not soft, just natural.

Nothing. It wasn't the lock. All she did just now was lock it, then unlock it.

But that's something.

She climbs her fingers onto the knob itself and pushes against it with the white nub of her finger, trying to roll it back to the left, the direction it needs to come.

It doesn't turn, but it does start to. The only reason it doesn't is because a smooth round doorknob doesn't turn from just one finger stump pressing on it.

Charlotte keeps that finger-nub in contact and grabs the knob with her other hand, cranks around.

It starts to turn, it likes and needs that dry white contact, but it needs more.

Charlotte stands there breathing hard, watching this knob.

It needs more.

"Fuck it," she says, and is already back to the top drawer of Mr. Wilbanks's desk. She comes up with his orange-handled scissors.

All she needs is an opposable thumb with some gription, right?

To be sure she goes back to the door, holds the knob with her stump, paying attention to where her thumb naturally falls.

She goes back to the desk, hikes her rear up onto it and hunches over her right hand, the scissors in her left, open wide, the shorter blade pressing to the base of the underside of her thumb.

"For Desi, for Ronald," she says, and, before she can stop herself, she scrapes it hard down and away, has to drop the scissors it hurts so much.

Her right hand trembling, she raises it.

The white isn't completely exposed, but there are scratches there for sure, a rip or two, and the skin around them is raw and inflamed, almost peeled up.

Charlotte slides down, staggers over to the door, grabs the knob in victory, and turns with her whole arm.

It starts to twist but won't go far enough.

"Shit!" she says, banging her left hand into the door, high up by her face.

Why did it sort of work before, but not now?

Because the lock isn't as big as the knob, she hears herself saying.

Because the lock isn't as big as the knob. Because the raw white she dragged open with the ragged blade of the lower jaw of the scissors is, in relation to the size of the doorknob, not as big or intense as the open part of her finger is to the locking button.

"I didn't cut myself enough," she says.

Which means *depth*, she knows. She didn't angle the scissors in painfully enough, was trying to do as little as possible to get the door open, the same as any sane person would.

This house isn't interested in as little as possible, though. It wants it all.

Charlotte looks down to the weak, timid scrape on the underside of her thumb, considers what even more violence there might feel like. But . . . the dog is here, isn't it? She looks down at it, still hates its aloof, thousand-yard stare. If it's here, though, then won't any cuts be temporary? Enough pain to make Charlotte pass out, sure, but, after pressing that pain to the dog's warmcold brass—*after* opening the door, after after after—all she'll have to deal with will be some mottled grey scar tissue. It's the price of passage. And it's worth it.

But that's later, too. That's after. Right now what she needs is more of her tofu white insides making contact with the metal of the doorknob. Simple as that.

"Don't, don't, don't," she says, stepping back to Mr. Wilbanks's desk.

She has to, though.

She pulls the left drawer open, turns around to put the center of her right palm on the edge of the desk such that her thumb wraps *inside* the drawer space, and then she steps forward all at once, slams the drawer shut with her hip, cranking her face up, away from the pain. Her neck won't go far enough to hide how much this hurts, though. There's supposed to just be dry nothing inside her, but she feels the stubby little bone in her thumb splinter all the same, then crack open, then tear away.

She falls to her knees, the side of her face pressing into the desk calendar. Her right hand is still clamped onto the edge of the desk. Just with less grip, now that there's nothing to oppose the fingers' pressure. Or, nothing connected enough to oppose that pressure.

Charlotte guides her left hand alongside a drawer, finds the edge, and works it back a quarter-inch at a time, dreading what she knows is inside: her thumb. It's not lying there like a prize, though, but's still hanging, her skin more elastic than she would have guessed. It kicks up a pencil drawing from one of her mom's Indian books, of the Sun Dance—of those leather pegs in the chest, leather straps tied to them, the skin being pulled out and out.

Charlotte drags her face down toward *her* strip of flesh and tongues it in, closes her eyes and bites down, having to saw her teeth side to side to sever the connection.

It goes with a pop. She pulls back, looks at her thumb curling there in the bottom of the drawer, on a legal pad, nudging Mr. Wilbanks's samurai-sword letter opener over.

"I'm sorry," Charlotte says down to it, and pushes the drawer shut gently, has already stood away from it when it registers: the letter opener.

She eases the drawer back open.

The letter opener is *brass*.

Steeling herself for the dog's sudden all-around bark—or maybe it's in her head?—she lifts the letter opener unmolested, even though it's as heavy as a gallon of milk to her.

She slides it into her back pocket, all one motion. It pulls hard at the waist of her jeans but screw it. The dog doesn't even know, either. It is real brass, though. Charlotte can feel that hot freeze radiating through her pants, and it's heavy like brass is on this side of the house.

"Smart doggy," she says down to the doorstop.

The dog's tail doesn't twitch.

Because it might make a difference how freshly exposed her inner white is, she jams the stumps of her thumb and index finger hard against the metal of the doorknob, presses them tight with her other hand, her left using the right like a rag on a lid, and twists.

It's still not easy, but this time the knob rolls, turns . . . the tongue in the strike plate clicks back just enough.

The door opens a crack.

Charlotte doesn't let it stop, keeps guiding it out with her left hand, and the first place her eyes fall is of course all the way down the hall, to the sound on the stairs.

It's herself, she knows. She remembers being on those stairs and seeing the office door open just this slowly. Before, after this bad moment, she thought it had been Nora Spinell opening this door. And then, by default, it had to have been Tia. But it was Charlotte herself.

She steps back, isn't sure she wants to have to see herself on the stairs. Which will be the real girl, right?

The door stops exactly where it stopped before.

Without looking down, Charlotte kneels, feeling with her left hand for the dachshund's long back. When she finds it, she crosses her body with her right arm, tightens her lips to a line, and presses the nubs of her thumb and index finger to the healing brass.

It hisses and spits, curls a line of that steam or smoke up, but Charlotte doesn't look down, even when the dog's growl rumbles up from the hardwood floor.

She brings her right hand up to inspect.

The white is . . . congealed over. Like pudding that got a skin overnight, over many nights.

She touches it with the tip of her left index finger and it doesn't hurt, is completely numb. She smells it, has to stop that immediately. She looks down what she can see of the hall and the light there falters, which makes the floor feel like it's dropping out from under her. She holds her arms out to balance even though her head's telling her nothing's really shaking, that she's not really falling, that she's just stepping over the threshold, into the hall. The light sputters again, sucking down to black for an instant. At the end of that blink—it can't have been any longer than that—Charlotte's standing in the minutes after midnight, she knows. In Halloween.

"*Three minutes . . .*" Charley calls from downstairs. "Are you here, babysitter?"

"I've caught up again," Charlotte mutters to herself in wonder. She steps all the way into the hall, the lights intensifying now, nothing but brightness all around.

"Three minutes," she says to herself, the fingertips of her left hand skating along the wall.

She doesn't stop for Ronald's bathroom or bedroom door, and only hesitates at the linen closet to be sure she's seeing what she's seeing: three BBs have rolled onto the hardwood. Meaning the tunnel *was* in the utility when Charley flung the jug at the wall.

Charlotte considers the possibility of the Featherweight vacuum waiting in the linen closet—surely it's back in there, right?—but shakes her head no about it.

She passes Desi's room without trying to get a look into the bathroom, to see what might be going on in there.

There's no headless women in the hall, no eyeless boys in the doorways.

She does stop at the master bedroom, though.

The closet's accent lighting is on again, or still.

Charlotte presses her lips together and makes herself cross the bedroom, tries not to track her lack of reflection in the mirror over the sinks. She can't help looking up once, though. At how insubstantial she is. At how not-there she is anymore. Like she's fading with each step.

Stop.

The closet is just Mrs. Wilbanks's clothes and shoes and boots and the little pegs she hangs her necklaces on. None of them moving, meaning nobody's hiding in and among, ready to spring out at her.

But there is something, isn't there? Behind the dresses still in dry cleaner bags, at or on the wall that should be the exterior wall of the house, if Charlotte's understanding the layout right.

It's like . . . a television screen? A big flat panel in the closet, suddenly on? No, it's a *window*.

Charlotte steps in between that thin clingy plastic, holds the dresses to the side.

A window, yes. It's foggy, but that's because it's . . . it's not glass, it's plastic.

On the other side is . . . not just an emergency room, but *the* emergency room, the one Charlotte used to have to do her homework in in elementary. She presses her face closer, so she can see the blurry forms scuttling back and forth in their teal scrubs and running shoes.

Her mom passes right in front of her, moving from the right to the left, and Charlotte reaches for her.

"Mom," she says, "what, what is it?"

Something about the look on her mom's face. The all-business straightness of her arms, her step a bit faster than it needs to be.

A moment later her mom is bustling back, pushing a gurney now, a patient on it.

Charlotte's mom is crying now, her eyes large and wet but staring straight ahead fiercely. Another nurse steps in to take this patient over for her but Charlotte's mom shakes her head no, keeps going, making herself do this.

When the gurney passes before her, Charlotte expects she's going to see some nightmare version of herself, chewed up and spit out by the house, or—or Arthur Lopez, flattened by some other bumper, dragged under the car and driven over, his back breaking backwards on the first roll, his teeth pushing through what's left of his cheek, the rest of his face just meat, one of his shoes still on but that whole leg twisted the wrong way.

Instead, it's Murphy. Her head's shaved, has come back to stubble, which isn't how it is now or how it ever was either, so Charlotte knows this is a look *ahead*. This is tomorrow night, this is next week, next month.

Murphy is just staring, the drool around her mouth crusted with overdose.

Charlotte runs her hand through her own hair, knows where Murphy's went: to grieving. When they first got together she was always asking Charlotte stupid Indian questions, probably dredged up from place mats in restaurants, from ill-advised stumbles around the internet. The result was Murphy saying that when Charlotte broke up with her, which was definitely coming, which had to come, which was already here pretty much, that Murphy was going to cut all her hair off then, because it's what you do when you lose your Indian girlfriend. It's what you do to mark the beginning of the next part of your life. You can't be who you were anymore, that person can't deal with not having the person she loves around, so you have to be somebody else.

Charlotte puts the palm of her right hand to the plastic window and pushes her face into it as well, screams into it, the window fogging from her breath.

Her mom wipes her tears on the back of her forearm and keeps going.

"Murph," Charlotte says, stepping to the side to try and track the two of them away, to hold on to them just a moment longer.

She crumples into the dry-cleaning bags, bringing some of them down around her, holding them to her mouth because maybe breathing them in would be easier, would be better.

She does once, on accident—breathes one into her throat, a thin wall of bubble reaching for her windpipe—but is coughing and gagging before she can even tell herself not to.

The closet lights go down around her and she's floating in crinkly blackness now, her breath hitching in and out, her nose snuffling. When she looks up, she completely expects the accent lights to come on in response, but she doesn't count that way anymore, does she? Babysitters who aren't really here can't turn on lights that are.

Still: Murphy didn't do that to herself because Charlotte was *gone*, she did it because Charlotte wasn't Charlotte anymore, right? If this was a look into the future, then that's the future it meant: the one where Charley's Charlotte, as far as anybody knows. And, either Charley's hetero, doesn't have any interest in kissing another girl on the porch after a date, or else Murphy was just too dangerous to have close, since she, of all people, would be able to clock the new driver at the mental wheel.

On the one hand this look ahead, if it's a real look ahead, means that Charley doesn't find a tunnel anytime soon.

On the other hand, it means this has to end, *now*.

"*Ronald, Desi . . .*" Charley's calling from the couch, and kind of laughing at the end of it.

"Oh yeah," she adds, speaking to the room, to Charlotte up at the balcony, "they can't hear me anymore, can they? Their babysitter's let something terrible happen to them, hasn't she? That's so, so *funny*, because, I mean—her references were practically radioactive, weren't they? That means 'glowing,' yeah."

She leans farther back into the cushions, her feet propped on the coffee table, and thumbs *SpongeBob* back into motion.

"I don't know where they are, Mr. Wilbanks, Mrs. Wilbanks," she goes on, just watching the screen now. "I put them to bed at nine just like you said. Maybe they're playing a joke? Do they ever do that? You say they hid dolls in their place? Sounds like them.

You did warn me about some big trick. Geez, can't believe they got that one over on me. Anyway, can one of you give me a ride, maybe? I don't know if I should be walking to the bus stop this late. Seems kind of like asking for trouble. My mom's always telling me that nothing good happens after midnight . . ."

Charlotte holds tight to the handrail with her bad hand, squeezing hard enough that the melted white at the end of her thumb splits, crumbles down into the open air. It's gone before it hits—snow that evaporates on the way down.

Charlotte tucks her thumb into her fist and turns to head downstairs, finish this one way or the other, and she only stops when a great shape rustles into the hall behind her.

"What now—?" she says, sure that she's ready for, for *whatever*: Nora Spinell, using the jack-in-the-box as her head, her hand to the crank to puppet her mouth open; *Mr.* Spinell, clean-shaven now that he's dead, his eyes just as punched through as his son's; Tad, hustling and bustling down the hall for some ghost-kid reason or another; a funny place opening its dark sucking mouth from the linen closet, its harsh shadow sizzling into the opposite wall, the vacuum cleaner floating in it like a bad special effect.

But—no way could Charlotte have been ready for *this*: the lizard, even more massive than last time. It's metastasizing in this between-house, is becoming more reptile than toy. Charlotte can tell from its dull eyes more than anything.

There are beanbag beads raining down off its blue scales. Meaning either it crawled up from there or it was nosing around in there, after a smell.

"What are you?" Charlotte says to it, too floored to even do anything grand and proper like fall backward down the stairs, away from this.

The lizard turns its great head to her, isn't quite through Desi's doorway yet, is too long now for that to be an easy turn. It's maybe going to have to roll over onto its side then curl up, claw forward with its front and back feet, stretching its chin forward to tighten its yards of belly skin.

The pearly drool stringing down from its harsh line of a mouth isn't drool, Charlotte knows. It's the life Mr. Wilbanks filled it with, spilling over, frothing up.

"Fuck you," Charlotte says to it, hopefully not loud enough it can hear, and watches her feet the whole way down the stairs, coming down all the way onto one before stepping down to the next, even though that great lizard could be about to slide down behind her, slurp her right up on the way, never a care what it's going to crash into right after.

So, now upstairs is more or less off-limits. Along with the outside world.

Charlotte shakes her head at how unacceptable all this is and takes her last step onto the first floor.

If she'd been thinking, she realizes, she'd have pinched those BBs up from beneath the linen closet, to plink one by one onto the coffee table. They've been through a funny place, taken a one-way trip like her, so that probably means they're still transitioning from one house to the next, are still visible and hearable by people in the real house.

That would be a petty victory, though, showing Charley what she missed in the utility, what she nearly had, what she could have had if she'd just been patient, and deliberate.

"I guess they're home any minute now, aren't they?" Charley announces with a dramatic teenage shrug, like she somehow knows Charlotte's with her again. "Maybe one of them knows CPR, you think? Or, will they expect me to administer that?"

"I'm not here," Charlotte says back to her, in the living room again at last, but not touching the television screen like she's supposed to.

She pulls the brass letter opener from her back pocket, inspects it. It's dull where it should be sharp, but the point still has some bite.

Charlotte looks over it to Charley. To Tia in Charlotte's body.

"I'm not letting you hurt her like that," she says about Murphy-on-the-gurney, and steps around the coffee table, plunks down right by Charley on the couch. She flips the heavy little letter opener around in her hand once to get its balance, takes a solid grip on its smooth handle, and stabs it into Charley's left thigh hard enough to drive it nearly all the way through.

Charley doesn't notice—or, she doesn't realize she's been stabbed, anyway. She does let her idle index finger scratch in a disinterested way at her pants leg, though.

Charlotte does it again, higher up, into what should be the hip joint—Charley doesn't scratch this time, just rubs with the heel of her palm—so Charlotte pulls it out to thrust it right into Charley's chest with both hands, but at the last moment she can't. Because it's her heart, too. The letter opener wouldn't do anything, she's pretty sure, but—just the idea. And . . . and she wants to be back *in* there at some point, right?

Charlotte lowers her face, presses her eyes shut, the brass warm against her face, probably sending tendrils of grey out from the contact. She lowers it, studies it again, holds the flat of the blade to where she opened her thumb stump. The brass hisses on the uncongealed spot. Charlotte works the blade over and back, making herself feel this, and flashes on Mrs. Wilbanks letting the eyeliner burn her just the same way.

Charlotte leans back, screams in frustration.

Charley just sits there soaking Bikini Bottom in, the kids dying, maybe already dead, the Wilbankses practically home. *The babysitter isn't the babysitter anymore*, Charlotte wants to write on the wall, but the words would never take, she knows. *This* babysitter, "Charley," she'll be skipping the SATs in the morning, she'll be breaking up with her girlfriend later, and she'll probably be offering to babysit for whoever lives here next, after these grieving parents have gone their separate ways. Because she needs to find a funny place she can burrow down into for eternity.

There's not one single thing Charlotte can do about any of that, either. She can't even hold a letter opener in a real way. All she can do, if she pays the price, if she can take the pain, is turn a doorknob, open a door. Maybe mess up an episode of a cartoon. Sacrifice herself to the giant plastic lizard pulling the long runner in the upstairs hall to it now, as it tries to scrabble its way out of Desi's bedroom.

Charlotte looks up fast to the lamp table in the upstairs hall spilling over from the bunching-up rug, the bulb popping in a blue flash that throws the distinct shadow of the lizard's giant head onto the big wall by the stairway.

Charley's eyes don't even flick at all this. The other house doesn't register for her anymore. Just the television.

Charlotte looks back to the screen with her, to SpongeBob giving the dragon jellyfish the Krabby Patty he's been carrying all along, saving all of their animated medieval lives.

If only, right? Still, she pats her pocket for if she's been carrying a magic Krabby Patty all along. All she finds is her useless phone. On it, a stack of text messages?

"Mom?" Charlotte says, swiping at the lock screen, the texts not moving from her touch.

The phone *Charley* has is buzzing now, though. Her stolen thumbprint unlocks it, no problem.

"Ah," Charley says, and Charlotte reads over her shoulder:
Here.
Here.
Here.
Here.
Here.

Here.

Here.

Charlotte stands fast, frantic, looking around.

As always, for safety, just standard operating procedure, probably even in chapter one of the babysitter manual, she'd given her mom the address of tonight's job. That's... she wants to say that's how Murphy found her, but really it's what Tia drank in from her memory: that Charlotte's girlfriend *could* have gotten this address that way. Still, the inescapable fact, the not-another-lie part of this, is that Charlotte's mom definitely does have this address. And now that her shift's over—midnight—here she is, Charlotte's ride, surprise, no thanks necessary, just being an overachieving single mother.

"*No, Mom!*" Charlotte screams, rushing to the door.

The doorbell rings on the way.

Charlotte shakes her head *no, no, please*, but behind her, *SpongeBob* mutes.

"What do you call her?" Charley says, all around. "Moms, maybe? Ma? There some Indian word the two of you use, like, a tribal thing? I don't want her to know right away, I mean. That would spoil the—the *fun*. It's better if she starts to clock small things over a week or two. And then thinks she's seeing me standing in her doorway at night, that kind of stuff—you know, you've seen the movies."

Charlotte bangs on the door and kicks it, opening her thumb and finger back up but who cares. As a last-ditch effort she pulls the closet door open, angles it across to catch on the doorknob of the front door when it swings back.

Charley inserts the key, hauls the door open, the closet door not immaterial, exactly. Just, shut again. Never open in the first place.

"Mom!" Charley says, so chipper, so surprised with this happy coincidence, with not having to walk to the bus stop, now.

It's going to be the Mr. Spinell scene all over again, Charlotte knows.

She falls back in agony, sits on the stairs then stands all at once, swaying away from the distinct noise of claws on wood. She turns fast, stepping ahead at the same time, sure the lizard's already going to be to her.

It is out of Desi's room, anyway. It's in the upstairs hall now. It's taking up the whole *length* of the hall. And—and it has a *tongue* now, long and iridescent and split, flicking in and out, slapping the air for floating molecules of taste, settling finally on the handrail that still has all-but-invisible white flecks of Charlotte on it. The handrail's probably even—to a lizard—still warm from Charlotte's touch.

"Why do you care about me now?" Charlotte says up to it.

The lizard either doesn't hear or doesn't care about sound. Just scent. Taste. The pieces of Charlotte she can't help but be leaving in her wake.

And why do you have a tongue now? she adds, to herself.

The answer is obvious: because it needs it. It's not a nanny cam anymore, it's not a spooge repository. It's becoming an animal. One that can eat. One that *needs* to eat, because it has actual insides, a digestive tract to siphon energy from whatever it swallows, push it out into the muscles so it can eat more. And—no.

Charlotte lifts her right hand to her nose, sniffs it.

Is the *grey* what the lizard's tasting the air for? It makes sense. The grey is like ash, is probably sloughing off at a faster rate than her usual skin cells.

Charlotte holds her hand side-up in front of her mouth and blows past it, sighing a good grey taste up the stairs.

The lizard stills into a statue, which has to be what it does when it gets that good scent reading, and then digs its claws into the hardwood, anchoring itself. If it were a hunting dog, it would be lifting one forepaw up under, to point. Since it's a reptile, it just lowers its face, angling its poor eyesight down the stairs.

Moving slow, Charlotte guides her cauterized hand behind her back.

It wasn't supposed to work *that* well.

She backs away carefully, sure the lizard can surge down the stairway at whatever point it gets its nerve up to try. It's probably never seen stairs, though, has it? Not at this size. Not when they're not giant wooden cliffs it had to jump up to, claw and scrabble over.

Still backing away, Charlotte bumps into her mom, who doesn't register the contact, is all eyes, studying this grand living room.

"How much they paying you?" she asks Charley.

"*That's not me!*" Charlotte screams.

"One year of college," Charley says with a daughterly smile. "Three more Fridays and I'll have a degree."

"Then you better not—" Charlotte's mom starts, playing along, but stops herself, seeing Mr. Spinell's blood on the couch. "What's this?" she asks, sitting down primp and proper on the edge of the couch and touching a dab of that tacky red with the pad of her middle finger.

"Fake blood," Charley says with a shrug, settling in beside her and snuggling in, her socked feet drawn up under her. "Mr. Wilbanks is like *super* into Halloween, right? He Scotchgarded under each spot, he said, I don't know. He promised his wife it would come right up."

Charlotte's mom cases the rest of the living room for decorations that could be in keeping with a random splash of blood on the couch.

She brings the pad of her middle finger up to her nose, gives it a smell.

"*Yes, yes, it's blood, Mom!*" Charlotte says, halfway across the coffee table.

Her mom rubs it away, says, "The kids?"

"Sleepy time," Charley answers, folding her prayer hands under her tilting-sideways head.

Charlotte stands, screams in her closed mouth in frustration, then dives for the television screen, rubs all over it, completely distorting the picture.

"Been like this all night," Charley says about what looks like a corrupt signal, a bad connection, and feels around for the remote, kills *SpongeBob*.

"*This* a decoration?" Charlotte's mom says then, impressed, hauling the jack-in-the-box over to inspect.

"Oh, yeah," Charley says, taking it into her lap. "Mrs. Wilbanks, like, restores them or something? She told me not to let the kids play with it, I don't know."

"Either know or don't know," her mom says back, on automatic. "Don't guess. That leaves room for people to make your decisions for you."

"Check," Charley says with an appreciative grin.

Charlotte rushes forward, over the coffee table, grabs at the jack-in-the-box to, she *doesn't know*, throw it across the room?

Surprising her and Charley both, the crank clicks over once.

Charlotte stops, holds her guilty hand up: the thumb and index finger stumps are both raw, open, new. And her right hand's the side the crank is on.

"Like the doorknob," she says in wonder, and pushes back from the couch breathing hard, trying to figure what this might mean, how this might help her.

The jack-in-the-box, it's—it's what Tia was initially trying to use to come back, isn't it? Didn't she say that? And the reason she could smuggle it across to Ronald from this between place, for him to crank a doorway open, was that Tia had made the jack-in-the-box from Nora Spinell's head in some twisted wrong-side-of-the-house way, so pushing it across, from house to house, was really just bringing it back.

It's special.

And, because it's special, because it came from the top house and slipped into the middle one, Charlotte's white insides can *touch* it. Not her real hands, just her white ones.

"Oops!" her mom says, about the single click. "Maybe we shouldn't, I don't want to get you in trouble on your first night with them."

"I kind of want to see what it does . . ." Charley says, speaking directly to the open air in front of her, a grin ghosting the corners of her mouth.

Charlotte's thinking hard, is making herself think.

If babysitter X can make the magic box move with just the whiteness of her thumb and index finger, then what could she do with a lot more whiteness exposed?

Before she can talk herself out of it, she spins the letter opener up from her rear pocket, fumbles it for a moment but catches it on its heavy way down, and, breathing fast five shallow times and then holding it in, trying to make herself stronger than she is, she stabs the point dead center into her open left palm—it feels exactly as bad as she expected—and then rotates the blade over, to drag the sharp point up over the heel of her hand, slitting the skin as far up the fish-belly part of her forearm as she can reach. Almost to the elbow.

White shrimp meat bulges from the incision.

"Old Indian trick," she says through clenched teeth, her whole left arm spasming with pain, her teeth grinding. "You fuck yourself up before fucking everybody else in the room up."

She hunches forward around the swirling vortex of pain her left arm is now. Her hand automatically starts to clench into a fist but that just amps the pain up even more.

Charlotte gags, the pain trying to find a way out, and the living room greys out before her, mutes itself.

"No, no," she says, and makes herself breathe in, makes herself focus, stay awake, not pass out, not give up.

The letter opener falls with a thunk. Charlotte tracks its soft bounce—it's so *heavy*—waits for it to come to a stop before turning back to her cut-open arm. Shaking her head no, she lowers her teeth to the flap of skin at the inner elbow end of that slit, and she pulls away, extending her hand from her teeth since she can't stretch her neck any more than it already is.

The pain is so deep she can feel her soul huddling up around itself.

Inch by inch, tug by tug, she works the skin of her forearm and wrist and hand down and off like removing a long fancy glove, one she's surprised to find is red on the *in*side. Underneath there's just white, like she's made of Styrofoam, like she's been this secret blank mannequin all along.

And, with the skin gone, it doesn't even hurt so much anymore.

She waggles her fingers before her face, looks past them to Charley. To Tia in a body that's not hers.

With one hand she's holding the base of the jack-in-the-box. With the other she's cranking it slowly, slowly, her head angled slightly away, her mouth ready to burst into laughter, infect Charlotte's mom with it.

Charlotte dives forward just as the flap springs, and—

Instead of that little clown popping up like before, what comes up is Charlotte's bloody arm—*red* muscle, white tendons, thin yellow sheathing it in places, blood all through it.

Her skeletal raw hand grabs Charley by the throat, pulls her head forward through the jack-in-the-box hole, into this hell with her.

Charlotte doesn't stop to think what her mom must be seeing. Really, the moment she pulls Charley through, her Charlotte-skin sloughing off, the lights blink like gulping this new person in, and it's just them on the couch, just them in the living room.

Tia is here now. The real Tia.

On this side she's scarred and torn and grey, seventeen years old, her hair long and matted, her clothes rags, her lips cracked deep, her eyes the eyes of someone who doesn't sleep anymore, who maybe hasn't slept since she looked around inside a funny place and realized it could be a home for someone like her.

She screams a guttural scream to be here again and comes at Charlotte like an animal.

They crash back into the television set, bring it down over them, pulling and tearing, screaming and clawing.

"No!" Tia screams right into Charlotte's face, into her mouth practically. "This isn't fair! I'm not supposed to be here! I got out!"

"You don't get to be me, Tia," Charlotte says, bringing her knee up into Tia's gut hard enough to drive her to the side.

Upstairs the dog is barking alarm, is loud enough to be shaking the foundations of the house, rattling the windows, making the spilled glass from the shattered television screen dance. Charlotte can feel its massive voice in the bone on the underside of her jaw on both sides, close to her ears.

She spins Tia away, scrabbles around behind the coffee table, falls over something that wasn't there before.

Mr. Spinell, lying where the couch spit him up.

He's dead on the floor, and now Charlotte's tangled up in him, trying to extract her right foot from between his arm and his side but trying to do so without touching him even a little.

She falls sideways, into the couch, and tries to roll away but

Tia's slamming the coffee table forward, into her, pinning her all over again.

Tia's calmer now, her rage burned off, replaced by something darker, and worse.

She grins, waggles whatever she's holding low down by the thigh of her ratty nightgown: the pruning saw she'd carried in to dispose of her dad with.

"This is *my* house," Tia says, drawing the wicked little saw back, its teeth like shark teeth, going every which way, hungry for the slightest bite of skin. "You're going to be so sorry, babysitter."

"I already am," Charlotte says, and surges sideways, under the slashing blade but not low enough that its grabby teeth don't latch into her hair, yank her head sharply over, something tearing in her neck—maybe her *skin* tearing. That's what it feels like.

She's already falling too, though, and her weight is more than Tia can hold with one arm, meaning Charlotte takes the pruning saw down with her.

It rips into her shoulder and her left hand comes up on automatic, grabs the blade the instant before it's to her face, her palm gouging open. She keeps kicking, no time to hurt, just have to get enough distance from whatever's next. It gives her enough space to pull her legs up onto the couch, try to climb the back. The pruning saw falls away behind the couch and then the couch itself is tilting back, nothing stopping it this time, no fake Murphy to take that weight. Charlotte goes with it, the cushions folding over onto her.

Right now would be a good time for a tunnel, she thinks. Except she's still in the wrong house—on this side, the bright shadow from a tunnel mouth will fry her.

Tia hauls the couch back down onto its feet and Charlotte can feel one of its big wooden feet crunch into Mr. Spinell.

"No, no!" Charlotte's already saying, but Tia's got her by the hair, is dragging her from the couch, across the valley of Mr. Spinell, onto the coffee table and then jarringly *off* the coffee table.

Charlotte reaches up to take Tia's wrist and manages to get it, but it doesn't matter even a little, just maybe saves her hair and her scalp some.

"Want to show you something," Tia says, dragging Charlotte to the kitchen.

Charlotte grabs at the doorway but she's not strong enough. She's crying now, and hating herself for it.

"I've been here so long I can *hear* them when I'm on this side," Tia says, throwing Charlotte into the island but not letting go of her hair yet. "It's like—it's like a place where there isn't any sound? Does that make sense, babysitter? It would have after a few years, if you lasted that long."

She drags Charlotte through the kitchen, into the utility, the mat in front of the sink bunching up under Charlotte, then speed-bumping under her when it goes upside down.

"See?" Tia says, jerking Charlotte's hair up so her face is parallel with the washer and dryer.

The dryer is spilling a thick beam of the bright shadow Tia can evidently *hear*, and—and Tia's right: there's not a sound, exactly, but there is a whooshing nothingness, sort of. A blowing absence. How did Charlotte not hear it before?

She tries to kick back, away from it, claws her fingers into this doorway with what she wants to be more strength, desperate strength.

Tia pulls harder, comes away with a handful of hair.

She catches Charlotte fighting back through the kitchen, alongside the island, and slams Charlotte's face into the tile, filling her mouth with powdery white shards.

"Know how hard it is to get your *gums* onto that idiot dog's back?" Tia asks. "You have to take its tail in your mouth, rub it around like a Q-tip. It doesn't bring the teeth back, but it does plug up the holes. And sometimes that's all you can ask for."

She laughs because this is so hilarious.

"You don't deserve anything this quick," she hisses down at Charlotte, dragging again, "but I don't have time for what you do deserve, for making me come back here. And don't worry, I'm pretty sure this'll *feel* like forever."

This time Tia jerks Charlotte hard enough ahead that she slings through the utility room doorway, into the wall that's right there.

"It likes the dryer," Tia says, stepping in, getting a grip closer to Charlotte's scalp, "I don't know why. Maybe it's the spinning, or the holes."

Charlotte pulls and fights and kicks at Tia's legs but she's not strong enough to keep Tia from forcing her into the distinct edge of the bright shadow. The freezing-hot burn starts on the left side of her face, her neck, her shoulder and arm, and it's pushing and pulling at the same time somehow, which is ripping her apart at levels small enough she can't see. But the result is her skin flaying away, flaking up into the air and disintegrating, leaving White Charlotte underneath like a Styrofoam mannequin getting slowly exposed. And the white doesn't burn away, it *melts* away, like pouring gasoline onto packing peanuts, like dripping water onto ash.

Charlotte screams, kicks some more, brings her ravaged right hand up to protect her face but her hand burns just the same, her index finger stump steaming like the barrel of a pistol.

Think like Murph, think like Murph, she tells herself, losing it fast, trying to crawl deeper into herself, away from the pain, away from Tia, away from this house.

What do you do when you can't get away? When your killer's stronger than you are?

You use that against her. Just like with the pruning saw on the couch. That was accidental, though, that was momentum, that was dumb luck. And—and Charlotte doesn't want to do this, can't imagine having to do this, having to *submit* to it, having to *choose* it, but there's nothing left for babysitter X.

Her only option is to move *with* Tia, not against her.

Instead of pulling away from the clean bright shadow the dryer's blasting, she pushes forward, *into* it, across it, the darkness boiling her right side on the way, stripping even more of her down to the white.

Tia screams when the shadow touches her, screams and finally lets go.

Charlotte crashes into the storage bins on the opposite wall and Tia pulls back the other way, holding her burnt arm to her, her eyes flinty mad.

"You bitch," she says.

"You don't get to have my life," Charlotte says back, from the safety of the other side of the bright shadow, her right side trailing vapor.

Tia makes to step forward, can't bring herself to step into that frigid blast of heat again.

"You can't stay over there forever," she says. "Or, you can, I suppose, but *it* won't."

As if on cue, the bright shadow sputters, fails. Five seconds later it's a thready wisp of exhaust, and then it's gone, ashing up into nothingness.

"Well well well," Tia says, stepping into that now-safe space, still holding her arm.

Charlotte reaches up, brings the fold-down ironing board down onto Tia's head hard, crumpling her down and back. In the same motion she's running, is pulling through the doorway, sliding into the kitchen, bouncing off the island with enough force that something in her hip gives in a soft, permanent way. There's no time to slow down, though. There's no time for anything.

"Babysitter!" Tia bellows right behind Charlotte, forcing her to sway her back in, away from whatever sharp thing's got to be coming for her.

It's not enough. She's just into the living room when a hand in her hair jerks her back all at once.

Charlotte goes down flat enough to whoosh the breath from her lungs, but she comes up with the letter opener she dropped.

It's hot enough that it cuts right through her hair, leaves Tia with a big handful of it, Charlotte spinning down, looking back to see which way Tia's going now.

She's just standing there, waiting for all of Charlotte's attention.

Moving like show-and-tell, she pulls the ripped-out hair up into her hand and then stuffs it into her mouth and chews its dry grossness in, staring Charlotte down the whole time, having to guide some of the strands up from what teeth she's got left. She swallows the tangled lump hard enough that it makes her eyes water.

"Watch this, now," she says, and opens her mouth, finds a tendril of unswallowed hair at her throat, judging by how much of her hand she has to force in. She pulls the strand steadily forward, working it out farther and farther, her throat clumping in reverse, like giving birth. She dangles what she's extracted up before her face.

It's . . . maggots? In the wet hairball?

They're wrong, though. They're shuddering too fast, and they're—they're too dry, is that it?

"No, please," Charlotte says, looking down to her mostly white left arm.

Its surface is already writhing.

She's not made of tofu, she's ghost-meat, and ghost-meat is dry, blind maggots.

They're what makes the doorknobs turn, *they're* what drives this place. Scratch the surface of the house on this side, it bleeds rot and ruin, decay and putrescence.

Tia smiles one side of her mouth.

"You think it was all rainbows and unicorns over here?" she says, then nods down to whatever's happening in this maggot hairball. Charlotte, shaking her head no, tracks down, down.

The soft whiteness of the maggots has hardened into roach-brown shells, which are cracking open at one of the tapered ends, and now one—no, two . . . *five* of these maggots are managing to struggle up and out of this transformation chamber, their long grey hairs wet, plastered to their bodies, their iridescent eyes sort of inflating. The maggots are shuddering into flies.

Charlotte falls back gagging.

Tia laughs, snatches a wet new fly from the air, her hand closing around it.

She turns her fist sideways in front of her mouth like to blow through it, but then sucks instead, taking the fly back in with a clear *pop*. She has to angle her chin up to swallow big enough to get it down, but it's a fighter, must be crawling back up her throat. She thumps her neck hard with her middle finger, making a hollow sound, then swallows deep again, finally bringing her chin down.

The fly's in her now.

It crawls across the backside of the white of her eye and she feels it, blinks it away.

"You don't have digestive enzymes over here," she says to Charlotte. "It's something I could have taught you. You have to . . . to co-opt some helpers, if you want to eat anything. And if you don't eat, well."

Charlotte throws up now, from deeper than she ever has. It's just inert bile.

Tia laughs about this, frees her fingers from the maggot hairball, and says, "You're just dragging this out, babysitter. You can't beat me. I killed my little brother, I killed my dear old dad, and I ran away with my mom's head before I was even in first grade. Nothing you can do even comes close to that."

She's right.

"I can help you find the tunnels," Charlotte tells her, stalling for time, scrabbling backwards across the living room. "We can go back, I can touch the television, show you—"

"Just because I was homeschooled doesn't mean I'm stupid," Tia says, advancing.

Charlotte pushes back with her heels, turns to run and falls immediately into the remains of the television. She fights out of that, her arm on fire, her face half-gone, her scalp crawling with new holes, her white arm just crawling generally, but she can fight her way upstairs to the brass she needs, she knows, to the aloof little dog that'll make everything right. She has to.

Except.

When she plants a hand on the stairway railing to pull herself around, there's a giant blue lizard stepping carefully down at last, its midsection not over the top stair yet, or else it would be sliding down fast.

Shit.

Charlotte shakes her head no.

The only place left to go now, it's outside, isn't it? To suffocate in the fake vinyl sky. And, and she never found the twins, and she doesn't know where her mom is right now, and Murphy's going to overdose when Charley dumps her, and and and—

"*The floor is lava!*" she turns around to scream at Tia, because maybe if she believes it enough, if she needs it enough, and if Tia can buy into it for just a flash, then it can *be* real, it can be true.

Tia stops between the coffee table and the fallen television, cocks her head over to be sure she's hearing Charlotte's last attempt right.

She even looks down, lifts her right foot away from the rug.

It comes up easy. Her bare, rotten foot isn't flickering with flame. It isn't even steaming.

"What if, right?" she says to Charlotte, and grins, her lips never leaving each other.

Charlotte falls back onto the entryway and it's slick with bubbles again, meaning she believed enough for *that* part, just, not the lava she actually wanted. She pushes back, back, and Tia shakes her head in amusement, steps forward but . . . she can't?

She looks back, down, Charlotte looking with her.

It's Mr. Spinell.

He's reaching under the coffee table, is bringing his other hand over now to clamp around Tia's ankle as well, his eye sockets hollowed out like burst from the inside, his lips sputtering, his skull split enough inside the sack of skin his head is that his two front teeth are cocked away from each other now.

"Is that you, T?" he manages to creak out. "Is that my little girl?"

Tia shakes her leg as if insulted, inconvenienced.

Mr. Spinell doesn't let go.

Tia tries to step forward, out of this, but her father's got her. Her chest heaves and her eyes get wild, desperate. She falls forward, still pulling away.

Charlotte latches onto the closet doorknob, pulls herself up unsteadily enough that the closet clicks open, swings her around a bit, which is lucky, since otherwise she might be falling into the bubble bath happening under her feet. From half behind the door, she looks up to the lizard on the stairs, its tongue slapping around in its blind way, lapping the air for the grey taste it's keyed on.

From the living room, Tia is reaching for her, needs Charlotte to pull her away, and the uncertainty and terror on her face is pure first grader, activating the babysitter in Charlotte, activating it enough that Charlotte actually takes a timid step that way, to save the girl who wants her dead. But she's still hanging onto the closet door.

She studies Tia's outstretched hand, looks to the lizard again, then steps neatly *into* the closet when the entryway under her goes full Jell-O. The lines of grout between the tile are sinking, swirling away.

In the closet, Charlotte moves away from the jacket arms brushing her back, but she's pressed up against the wall now, is suddenly sure the back wall is going to go window, is going to deliver her to a funeral scene, a series of them this time: her mom, Murphy, Arthur somehow. And the twins, shit.

She pushes the door open again and rides it out, giving as much weight as she can to the doorknob, until her reaching left foot can come down on the lip of wood that's the first step of the stairway, her eyes instantly locking on the lizard's to see what it might be about to do.

"I'm nothing, I'm nobody, not even here," she says to the lizard, keeping the grey sides of her hands down by her legs, hidden. She steps across the bubbly top of the water, her right foot landing in the living room, the closet door shutting behind her when she pushes back for the last *oomph* she needs.

The lizard takes another step down in response, keying on her *movement* now, maybe. It lowers its wide nose to the bubbles mounding up from the entryway. The breath from its great nostrils launches tufts of the white up into the air and they hang, drift.

"*Help me!*" Tia is saying to Charlotte.

"Why?" Charlotte says, close enough to take Tia's hand if she wants.

"I can show you how to get back!" Tia says, almost crying now.

"The jack-in-the-box?"

"There's another way, it's—it's upstairs."

"The dog?"

"Fuck the dog, just . . . here, please."

"Where are the twins?" Charlotte asks, stepping closer, her shins just shy of Tia's grasping fingers. At least until Mr. Spinell's fingers dig into Tia's calf. And she has actual blood inside of her now, maybe from visiting topside. It's black and too thin and somehow dry, maybe too floaty too, but still, it's blood. It spurts up. Tia screams in agony, slides back. Mr. Spinell is pulling her calf to his mouth, now.

"He *was* hungry," Charlotte says, impressed.

"Please!" Tia says, reaching.

"Where are they?" Charlotte repeats.

"I put them in the, in the wall!" Tia says, pleading. "In the closet, upstairs! It's the—the first place I went. It's still there, behind the wallpaper. Please! I told you."

Charlotte looks up, over the perfectly scaled back of the lizard on the stairs. It's testing the waters of the entryway with its right forefoot, now.

She considers the closet up there. The one she was just in.

"I'm gonna hate myself for this," she says, and reaches down, takes Tia's hand in her stripped-white left, and she can practically hear her mom over her shoulder, whispering to her to never be a Pocahontas, to never give the enemy a hand, never give them a foothold.

She leans back, jerks Tia away from her father's grasping fingers, from his tearing mouth.

Tia climbs Charlotte's frontside so they're practically hugging, Tia weak and spent and gasping, all her weight on her good leg, Charlotte burned on one side, her left hand mannequin-slick, her hair half pulled out, half cut away, her teeth gravel, her arm sloughing off into maggots.

She leans down into Tia's ear, says, "I was just upstairs *in* that closet? And guess what? No Desi, no Ronald."

Tia pushes away, still in Charlotte's arms, and looks her in the face, sputters a laugh, says, "I told you, babysitter, you can't win, this is where I live, this is where I'm—"

"Shh, shh," Charlotte says, taking Tia by the shoulders, her white left hand screaming from the contact with all that scarred-up grey, "while your mom's gone, the babysitter's in charge, right? And guess what, Tia? It's bath time."

Tia shows confusion in her eyes for maybe the first time and tries to push farther away but Charlotte's already coming around, is stepping into her, driving her back hard.

Her heels catch on the step up to the entryway and she trips backward, arms wheeling, and splashes ass-first into the short, square bathtub the entryway is by now.

It gulps her right in.

Charlotte steps closer to be sure, and, when Tia's hand breaks the surface like she knew it was going to, when it slaps and slaps, finally finds the edge of the step, when she pulls her head out of the water, her mouth open and gasping and screaming air backward into her starving chest, Charlotte leans across for the doorknob of the closet door and twists it, pulls hard, the bottom of the door spatula-ing through the bubbles but stopping hard at the *clunk* Tia's head is.

Blood from her mouth and nose blooms black on the surface of the water and Charlotte looks up at what she thinks at first is a fly buzzing near her face.

It's the split tongue of the lizard.

"All yours," Charlotte says, and steps back.

The lizard lowers its left forefoot delicately into the water, and then it slides in, taking a full fifteen seconds for the bathtub to take all of it. The water surges over the lip of the entryway, washes across the hardwood, past Charlotte's feet.

On the way down the lizard latches onto Tia's body with its wide flat mouth, pulls her into the depths with it.

Charlotte stands there until the entryway hardens back to tile, gets its dusty grey lines back. She tests it gently with her right foot, and when it can hold her, she steps up onto it all the way, to survey the thoroughly trashed living room. The one that should have reset itself, since she can't actually do damage to real things.

Meaning she's all the way over, now. All the way under. All the way gone.

"Desi?" she calls timidly. "Ronald?"

Tia was lying about them being upstairs, of course, but Charlotte has to see.

She takes the steps two at a time, pulling hard with her left hand on the handrail.

The wall in the master bedroom closet is solid, but just to be sure she finds the corner of the wallpaper, peels it up, just finds the drywall she was expecting. Next, Desi's bed and bathroom— nothing. Ronald's is empty too. The office door is still open, though. Charlotte holds on to the doorframe, leans in, says the twins' names to all the corners, to the hidey space under the desk.

She stands in the hall for a long moment afterward, her eyes closed, her chest shuddering with either laughter or crying, she can't exactly tell. She won, but she's still losing.

What else is there to try, then?

She considers the linen closet, even looks in, but it's just games and sheets and that little vacuum cleaner.

Five steps later she's standing in Desi's doorway again. All the My Little Pony eyes stare back at her so hopefully, like they all know the secret answer, are just waiting for her to figure it out.

"What already?" she says, and steps back in to see.

Is Tad under the bed, perched on fingertips and toes, his head cocked to drink her in with his ears? Charlotte stands with her feet right at the skirt, waiting for a decayed little hand to swipe out, grab her ankle, but it doesn't happen.

All that's left, then, is the beanbag.

Charlotte stares and stares at it, finally looks behind her to the hall, for Nora Spinell, to the open door of the bathroom for Mr. Spinell.

She's alone.

All around her, the house is holding its breath.

"I can't believe I'm going to do this again," she says finally, and unzips the beanbag, wades into the spider eggs. Before nestling down into them she looks behind her, to the mirror. It isn't showing the past, but it's not reflecting Charlotte either.

For all she knows, Tia will be in the beanbag once it's zipped up. Or Charlotte will be *in* the lizard, unable to find the zipper tab again, just sloshing back and forth through all Mr. Wilbanks's pearly whiteness. Or she'll be back in the Lopezes' kitchen, Murphy's hands feeling for the button on her pants.

There, she decides. That's a good place to start this all over.

Slowly, like a ritual she's just making up, she settles down into the spider eggs, lies back, and, because this is all that's left, she zips it up over her face like a body bag, closes her eyes, and right when she does, the baby spiders come alive around her, a thousand hatchlings, but it's not hatchling arms that rise up from the depths to embrace her face and chest, her stomach and legs. It's the sharp-legged *mother* of all the spiders. Charlotte's lying with her back to its belly. She arches away, knows she's just being held still like this so the pincers can come down, dig into her skull, or into her inner thigh, her crotch—her *crotch*. She's laying on the spider upside down. She can tell because of the sawing and crunching at her hip, *in* her hip, the . . .

The buzzing in her pocket?

Her phone.

She works her arm down through the cascading beads, digs her phone up with her left hand, which is complicated, and then she brings that glow up to her face to see who's texting her.

Mom.

b2u in 10, love.

Charlotte bursts up from the beanbag holding her phone, looking around the room desperately.

Desi's still not a mound of cuteness in her bed, but, but—

Charlotte falls forward with happiness, with success, with escape.

Her reflection, it's *in the mirror*!

She crawls and falls across the room, flicks the light on to be sure, brings her face close to her reflection, touches the her in the glass.

It's just a normal reflection, like a thousand times before. Like always. No tricks, no weirdness.

She rushes out into the hall, to Ronald's room because sometimes kids really do end up in the same bed. It's empty, but the office door down there, it's closed. Closed closed closed.

Charlotte steps down there, wraps her hand around that knob, and twists.

Locked, even. Or, still. But that's the only reason it's not twisting.

"Yes," Charlotte says, and turns, runs downstairs, is about to race across the living room when she remembers, just normal-walks past the television, only glancing over there once, casually, to be sure there's a lizard with a glass throat positioned there, keeping watch over her.

There is. She's never been so happy for a nanny cam.

She stops in the kitchen doorway, clocks all the clocks on the appliances.

12:28 blinks back at her.

"Okay, okay," she says, looking around fast, with SAT eyes. If—if Tia was trying to mislead her about where the twins were, and she said upstairs, then that means they're actually *down*stairs. And they're not in the living room, unless—

Charlotte walks mechanically back through it, calmly opens the closet door by the entryway, checks the space behind the couch, even opens the cabinet under the television.

No twins.

Okay, good. Think.

If they were in the utility, then Charley, Tia *as* Charley, would have scared them awake when she threw the jug of BBs.

The kitchen, then?

Charlotte goes back to it, her fingertips to the island, her eyes everywhere.

Calmly, methodically, she opens and shuts each cabinet, even looks in the top and bottom ovens, in case this is some ridiculous fairy tale. The refrigerator is side by side but she checks it anyway, imagining one twin in the refrigerator, one in the freezer.

No Desi, no Ronald.

She pats her pocket, has the deadbolt key again—*still*—meaning they didn't go out that way either.

"So?" she asks herself.

So . . . Charley. Tia. She knew about the pruning saw Charlotte left on the floor of the garage, didn't she? She said she'd had to hang it back up? But—*why* hang it back up?

"Because if it's on the ground," Charlotte says, already going there, "then it's the first thing the Wilbankses will see when they pull in. And then they know somebody's been there, in the garage. And they're not supposed to know that, are they? Nobody is."

Now Charlotte's running. She crashes into the garage, slaps for the light, finds the button that grinds the door up but screw it. Where where where.

"No," Charlotte says when she sees it.

The chest freezer.

What if Charley, when she was Murphy, told the kids it was another funny place, that it was the last one before bedtime, that it was the best one of them all, that Charlotte would never find them there?

Charlotte rushes across, flips the heavy white door up, and there's an Indian princess curled up on top of a 1940s nurse, their hair frozen sharp, faces frosted, lips blue, eyelashes ice-welded to their chubby cheeks.

"No no no," Charlotte says, and hauls Desi out first, then Ronald.

Desi writhes but doesn't open her eyes. Can't. Her lashes are frozen to her cheeks.

Ronald, though. He doesn't move, was the bottom of the two, got double the cold, probably.

"Ronald!" Charlotte says, her face right to his tiny one, "Ronnie, Ronbo, Veronica!"

Nothing.

Charlotte stands, doesn't know which way to go, what to do.

"Here, here," she says maybe five desperate seconds later, and collects them both in her arms.

This can work. It's not too late.

She staggers them inside, rests Ronald on the island to rebalance their weight, and then, lizard be damned, she's making her way across the living room, over the entryway, is plodding upstairs.

Desi's bathroom.

She strips the twins down, nestles them into the tub and turns the water on. Not too hot—they're kids—but, compared to how cold they are, even cold water would be warm.

"C'mon, c'mon," she says, a hand to each of their faces, to be sure they don't inhale any of the not-hot, only tepid water, her left hand and arm red from guiding sluices of water down to the twins. Except . . . it's not hot water, right?

The red's like a sunburn, but it stops neatly almost at the elbow.

It's the skin she peeled off. Her arm still remembers.

She'd peel it off again right now with her teeth if the twins would just thaw, though.

Ten agonizing minutes later, Charlotte crying and breathing all the hot breath she has onto them, guiding more and more water over their shoulders, into their hair, Desi gasps awake, splashes her hand down in that panicked way kids have, like they're just waking from a falling-dream.

But then she realizes where she is, who she's with. She smiles maybe the best smile in the whole history of smiles.

"Is he sleeping?" she says about Ronald, her voice creaky enough that she touches her throat to feel that sound.

"Just wait," Charlotte says, crying silently but smiling for Desi.

"Shh," Desi says then, conspiratorially, and snakes her hand up to the bathtub's ledge, dunks the squeeze turtle in, and raises the head just enough to spurt a line of water up at Ronald in a way that takes Charlotte's breath away. The last time she saw this, the result was . . . bad.

Sleeping frozen Ronald takes it for maybe four seconds, and then he sputters, gasps, pushes back from whatever this is.

Charlotte leans in, never mind her flannel shirt, hugs the two of them to her tighter than a babysitter should, longer than they can take, almost.

"Is it tomorrow?" Desi asks.

"Halloween," Charlotte says, bopping her on the nose. "Trick-or-treat, little girl."

"I'm a nurse," Ronald says. It's his first words.

"Listen to my heart," Charlotte says, batting away tears, and hauls them up and out, dries them, pajamas them, and tucks them each into Ronald's bed together, smoothing their hair down at the very end, and not wanting to have to stop doing that.

"You're a couple of great kids," she tells them.

"Are you coming back again?" Desi asks.

Charlotte turns her head to the idea of that and shrugs, says, "If your parents still want me, yeah. Now, new game. Pretend to be asleep, can you do that? For when your mommy and daddy get back?"

Ronald nods, shuts his eyes tight, and Desi giggles, can't even pretend to pretend.

Charlotte squeezes her foot under the blanket like a hug and stands to leave, sits back down fast when something bites her. No:

when she stepped on something. One of the tacks from the vinyl poster she pulled off the wall a lifetime ago, that she couldn't find.

Charlotte goes to her knees, finds it and the other three tacks, then wrenches the sole of her foot up to see it, has to smile: there's a single dot of wonderful red blood.

She lowers her lips to it, kisses it away, then leaves the door open a crack, the hall light already on. The hall is just the hall again, is just any hall, every hall.

"Stay good," she says to the upstairs, and follows the handrail down, stops when the garage door grinds . . . not up, but down again, *then* up. Which she has no explanation for, if asked. Maybe the Wilbankses will be tipsy enough or postcoital enough to blame themselves. Premature button-pushing. It's a thing.

Charlotte cases the living room to be sure it's in order—the last chapter in the babysitting manual—and she has to laugh, shake her head.

Not even close. The television is where it always was, but Mr. Spinell's blood is on the couch, on the rug. The house ate him, sure, but it didn't wipe its mouth afterward.

Charlotte breathes in, breathes out, and vaults down the stairs, runs hard for the kitchen, pulls the last container of lasagne out.

At the exact moment the door from the garage into the kitchen opens, the lasagne is arcing through the air in what feels like slow motion, to splash all around the living room.

Charlotte tosses the little storage container behind the couch and stands there as if waiting for them, so she can claim this mess.

"Um," Mrs. Wilbanks says, about it all.

Her hair is mussed at the back, her eyeliner smudged.

Mr. Wilbanks has to suppress the smile that wants to happen.

"There was a, a *food* fight," Charlotte says, chin up. "It's not their fault. I started it, I'm sorry. You don't have to pay me, I understand. And—and I'll come back, clean this up. Or pay for any cleaning, whatever you want, whatever works."

She looks from face to parental face and stands there awaiting her judgment.

After a moment, Mrs. Wilbanks steps forward to touch a smear of the lasagne on the arm of the couch. "Was it—was it good, anyway?" she says, as if considering putting that finger in her mouth.

Charlotte has to look away from this, and in looking away she catches Mr. Wilbanks at the bookshelf, using the back of his index finger to wipe a crusty smear from the lizard's mouth.

It's bubbles, Charlotte doesn't tell him, just letting this pass. But, thinking about the nanny cam, she realizes that there won't be any food fight on the recording, will there? What *will* there be, though? A babysitter smuggling two popsicle children across the living room?

But that's all later, and Mr. Wilbanks can hardly call her on it if he was spy-camming her, can he? Or do babysitters not have privacy either, in his world? In his house?

Charlotte presses her lips together, hiding her smile as well, and says, "I'd never had homemade lasagne, ma'am."

"'*Ma'am*,'" Mrs. Wilbanks says, poo-pooing that away with her hand, like she's holding an imaginary handkerchief. "And the kids? Aside from this disaster, I mean?"

"Little angels," Charlotte says, stepping over to collect her backpack, trying to affect a contrite posture, or step. Something. Mostly? She's just happy to be alive. No, not just alive. *Here*. Back in the real world. On the good side of the house.

"Kids need to have food fights every once in a while," Mr. Wilbanks announces, pushing away from the incriminating evidence at the bookshelf.

"Maybe in the back*yard*," Mrs. Wilbanks corrects with a tone of warning, punctuating it with the playful/not-playful cut of her eyes.

"Thank you for letting me get to know them," Charlotte says, hiking her backpack up onto her shoulder. "Really."

"Did you get some good study time in?" Mrs. Wilbanks asks, holding Charlotte's eyes with hers.

"SATs . . ." Mr. Wilbanks drags out both ominously and with excitement.

"I learned a lot, yes," Charlotte says, in the entryway now. Which is solid, normal, perfect, never mind the toeprint smushed into the grout by the closet door.

"Hey, listen, let me drive you—" Mr. Wilbanks offers, stepping forward like to . . . what? Take her backpack, lead her to the car in the garage?

Charlotte works the key up from her pocket, twists the deadbolt back and shakes her head no, holds her phone up and says, "My mom's almost here already, thanks." She waggles the screen awake like proof.

Mrs. Wilbanks steps brusquely ahead to enter the code into the alarm's keypad, careful to enter the temp one, Charlotte's pretty sure. The one it doesn't matter if the babysitter sees.

"Well," Mr. Wilbanks says, opening his hand to release Charlotte into the big bad night.

"Was it a good time, your date?" Charlotte asks as farewell, standing in the open doorway, and Mr. Wilbanks nods, Mrs. Wilbanks presses her lips into an embarrassed smile, and with that—with no money changing hands, but Emergency Services not called either—Charlotte steps out, closes her eyes and steps off the porch, into the *actual* front yard, not against a child's cartoonish imagining of it.

She breathes the crisp air in deep, holds it as long as she can.

It's over.

She made it.

She wasn't supposed to, she shouldn't have been able to, but she did.

If she can do that, then the SATs will be a snap, won't they? Tonight, this, it was the real test.

Behind her the deadbolt locks, the key retracts, and, presumably, the real code for the alarm's being punched in.

Charlotte can't help but laugh. She hugs her arms to the wet flannel shirt she shouldn't be wearing in this chill, and shakes her hair out behind her, crosses the Wilbankses' lawn, only twirling around in little-girl celebration once, maybe twice. She steps over the sidewalk and off the curb, the streetlight flicking unsteadily above in such a wonderfully real way. A not-fake way.

She walks the direction her mom will be coming from—the hospital—and her phone buzzes with a stack of texts, the beginning of each new buzz overlapping the end of the last. They're all from Murphy.

She starts with *studybuddy?* and, over the course of nearly thirty messages, graduates to more genuine concern, and finally just a long line of question marks with a stick-figure shoulder-shrug-with-upturned-palms buried in there like Murphy can do without having to even think about it, like her fingertips bleed emoticons.

Charlotte taps a simple red heart in, no punctuation there she can break, and sends it with finality, then looks up into headlights. Not about to hit her, just easing up, lighting the street between her and them, to be sure she doesn't trip coming to the passenger-side door.

"Mom," she says, lifting her right hand to wave her fingertips.

Her mom opens her hand to the passenger-side door but Charlotte doesn't come around yet.

Did she just hear something?

Her mom taps the horn to hurry her—she's from the city, so horns are just another verbalization to her, even at nearly one in the morning, deep in the heart of suburbia—but Charlotte holds her hand up, asking for a moment, a quiet moment, please.

Click.

Charlotte looks around, but this . . . it's not dog claws on concrete, isn't somebody out for a night walk. It's not the car's engine, ticking down, or some loud part of a belt under the hood. It's not a transformer on a utility pole and it's not a late leaf spiraling down from its tree.

Click.

It's not even in the air, really, is more like a sound Charlotte is feeling. In the ground. Through everything.

Click.

Her face goes slack, her eyes heating up instantly.

It's a giant crank turning. A giant jack-in-the-box crank.

Charlotte drops her backpack, looks around fast now, at everything.

"No," she says.

Click.

"*Mom!*" she screams, reaching forward, and her mom leans over the steering wheel like to see better. To understand.

Click.

When the spring pops at last, it's huge and strong and unavoidable, and it's under her mom's seat.

She smushes up into the headliner and windshield, is smashed into chunks and smears, spurts and gouts, some splashing out the window, dripping red down the side of the door, some just sliding down the backside of the windshield, the rest bobbing with the seat as the spring winds down, its job done.

Charlotte falls to her knees, pushes away from this, runs for the safety of the sidewalk, but that whole side of the street—no no no—it's a vinyl *sheet* hanging down, the streetlights just paintings all along it, right at the curb. No, *including* the curb! Charlotte falls back, pulls her buzzing phone up to her face, desperate.

"Mom, Mom, is that you? Listen, don't—"

It's not her mom, though.

"Really, this is too much," Charley is saying not so much into the cell at the other end as in the area *of* that cell.

"No, you were worth it," Mr. Wilbanks says back, his voice different now. More creaky. "They were safe in bed. You can't believe how nervous my—how nervous Regina was all night."

"I only hope the two of you had a good time," Charley says. "Here, you can cut across here."

They're in a car. He's giving her that ride home.

Charlotte stands, switches ears.

"*No!*" she screams into the phone. "That's not me!"

"And they really were little angels," Charley says. "I hope my kids someday are—well. I mean, I wish Ronald and Desi were already mine? But that would mean that you and me would have had to . . . never mind. I'm thinking stupid. It's not like—nothing, sorry. God. Can you make this any more awkward, Charlotte?"

"Here?" Mr. Wilbanks says. "This your bus stop?"

"Your car is so *clean*," Charley says then, like changing away from subjects that don't matter. "How do you keep it like this?"

"You know," Mr. Wilbanks says. "Car wash. It's easy."

"Car wash?" Charley asks, her voice practically blinking its eyes. "Can you show me?"

"The car wash?"

"My mom isn't expecting me home until one," Charley says. "But she'll be asleep anyway."

"The car wash," Mr. Wilbanks says, in a distinctly more satisfied way. The slimiest purr makes it up to wherever the cell tower is, burrows the tip of its tongue right into Charlotte's ear.

"*That's not me!*" Charlotte screams into the phone again, and then is plunged into darkness when her mom's headlights die down.

She looks up to the painted-on streetlight but now it's flickering and wavering too, sucking its light back into that flat bulb.

Charlotte falls to her knees, hears another sound from her phone so pulls it up and then away again, fast.

There are fast little spider legs reaching out from the speaker, the mic. One of them births up, dives for the ground, Charlotte's open hand dropping the phone right alongside it, since that's what your hands do with things that are full of spiders.

When the phone hits the little lip of concrete where the curb meets the sun-faded blacktop, the screen audibly cracks and it's like the light it had been holding in strobes out, bathing the vinyl wall shimmery silver.

Lit up like that for that slice of an instant, Charlotte sees . . . that little spider's shadow, suddenly large.

But she tracks it back to its tiny self, sees that it's running for the vinyl backdrop not because it thinks it's real, but because its cluster of eyes must see in a way Charlotte's eyes can't. That strobe of escaped light from her phone, though, it sort of showed her: there's the lightest tracing on that vinyl, isn't there?

This desperate spider skitters *into* that tracing, showing it to actually be a crack, a cut.

This is a doorway.

"Oh," Charlotte says, reaching to flap it open.

Real night air breezes through, chilling her wet shirt against her skin even more.

"I don't—I can't—" Charlotte says, as if speaking for an audience, some imagined listener, but this is no time to try to think her way through out loud.

If she waits for this to make sense, it'll stop making sense, won't it? If the funny places don't last, then escape hatches have to be even more fleeting, don't they?

She steps forward, into the doorway, and it's a flap, still, but it's also heavy and stiff, is . . . it's metal on the backside, somehow. And set into the side of one of the stalls at what has to be the car wash.

It has to be because what Charlotte's seeing is Mr. Wilbanks's Audi—of course the Audi: Mrs. Wilbanks's Lexus or whatever *already* smells like sex.

The windows are steamed up, and then a hand slaps into that steam, smears down.

Charlotte's hand. What used to be her hand.

She shakes her head no, no, this isn't right, this isn't something she would do, and is stepping through to stop it, the door still open behind her, when something slaps at the side of her left leg.

She flinches up, sure that that little spider that ran through has swelled up to dog size here in the outer world, to match that big shadow it was throwing, but it's just an old yellowy newspaper.

Charlotte reaches down to dislodge it, step through, let it continue on its nighttime whatever, but, right when she's letting it go, she sees her own name there. Her last name.

But, in front of that last name is . . . her *mom's* name?

Over the top of the newspaper, the Audi is rocking back and forth, either a suspension spring squeaking or a seat in there squealing, and Charlotte watches it for a moment, like daring that passenger-side door to open. When it doesn't, she scans the article like Murphy taught her, sort of speed-reading for details she'll need to answer the inevitable questions and realizes it's no accident that this paper found her. Either this edition is blowing around in every direction she could have stepped, or it had been snagged at the edge of this stall, waiting specifically for her.

Which doesn't matter.

What does is that, according to the article, in this world, this version of the world, her mom, coming to get her from the Lopezes' that babysitting night, *did* run over Arthur.

Charlotte lets the paper go.

It blows across the Audi's roof, is gulped in by the vast night on the other side, its assignment completed.

"She didn't, she wouldn't," Charlotte is saying, shaking her head no.

But she understands, too. Yes, here, now, she can haul the

door of this Audi open, stop what's going on inside, either kill Charley and stuff her body back on the other side of the vinyl, or—or climb back *into* it—but what she can't do is go back in time, not be fooling around in the Lopezes' dining room while her babysitting charge sleepwalks out into the street, into a pair of headlights.

That's done. It's the price the house exacts, for letting her step back through, into her life.

"But—" Charlotte says, a bare foot pushing hard against the glass of the car now, a long crack shooting up and down from it, which makes her feel weird inside, and all over.

She has no real objection to what the house is offering, though. Or, she gets it: nothing's free. Or, to look at it in SAT terms, in college terms: how bad do you want it? what are you willing to sacrifice to get it?

Charlotte closes her eyes. A tear slips down her cheek. Her throat is swelling. Her right hand is a fist at her throat.

"Mom?" she says, looking in the direction of the hospital.

Thing is? Her mom, to let her daughter blast off into the future, would willingly take this hit, would go to jail for the rest of her life. Or, if running Arthur over wasn't her fault, she would *make* it her fault, to let Charlotte get away.

Charlotte shakes her head no, though.

"Not like this," she says, her voice cracking, chest shuddering with the finality of this, and reaches back, catches the dull blue door to the office of the car wash right before it would have closed, trapping her here, on what's now the wrong side of things.

She holds her lips together and breathes in this crisp real-world air one last time, looks as far as she can out the bay of the car wash, out at the glow of the suburbs, the pinprick light of real stars way up there, the distant buzz of an airplane. A dog, barking.

But the barking's coming from the doorway behind her, isn't it?

The barks are deep and urgent.

"I'm sorry," Charlotte says to the her in this Audi, to Murphy, to her mom, and then she pivots on her right foot, forces herself to step back through. Not into the car wash office, but back onto the street.

The door shuts behind her, the crack becoming just a tracing again, then sealing into nothing, like it never even was.

Charlotte can't help but sob, fall to her knees, and lower her forehead to the asphalt. When she looks up to the new silence pressing in, it's like she's on a stage at the end of a play, after the theater has emptied out.

Up and down the street, the lights are all dying down.

Except one.

The Wilbankses' porch light.

Charlotte shakes her head no, please, no.

It's the only place left, though. It's either get swallowed by this encroaching darkness, or, or—

She scrabbles forward, picks her phone up on the way. The screen's still cracked, but not that bad. She can still see the time, just one jagged line bisecting it: 7:59 p.m.

Well then.

Charlotte stands, her posture braver than she feels, and slings her backpack over her shoulder. She looks up into the obviously fake sky—planets with cartoony rings, the same way a kid would draw them—and then, each step shaky and uncertain, she crosses the lawn, uses the railing to pull herself up onto the porch, and holds her index finger a shade away from the lighted doorbell button long enough to reconsider, to do anything else.

But this is all there is.

Hi, I'm your babysitter! she practices in her head, jaunty delivery and all, and wipes her eyes with the sleeve of her shirt, noticing the flannel's dry after just having been wet from the bath, but never mind, she was supposed to be here ten minutes early for the big walk-through, and it's already eight, so she pushes that glowing button in, can just hear the distant chime in this pale giant of a house.

Footsteps hurry down the stairs and then the doorknob turns, that little brass tongue retracting from its brass strike plate with an audible *click* that Charlotte almost remembers, she thinks, but from where?

It doesn't matter. But remember that there's brass in the *door*, the *door*, she tells herself, trying to get it to stick. When this house was updated from the nineties, all the visible hardware went pewter and silver, but this hidden strike plate and tongue are throwbacks, are from the before times. They're how you can make this time through different. They can change everything.

"The door," she says out loud, in private, and then pastes a pleasant, innocent smile on her face, the skin around her eyes crinkling just enough to sell how earnest she is, what a good and perfect babysitter she's going to be.

"Hi, I'm Charlotte!" she says to the opening door, coming up onto her toes, her shoulders rising a bit, the warm air of the house breathing out across her.

I'm Charlotte, and you have something in your door, something I'm going to need later, just give me a moment to remember what it is.

But the night's already starting, isn't it?

Again, Charlotte thinks, wilting inside, but then, once the ball of her right foot touches the tile of the entryway, that's just a leftover word rattling around in her head. One that doesn't touch the smile pasted on her face.

She looks up the stairs, blinks twice.

"Beautiful home," she says, and her back doesn't even straighten when the door slams shut behind her.

ACKNOWLEDGMENTS

Those time-lapse loops of a rose blooming, and blooming, and then blooming some more, like it's got an endless spiral of pedals inside it somehow? That's what writing this novel was, for me: it just kept opening up and opening up. I never have much idea where my stories are going, but this one really kept me guessing, in the best way. Years back, someone explained American Naturalism to me as... if, early in the book, the writing veers over here to get some old gnarled tree with a cool and portentous shadow halfway on the page, then you can rest assured that that tree is going to be important later on in the story. I never ran down American Naturalism to see if that's an accurate statement or not, but, all the same, when this person told me that, it kind of struck a Nick Carraway tuning fork in my head, and my heart: that's how I write! I wring twice, I recycle endlessly, and then I sift the ashes of whatever I've burned, in case I missed something. To say it another way: use every last part of the buffalo, Steve. Don't keep moving on and inventing new things until you've drained what's already there. And, it nearly always turns out that what's already there is completely enough.

Which is to say: I was as surprised by that toy lizard as Charlotte is. And the bubble bath. And the dog. Man, that dog; it's based on a series of dachshunds my grandparents had—"wiener dogs" to us. Or: the only dogs that could get hit in the face by a rattlesnake and not crawl into some place dark to die. They just shake those bites off, I have no idea how. Just meanness, I guess? But, really, all this—the lizard, the bubble bath, the dog, the master bedroom closet, the railing, the stairs, the entertainment center, the kitchen island—it all came just from that initial walk-through, which is baked into the genre. Once you know it's there, that the first beat of this story is for us to get a sense of the floor plan, and all the devious possibilities there, it's hard to miss it, isn't it? For figuring that floor plan and the rest of those beats out, though, I have both books and people to thank. First, all the amazing haunted house novels that came before, that got that magical pattern locked in. I can't list them all, but: *The Haunting of Hill House*, *Hell House*, *Burnt Offerings*, *The House Next Door*, *The Shining*, *Solaris* (yes, *Solaris*)—you can learn about all you need to from those six. But I'd never thought about them in the right and helpful way until, first, an independent study with an MFA student, Nick Kimbro, who was writing a legitimately scary witch novel, but was deep-diving into all things haunted housey . . . maybe because he was interested? Maybe because I was? I don't know. But, I do know that, together, we went down all the halls, opened all the closet doors, and listened close for the attic, the basement, the porch, that creaky swing. Next there was a grad seminar I was lucky to lead, with thirteen students along, each of whom got me thinking about the haunted house in a different way. Matthew J. Pridham was the one who first lobbed out the idea that each haunted house has a "hub" of sorts—a central place, the innermost, most dangerous chamber. His story "Renovations" (*Weird Tales* #348, 2008) shows he was there in hub-land long before I was even considering it.

Thanks too to Mike Flanagan, for not doing *The Haunting of Hill House* series until I'd written this. Not sure I would have, had that already been in the world. It's that good, yes. It doesn't leave a lot of shoulder room for other haunted houses, I mean. So cool when a work can be that instantly canonical, that iconic, that

ACKNOWLEDGMENTS

formative, never mind if it comes late in the game. The game's always changing anyway. Thanks, obviously probably, to Chutes and Ladders. I don't have the temperament for most board games—okay, Settlers of Catan—but I'll play some Chutes and Ladders. Well, with a kid, I'll play. I love how it makes them smile. Thanks as always to my early readers: Mackenzie Kiera, Michael Somes, Kathryn E. McGee, Reed Underwood. Bree Pye, you read it too, yes? I keep searching my inbox to find out who all helped me with this, but I talk about "The Babysitter Murders" so much that I get too many results. Thanks too to one of my uncles, for haunting my grandmother's house when I was . . . I don't know: four? five? This uncle told me how when the house was being built, a construction worker had lost his arm, then died, so now, if I went out into the hall at night, I might hear that worker walking along in front of me, looking for his lost arm. I was a terrified-of-everything kid (who grew up into a terrified-of-it-all adult), and this was maybe just what I needed to push me over into horror for the rest of my life. Thanks to a porcupine, too. I never knew its name, but one day, miles and miles out in a West Texas pasture, which was my happy place always, I chased this porcupine into a fallen down house I knew my granddad had lived in, probably fifty or sixty years ago. Or maybe I had it wrong, and it was his parents who had lived there? This place was old-old, I mean. The walls had collapsed, so the house was pretty much just a rotting roof in the mesquite, home to snakes and pack rats and maybe even bobcats and badgers, and definitely wasps. Still, I wanted to catch this porcupine—it's hard to have good ideas, isn't it?—so I wormed in right after it dove into the darkness, squirmed through all the rat droppings and grime of decades, finally cornered this porcupine that thought it was safe. Of course by then I'd had to use pliers to get quills out of dogs' faces, and knew I didn't want to have those same pliers used on my face, as one of those quills might come out with my eyeball shish-kebab'd on it, but . . . I really wanted a quill. I had the idea that this was a test, that I would be even more "Indian" if I could do this, and get away. So, squinting, looking away, trying to protect these congealed balls of jelly I call my eyes, I reached ahead and . . . plucked a single quill off the back of that porcupine, then scraped my way out of this ancient place like Indiana Jones, ran away fast with my treasure. To immediately lose it, of course. But at least I have the story of it—I was only two years away from *Mongrels*, yes. More important than the quill or its story, though, what this fallen-down place taught me was that a house can be dangerous, yes, it can be as dangerous as anything, but that doesn't mean it always eats you. Even when it really-really wants to. Sometimes it will—if I'd gotten a face full of quills, or opened my back on a square tenpenny nail, then I maybe bake dead out under that roof—but not always.

There's hope when dealing with a haunted house, I'm saying. There's the thinnest sliver of light waiting up ahead, at the end of this ordeal. Without knowing that, I bet Charlotte comes together differently, and this novel's not even a little bit the same.

Thanks also to a guy I grew up with, Cory Hopper. Cory was older than me, and way bigger and meaner than I'd ever be, and was the kind of white that was reflective, practically. Nowadays he'd be a ginger, but that term wasn't in circulation in 1980-whatever this was, and if you'd tried it on Cory, you'd wake two days later with your face significantly altered. To say nothing of your teeth. That's how Cory dealt with people. He'd smile and laugh and have a good time, but he was quick to come at you, too. Anyway, one Halloween night in Stanton, Texas when we'd sneaked into the abandoned, supposedly haunted convent's cemetery to play around like you do, Cory—who wasn't with us kids—he jumped up from behind a headstone waving his arms and yelling and pretty much glowing in the darkness, and I kind of thought my life might be right-then over, because no way could my heart ever think about beating again. This kind

ACKNOWLEDGMENTS

of spiked terror—not dread, just pure, unadulterated, mindless terror—into any haunted-house stuff, for me; I never was brave enough to actually sneak into that convent, no. Very glad I never did. Haunted houses up on the hill are fine to run past, to tell stories about, but if you ever ring that doorbell, then you're asking for it. I try not to ask for it. Anyway, Cory's gone now, but that jumpscare he gifted me with, it remains, and keeps remaining, even when I wish it wouldn't, please.

Thanks as well to a house I lived in for the longest of any house, from the time it was frame and tar paper until it had stucco on the outside. I had so many nightmares in that house—*The Only Good Indians* comes directly from one of them: four strikes of black lighting at all four directions, and then a deer-person standing up, his antlers rending the sky open—and so many injuries. One morning I woke with wasps all over my neck, biting me. Another time I saw my stepdad run a circular saw across the top of his thigh, and then had to help him try to hold his skin together until the ambulance got there. I did a ceremony there with black widow spiders and candles and Max Headroom—think you can find that on one of my early *Kingcast* visits? My first and most favorite dog of them all, Shasta, she got buried alive there in a plastic bag, breaking my heart forever. The way we can ever only know the emotional contours of a single place, finally? I think we might only ever really know the doors and hallways and rickety staircases of a single house, too. That house, for me, is on County Road 1120, in Greenwood, Texas. I still drive by it about once a year, when I'm back in Texas. Just to remember where I'm from, and where I don't want to have to be again, because I can't handle the dreams. They would break me, I think.

Thanks as well to my agent, BJ Robbins, and thanks to my editor at Saga, Joe Monti, for pushing me (as Michael Somes had) to modulate the ending a little. It was less about changing things, more about changing the feel of those things, if that makes sense. And thanks to Caroline Tew, for dialing up the audio of this and typing it in so I could mess with it for this edition, since of course, like that porcupine quill, I'd long ago lost my file of the acknowledgments. Ralph Berry—who started this whole "writing career"-thing for me by offering to publish my dissertation, *The Fast Red Road*—he opens his amazing story "Metempsychosis" in *Plane Geometry and Other Affairs of the Heart* with the line "Dougherty dreams of second chances. He doesn't feel cheated so much as simply baffled by irreversibility. Things happen. They don't happen again." That's sort of how I feel about files, and porcupine quills, and everything in between: their presence and then sudden and unaccountable absences baffles me. Why, right? I have no answer. But I still find sharp things to poke myself with; please don't ever worry that I'll run out of sharp, poky things, or blood to let out with them. And as long as I'm working with amazing people like Caroline, I may never want for lost files, either. Thanks as well to Christine Calella and Savannah Breckenridge, for getting this flip book on all the shelves, all the lists, in everyone's hands—and me on all the flights, all the Lyfts, all the stages of the world. And of course thanks to Charlotte, for being Laurie Strode here, and watching out for the kids first. It's easy to cut and run, but it's worthwhile to stick around. I like people who stick around. Like . . . my wife, Nancy.

    Nan, you and me, we've lived in so, so many houses these last thirty-four years, haven't we? I'm not sure I can even remember them all. But that's a lie. I'll never forget a single place I've lived with you. You're all my best times. And, who cares about houses, anyway? You're my home, and that's so much more important. Wherever you are, that's where I'll be.

S
G
J

SGJ